PENGUIN METRO READS

THE PERFECT US

Durjoy Datta was born in New Delhi, and completed a degree in engineering and business management before embarking on a writing career. His first book—*Of Course I Love You . . .*—was published when he was twenty-one years old and was an instant bestseller. His successive novels—*Now That You're Rich . . .*; *She Broke Up, I Didn't! . . .*; *Oh Yes, I'm Single! . . .*; *You Were My Crush . . .*; *If It's Not Forever . . .*; *Till the Last Breath . . .*; *Someone Like You*; *Hold My Hand*; *When Only Love Remains*; *World's Best Boyfriend*; *The Girl of My Dreams*; *The Boy Who Loved* and *The Boy with the Broken Heart*—have also found prominence on various bestseller lists, making him one of the highest-selling authors in India.

Durjoy also has to his credit nine television shows and has written over a thousand episodes for television.

He lives in Mumbai. For more updates, you can follow him on Facebook (www.facebook.com/durjoydatta1) or Twitter (@durjoydatta) or mail him at durjoydatta@gmail.com.

The Perfect Us

DURJOY DATTA

Penguin
metro reads

An imprint of Penguin Random House

PENGUIN METRO READS

USA | Canada | UK | Ireland | Australia
New Zealand | India | South Africa | China

Penguin Metro Reads is part of the Penguin Random House group of companies
whose addresses can be found at global.penguinrandomhouse.com

Published by Penguin Random House India Pvt. Ltd
7th Floor, Infinity Tower C, DLF Cyber City,
Gurgaon 122 002, Haryana, India

First published in Penguin Metro Reads by Penguin Random House India 2018

Copyright © Durjoy Datta 2018

10 9 8 7 6 5 4 3 2 1

ISBN 9780143426592

Typeset in Bembo STD by Manipal Digital Systems, Manipal
Printed at Thomson Press India Ltd, New Delhi

www.penguin.co.in

The Perfect Us

1

'We are here.'

Deb heard the dulcet voice coming from beyond the darkness, the biting cold and the blinding pain.

'Open your eyes, we are here. You don't want to miss this.'

The voice kept getting louder, pulling him away from the exhaustion and disorientation he was drowning in.

'Any second now, please open your eyes,' he heard the voice dance in his ears.

Deb's eyes flickered softly. He saw no light. She patted his face, at first lightly, and then urgently. The pain had seeped down to his very bones. Lying helpless and splayed at the summit of Mt Kilimanjaro, the past five days seemed like a mistake to him. Struggling to draw himself out, he cursed the moment they decided to come to Tanzania.

Stranded in the Dubai airport a week ago, bumped off their flight to Bali, the ground staff in her beige uniform and a kind smile asked them what they wanted.

'The airlines will give you a hotel voucher and put you on tomorrow's flight to Maldives. Or we can give you a flight coupon which you can avail today to a destination of your choice. You can check the board for flights departing soon and let us know,' she had said.

Waiting for a day would have meant spending their anniversary in a flight, middle of nowhere.

So they stood in front of the flicking board of flight information, their powerless Indian passports in hand, checking if a flight that left soon went to a country that didn't require a visa beforehand.

TANZANIA.

'We travelled so far for this,' she said, her voice smooth as honey, as the fur of baby unicorns.

It battled with the sharp pain that rose in his head.

They had been warned about this—the headaches, the cold, the snow, the blisters on the feet, the worn away muscles, the strained ligaments, the regret. When they landed in Dar-es-salam, Tanzania six days ago, it's the first thing they were told after their passports were stamped. The charming tout outside the airport who tried selling them a tour, taxi and guide services had predicted this.

'*Jambo, jambo poa.* Brother, brother, listen to me, brother. Where you go, brother? Me best in town, give you best deals. Come to me, sister. Go to Moshe town, brother, to see the safari. Lions, you like? You do? But for now, see the Dar-es-salam. Best city in the world, sister. Let me show you around. Europe people? They go that mountain, fit, run. Indians, not so much. They relax, they can't. They don't do this mountain business, sister. Headache, tiredness, no chai on the mountain, too much for them, sister. They chill,' said the tout, pointing to the billboard with a picture of the snowcapped Kilimanjaro.

A day later, they were at the base camp bunched up with a group of young boys from Australia, all college athletes, all of whom had prepared for months for the five-day climb to the top.

'We can do it right? You're sure about that?' Deb had asked her.

'*Bharat Mata ki jai, Deb, Bharat Mata ki jai.* This is for our pride, for us and for all Indians,' she had answered.

For the next five days, they climbed, hiked, hopped all day under the unforgiving rain, lugging their backpacks, spending every night in a tent. Deb wanted to ask her to turn back, leave the relentless mountain and the tasteless food behind. But he would find her unpacking and packing their rucksacks, scraping their climbing shoes, filling their bottles with hot water, spreading out the sleeping bags like she had grown up there. Sometimes, he would wake up in panic. It would take him a few seconds to register why he was bunched up in a sleeping bag and in a tent in the middle of nowhere. He would go outside and find her sitting in pitch darkness, neck craned upwards, sitting by the side of her camera capturing a time-lapse of the shifting stars. She would look at him, ask him to sit next to her hoping he would appreciate it as much as she did.

'It's beautiful,' he said once to not disappoint her. 'But why look at it for hours?'

'Everything that we have built, everything we have made ourselves believe in, is a lie. The jobs, the money, the buildings, and the coffee and the media and the clothes we wear. We invented things and let them take over our lives. It was only meant to be this. Us and this world. You think it's nonsense, of course. What you do still has some legitimacy. Art always does.'

'I wrote a few bad novels and worse television shows. You can hardly call it art.'

'Cave paintings were probably made by children but it's called art too. I move money. Money that often doesn't exist. It's notional, numbers on the stock market screen, on papers. What you do is real.'

'What I really think is that the lack of oxygen at high altitudes does impair brain activity,' said Deb.

And every night he would fail at asking her to turn back, go to the jungle resort instead, dip their aching feet into a pool and try to have sex in it.

'It's coming now! Wake up. C'mon Deb, we promised each other we will see this together. Bharat Mata ki jai, remember?' she exclaimed.

Deb drifted back to reality. He mustered his remaining strength and opened his eyes. Light flooded in and blinded him for a moment.

'Look! Look there! Oh my God, it's beautiful, it's so beautiful,' he heard her exclaim.

His vision cleared a little.

'It's the most beautiful thing I have ever seen, Deb!' she said.

He could see now; but not what she saw.

He saw her face, lit up from the first rays of the morning sun atop a dormant volcano, 5895 m above sea level, closer to heaven than earth and he knew she was right. Like the skies had burst open and a rogue angel had sashayed out to the world. It was the most beautiful sight he had ever seen. *Avantika*. That childlike smile, the sun and the glint in her eyes, those long, curved eyelashes which swept in the night if they fell, those perennially half-opened lips, full and red, those slightly uneven teeth as if they were a little joke she played on others to show she was imperfect too, and that tanned olive skin. Her hair fell across his face in big waves, the hair he loved to wrap around his fingers in the night, so she couldn't move without tugging him. 'Why do you do that,' she would often ask in her sleep. 'I'm scared you will leave in the night,' he would answer. She was still the girl he had fallen in love with ten years ago when he had gasped and fumbled and found words deserting him just like it did today. He was not the same person, neither was she; yet he felt the same—inadequate and in love. His falling in love wasn't a past event, it was always present continuous.

'It's incredible,' gasped Deb, using what seemed to him like his last breath. *What a beautiful way to die*, he thought. *What a fucking beautiful way to die.*

Avantika helped him get up and turned him towards the sunrise. It was what they had spent the last five days for—to catch the sunrise at the top of the highest mountain in Africa. Instead, he watched her. All the world was a lie, things we had invented and built, but she was real and his love for her was real and it was beautiful, and she was beautiful and he would climb a billion mountains, dive into a thousand seas to look at her once more.

He heard her scream, 'Bharat Mata ki jai,' to the confused white boys.

'You were right,' said Avantika as she walked past the stretcher they used to bring Deb down from the mountain. 'At high altitudes, the brain is affected. I shouldn't have done that. But damn, did you see how beautiful it was?'

'I saw what I needed to see,' said Deb and passed out with a stupid grin on his face.

Deb was admitted in a hospital for exhaustion. The forms were filled, the flight tickets were rescheduled, and Avantika applied for more sick leaves.

'I will be back in an hour. I have to make some calls to the office,' said Avantika.

'I have seen it in the movies. The heroine or the hero attending to their sick partner sleeps in the chair, changes the flowers, reads the newspaper, adjusts the blanket, all in the hospital room. They don't move for days. Entire songs are sung, and they are always there, and you want to go after just six hours?'

'Did I tell you I have to make work calls? Oh ho, my bad. What I meant was that I need to crawl up the stairs of the mandir and pray for your well-being. Can I go now?'

In the couple of hours that passed when Avantika wasn't there, Deb lucidly dreamt and checked the depths of his love for her vis-à-vis his love for others.

In a multitude of ways, he imagined both his sisters and his parents dying in a fiery car crash, a quick painless death, charred to a bone within seconds. He would imagine his best friend, Shrey, getting stuck in a lift, his body ripped into two, guts spilling out. Or Vernita, his other best friend, dying slowly of cancer, of him holding her bony, spotted hand when no one would. He found himself tear up thinking of these hypotheticals.

Then, it was Avantika's turn to die.

He mulled over dozens of ways she could die but none of the imagined situations came to fruition. She was the lone survivor of a plane crash and defeated cancer twice. In his fantasy world, she was immortal.

He gave up. He couldn't imagine her not being around. What he could imagine was what would follow. He would be standing atop a building to follow Avantika in death.

He often wondered if Avantika loved him as much as he loved her. Of course, she was the perfect partner, far better than Deb was, but was she equally in love with him as he was with her? In Deb's opinion, she wasn't. If he were to die, she would carry on, tragic and beautiful and unmarried for the rest of her immortal life.

That didn't make him sad.

He was proud to have done one thing right in his life. He loved her and he loved her like no one loved anyone. That was something that would never change. They would always be enough for each other.

Little did he know, that this was about to change. There would be someone else who would threaten to rip them apart.

2

'Did you think about it? I don't want to put pressure on you but I need to know. This is important for me,' Avantika asked, her voice much sterner than usual.

She had given Deb a year to think about it and he had loved her more fiercely in response and waited for her to forget the question. He had other questions in his head. Were they not enough? Were they out of love? What more could he do?

'Of course, I thought about it. What are you talking about?' he argued. 'Why would I not think about it? You asked me to do something and I did.'

'Don't get defensive, Deb. I'm just asking.'

'Your tone made it sound like an allegation. As if I didn't think about it, when in fact I did.'

'So what did you think? There's a timeline to these things. We need to decide soon.'

SOON. TIME RUNNING OUT. There were those words again.

Cradling his cell phone in his hand, Debashish Roy, Deb to everyone around him, felt like a gnarly old banyan tree at the *nukkad*, the street corner, like the old uncles from the neighbourhood who hate bachelors and their imagined debaucheries, like the men who don't mind paperwork at the bank and call photocopy 'cyclostyle', like his *mesho*s and *kaku*s who wore monkey caps in June and wrote consumer complaints about broken Aquaguard machines in perfect English. For many years, he had virulently fought against the impending blight of old age, and yet the numbers irritably ticked on.

He knew that nostalgia and time smoothen out the kinks and the mishaps from one's memory. But even then, he missed being younger, when these questions didn't even cross his mind.

'It's not an easy question to answer, Avantika, and you know that,' Deb replied with the feeling that he would grow older even by voicing out the question.

'I just want to know what you're thinking. I don't want you to commit to it. Just want to know the direction of your thoughts,' said Avantika.

At that moment Deb's thought was—*how did we get here? How did so much time pass?* The early twenties were a steep learning curve with jagged ends for Deb. While at twenty-one, Bhagat Singh was pumping bullets into colonialists, writing about atheism and socialism and in general being a legend, Deb at twenty-one was battling the raging hormones of a delayed puberty and his own recklessness. There was all but one thing on his mind— getting laid—and he acted foolishly and with moderate success in that pursuit.

And when the waves of horniness ebbed, and the bleak future of cubicles and shackles of a corporate life loomed large, it seemed like the right time to find an escape in love, and boy, did he fall in love. He met Avantika Sharma in the second year of engineering and the girl changed him. She clawed her way into the deepest recesses within him and tinkered with everything that made him. He shed his old self like a snake and came out shining anew. Avantika swore he had done the same to her. Their love was all-consuming, the irritating kind, with mushiness that made others gag and envious at the same time. Avantika was the love to beat all loves. At least, in their heads that was so till they (mostly Deb) made mistakes and realized it was love like every other love—fraught with problems, doubts, heartbreaks, but at the end of it all, worth it.

'You have had enough time, Deb. I deserve an answer,' said Avantika.

'I'm just looking for the right words,' said Deb, staring at what seemed like an irreversible, life-altering crossroads.

Why hadn't he seen this coming? Why hadn't he imagined standing where he was right now? The answer was simple. He thought time wouldn't move as swiftly as it did. The mid-twenties were a blur of ambition, alcohol, moderate-to-earth-shattering sex, flitting endlessly between cities and jobs. At that time it seemed to him that he would never get old; that this time would last forever, with his friends and him being the masters of their own lives, powerful enough to mould life the way they wanted to. They were past their middle-class and lower-middle-class lives. The oppressive pressures of entrance examinations and internships and job interviews had borne fruit and they had money that they could spend on clothes and mobiles; their hearts and minds were healthy and full of life and they could do no wrong. They could go out, eat, drink, party and their young, lithe bodies would metabolize everything leaving them to conquer the world again the next day.

But then came the questions.

'You didn't think there would be a time that you would be faced with this question? Do you want me to believe that this is the first time you have had to think about this?' asked Avantika.

'Yes,' lied Deb, who had sensed things change way before that day.

It hit him at the end of the twenties that there had been a seismic shift, that they weren't as young any more. The hangovers lasted longer, the joy of a plan getting cancelled was unparalleled, coffee became an essential fatty acid, and he knew that mutual funds were less secure than fixed deposits.

When Avantika and Deb got married, they made conscious choices to not slip into the social coma that is the fate of many couples when they touch twenty-eight. They travelled, partied, had people over all the time, and reinforced their belief that there was a life still to be lived after twenty-five.

It was a lie.

They started liking their alone time better. They slept early on Friday nights, and even earlier on Saturdays. They liked their house clean. And that was the end of their house parties.

Time ticked on and somewhere unbeknownst to Deb, Avantika seamlessly slipped into the role of a proper functioning adult. Deb was left alone to deal with the anachronism of his body and his mind and his age. He would want to get drunk and hammered silly but would be scared of the hangover, he would want to plan backpacking holidays but get lazy, he could tell a good-quality duvet apart from one that would become lumpy after a year and yet not want to know he knew it.

'Why do I feel like you didn't take it seriously?' she asked, breaking Deb's nostalgic train of thought.

'Why would you say that?' said Deb.

'Because that's what you do,' said Avantika.

The worst part about growing old was that he didn't feel old in a sage-like way. He felt old in an unattractive way where difficult questions were still difficult—none of the sexiness of George Clooney or the wisdom of Gandalf the Grey.

'I talked to Shrey. We had a long discussion about it.'

'You talked to Shrey about it?' she asked incredulously.

'He thinks conceptually it's a great idea. A brilliant idea. Genetically, it's perfect. Like there's no reason why not to do it. You know, because, our genetics, it's perfect. It's so perfect. You and me, me and you, perfect, just perfect.'

She sighed tiredly. 'You lost me at Shrey. He's the last person whom you should talk to about this. Leaving floaters in my bathroom is his idea of a prank.'

'Well, there's also something else he pointed out. A few months of relief . . . errm . . . protection-wise. So that's something to consider. And it's on my list of things . . . you know to be considered while taking a decision like this.'

'Relief? Is that what he's calling it?' scoffed Avantika.

'He's not very strict with terminologies. What do you want to go with? Let's say we don't have to be careful any more.'

'Debashish, I need a decision soon,' said Avantika irritably.

'Something tells me it's not a discussion any more. Should we talk about that first? How you're the one making all the decisions? I didn't even want paneer yesterday and yet we had that. Can we discuss that first?'

'I just want to know where you're on this. You can't joke around about this. You know that, right? I have always wanted this,' she said, her voice suddenly sincere and soft. And how that pathetic, lovelorn voice broke his heart! That soft velvety voice wrapped itself around him like a bathrobe with a dense thread count.

'Avantika—' he attempted.

'This matters to me, Debashish. Also, Shrey, it's been ten years you have been eavesdropping on our conversations. You should stop. Bye, Debashish!'

Click.

She had taken Deb's full name twice in a space of two minutes during their conversation. That only meant one of two things—he was great at phone sex or it was the beginning of a nail-biting, cold war.

I have always wanted this. The words rang in Deb's ears all day. If it was the truth, what about all the times she had said she had Deb and it was all she ever needed. Had that time passed? After ten years, had her love for him finally abated? Had she finally realized she was too good for him? Or was his love not enough for her any more? Was he no longer her saviour as she often put it? Why did she need someone else now? He understood a family was what she always wanted but why wasn't he enough?

3

'You shouldn't let her bulldoze you like this. It's your decision too, bro,' said Shrey.

'Don't call me bro. And she's not bulldozing me, I have an equal say in this. We take decisions as a single unit. That's how marriages work.'

Shrey laughed and leaned back into his chair. 'She has you by the balls, bro. Be a man now and deny her sex. Plain and simple. Don't fall into this trap, I'm telling you. Mark my words, otherwise this will be the end of your life.'

'You're blowing this out of proportion. End of my life? Really?'

'I knew you would say that, Deb, and hence I made a presentation for you. Just to show you how right I am and how wrong you are. I will also mail it to you and CC Avantika on it. If she takes it seriously she will rethink her decision too,' he said confidently, opened his laptop and clicked through to a presentation.

'By the way, did you send the mails you had to send last week?' Deb asked.

'Why would you think I would prioritize that over saving my only friend from certain ruin? I'm not a jerk no matter what your wife thinks of me. I care about you, bro,' Shrey said.

A sharply made presentation filled up the screen—*HOW BABIES RUIN EVERYTHING.*

Deb animatedly rolling his eyes did nothing to dampen Shrey's enthusiasm. Instead he looked enthusiastically at the list of names that had popped up on the first slide with their stud ratings, their childish invention from the past. A stud rating was a gender-neutral, weighted rating that was given to every boy and girl around them under four clear heads—Fitness, Sartorial Choices, Social Media Behaviour and Interests.

'Nonsense! This rating is juvenile. You can't put numbers to people—'

'Deb! Concentrate,' Shrey said pointing to the screen. 'Remember Aman Nagpal? Rini's friend? Ripped, marathon runner, barely posted on social media because he was too cool for it? Knew how to get into any guest list? Partied like a fucking stealth bomber?'

'He was a solid 9,' said Deb, remembering how he'd wished the worst on this perfect human specimen back in the day.

'Quoted Marx at will? Milind Soman potential?'

'Get to the point, Shrey.'

'He is a 3 now. Even at your worst, Deb, you were never a 3. Maybe 4, but not 3.'

Shrey and Deb, despite strictly being in the middle of the social hierarchy of appearances, had taken care of themselves and their bodies and made sure they never strayed to the dark side of 5. They rated themselves as dependable 6s. Shrey had ways to hide his averageness—he was tall and his curly, poodlish hair could pass him off as a hipster. Deb, in his turn, had learned to smile a lot and distract attention from his poor features and direct them towards an evolutionary anomaly—his dimple.

Shrey tapped to the next slide. A before–after comparison of Aman Nagpal. Once an elite-stud he was now unfit, badly dressed, had put up albums with twenty pictures each of jaunts to his relatives' houses. There were selfies taken from below eye level capturing his cavernous nostrils. That's what age does to you—it reduces the angle from which you click a selfie. There was an entire album with thirty-three pictures named *karwa chauth* from a few months ago.

'He voted for the fanatical Hindu. Even tweeted *Mandir Wahi Banaenge* and nagging wife memes. He's gutter now,' said Shrey, clicking through screenshots of his tweets and Facebook posts.

'Remember Rini Biswas?'

'The McKinsey girl?'

'A solid twelve, wasn't she? Dancer, talked like a bullet train, clothes so sharp they could cut you, knowledge bank deeper than the Mariana Trench. Barely one post every six months on Facebook, but tweeted like a maniac about DBA and feminism and what not. So cool she could undo global warming?'

'Didn't two boys beat each other half to death over her? She got them expelled, filed police reports too, didn't she? Now where's she?'

'BABY PICTURES. ALL YOU SEE IS FUCKING BABY PICTURES!'

A helpful hyperlink took them to Rini Biswas's Facebook profile which corroborated Shrey's research. A hideous baby with a ginormous black smudge on his forehead stared back at them.

'That baby doesn't need that kala tikka, no one's putting a *nazar* on him,' Deb murmured.

'And *that* is why you're not ready. Once every child seems cute to you is when you're ready for your own. It's pure science. You can't deny it. Look at the comments on the baby pictures. Every one of them is from someone who is either pregnant or has a baby of their own,' said Shrey.

The pattern in the profiles the presentation threw up at Deb was undeniable.

'It's what babies do to you. They are little dictators who take over your life and ruin everything. They destroy your bodies, your careers, everything,' said Shrey. 'You can't have a child, Debashish. Be a child yourself. Don't lose that.'

Deb looked at him.

'Did you see what I did there? Used your name in a sentence to make it sound serious like she does.'

'It only works when she says it,' said Deb.

Later that night, Shrey called Deb to check if he was using protection.

'I told her I wasn't ready and she took it well,' said Deb.

4

'Are you sure you're okay?' Deb asked her again that night.

He had been asking that quite often to make sure Avantika had been okay with what *they* had decided. Weeks had passed since Deb told her he didn't want anyone in their lives; they were not ready for a child. Avantika had taken it surprisingly well, so well, it seemed suspicious to Deb.

'We are still so much fun, Avantika. A baby will wreck all that and I don't want that to happen. I want it to be just us. If you want someone to fuss around, trust me, I can leave the house dirty and pee in corners. It will be just like you had a baby,' Deb joked again to test the waters.

'Aw, that's so cute,' she said. 'You don't have to keep explaining yourself. If you don't want it, there's no point having this discussion. I'm happy that you know what you want or don't. That's important.'

When Avantika slept that night and Deb stumbled on Avantika's unlocked laptop, mostly out of boredom, and partly because he wanted some dirt on Avantika, he snooped into her browser history. He remembered the time she had sneaked into his phone and found him uploading stellar, 5-star reviews from different accounts for his old books. She still mocked him about it. That duel was still on. He started looking for embarrassing Google searches. Shirtless Bobby Deol pictures? Justin Bieber song lyrics?

There were mountains worth of drivel for him to wade through to the good stuff. Tons and tons of searches of investment instruments, company annual reports, images of pie charts from financial newspapers and what not. As much as it confused Deb as to how much she liked what she did, he was thankful for it.

Between Deb's publishing venture—he had set out to find young writers, and strike gold with them—shutting down, his lacklustre writing career, and their bad investment choices, Avantika's salary from the investment bank kept them afloat.

Once his eyes got used to filtering out the money-related garbage, a few searches started to stick out. At first he didn't pay much attention. But then a pattern emerged, and he started to track them.

The first Google search had been made three years ago. *THREE YEARS AGO!* They were still tirelessly partying and cursing older people at the time.

'*When do you think you're ready to have a child?*'

She had clicked through five websites with 2,500-word essays by women who had kids too early, too late, or didn't have them at all. Deb wondered what he was doing while his wife was searching through the net. A few days later, there were a bunch of other searches.

'*How to tell if your husband is ready for a child?*'

Nightmarish horror stories about careless, clumsy husbands who thumped their chests about not knowing how to cook or clean up after themselves. She had bookmarked three pages. Was she putting him through the test? Did he pass? Of course, he passed.

Another bunch of searches.

'What will a child do to your career?'

Depressing articles. A bunch of feminists laying out the truth. All the talk about motherhood being gratifying and noble, about sacrifice and pain and what not, and yet the continual terrifying treatment meted out to pregnant women and new mothers at workplaces. There were no searches for a few weeks. Deb knew her office was infested with men who would guiltlessly destroy a woman's career over nothing. Pregnancy was the easiest pretext of them all.

The searches started again, as it was a pattern, late on Monday nights. Was her tyrannical work life driving her to this? Finding an escape route?

'What should you eat if you're planning a child in the near future?'

Scores of visits to diet and nutrition websites. Deb checked the month. Was it the same month she insisted they go for full-body check-ups? Was it around the time they cut out white bread, processed sugar and machine-polished rice from their diet? Maybe, maybe.

'How painful are deliveries?'

She'd read just two articles. She would have told herself she could do this. Last year, sitting in front of an orthopaedic doctor with a torn off meniscus, it was Deb who'd cringed when the doctor had brutally twisted her leg back into shape.

'On a scale of one to ten, how much is the pain?' the doctor had asked when he'd seen the leg. 'You can't just keep saying the pain's bearable. This looks in really bad shape. How did you manage to get the entire meniscus torn off?'

'Why don't you tell him, Avantika? He's a doctor, he needs to know. C'mon now, tell him.' Earlier that morning, Avantika had slipped and fallen while trying to beat Deb's skid distance on the freshly polished marble of their society's reception.

More searches.

'Do you ever lose your pregnancy weight?'

'*After a ceasarean?*

She must have gotten bored after three articles, all three of which asked women to not worry.

And this is where it started to get heartbreaking for Deb.

'*Babies.*'

She saw pictures of babies every night. Brown. White. Black. Cute. Not so cute. She clicked through hundreds of images. This was also where Deb got a little jealous. There was no way he could ever compete with the babies she was looking up online. Those annoying marble eyes, filled-up cheeks and those little paws.

Talking of paws, there were also a bunch of searches for '*Babies and puppies*'.

Deb recalled seeing one of the images on a wallpaper she had put on her phone. He had changed it back to his picture.

Deb scrolled down.

'*Pregnant women.*'

At this point, Deb started to feel bad. Why couldn't she have shared this with him? They could have talked this out and then he remembered how long he had taken to answer a simple question.

The clicks took another turn. Deb wasn't the first one to spy on Avantika's online activity.

Google, Facebook and other platforms had started to prey on Avantika, a girl wanting to be a mother, gawking at pictures of babies in the middle of the night, melting into a puddle. They must have started inserting ads, sponsored posts on her timelines about baby-related things—childcare hospitals, doctors, baby clothes, maternity wear, breast pumps, and those sort of things. But what Avantika had clicked through were ads from NGOs sourcing funds for dying and starving babies.

He switched off the laptop having seen enough. His spying had led him into a trap. How could he deny Avantika something she had wanted for the past three years? Or was it more? Coming from a family that was never really one, she always told Deb he was her family. But what if she always meant it like he was family for *now*? He crept into bed and snuggled next to Avantika. He looked at the clock. Five hours before she left for the gym; five more hours and then the world would have her. Having a child seemed unnatural. Why would he want to share her with anyone? Why would he divide her love?

'I love you,' he whispered in her ears.

And like every time he did that, no matter how fast asleep she was, she replied, 'I love you too.'

Was he overthinking, or did she sound different this time? Did she love him less because of his decision of not wanting kids right now? There were no searches after the decision, so it seemed like she had taken it well.

Then why was he stressing over it? She would do fine without a child between them. Wouldn't she? He loved her, that's all that mattered.

5

'Yes, you're overthinking, Deb,' said Shrey.

'You don't know Avantika. Even if she did feel bad or is continuing to feel bad about it, you would never know.'

'So what if she's feeling a little bad? We got what we wanted. We can still be children sometimes if we don't have them. Today you will have a child, tomorrow you will wear sports shoes with trousers. Where will it end?' said Shrey.

Shrey's words did nothing to mollify Deb's position and he followed her around to find out if her smiles were fake, if she was truly over the idea of being a mother, and if there was someone she was talking to about Deb's decision. There was only one place other than home and office that Avantika went to—the gym.

That morning was Deb's third attempt to go to the gym in the morning with Avantika. The first was when they had first joined it and promised each other that they would be fighting fit within three months. She held her part of the bargain.

The last time was when he had overheard a locker-room conversation:

'You should come in the morning, bro. The chicks, bro, the chicks . . . There's one who does, like, these deep squats. Her quads are like granite, bro,' said a boy.

Seven–eight years ago, he would have backslapped his way into the conversation of the three boys, wanting to hear more about the deep-squatting goddess, but now he knew better than to be a part of them or to confront them.

The boy continued, 'You should totally check her out, bro. Ass like melons, bhai, spring time melons. She does crazy hang cleans and squats till her ass is touching the floor, bro. You got to come, bro.'

No one he knew in the gym did hang cleans and squats like Avantika did—perfect shrug, below parallel and butt to the floor, back arched all the time.

The next morning, the three boys ran on the treadmill behind Avantika's. Like a self-respecting snitch he pointed them out to Avantika. She sashayed up to their treadmills—they had all cranked theirs up to 14 km/hr trying to impress the women around them—and slammed her palm into the EMERGENCY STOP buttons. Their belts stopped with a jerk.

All three boys, one after another, propelled by inertia, got their faces slammed against the treadmill console. They crumpled to the ground, bleeding from their noses. Avantika had laughed heroically. The women in the gym had smiled at each other as if they were tapping into the same neural networks and they knew what had just happened.

That day was the third time.

While Avantika went pottering around weights, Deb cycled next to an old, sprightly uncle who was in a chatty mood.

'Lift your knees to at least 95 per cent to burn more fat,' he said and added with a wink. 'Will keep your wife happy too!'

Deb smiled and plugged in his earphones. Avantika had looked cheerful while doing the Zumba, bored on the cycle and angry during the deadlifts. Maybe she wasn't disappointed after all. Maybe there was nothing to hide.

She was cooling down on the treadmill with another girl when Deb heard the word 'baby'. His ears pricked.

'He's so sweet when he latches on my breast!' squealed the girl. 'Look at his pictures!' Avantika looked on, a twinkle in her eyes. Deb wanted to throw his sipper at the girl who was scrolling through what seemed like a billion pictures of her child. The girl continued, 'Are you trying? If you are, make sure you get a date from the pandit for the sex—'

'We are not ready yet. There's a lot of time,' Avantika responded.

'Of course, of course. You can't have a child unless you're ready for it. Though don't wait too long. You don't want your parents to go without seeing a grandchild. It's the greatest love in the world. You don't know love till—'

'I'm pretty sure I know what love feels like. He's Deb and he's the greatest love of my life.'

He came back home, troubled and proud. To have her declare him the love of her life still gave him goosebumps. A decade had passed and he was yet to get used to walking next to her. Sometimes he would get a childish impulse to stare back at the men and women who would look at them strangely and snap back, 'We are having sex, okay! She loves me! Ask her!'

But even as he walked around all day, chuffed, calling himself the greatest love of Avantika's life, he couldn't forget how she looked while looking at the pictures of the baby.

Later that night, Deb snooped into her laptop again. He realized he had made a rookie mistake. There were two browsers, two search histories, and more troubling searches, the most damning of them were made that evening.

'How does breastfeeding feel?'

'Where can you play with babies?'

'Sponsoring babies—NGO.'

'After what age does getting pregnant become difficult?'

Deb made a few searches of his own.

'How to not feel guilty about not wanting a child as much as your wife?'

6

'You can't have your cake and eat it too,' said Shrey. 'You can't get what you want and want Avantika to be happy about it. She will get over it eventually. Stop stressing over it.'

'I'm not stressing, I'm just angry at her. Why can't she make do with me? Don't I make her happy enough that she wants a child? What can a child do that I can't?'

'Umm . . . that's a strange question for you to ask me and I would like this conversation to be over because I'm thinking breast and milk and you and Avantika, so, SHUT UP,' said Shrey and put on his headphones.

Avantika's lie of having accepted Deb's decision without a groan ate at him. But as Shrey said, he waited for her to get over it. He continued his snooping and spying and things seemed to get better. Until that day when Avantika didn't ask for a second helping of the *poori–bhaaji*. She would pick his poori-bhaaji over a solution to climate change, over Hogwarts, over a private one-to-one with Shah Rukh Khan. On other days, she would crib about the oiliness and yet keep stuffing herself endlessly and then declare, 'You know what I really need now? A cup of tea and a nap.' These words always gave Deb almost as much satisfaction and raw pride as making her orgasm thrice and leave her shaking. And making poori-bhaaji was always easier, and the reaction harder to fake.

That particular day, however, Avantika didn't complain about the oiliness, or make a mound of pooris on her plate. She nibbled at it like a bird and left without a word. Back at the office, he made Shrey taste it and ratified that his poori-bhaaji was saturated fats heaven.

Through the afternoon, Deb left her worried texts and got one-word answers as replies. No heart-shaped smileys, no goofy boomerangs.

'She must be on her period,' said Shrey.

'Did no one slap on your face the book on what's not appropriate any more?'

'Where's your pink shirt? Vanguard of feminism that you are, where's your crown?'

'Not a dick is how I would define it.'

And then it struck Deb.

She wasn't on her period. What if . . .

'Could she be . . .' Deb's voice trailed.

An otherwise efficient bather Avantika had taken enormously long that morning. Deb knew little about the mechanics of sanitary pads or tampons and how much time it took to get one in place, but he was sure Avantika would do it lightning fast. On the other hand, a home pregnancy test . . . that could take time. Had she taken one?

Deb rushed back home.

He upturned dustbins, rummaged through drawers, pulled the house apart for tell-tale signs. Instead he found a condom from three days ago. Deb held it beneath running water to check if it leaked. Nope, no chance.

She didn't call in the afternoon. It was a tradition—their lunchtime calls. Deb had come up with it long ago. He had always been insecure of Avantika prancing around in her shockingly well-fitted suits in an office with other overachievers in equally sharp suits and healthy bank accounts. To counter his discomfort, he made sure every afternoon he engaged Avantika in a long conversation where he made her say sweet things out loud to him. Sometimes, he would dress up for video calls so others around her knew she was with someone who could occasionally look cute.

Deb paced around, tried to count days, Googled signs of pregnancies, let his imagination run away from him. He went cold.

When she got back home and behaved normally, Deb hatched what he thought was a carefully laid trap. First, he would ask her if she would be going to the gym the next morning and they could do some snatch pulls mixed with some heavy, relentless deadlifts. Then he would ask her to go clubbing that night, get drunk till they vomited their guts out, wake up with a hangover and then cut that with another drink. But he could barely keep it in and blurted out, 'I know you took a pregnancy test. All the signs are there. I know you did. You didn't eat the poori-bhaaji and then you didn't call in the afternoon. You thought I wouldn't know but I do. You took it, didn't you?'

In the few seconds she took to answer him, he felt his heart stop.

'I didn't,' she said and before Deb could calm down she added. 'But I should have gotten my period three days ago and I don't feel anything right now.'

It wouldn't be the first time her period was late. Every few months, they would have a scare like this—sometimes she told Deb, sometimes she didn't—but most times they were sure the contraception had done what was asked of it.

'It must be because of stress at work. Don't worry about it, it will be nothing,' she said.

Deb woke up twice that night and found Avantika working. He asked her if she was doing okay and she nodded and told him to go back to sleep.

'Do we need to take a test? What if you're pregnant?' he asked.

'Three days is not a long time. We can wait for a couple of more days,' she said looking at him. Then she stared back into her laptop. Deb wondered what emotion would she have betrayed had she not broken her gaze. Deb knew her enough to understand what she was saying and what she really wanted.

She wasn't waiting for her period. Could someone want a child so bad they could fail contraception? What nonsense. He closed his eyes and prayed to the condom gods.

Sleep evaded Deb for a while. He closed his eyes and imagined what it would feel like if Avantika was pregnant after all. What would he say to her? What would he feel? Who would he first call?

She didn't go to the gym in the morning. They spoke very little. Deb couldn't think of the words that he could say to her. The silence between them ate at Deb. Avantika's secret hope and Deb's fears were at odds with each other.

Deb called Shrey from the bathroom. Shrey held his silence for a long time before he said, 'Now that that damage is done and you have ruined your life, tell her that you will support her no matter what. She needs to hear that right now. Put up a smile and just say the words. Fake it.'

'Fake it? Really? She could have a child inside of her right now! A living human that I would have to raise and take care of! How am I supposed to hide my reluctance to do that?' said Deb.

'That's what marriages are about, isn't it? Go out there and talk to your wife.'

Their marriage was not about that. Would he have to lie? Like Avantika was lying the past few days about how Deb's decision affected her?

'I have to go,' said Deb.

'What are you going to tell her?'

'I don't know yet.'

He disconnected the call. By the time he left the washroom to talk to her, she was gone. A Post–it was stuck on the refrigerator.

Urgent call from work. Had to leave. Love.

He thought of doing what Shrey had asked him to do; typed the words in a message and deleted them twice. It didn't seem right.

Back in the office, he paced around, torn between feeling what he did about the possibility of Avantika being pregnant and pacifying Avantika. Shrey looked on, angry and irritated.

'You don't look like a person who could get someone accidentally pregnant.'

'Of all the times, you think this is the time to joke?'

'I have told you what to do. That's your only option,' said Shrey.

'I can't lie, not about this,' Deb said to Shrey.

'So if she does find out she's pregnant what will you ask her to do? To get the child aborted? If not then you will have to learn to lie. To her at first and then yourself. You can't be bringing a child into this world thinking that you didn't want him or her in the first place,' said Shrey.

'Stop embarrassing me. I fucking hate it when you talk sense. You're the last person who should think clearly.'

Just then, Deb's phone rang and it was Avantika. It wasn't lunch time yet.

'Where are you?' asked Deb.

'In the office washroom,' said Avantika, and added after a pause. 'I have a pregnancy test in my hand right now. I had to know. I couldn't help myself. I wanted to talk to you before I take it.'

'What do you want to talk about?'

'Deb? What if it's positive? What if there's a baby inside of me? I saw how you reacted yesterday, you were terrified. I want to know what you were thinking.'

Deb felt uncomfortable by this sudden turn of events. Like the kind of inconvenience you feel when your relatives drop by suddenly and stay for a little longer than necessary.

She continued, 'If it's positive and I have a child inside me, it wouldn't be fair to you. But I will keep the child,' she said.

The rehearsed and taught words dribbled out of his mouth, 'I feel I would be ready to be beside you no matter what happens.'

'You say it like I have cancer.'

'Not cancer. But tumour, maybe? A little tumour in your womb?'

'I may not be pregnant but all your jokes are dad jokes,' she said and chuckled sadly.

He heard her put the phone aside on speaker.

'Are you peeing on the stick? What if you miss?' he joked nervously.

'DEB!'

'As the father of that unborn child I need to know what the first secretion was. What's the colour? The projectile? I'm just being with you every step of the way,' joked Deb, not to lighten Avantika's mood but his own. Who knew, it might sound less daunting then!

Deb heard the tinkle. His pulse quickened.

'So? What's it? What happened?'

'Wait.'

'Now? Is it positive? Is it?'

'WAIT, DEB!'

He knew his worst fear would come true and the test would be positive. When had Avantika failed? She would ace this too, she would be so pregnant, so immensely pregnant. There was no doubt. He would have to live with that. He imagined a little embryo kicking around in her uterus. He didn't imagine a small homunculus but a tiny seahorse floating around.

A couple of months later, her bump would start to show. She would no longer be the girl whose abs were the envy of everyone at the gym. She would freeze her membership for a year. Such a waste of money. Instead, she would have to stay in bed longer with him, cuddling, wasting time rather than being fit.

From being fiercely independent, she would need Deb to hover around her for everything. She would throw tantrums and it would be up to him to keep her in good spirits and he would do that. He would make her happy because what else would he do. He would have to fuss over her constantly, not let her pick up heavy things and exert herself. He would have to give her a dressing down every time she would try to do something on her own.

She would have that pregnancy glow people talk about. What good could that do to her? Would she become even prettier? Was that possible? There was no question she would rock her maternity too. Other pregnant women would flock to her and ask where she got her clothes from. Embarrassed husbands would gawk at the glamorous, pregnant Avantika and Deb would look at them and mouth silently, yeah, I did that, we had sex, mad sex. There would be so many awkward conversations.

He would have to love that little foetus inside her. He would have to talk to him or her, tell stories, sing songs. He would tell him or her how lucky he or she was to have an awesome mother like her. He would tell him or her all the stories of them much to the chagrin of Avantika. 'Shut up! Don't tell her that,' Avantika would complain. He would describe Avantika to him or her and would hope the foetus looked like her.

Avantika would apply for a maternity leave, he would stay back home and they would spend entire days together talking about the future and the past. Together they would binge on every Netflix series, watch all the Shah Rukh Khan movies and cry, spend more time together than they had done in years. They would go swimming and pre-natal yoga together.

He would keep telling her that despite the weight she's sexy and she would always be. He would have a little belly himself and they would click a picture together with their bellies touching, look at the picture repeatedly and go . . . Aw! He would massage her feet after a long day, try to seduce her in the process but she would be fast asleep with her mouth open, saliva dribbling, and she would still look cute. He would sit up wondering if the baby had fallen asleep too, and just to pass the time, he would have to talk to the baby the entire night.

He would make elaborate lunches to feed her and the growing child inside of her. He would insist she finish. He would hold up her hair at three in the morning when she would vomit. He would clean up after. He would fire their house help for leaving water on the floor and then do it all himself there on after.

They would go out to shop for the baby, fight on what colour his or her room would be. He would buy the best cot and Avantika would advise against spending so much. They would debate what the name would be, and whether he or she would take his surname or hers, and Deb would insist on his. Every week she would pose and flaunt her baby bump and he would click pictures. They would have sex later because it would get too intimate. She would sleep and snore and he would keep his hand on her swollen belly. She would keep asking him if he still loved her? If he loved her baby? He would answer without thinking, the answer always at the tip of his tongue. How could he not love her new body? Or what it carried inside? A part of her, and a part of him?

She would be pregnant, and their lives would change.

Deb broke out of his reverie, deeply confused. *What's happening? What was I thinking?*

'Is it positive?' he asked.

'It's negative.'

Nothing was brewing in her belly.

Shrey exulted in the background, 'I KNEW IT! I FUCKING KNEW IT! YOU SHOOT BLANKS, BRO! YOU SHOOT BLANKS!'

Later, Deb searched for what embryos looked like and found out they look nothing like seahorses. Shrey ordered butter chicken to celebrate and Deb complained about how it tasted like ash.

He kept going back to those few seconds when he had imagined an alternate future. Was it all that bad?

7

'Do I have to go too? You can't go alone? Tell them I'm dead and will be unavailable till further notice,' said Deb.

'For the last time, you're coming with me. Vernita has insisted that you come. She's your best friend and how long has it been since you last met them?' asked Avantika.

'Excuse me? I met her just last week,' said Deb.

'You didn't meet him though.'

'I have nothing to do with her husband. Had she married well I would have thought about it.'

'Deb, behave. He's my brother.'

'Why would I want to meet him? I don't know if you have noticed but I don't feel comfortable meeting that *saala*.'

'Don't call him that.'

'But that's what he is. He's your brother, so, S.A.A.L.A.'

'Don't.'

'S.A.A.L.A.'

'After we come back we will have to discuss why we got married and before you say it, it's not because you're a good kisser. You're coming and that's final. It's an important day for him and he wants us to be there.'

Deb scoffed. 'What's new?'

Tanmay Sharma, Avantika's brother, had had important dates every few months since the past few years. Promotions at work, fastest North India Ironman, fiftieth blood donation, and days he took out to feed orphan kids . . . his years were peppered with achievements.

'Is that foundation on your face?' asked Avantika in the cab.

Deb didn't dignify her question with an answer.

'And did you use an entire bottle of Engage Deo on yourself?'

Deb said, caught, 'All 250 sprays of it.'

'Well, at least you're going smell better than him.'

'He can give his best shot.'

Tanmay Sharma was Deb's senior in college, and he'd broken Deb's stud-rating system when Deb and Shrey had tried rating him. He was then and even now an improbable being, a chimera—proficient in sports, academics, professional life all matched with symmetrical facial features which are the benchmark of attractiveness.

Deb, Shrey and Vernita—best friends in college—first saw Tanmay at the inter-collegiate swimming competition. They had heard a lot about him and Vernita had dragged them with her to the swimming pool to find out more.

'How hot can he be?' Deb and Shrey had said cynically, both of whom crushed a little over Vernita—not without reason—at the time. Vernita, herself, was stereotypically hot, the kind of girl both alumni, juniors and prospective students talked about. She was in mechanical engineering, no less, one in a billion occurrence, and that made her the inspiration of choice for toilet caricaturists across college who would draw her with big breasts, wide hips and full lips. She was to model, her features quite conspicuous.

They had to eat their words when his entry was marked by gender-neutral gasps around the pool. He glided by the pool-side, his abs so unnaturally thick it looked like someone had modelled a mountain range on his stomach, his quads and calves flexed as if they had a life of their own, and no one missed the significant bump in his swimming costume. He dived and cut the water like an eel. He backstroked the last lap in a freestyle race and won. When he emerged from the pool, the costume clung to his butt like his second skin, and everyone felt a bit turned on.

'He's going to get a blowjob today,' Vernita had whispered in their ears.

What Deb and Shrey had thought a generic statement—like he deserves a blowjob, or there might be someone who would give him a blowjob today—was not one.

Later that evening, Deb and Shrey were standing guard outside the electronics engineering classroom while Vernita made Tanmay fall in love with her. It took her half an hour. When Tamnay emerged with a grin on his face, his arm linked around Vernita's, who wiped the dust off her knees, fixed her hair and hid her trembling, glistening lips, he patted Shrey and Deb's shoulders and thanked them. They had never seen Vernita that tired. They hated him ever since.

After that day, Vernita gave up years of promiscuity for this piece of pure muscle and brain. The collective breaking of hearts in their college had resonated between the walls for years.

Tanmay and Vernita seemed so much . . . in lust and love that it grated on all of them. The carnality of the relationship was raw, aggressive and hard to miss. Their embraces looked like the interlocking of two Greek sculptures. It was painful to look at their combined gorgeousness. Their kisses seemed to make the earth rumble. If someone would tap them like rubber plants, by making a small incision, you could collect sex in a vessel. There wasn't a more perfect couple.

Over the years, he had grown even more fiercely alpha-male of the feminist kind. He had raked up crushes of precocious teenagers and old women alike with his hair that was prematurely grey and the skin that had gone rough with shaving every day.

'Don't stare at her, Shrey,' said Avantika when they reached their doorstep and pressed the bell.

'That's a baseless allegation you are making and I will not stand for it,' said Shrey, pretending his feelings were hurt.

'You know you do and then you enlist my husband too,' said Avantika.

'I can't talk about your husband but I'm not sure you can blame me. It's conditioning and evolution. Even you know, Vernita was the hot bhabhi even before she became a bhabhi.'

'Why are you friends with him, Deb?' said Avantika.

'I don't subscribe to his views,' said Deb.

'Of course you do, please don't tell me you find absolutely no parallels between her and Savita Bhabhi.'

'I don't know what you're talking about,' said Deb.

'A, Deb, you're quite bad at lying, and B, Shrey, she looks nothing like her!' Avantika said hotly.

Vernita opened the door. Vernita had grown into an amply-bosomed, child-bearing-hipped woman at eighteen and stuck out like a sore thumb in their engineering college back in the day. She wore her sexuality like a badge, and there were students back at Delhi Technological University who were still talking about her ten years later.

'Maybe she does,' muttered Avantika under her breath. 'I thought you wouldn't come, chuti . . .' said Vernita and lunged at Deb. She hugged him first and then Avantika. 'Don't tell Tanmay I swore. You know how he gets,' she whispered into her ear as they hugged.

'YOUR WIFE JUST CALLED MY HUSBAND CHUTI . . .' shouted Avantika.

'Bitch,' grumbled Vernita.

'SHE CALLED Avantika A BITCH,' said Shrey.

As they all laughed, Tanmay walked out of the kitchen, his sinewy arms in sharp focus.

'He needs a pressure cooker to explode in his face,' said Deb.

'A splash of hot oil will do too,' said Shrey.

In Tanmay's hands were little pakodas, fried perfectly, smelling like they should be eaten that instant.

Tanmay hugged Avantika and said, 'I believe the guys didn't want to come, did they?'

He stepped closer and swung a mock punch at Deb's face. 'Why are you so scared of me?'

Deb swayed out of the way, putting up a masculine, unafraid smile. 'Scared of you?' he chuckled and battled to come up with a wicked repartee. 'I would rather be scared of . . . nothing.'

'Wow, Deb, just wow,' said Shrey.

'That made no sense,' said Avantika.

'That's true,' said Vernita.

'It wasn't supposed to. It was meant to confuse you. Which it did.'

'Err,' said Tanmay.

'What happened to you?' asked Vernita mockingly.

'You are tragic,' said Avantika.

'I'm so glad to be Shrey and not you right now,' said Shrey.

No one mentioned why Deb thought that mock punch was only a part-mock. When Avantika and Deb had first kissed back in college, Tanmay had punched Deb, and not without reason. Deb had been dating Smriti, a cute, petite medical student he wasn't in love with. Hence Tanmay and Vernita had asked Avantika and Deb to stay away from each other, but they hadn't listened.

'You will destroy her life. You're the last person a girl should date,' Vernita had told Deb who had been quite unlucky in love at the time. He would think he was in love for a moment and then orchestrate elaborate break-ups when he found out he wasn't.

'You're too fragile to be in love again. And especially not with him. You are you and he is him. Have you seen him?' Tanmay had told Avantika who had been trying to move on from an abusive relationship.

When Vernita and Tanmay found them mucking around behind their back, Tanmay had pummelled Deb. It had taken years for her relationship with her brother and Deb's with Vernita to heal. If Deb had known that the healing of their relationship would mean combined lunches celebrating Tanmay's achievements, he would have preferred to remain strangers.

For Deb and Shrey, it was rather annoying to be in the company of these three smart, ambitious people who talked tirelessly about their offices, new investment vehicles and the state of the economy.

Usually, Deb and Shrey timed their meetings with Vernita for when Tanmay was not around. She was a different person around him. With Shrey and Deb, she was her usual foul-mouthed, back-slapping, cynical self who they liked more.

They all sat around a tasteful dining table and ate what was begrudgingly one of the best meals Deb had had in a long time. It was only Tanmay who hadn't touched anything. He seemed to be visibly beaming, barely being able to contain the impending news.

'There's a development . . .' said Tanmay with a bit of hesitation.

'We can't wait to hear about it,' Deb muttered.

'Both of us could barely sleep last night. Please tell us what it's about,' said Shrey.

'Will you tell them, or should I?' Tanmay asked Vernita.

'You should,' said Vernita disinterestedly, looping a long strand of pasta around her fork.

'Are you sure?'

'Of course. You're the one who did it,' said Vernita, slurping the long noodle.

Tanmay's words dropped like a hammer.

'*We are pregnant,*' said Tanmay.

8

Vernita, Deb and Shrey were at the brewery where they met once every two weeks and indulged in some light nostalgia and talked about how it was only yesterday that they were in college.

'Vernita, how strict is your alcohol ban? Are there conclusive studies that you can't drink? Or is it just "let's be careful about it" stuff?' asked Shrey who'd ordered tasters of all the beers the brewery sold.

'I'm pretty sure the studies are conclusive,' said Vernita, irritably.

'Why are you being a jerk to her?' said Deb.

'Yeah, that's a dick move,' agreed Vernita.

'Are you allowed to say that? Pro-life activists argue that even sperms can listen to what we are saying. I don't think you should swear,' said Shrey.

He had lined up tasters of all eight beers in front of himself and was now gulping them one by one, never losing eye contact with Vernita.

'*Somras*. *Amrit*. Life! I feel sorry for you,' he said.

Then he tried to order a few more but Deb stopped him.

'Enough!' said Deb.

'Someone would think you're pregnant not her.'

'Can't we be supportive of her at least?' said Deb.

'That's weird. When have we ever been supportive of the stupid decisions each of us have made? And this is by far the stupidest!' said Shrey and licked through the last of the tasters. 'Why did you do it? *Is mein* overachieving? It's not a competition, both of you know that? It's not something you can pin on your wall.'

'Your husband seemed awfully kicked about being a father. Wasn't he nervous? Or was he this chirpy from the get-go?' asked Deb.

Shrey and Deb never took Tanmay's name. They called him *her husband* like it was a position that could be filled by different suitors at different times.

'Global warming, no freedom of the press, religious fundamentalism, men being assholes, and there's talk about alcohol prohibition. All I have to say is that you don't want to raise your child in a world like this,' said Shrey. 'Not when the world is going to the dogs.'

'Thank you for that, Shrey! I would have never known had you not told me,' snapped Vernita.

'Is this a hormonal reaction or are you genuinely pissed at me? What do you think, Deb? Since you are being so supportive of her?' asked Shrey.

'I'm right here. Ask me,' said Vernita.

'Isn't asking whether behavioural changes are linked with hormones offensive? But in hindsight, Deb thinks of himself as a feminist ally and today even more so, so I should be more worried about offending him than you,' said Shrey.

Vernita sighed deeply.

'How does it feel to be pregnant? How did you react when you first found out? Weren't you nervous? Felt like you were not ready?' asked Deb.

Shrey shook his head. 'Can you stop with these questions? How does it matter what she felt like? Oh, wait! Deb? Are you thinking . . . are you changing your mind . . .'

'I'm having a conversation. Do you mind?' retorted Deb. He looked at Vernita. 'So? What was it like? That moment?'

When Vernita didn't reply, Shrey banged the table animatedly. The little glasses clinked. He pointed a finger at Vernita's face and said, 'Caught you! You didn't want a child! That's it, isn't it! This is sacrilege! What kind of a feminist are you? That's emotional abuse, Vernita. You should be ashamed of yourself. You got pushed into having a child! I should write a Twitter thread about it and go viral.'

'You think it's okay to joke about this?' asked Deb sharply.

'No Sherlock, I think we all should be freaking out, but since clearly I'm the only one who's in that boat I might as well joke. It's a child that's going to be around forever, and having children is the most thankless pursuit in the world, only topped by being a wife. Look at us. We are horrible kids, aren't we? You want another one of us? And look at you being all understanding with her because right now it feels like you're considering having one yourself despite that scare literally days ago!' exclaimed Shrey.

'Why don't you order something and shut up for a minute?' said Vernita.

Shrey did precisely that.

'You won't be the first one having second thoughts,' Deb said.

'Yeah, Avantika told me how you had freaked out about that missed period. I had expected you to tell me about it. Instead you tell Shrey everything. Never mind,' said Vernita.

'See? A mood swing,' said Shrey.

'You're always home with him and he's always around,' said Deb.

'I thought it was because you love me and not because it was convenient for you. Anyway, look, there's still time for both of you. Get out of these baby-wanting marriages while there's still time. These Sharmas are crazy!' said Shrey.

'What's crazy is there's a life growing inside of me,' said Vernita. 'The only thing I have successfully grown is a fungus. It's not as if people less competent than me haven't raised kids but it's still freaking me out a little. The worst is what if I don't love the kid enough? That would be really scary, no? What if I'm a really bad mother?'

The strangeness of the sentence brought a gloomy silence to the table. In their heads, they were still in college, at least a part of them was.

'A mother?' sighed Shrey. 'Seems like only yesterday you were giving blowjobs to people in electrical engineering classes.'

'It was electronics and it wasn't people, he is my husband.'

'Technically he was just people back then,' corrected Deb.

They all looked pensively at the younger people at adjacent tables as they finished their mid-afternoon perfectly avoidable beer.

Shrey had to leave urgently when Vernita asked him to help her pick her maternity clothes.

'It's against my principle. I don't support children or their parents putting on extra weight,' Shrey said before leaving. 'Are you coming?'

'No,' said Deb.

'You know what? I'm scared Vernita is going to drag you down into this baby-making business. You know how we are.

We drag each other into our miseries. Be strong, okay?' said Shrey.

'Fuck off,' said Vernita.

Through the evening Vernita twirled and twirled looking at herself in the passing mirrors and kept worrying about the future.

'I have heard bodies turn maternal once they give birth. It's mostly auto-pilot. I'm sure I'm going to be fine. All this worrying will come to naught,' said Vernita.

'Isn't having a child based on pseudo-science a risk?'

'There's a baby inside me. Everything is a risk, Deb. Anyway, how are you holding up?'

'Everything is fine, why?'

'Do you think so? Are you sure?'

'Why would say that?'

'I have lived with a guy who wanted a child when I didn't and I know what it's like. Everything can't be fine.'

'Tanmay is stubborn, Avantika is not.'

'So suddenly she doesn't want a child? Is that what you're saying? She changed as a person, did she? That makes absolute sense,' she said.

'She might not have but she has changed me and that's what I wanted to talk to you about.'

'Wow, not Shrey! Should I be honoured?' mocked Vernita. 'Go on. What's it about?'

'I seem to not hate babies any more. Whether it's because I know it will give Avantika happiness or she opened something in me, I can't figure. It's irritating me now. I can't think of myself as a father but I keep seeing Avantika as a mom. How great she would be, no? I can't get that image out of my head. I don't see her pregnant, or like breastfeeding or changing diapers, I keep seeing her as someone who a little baby would look up to, want to be her. That picture in my head looks complete. Like it's meant to be. And then I feel like I'm the one who's preventing that from happening.'

'Where are you in all these images?' asked Vernita.

'I'm just there, melting into the background, you know. I feel I'm happy in these images but I'm not sure why,' said Deb.

'You're a stupid boy and you take stupid decisions. Don't hurry with this. Most likely Tanmay and I will bring up a beautiful, smart child because, well, we are perfect, and I will find it in myself to tide through this. How hard can it be? But you . . . well, Avantika is flawless because she shares genes with my husband but you . . . you know you can't screw this up. Just know for yourself if this is something you want as well. Don't do this because Avantika wants it and you want her to be happy. Do it because you want it.'

'Should we crack a joke now to pretend we didn't have an adult conversation?' asked Deb.

'I can't believe Avantika wants a child with you. What if it looks like you?'

'You're an asshole, Vernita. I will make sure your child knows that. I will whisper that in his or her ears every night before going to bed.'

'Then you will be the uncle he or she never meets.'

'When did we become so old that we have to decide what kind of uncles and aunties we have to be?' asked Deb.

'I have no idea how Tanmay and Avantika own their age,' said Vernita. 'By the way, Tanmay discouraged Avantika from having a child. He still hopes that you two . . . you know, won't last.'

'Of course, he hopes that. Go home and tell him that Avantika and I will have wild, dirty sex tonight.'

'I won't.'

'That sounds about right. I don't want him to Hulk-out and punch through the wall mid-sex. Whisper it softly in his ears that his sister and I will have mad sex tonight so that his subconscious knows though?'

Deb and Avantika couldn't have sex that night. Deb kept thinking of Tanmay barging in through the door.

৯

Deb learned quickly that when one's in the television business, there are a lot of meetings that are a monumental waste of time. Most times it's the producers testing how quickly the writer can suspend his or her disbelief and turn the girl's mother into a *chudail*. A moment's hesitation, the mention of an obscure novelist or a filmmaker, even the suggestion of a functioning brain can cost the writer their job. It's an effective way to weed out unruly writers who have nothing better to do than tell logical stories in the cash-strapped market. A writer who doesn't think is an asset in the television industry. If the audience can believe in a thousand gods with a million arms, they can believe in the stories the daily soaps tell.

Shrey and Deb, both washed-up novelists and failed publishers of sappy college romances with a smattering of smut, had it even worse than other writers.

Shrey and Deb had both answered their calling to be writers after their management college stints. They worked hard at it but little did they know at the time that they missed a crucial element—talent. They learned in the initial days that their books wouldn't sell so they pooled in money and started a publishing house where they aimed at publishing others who wrote better than they did. After early signs of success, it dawned on them that it was a lost cause, that reading books was on a downward spiral. They turned to the last refuge of any writer in India—the immoral but well-paying world of *saas*, *bahu* and drama. Writers in Indian television earned more in a year than novelists could hope to earn in their entire careers.

While the literary world thought of them as hacks, one-book wonders who couldn't write to save their lives, the television producers—most of whom hadn't read a book in their lives— thought of them as too intellectual, too eccentric for daily soaps. In the past four years, since they'd written their first TV show, they hadn't been able to hold down a job for more than a couple of months. Sooner or later, one of them would buckle under the pressure of moulding the storyline according to what the TAM ratings said about the show and say something crazy like, 'What if we don't take an eight-year leap?' They would immediately get fired.

One would think being a genius or a moron is tough, try being mediocre.

'It's a big show. They are taking a fifteen-year leap, and they want writers with a vision,' Shrey had said before setting up a meeting.

'Did you tell them our vision is not having empty bank accounts?' Deb had asked.

Avantika made him eat dahi-shakkar and packed him lunch like he was a schoolboy. 'You will be great,' she said and kissed him.

'You know it's going to be bad, they will want something, I will say something else, something will go wrong and I will come home with a drooping face. That's the drill. I should just stop trying, no?' said Deb, who became insufferable before every important meeting to not raise his or Avantika's hopes; he only half believed it.

'You and I both know that's not going to happen, baby. Even while you're writing the worst television show, you're still happy because you love telling stories. Don't tell me you haven't already daydreamed of ten ways the meeting will go and how our lives will change post that.'

Deb smiled and said, 'You should hear the one where I impress them so much today they make me the content head of the channel and a year later I'm heading Fox worldwide and the board is undergoing a rift because I want to shift my office to Bhutan. The board is split but you have your mind set on Bhutan and I leave the job and we move to Bhutan. You love it so much, that place.'

'See how your eyes light up?' said Avantika. 'I notice how all these stories end with me. You will do great, I know.'

Shrey, for once, picked Deb up in a cab.

'Let's go over the rules one more time?' said Deb.

'I know, I know,' said Shrey.

'We are not going to act smart. We are going to nod and tell them that the show is great, and we watch it with our families. We tell them we loved when the plastic surgery of the bahu went wrong and she turned up with the face of a man and how it was a nod to the LGBTQ community. And when we get the chance, we bitch about the slot leader show, *Bahu Sasural Mein, Damad Maike Mein*, and their irrational story tracks.'

'You don't have a soul any more, Deb. You will do anything for money, won't you?' said Shrey, shaking his head. 'Park there,' he told the cab driver and pointed to the parking lot of a nursing home. 'I got to see my cousin. She's admitted there. Will be back in a second.'

'Your cousin?'

The last Deb heard, Shrey's family—parents, brothers, aunts and cousins—had abandoned him en masse a few years ago when he had fallen in love and moved in with someone from the same *gotra*, genetic lineage. His family had called up the girl and accused her of being a whore who had ensnared their innocent son, even landed up at the girl's house and thrown faecal matter at her parents.

'She's like your sister. What will people say? Choose her or choose us,' his parents, whose proud bania heritage had been sullied, had said.

He vowed to never see his parents, brothers or cousins again. He broke up with the girl a few months later but never reconciled with his parents.

But every few days—primarily to put his parents through the loneliness and abandonment he felt—he called them and asked for his part of the inheritance. His parents would curse him, call him ungrateful, and he would laugh and curse them back.

As Shrey jumped out of the car and strode towards the nursing home, Deb followed him.

'Ms Gupta,' said Shrey at the reception, put in an entry and walked in.

'How do I not know about her?' Deb asked.

Shrey didn't answer, and neither did he go in the direction in which the nurse at the reception had pointed.

'Where are you going?'

'There,' said Shrey and pointed at the board.

MATERNITY WARD.

'She's pregnant?'

'No, she's not.'

'Her friend's pregnant?'

Shrey turned and held Deb. 'How do you never catch me lying? That only makes me scared for the times that I'm not lying and you don't believe me. But you're a good, gullible friend, and for that I love you.'

'What are we doing here?'

'We are here to show you how helpless, useless, time-intensive, joy-sucking pieces of shit little children are,' he said. 'Wouldn't you want to see the product before ordering it? Vernita told me what you were going through and we thought it was necessary to do this.'

Deb wanted to bolt but he had always had trouble extracting himself from situations Shrey put him through. They turned towards the OTs where a bunch of scared husbands were huddling around.

'Look at these terrified bastards. They can't bear to see their wives birth a full-grown baby from their vaginas and yet they want to be fathers. Hypocritical nonsense,' said Shrey.

The mothers and mothers-in-law prayed silently and strained their ears to hear a child's cry.

'I'm sure they all want grandsons,' Shrey added.

The door to the operation theatre closed and opened as doctors, nurses, husbands poured in and out of it.

'Do you see that door? Now wait for the babies to come out. If you feel something looking at the slime-covered little worms you can continue to indulge in the images in your head. If not, you will always have this moment to remember. When you saw a baby and felt nothing,' said Shrey. 'It's mostly Vernita's idea. That's what she did and decided to get pregnant.'

Deb saw no babies.

'How difficult is it to get a baby delivered?' muttered Shrey impatiently. 'Deb? Deb? Where are you going?'

Deb walked inside the changing room where only overworked, bored doctors and anxious husbands of the pregnant women in question were allowed. Deb started to change. Shrey looked at the mirror. With scrubs and masks on their faces, they could turn into anyone. They could be husbands who changed their minds about missing the most important moment of their lives.

'Why am I such a bad influence?' he asked, changing into scrubs himself.

'We will be husbands who found the courage to see their wives being operated on. So now we find our wives.'

They walked through the line of operation theatres, and peeped inside. Women were being sedated before their children were brought to the world.

Deb found a woman moaning, doctors crowding over her body, and entered the room. He stood quietly in the corner, a sense of dread coming over him as he watched the doctors work on her. The stench of blood was overpowering. The woman flitted in and out of consciousness, more white than black in her eyes. A green cloth was set as a curtain to keep the woman from seeing the doctors who were elbow deep inside her stomach area. It wasn't elegant; it didn't look like a miracle, it was bloody, messy. The doctors looked like they had dropped a scalpel inside her womb and were pawing around looking for it.

'Who are you?' asked an assistant doctor who spotted Deb.

The anaesthetist repeated the question. 'Are you supposed to be here?'

Deb had the mask on his face. He pointed at the woman on the table and then at himself—the dumb charade meant to say he was her husband. The heavily sedated woman who lay with her legs away from him, looked at him with her drunk, tranquilized eyes and smiled. She'd also mistaken him for her husband.

'Sit here, she needs you,' said the assistant doctor.

He was guided to a chair. He shifted it just outside the vision of the woman who seemed to be in pain despite the sedatives. The doctors kept talking to her while shifting her organs around like they were little Lego pieces.

'Just a little more!' said the senior doctor as if it was his first time as well. 'We can see the baby now! We can see the baby!'

Deb heard the anaesthetist say, 'Are you feeling hot? Are you? Okay. You're doing great.'

The woman sweated rivers. She reached out for her *husband's* hand. Deb was made to give his. She didn't notice. She held it tightly.

The assistant doctor said, 'We are now getting the baby out, we are now getting the baby out!'

Both doctors were still at work. They were like a cheerleading team egging the woman on.

The senior doctor said, 'WOW! It's a big baby! We are almost there, we are almost there!'

The anaesthetist said, 'You're doing great! What are you feeling? Hot? Cold?'

The senior doctor said, 'We are pulling your baby! We are pulling the baby out!'

The assistant doctor said, 'It's almost there, it's almost there!'

The anaesthetist repeated, 'You're doing great.'

And just then, a cry pierced through the room. A loud, solid cry. The woman let go of Deb's hand and looked up. The senior doctor raised the baby out from behind the green partition and said, 'It's a boy! It's a beautiful boy!'

The baby was covered in grey slime and didn't look pleased with the doctor getting him out of his hotel womb. The assistant doctor and the senior doctor helped keep the baby on her chest. Such a delicate thing and yet they, who would see five of them in a day, held the baby like it was a toy.

'He's perfect,' said the assistant doctor.

'He looks perfect,' said the senior doctor. 'Do you want to see your baby?'

The woman nodded, once, then twice, tears pooling at the base of her eyes. She stared at the ball of slime unwaveringly. With great effort, she held the baby close to her chest and then nervously kissed it. Deb watched her tiredness melt away. She laid back, closed her eyes, and an inexplicable glow crept up on her pale face.

'We will clean up the baby and get you ready,' said the assistant doctor. 'Try to sleep if you can.'

The woman nodded. The nurse pointed Deb to a table. The woman tried to look at Deb but her disorientation and euphoria had heightened, and she couldn't catch a good look at him with all the nurses running around.

Deb was made to stand near the tray where the baby was cleaned of blood and the grey slime as it continually bawled. The time was noted down, a hospital tag slapped around his feet that said Mrs Chugh, the weight and the height measured. He was wrapped up and given to Deb in a green cloth.

'Here's your baby. Congratulations!' said the paediatrician.

'Congratulations,' said the nurse and pulled Deb's mask down. 'He looks like you.'

'Wouldn't that be a scandal?' Deb muttered to himself and put the mask back on.

'He's so cute,' said another nurse.

That much was correct. Helpless, he simultaneously looked like he was in love and was irritated with Deb. He stared at Deb, blinked once, blinked twice, and squinted under the harsh OT lights. He started to cry and then quietened down when Deb whistled to him. He moved in the direct path of the OT lights, held his hand over his big eyes and started singing a lullaby he didn't even know he remembered. The baby's lips curved into a little smile. Is that what new fathers do? Whistle and sing? Did he smile?

'Seems like he likes you!'

'Does he? Can you tell?' Deb asked.

'He's ready to meet his family,' said the paediatrician who deemed the baby fit to be shown around. 'Bring him back as soon as possible.'

And just like that Deb was holding a three-minute old baby. He was little, fragile. Deb thought he might break those little baby fingers, that tiny body that wiggled in his hands and eased his grip a little. It kept looking questioningly at him, as if asking him if he would take care of him. Deb had never held a baby before; he would go to unnatural lengths to avoid picking them up and here he was, holding him, not wanting to let go. Deb walked towards where all the husbands were.

'Mr CHUGH?' he shouted out, voice stuck in his throat. He tried again. 'MR CHUGH!'

'YES, doctor!' a fat man came hobbling towards him, wide smile pasted on his face.

Behind him was an old couple who seemed equally ecstatic. They looked like the kind who had decided the only thing keeping them from certain death was seeing the face of their grandchild.

As the husband reached out and took the baby away from him, Deb felt something tugging at him.

'I will take it, don't worry,' said the husband.

'Take care of him,' he said, a sense of sadness piercing through him. He unclasped his arms and time slowed down as the baby left and cried hoarsely in his father's arms.

The husband rushed inside with the baby.

Shrey and Deb changed out of the scrubs, left the hospital and walked solemnly to their cab.

'Did you see it, Shrey? Did you hold a baby?' asked Deb, his voice a whisper.

'They didn't let me inside,' said Shrey. 'I saw you carry that baby.'

'It was an experience, that much is for sure.'

'I shouldn't have listened to Vernita. This was a bad idea, the worst, the fucking worst in a long, long time. I have seen you struggle at an engineering college, seen you embarrassingly pursue women and careers, seen you try your hardest and fail at businesses, seen you achieve moderate success at holding down the love of your life, but I have never seen you look this . . . perfect? Right? Complete? You were at home for the first time. The only thing that beat watching you hold that baby is—and I'm only going to say this once and never again—seeing you hold Avantika and that's quite a sight. Goals, as the kids would call it. I never thought I would say this but I think you're ready to be a father. Go home, Deb, and have unprotected sex. Just give her the good stuff, you know just pump it—'

'I get your point.'

It was middle-of-the-night-can't-sleep-so-let's-have-sex sex. They were getting their foreplay out of the way, like French fries—essential, but not the mainstay. After a decade, it was like well-oiled machinery. They would gauge who was less tired, and that person would take the onus. Since the nursing home experience had left Deb emotionally wrecked, Avantika initiated it and took it forward. She had just lunged at the bedside table for protection when Deb stopped her.

'Let's skip that,' he said.

Avantika bit his ear, swirled her tongue inside his ear, gross and just like Deb liked it and said, 'Neither of us are nineteen. You can't convince me into taking an I-pill.'

'You don't have to take that either,' he said.

She slightly pulled away from him.

'Let's see what happens.'

The words seemed strange on his tongue. *Let's see what happens.* It's what age tasted like, perhaps.

She didn't speak for a bit and he waited, buck naked, for her to take him seriously. Maybe he should have picked a better time. Her face as if went through the nine-rasas with lightning frequency and settled somewhere between elation and shock.

'Are you still turned on because I still am?' she asked.

He nodded.

Then they had egregiously bad sex. How could they do it when they had procreation as the end result? How could he when he couldn't get that newly born little boy's face out of his mind? Deb thought it was wrong to start a child's life with lacklustre intimacy. But he wondered if he would feel any better if it were earth-shattering sex? Deb knew this would have been on her mind too because they did it efficiently not enjoyably. They timed their orgasms, and it was over rather quickly. They tried not to think they had possibly started the first step towards conception. They kissed ceremoniously, smiled, turned to their sides, tired and a bit muddled.

They were awake till late thinking about the little tadpoles making their way to Avantika's fallopian tubes. Deb was telekinetically willing them to impregnate the hell out of Avantika's eggs. Not too much though; he wouldn't want septuplets on his hands! Deb wondered if it were one of those days she was ovulating? He counted the days and it seemed about right. He then touched his toes with hers in a futile attempt to know if her basal temperature was higher than usual. He counted nine months from today.

They both slept quite late.

Deb flitted in and out of his sleep. He dreamt of holding a pregnant and gorgeous Avantika, of her giving birth, of them holding their baby.

When they woke up in the morning they found the AC temperature to be too low, freezing their room, and their bodies intertwined with each other, like two entangled squids. They were both reminded instantly of what they had done the night before. It felt like the morning after the first time he had gone first base with her, a decade ago, and felt her breasts for the first time—embarrassed, exhilarated and nervous of what would come next.

Avantika, who usually backslapped him in the morning if the night before had gone well, was shying away too.

'Do you feel something?' he asked.

Avantika took his hand and kept it on her stomach. 'Do you?'

'Is there something?' he asked, curious, his skin tingling.

Avantika's face glowed with all the brightness of the sun.

'I think so, six hours is all it takes for the child to grow,' she said.

'Whatever. When will we know?' he asked.

'Arre? We just tried once. Give it some time. People try for years.'

He held her and said, 'It won't take us long. I can already feel something.'

'You're so cute.'

Just then, the house bell rang. A boy carried two bouquets of flowers with a card addressed to them from Shrey.

Congratulations! Here's hoping you guys are naked while you're reading this. Avantika, get your legs in the air to help it along.

10

Their streak of unprotected sex continued. They weren't calculating the days when she was ovulating any more. The awkwardness had abated and they were doing it as if God wanted them to. Every morning Shrey would slap his ass, fist bump, chest bump, wink, whatever he felt like on the day.

'Soon, bro, soon,' he would say. 'Did you take that Ayurvedic medicine I gave you yesterday? And don't be nervous. You think I would ever give it to my friend without testing it first?'

'You what?'

'I came like . . . uff. Vats full of the good stuff.'

'You need to stop talking,' Deb said and stuffed his earphones in. Shrey pulled them out.

'I will gut punch you if you pull them out.'

'That's what she said!' Shrey said and chuckled. 'You see what I did there?'

'I know how "that's what she said" jokes work.'

'But you don't know how this medicine works. I went to a clinic, saved my stuff. You know, just in case cell phone vibrations mess with . . . whatever . . . they tested my stuff. Said it was teeming with sperms. Like, literally, they said that. Only second to Changez Khan. Well, they didn't say exactly that, but I saw it in their faces. The nurses were impressed. Wouldn't be surprised if they took some of it home.'

'Ugh.'

'Now imagine if I were getting laid, how impressed would my girl be!' he said and leaned back confidently into his chair, grinning.

'You haven't told anyone, have you?' Deb asked.

'Cross my heart and hope to die,' said Shrey.

It had taken emotional blackmail, threats, the promise of setting him up with a friend of theirs, for Shrey to keep it to himself.

Deb and Avantika were tight-lipped about them trying to start a family. They even kept it from Vernita, and told her that Deb was still mulling over the decision. But the cagier they were, the more people asked them if they were thinking about a baby.

'Did you tell your parents?' asked Shrey.

'I think Maa knows. Earlier she used to ask about us having a baby all the fucking time and now silence. Not a word.'

'Moms, bro. They are soothsayers. I won't be surprised if Aunty is already knitting sweaters and asking your father to melt her jewellery into little *katori*s. You should tell her, make her happy,' said Shrey.

'You think that's easy? How do you tell your mother that the son she birthed, bathed, fed and had wrapped around her finger was now in someone's bed doing unspeakable things to a woman? There's no way I'm telling her that every time she calls either before or after sex.'

'Send her a text,' said Shrey.

Avantika meanwhile, the more careful of the two, had been reckless in her behaviour with their secret. Every mall that they went to, she stopped a little more than necessary in front of baby shops, gawked at the tiny clothes, like a child outside a pastry shop. Despite Deb's warnings, she had been picking up stranger's kids and babbling to them as if they were her own. A few friends of theirs had raised eyebrows every time she did that. She would tell them it's because Tanmay was having a baby.

That night, after sex, when they were heating up some leftover pizza she suddenly looked pensive. 'I was thinking,' she said. 'What if we have a boy?'

'He should be at least eight years old at birth so we can play cricket straightaway.'

'An eight-year-old girl can do so as well. But you know what you can't do with boys? Dress them up cutely,' said Avantika. 'Did you see their clothes at the baby shop? Restricting. It's either blue or black or stuff with sailors and whatnot. I know we can dress him up in pink, be subversive, but little boys are hooligans. They aren't even cute.'

'I was cute!'

'But imagine if you were a girl? In a little frock and bow?' said Avantika, biting into her pizza. 'You, as a girl, would be cute beyond words. I want her to be a mini you.'

'I take strong exception to that. If she should be like someone, it should be you. You're . . . gorgeous.'

'But you're cute. What will we do with a gorgeous baby? I want a cute, cuddly girl. Someone who will cling to me like a chimp and never leave. I want her to be obsessed with me. Like you are.'

'A, that's presumptuous because I'm not obsessed. At most I have a keen interest in you. B, I'm far from cute. If anything, I am rugged, forged in evil dungeons from Valerian steel and blood from fallen warriors.'

'More like from your mother's sweetmeats, *nolen gurer shondesh* and *patishapta*,' she said and laughed.

'Dynamite and concrete.'

'*Roshogolla* and *payesh*.'

'Demons and darkness.'

'Puppies and velvet.'

'We are not playing this game,' Deb said.

When they went to sleep later, he prayed silently for their child—girl or boy—to look like her, act like her, be like her. He slept imagining a future where an androgynous child, a spitting image of Avantika, bounded about cutely, pulled at their hair, laughed and solved calculus and read poetry to them.

In the morning, Avantika found Deb already awake.

'I have something to ask you,' he said. 'Answer it truly. If she grows up and looks like you, will I look odd walking with the two of you? Two beautiful women with an odd-looking man?'

'You're beautiful, Deb.'

'I'm not finished. Will I be the embarrassment of the family? People say that the girl's lucky if she looks like the mother? Will the two of you love each other more than you love me? Will your world start to revolve around her because that's unacceptable. That's not what I signed up for. I need to be sure of that.'

'I love you more than I love myself, so, if only, and only if, she looks like you is there a slight chance of me loving her more than I love you,' said Avantika.

'I will have more questions when I think of them.'

'Come here,' said Avantika and wrapped her arms around him.

11

Avantika's period was delayed.

Deb had tracked it and for the first day he skirted the question and didn't bring it up with Avantika, scared that he would jinx it. Instead, he checked every few hours if Avantika had used a sanitary napkin. Avantika, herself, intentionally worked harder to not think about it too much but failed. How was she supposed to think of anything else? It was nothing though; a day or two here and there was more the norm than the exception. She watched Deb disappear into the washroom, heard him open and close the cupboard and smiled to herself softly.

The second day, the nervousness was writ large on their faces. Their anxiety was an open secret now. Deb's tea bubbled over; Avantika overfilled her coffee cup; Deb closed his Word document without saving it; Avantika CCed the client on an internal mail. There was no point any more in trying to hide it from each other.

Every twenty minutes, Deb texted Avantika asking her if she felt she would start chumming. Avantika replied in single-word answers, trying extra hard not to be happy. Deb failed to concentrate on anything. Through the day, their hearts pounded against their chests. Avantika could tell the grumbles in her stomach weren't an oncoming period but impatience and uneasiness. There was no period coming. A woman knows, doesn't she? That's how these things work.

This was *happening*. This was *too soon*. Were they always this close to a baby? Had they not been careful all these years, she would have been pregnant quite a while ago. She thought of Deb and how he had changed over the past few days. He wanted *this*, and that made her want the baby even more. A little girl she could call family. A girl she could be a role model for, someone she could truly call her own, by heart and by body.

They both pulled their old baby pictures from Google Photos and wondered what she would look like. They sighed and smiled and worried about what was to come. They kept wondering if going that far in their heads on the second day itself was an overreaction. Earlier as well, there had been times when her period was delayed by a couple of days but never had they reacted like this.

The third day, Avantika stood in front of the calendar and counted the days again. Deb marked the date of her last period. They both tried remembering the last time she was three days late on her period. Their pulse never settled.

'A couple of years ago,' said Avantika before Deb could ask.

They hid their nervous smiles. Every time she visited the washroom he nervously waited outside. There were no cramps, no headaches, no severe mood swings. She found herself keeping her hand on her stomach, and he found himself looking there. Things were looking good.

At the office, Shrey backslapped him, and congratulated him for his strong swimmers. Deb found it hard to concentrate on the *Teen Saas, Do Damad, Kya Hoga Simar Ka* concept. They had had to submit the initial concept note to the production house two weeks ago.

The fourth day, Deb woke up and was sure Avantika was pregnant. She looked beautiful beyond words. It broke his heart to see her leave the house for office. What would it be if not the pregnancy glow?

'Going by your words, Avantika has been constantly pregnant for the last decade. When has she not "glowed" for you? Nonsense,' said Vernita when Deb shared his anxiety with her.

Deb spent four hours in a bookshop browsing books on pregnancy, Avantika searched her office's internal database for maternity leaves and compensation. Deb stopped at Mothercare and let his heart be stolen by a Stokke stroller. He wondered if he should buy a data card, to accommodate the pictures he would take of Avantika every day of her pregnancy to compile them into a hyperlapse later. Avantika Googled all the things she had to avoid from then onwards. When Deb didn't turn up at the office till late afternoon, Shrey bought nine bouquets for nine months and sent them to their house. He sent congratulatory messages to both of them; they read them, smiled and superstitiously didn't reply. Shrey then checked office property rent near Deb's house because with the kid coming he might not be able to travel as much. Deb, on the other hand, was ready to let go of the office. He made rough calculations of how much they would spend extra on the baby every month. He searched and found the things they would need—cribs, curtains, clothes, toys, tissues, insurance. The list was endless. He felt a little sorry that everything would come from Avantika's credit card. He felt himself steeling up—I will pull my socks and contribute to this family no matter how. He started to feel responsible; as if overnight he had sprouted a few grey hair.

By the time evening came, Avantika could wait no longer. She bought a home pregnancy kit and rushed back home. She almost jogged up the stairs. *This is it. This is it. I'm going to be a mother. I'm going to have my own family, my own flesh and blood. I will love her like no one loved anyone. Finally, finally.* She felt herself tear up a little. *This will change everything. Thank you, thank you so much, Guruji, thank you, God.* She clutched the pregnancy kit harder. She was going to save it for all of eternity. She wondered if she should have got a better brand. Or two of them, one for Deb, and one for her. *Should I get a scrapbook? Do we need to go to a doctor today? Or tomorrow? Which doctor? How would Deb react?* She smiled shyly—a new thing for her—when she thought of telling Tanmay the news. She thought of calling Deb home but didn't. *It will be a nice surprise.* She took a deep breath as she entered the house. She saw the centre table, its pointed corners and said to herself, *this needs to go, the baby is going to crawl*. She could feel the baby in her belly. It was there, getting ready for Deb and her, and they had to be ready for her when she arrived. For a moment, she toyed with the idea of doing this with Deb. No, she thought. There was no point in waiting any longer. If this had to happen, the journey better start as soon as possible.

When Deb got back home, he found the lights on. Avantika was home early from work, and she was never early from work. *It was happening, it was really happening.* He clutched the pregnancy books and music CDs for pregnant women he had bought earlier that day. He closed his eyes and breathed deeply, he told himself he would be great at this. *You're ready, Deb, you're ready.* He said the words, mother of my child, Avantika, and he felt silly, and he was smiling now, happy tears flooding his eyes. *Had she taken a test?* His heart thrummed. *Is this happening?* She wasn't in the living room. No balloons coloured pink and blue, or an alphabet string screaming *Congratulations!* on the wall. No friends hiding behind couches and pillars waiting to spring up a surprise. There wasn't a teddy bear on the table with a little red ribbon around it, or a cake with the words, *You're Going to Be a Dad*. Deb thought that maybe she was making it a personal affair. A day they would look back on, romanticize when they were old and their son or daughter was away for work.

In the future they might not think of their birthdays to be of any consequence, but this day would always be special. There would be no celebration because how do you celebrate the day you found out you were pregnant? A happy kind of anxiety flooded him. How long before he could tell his parents? Two months? How long before he told everyone? Three months? He was already imagining Best Dad coffee mugs, complaints about not getting to sleep enough, PTA meetings where the English teacher would crush on him, him catching her on late-night sneak-outs, and then encouraging her and covering for her in front of her mother.

The door to the bedroom was open. He calmed himself down, knowing fully well he would melt into a puddle of tears. In the past four days he had often wondered what was he looking forward to more—to have his own child or experience having a child with Avantika, to hold her hand while she delivered, to be with her while she raised an impeccable human?

He would stay awake till late in the night wondering how their life would change and how he would change with that. His daydreams spanned years and decades, well into his grandsons and granddaughters. In all his daydreams they had a daughter. And in all his daydreams, Avantika still loved him more than she loved their daughter. But what he really got a kick out of was Avantika complaining that Deb had found someone to love more.

He hadn't told Avantika yet, but he had decided on a name—Nayra. His first choice was Rayna but an annoying friend had already named his daughter Rayna so he settled for an anagram. Nayra, he Googled had it; it meant *beautiful*. His behaviour bordered on obsession.

Deb found Avantika on the bed, in semi–darkness, hunched over. Was she nervous? Scared of the future? Of the kind of parents they would be? Deb knocked on the door. He started constructing the sentences he would say to her to make her nervousness ebb away. *We will be great parents, the best.* She looked up and met his eyes. Deb smiled, the practiced dimpled smile that he always used on Avantika, the first of the few sentences he would say on the tip of his tongue.

'Hey?'

'Deb.'

'Avantika.'

'I . . . I got my period.'

No.

Why?

Deb's face flushed red. He had heard these words before. They always brought a sense of relief. But this time, the way the words left her lips, the despair in her voice, made him feel like they had failed, like something had been snatched away from them.

But how can it be? We were pregnant just moments ago.

Unknowingly, in the past four days they had built an imaginary world, started dwelling in it, and it became a part of their being. They were already Nayra's parents.

Avantika looked at him; they both struggled to say something to lift the gloom, anything to make it all right, because it was all right They were being hard on themselves, overreacting, over-feeling.

'If it took me more than one attempt to clear an entrance examination, then this is much tougher, isn't it?' he said. 'Seems like Nayra has to wait a little bit.'

Avantika smiled.

'You're really committed to that name, aren't you? You think I haven't noticed you scribbling that name everywhere,' said Avantika.

'I don't know what you're talking about. I'm sure you do it and forget,' said Deb, smiling.

He switched on the lights, confused at how such a little thing could suddenly chip at their happiness. It was infuriating that something so basic had shifted within them in the past few weeks that they would react this way. They had been trying for just a month. They had assumed they wouldn't be those people who had to try.

'There's only a 25 per cent chance every month of getting pregnant,' said Avantika as if reading his mind. 'I checked.'

'It must be hard for a nerd like you to not be in the top 1 percentile. You know what this means now, right? We get to have more sex. All the time,' said Deb and chuckled.

The vacuous words, the bad jokes, didn't make it easier. He put his arms around Avantika who smiled softly.

'I shouldn't be disappointed but I had built my hopes in the last seventy-two hours. I just gave too much energy to the thought that I was pregnant. I was getting ready for it. I thought it had too,' she said and she snuggled close.

'So had I. It was like the courier guy called and said he would be here with the Amazon package and didn't turn up. But he always does, sooner or later, doesn't he?' he said and Avantika smiled weakly. He asked, 'Is it time for *it*?'

They ordered biryani and watched their wedding video; that was their go-to mood-lifter, it always made everything alright. Most of the video was shot on phones because the video guys had run off before the wedding; Shrey had spent months fetching videos from the guests and stitching them together. The video always made them cry and left them in a happy, giggly mood.

Deb always remembered how conflicted and turned on he was on the wedding night seeing the thick streak of violent red sindoor on Avantika's forehead, the demure tears in her eyes. It meant she was *his* to keep in an archaic, oppressive, patriarchal kind of way; he was the *husband*.

'I feel much better,' said Avantika, licking off the raita from the bowl.

Deb burped and said, 'So do I. We shouldn't have eaten that much. And why the fuck were we so upset? It was absolutely unwarranted for. We need to chill a bit, okay. Back there it was like someone had died.'

'I got sadder looking at your face,' said Avantika.

'That's my bad but if you were not sitting in the darkness like that, and talked to me in a voice like you did I wouldn't have got that sad.'

'Let's call it a draw, then?' said Avantika and smiled.

They were making the bed, when Tanmay and a four-month pregnant Vernita Facetimed them.

'Tanmay, show it to me!'

Tanmay held close to the camera what was a little picture of an ultrasound. It was white spots on black paper. Avantika tilted her head like a puppy.

'Wow, that's hideous. It's gone on you, Tanmay,' Deb said.

Avantika nudged him.

'Do you see that?' said Tanmay. 'That's the heart. We heard it beat. It went like whoosh, whoosh, whoosh . . .'

'Were you sleeping with Skrillex, Vernita?' said Deb.

Vernita rolled her eyes.

'The doctor said the child is healthy and growing well,' she said.

'Hold up the picture again!' said Avantika. 'I need to take a screenshot of my niece.'

'Or nephew,' said Vernita, holding up the picture.

'Looks like potty. Are you sure it's not the intestine you're showing us?' Deb asked.

'Just shut up, yaa. And let Avantika see it,' said Vernita.

'It could be just gas, you know?' said Deb.

'Can you please let us enjoy this moment, Deb?' said Tanmay in a voice that always scared Deb.

The video call went on for twenty long minutes. Deb noticed a slight change in Vernita, the way she held the ultrasound, the way she talked about the pregnancy, about her maternity leave, about Tanmay's tears in the scan room.

'I noticed that too,' Avantika said later.

'It seems like she's getting into it now,' said Deb.

They both stared at the screenshots of the video call; the happy faces of Tanmay and Vernita holding up the ultrasound, the forced smiles on theirs.

'Deb? I think we are needlessly festering in our sadness. We are making this a big deal, don't you think?'

'Absolutely,' said Deb.

'Can we decide on something? Let's not talk about the pregnancy till the time we get a positive result? If it takes one month more, great, if it takes more, then we don't stress about it? Let's not hope for anything too quickly. When it happens, it happens? Let's take it as it comes? We will put in the work and wait,' said Avantika.

'When you say work, you mean sex right?'

'Yes.'

'Can we start tomorrow? I think my stomach's a little upset from all that biryani.'

'I am glad you said it before I did.'

12

While the months crawled on slowly for Deb and Avantika, Vernita's pregnancy seemed like it was on a fast track. It was as if within a blink of an eye, Vernita was seven months pregnant though she looked nine and ready to deliver any moment. She couldn't stop crying hoarse about the possibility of snaking stretch marks showing up any moment. Nothing would calm her down. Every ten days she would take either Deb or Avantika for the doctor's visit.

Avantika and Deb had spent the entire day looking for something to gift Vernita on her baby shower and came up with naught.

'How do you even pick something? Everything is so cute,' groused an exasperated Avantika, sitting in the food court of yet another mall. They had spent hours rubbing pink socks against their faces, sniffing them like cocaine, and yet couldn't decide on anything.

'It's trickery. They want us to buy everything. They are taking advantage of how unbearably cute baby things are. It's a scam!' said Deb.

They were stress-eating their way through their second burger and drinking their fourth coffee that day. It was worse because both of them couldn't stop wondering when they could buy those things for Nayra.

Getting pregnant was so basic. Their grandparents had churned out kids every year like an assembly line. To want it and want it desperately sat uncomfortably with them. Four months had passed but they had stuck to their rule of not talking about it.

How far along Vernita was in her pregnancy was how Deb and Avantika kept count of the time that they had been trying for. It had been four months, and Nayra had refused to implant herself in Avantika and their lives.

They tried not to dwell on it too much, and told each other that the threshold of when one should start worrying about conceiving, a year, was still very far.

The signs of a successful implant and period pains feel the same and that made it worse for them. Four times, their hopes had been dashed when they didn't get pregnant. For the most part, Deb felt bad about Avantika because it was she who had to go through it at the end of every month.

'So jealous of these post-millennial kids. All I had growing up was hand-me-downs from my sisters. They still mock me for it,' said Deb. 'You, of course, don't know what I am talking about. Tanmay and you must have had your handcrafted cribs flown in.'

'And I'm sure I stayed in that crib while Tanmay enjoyed the lap of my parents,' said Avantika solemnly.

'I'm sorry I brought that up,' said Deb.

'You don't have to be, you're the one who saved me,' said Avantika.

'Are you sure it was me? And not the bearded Guru?'

'I'm going to throw this coffee on your face if you say a single word against Guruji or Spirit of Living,' said Avantika, who had turned to the Guru after her abusive ex-boyfriend and her parents who had always wanted to trade her off like cattle to a suitable suitor had driven her down the spiral of alcohol abuse and drugs. 'He helped you too.'

'Do I need to remind you that I only went to him after he asked you to break up with me?' said Deb.

'He had only alluded to it, not specifically asked me to do it.'

'Because that's how gurus talk!'

'Can we get back to what we need to do? I don't want to disappoint him. Don't tell me that the thought counts.

Tanmay has a lot of friends coming and I don't want to give him something someone else does too,' said Avantika, worrying.

Despite her anger towards her brother for not standing up for her when her parents were unfair to her, she never stopped clinging to him. After she snapped ties with her parents, he was all she could call family.

'Should we make them something?' he asked. 'Like a scrapbook? Remember how I made that card for you when we had completed fifty dates? With illustrations of what we did on every date?'

'You were so cute.'

'You have no idea how unreal it was for me to date you. I brought on my A-game,' he said. They pulled out that card when they got home. That card didn't age well.

'The thought is what counts,' she said, smiling at the card.

They spent the entire night making and unmaking a massive 3 foot by 3 foot scrapbook for Vernita and Tanmay's unborn child. They skimmed through a copy of *What to Expect When You're Expecting* to get the stages right. Every now and then Deb would catch Avantika, glassy-eyed and lost. She would break out of her reverie and then smile at Deb as if it was nothing.

When they finished it looked like a grimoire straight out of *Vampire Diaries*. It had spaces right from where they could stick their first test result to the first report card to the pictures of the baby's first vacation. Avantika teared up when she wrapped it up in gift paper.

'I'm going to love that baby so much,' she said, cradling the scrapbook.

Deb dug in deep, and searched for love for the unborn baby and came up short. He wanted his own; he wanted to make a scrapbook for his own baby, and that, that he would make it with all his heart, all his love—it would be the scrapbook to beat all scrapbooks.

They spent the rest of the night going through their first fifty dates. Deb was surprised by how much he had forgotten and how much Avantika remembered.

'I was way more smitten with you than you were with me, Deb,' said Avantika. 'You didn't know and I didn't tell you but you became my everything pretty damn quickly.'

13

However, it wasn't all bad news.

For the first time in years, Shrey and Deb had completed two successful months at a TV show. Deb had kept his and Shrey's impulses in check. Success has many fathers, and since the show had taken off, everyone wanted to tell Deb and Shrey how to write it.

'Let them meddle. As long as we are in the show I don't care what we put on screen. If your conscience doesn't allow it, let me write the episodes,' Deb would say before the meeting every week.

That week the saas had her family heirloom, a pair of *kundan* bangles, stolen by a snake. A CGI snake wrapped itself around the clicky round dial of the safe, literally wore the bangles and slithered out of the room while the saas slept soundly. It was caught on a CCTV camera of the Kapoor household. It rated highly for them. The special effects were reminiscent of old Ramsay classics. And precisely then the question of how to sustain that spike in TRP was raised.

'What's the twist though?' the programming head of the channel asked.

They wanted to go with a simple conflict-resolution storyline. The saas suspects that the bahu trained the snake into stealing it, the bahu proves her innocence by learning to play the *been* alongside her householder duties and brings down a nexus of snake charmers with trained ninja snakes who robbed at will.

'Cliched, so cliched. Doesn't work for me at all, guys. We can be so much better than this, can't we?' said the programming head, whose every sentence was a statement but also a question.

Shrey tried to sell it.

'Isn't this women empowerment though? If you can bring down a notorious snake-charming–robbery ring, is there anything you can't do? Deb? What do you say?'

'Precisely. It's an allegory of what women can achieve these days. Anything. There's nothing they can't achieve,' Deb added.

'Debashish, our audience sitting in the *kasba*s and the villages don't care about this detective type storyline any more, do they? Done to death, isn't it? Think something new, can we do that? Haven't you read the consumer report?'

'We didn't get that email,' said Shrey.

The programming head threw an icy look at her juniors.

'Send it to them, will you? How will they write if they don't have the basic insights? They need to know what's the pulse of the audience.'

A junior tried justifying his salary.

'Actually, I told them we needed to put one *devar*–bhabhi scene in every episode. I thought—'

'Just send them the report. Don't stifle their creativity,' said the programming head sternly.

Then she turned to Deb and Shrey.

'So yes? What can we do?'

'Deb?' Shrey looked at Deb.

Deb rummaged through the garbage bin of ideas and found one. 'What if. It's just a wild thought. I'm thinking aloud really. What if the saas doesn't suspect that it's a trained snake.'

'I'm listening. I'm all ears,' said the programming head, eyes lighting up.

'What if she thinks that her bahu is the snake herself?' Deb said.

There were gasps around the room. The programming head had a degree from TISS, the two juniors were English honours graduates from St. Xaviers and Hindu College; they were all impressed.

Shrey leaned forward, and dramatically continued, 'The saas accuses the bahu! Trolley, trolley, trolley, pull focus. Tension builds! Builds, builds, builds! We charge on everyone. We build it up! The *sasur* clutches at his chest. Drama! The *nanad* jumps in. Tight close-up of her eyes. They twitch. Build-up, build-up, build-up! And then . . . the saas asks the bahu to prove that she's not a snake!'

'Then?' said the programming head, drooling.

Deb continued, 'A new villain enters! A *sapera*. It's the sapera and the saas on one side, the bahu on the other. And the husband . . .'

The junior spoke again, 'We don't need the husband to side with anyone. Make the heroine vulnerable.'

'Brilliant, that's brilliant, isn't it? What will the husband do? Make him the wallpaper, a mute spectator, the housewives will love that,' said the programming head.

'That's exactly what I was going to say. The husband is a wallpaper and then . . .'

'Stop, stop,' said the programming head. 'Let's just lock the story till here, okay? We will see how the TRP is and then decide what we need to do. How many episodes do you think this is? From the stealing to the accusation?'

'Eight,' said Shrey.

'First two, the snake opens the lock, the snake leaves, the saas wakes up and finds the bahu in the room. Next two, she finds that her heirloom is missing. Next two, will be an accusation scene. Last two will be the entry of the sapera. We really need to juice the storyline,' Deb said.

'Sounds good. Make sure you give the sapera a personality,' said the programming head. 'We don't want a cardboard character. Give him depth. He should have a backstory. A flaw, a block, a wound.'

'Of course, you know us. The audience will love to hate the sapera. It will be like *Breaking Bad*'s Walter White but with snakes,' said Shrey.

'This show will create history, I'm telling you,' said the programming head.

They left the meeting happy men. Their audacity didn't even surprise them any more. It took them two dedicated months to lose all their conscience for money and stability.

Deb came back home and couldn't stop irritating Avantika with snake references during their foreplay. *I want to snake into you! Show me my snake's burrow! Do you want to pet my snake?*

'These jokes are funny but you're more caterpillar right now than snake,' said Avantika and nibbled at his ears. She inched lower and unbuckled his jeans. She took his mostly-limp penis in her hands and said, 'I need you to be a python.'

They both burst out laughing.

14

Vernita's water broke a week too early. Tanmay had made the call while they were driving to the hospital. Vernita screamed like a banshee in the background refusing to let the baby out of her vagina unless Avantika was around.

'I WANT YOU HERE!' she shouted.

'BHAIYA! JALDI!' Avantika shouted in the cab driver's ears.

It was too late by the time Deb and Avantika got there. Vernita was already inside the labour room and they didn't let Avantika inside. Avantika threatened the hospital staff with mutilation and death if they didn't let her in.

'THAT IS MY NEPHEW OR NIECE IN THERE AND I NEED TO SEE IT GET BORN! I WILL RIP ALL OF YOUR THROATS OUT AND EAT THEM!' she screamed in the nurse's ears.

It wasn't until four security guards appeared with batons and stiff faces that she quietened down. A little later, Shrey reached the hospital too, grinning and impatient.

'Is she birthing a bear? How long will it take?' Shrey complained when it was already an hour that Vernita had been inside.

Avantika threw him a murderous look. A multitude of screams came from the labour rooms and the loudest, most filthy was Vernita's. With every scream, Avantika's panic reached a new peak.

'As long as she's using expletives, she's fine,' said Shrey.

'If she's silent, then there's something wrong,' added Deb.

Another hour of screaming had passed when the door to the labour room opened and a scared, haggard Tanmay walked out. He was looking down at his hands. In his hands, wrapped in a dark green cloth, was a baby crying his lungs out. As he came closer, Deb heard a little gasp and watched. Avantika shifted a couple of steps back, both her hands on her agape mouth. Deb saw the little hands and balled up fists sticking out from the wrapper.

'My nephew,' said Avantika, taking the baby in her trembling hands, tears flooding her eyes. She kissed the baby and then her brother.

The baby squinted and cried loudly, brought his little hands to his eyes.

Avantika's lips quivered for a moment and she cradled the baby closer to her chest. She closed her eyes and said a little prayer. She mumbled softly to the baby.

'Aw, you're a little cub, a little tiger cub. Aw, look at you, look at your eyes, your tiny, tiny feet. So cute you are, baby. Aw, don't frown, I'm your *bua*, your *pishi*, you can call me *peepi* . . . okay, peepi, I will always love you, I will always hold you close, always remember that. I'm your family, okay, I'm your family, your peepi. I will always be your peepi.'

She wept softly as she stared unblinkingly. Tanmay reached out twice to take the baby from her hands but couldn't make himself do it. Avantika kept rocking the baby in her arms and sweetly singing to it. A little later, the paediatrician and the nurse came looking for the baby.

'We have to go,' said Tanmay.

Avantika nodded and reluctantly handed over the baby to Tanmay. 'We will be right outside,' said Avantika and kissed him on the forehead. 'Congratulations, Bhaiya. Take care of him.'

Tanmay disappeared behind the door and she hugged Deb. They waited outside for twenty minutes for Tanmay to emerge but when he didn't, Avantika got up and said, 'I need to see him.'

She ran inside.

Deb and Shrey went to the hospital canteen and idled there when she didn't come back for an hour. Shrey said wistfully, 'To think of the girl who we had a crush on ejected a full grown baby . . . from her vagina.'

'Hmm . . .'

'Is that them?' said Shrey, putting his cup of coffee down, and pointed towards the lift.

It was *them*.

The resemblance was uncanny. Tanmay was a carbon copy of his mother, Avantika of her father. Why hadn't it struck them that they would come here? Of course they would, especially knowing that Tanmay had a son.

'Is this the first time you're seeing them after the wedding?' asked Shrey.

'Thankfully, yes,' said Deb who alternated between being terrified and angry.

Deb and Avantika's wedding was supposed to be a small, cosy affair, over in half a day. They had booked a tiny resort on the outskirts of Kolkata. It was all hush-hush. None of Avantika's family were told except Tanmay. They couldn't have afforded Avantika's parents to know lest they try to disrupt it.

'I'm sorry it has to be this way,' Deb had said.

'I'm getting married to you, what else could I possibly want?' asked Avantika.

'500 guests? A filming crew? Sangeet from your side of the family? Dance performances? Things that happen in every wedding?'

'I'm getting something that doesn't happen in anyone's wedding. A stupid boy who's fussing over me, and my in-laws who behave like they don't have a son, only a daughter-in-law. I think I'm set,' said Avantika.

'You're not saying that just because . . .'

'I mean every word of it. After all, from today onwards I will able to ask women to back off by saying he's my husband rather than the lousy guy I'm dating.'

'You will have to imagine the women part of it to use that. No one apart from you is interested,' said Deb.

'Come here,' said Avantika.

'I should tell you I'm strictly against pre-marital sex. It's against our *sanskriti*, but I am a proponent and pre-marital blowjob extremist,' said Deb.

On the day of the wedding, there were twenty people in the restaurant of the resort which doubled up as the *mandap*. Deb and Avantika had just sat down, holding hands, a strange sensation pulsing through their bodies even though they had touched a million times and in places much more intimate than the back of their hands, the pandit had barely started uttering the slokas that would supposedly bind them for life, when ten men barged into the hall armed with chains and hockey sticks. Within minutes they had pulled down the flower arrangements Deb's sisters had spent all night putting up, trampled on all the gifts they had received, broken the tables, upturned the chairs, thrown water on the matrimonial fire, flung waste on the walls and taken away the pandit by force. Then they went back without a word leaving behind a crying Avantika and the battered trio of Shrey, Tanmay and Deb who had heroically and foolishly jumped in the way of the men's hockey sticks and rods. No one moved for the first half an hour. And then suddenly, Deb's mother wiped her tears, adjusted her bright saree, put on a bright smile like nothing had happened and sent Deb and Avantika to their rooms. His mother had six hours.

'I'm sorry,' Avantika had said. 'I don't know how they found out we were getting married.'

She cried while Deb held her hand. A little later, Deb's sisters—Sonali and Moushmi—came and screamed at Avantika for spoiling her make-up. She sent Deb outside the room and re-did the make-up.

'I'm sorry,' Avantika told Deb's sisters.

'We don't have time for talk. We need to hurry up and make this happen,' said Moushmi who had come all the way from Sweden for this wedding and had been grumbling at the small scale of it.

'She has the perfect pretext now, our mom, for having the wedding she wanted,' said Sonali, before re-doing Avantika's make-up.

'The wedding we wanted,' Moushmi corrected.

Maa marshalled her daughters, nieces and nephews before the auspicious time went by and had the garden outside set up for a wedding. Vernita, too, had taken it on herself to whip the lazy Bengalis and an embarrassed Tanmay into working, spewing expletives left, right and centre, regardless of gender and age. The videographers had run off so it was up to Shrey, armed with cameras and phones to record the entire wedding.

'They are ready for you,' said Sonali before leading Avantika out.

'You're going to love it,' said Moushmi. 'I hope your friend, Shrey, is as good a videographer as he claims.'

'He's the fucking worst,' said Vernita.

Avantika let out a little gasp when they saw what Deb's mother had done. Instead of a paltry fifty people, hundreds crowded the little garden. They were dressed in the finest of clothes, bright smiles on their faces, and they all looked at Avantika with love.

'Your mother-in-law also wanted a big wedding. She called everyone she knew. She threatened them, made them wear their best clothes,' whispered Sonali in Avantika's ears.

Avantika felt a déjà vu grip her and wondered if this was the wedding she had dreamt of—under the moonlit sky, bloody, imperfect, beautiful.

Maa bullied the pandit into shifting the *mahurat* to a time she was to decide. When the pandit acquiesced, the anger on her face that had been there for the last few hours melted and was replaced by a bright toothy smile.

'There were performances to be performed,' she told a confused Baba who didn't understand the need of it.

Deb's mother kicked it off by making Baba stand bang in the middle of a makeshift stage, straight and awkward and smiling, while she danced to *Jab Pyaar Kiya to Darna Kya*.

'I'm sorry about this overreaction from Maa,' murmured Deb into Avantika's ears.

'This is the best thing anyone's ever done for me!' squealed Avantika before putting both her fingers inside her mouth and whistling for Deb's mom, who spurred on by this encouragement danced to two more songs. Maa twirled wildly, and the crowd erupted in applause. She set the mood for the rest of the evening, where now every couple wanted to dance. Avantika, for the most part of it, was standing on the chair, clapping and whistling wildly for every couple like a roadside ruffian.

'*KHUB BHALO! KHUB BHALO! DARUN! KI LAGCHE! EK NUMBER!*' she kept shouting at everyone. '*FATAFATI! FATAFATI! BANGALI LOG KHUB CHANGA!*'

Morning was only a few minutes away when it was time for the last performance of the day—Avantika's. Deb had almost dozed off in his chair but when she started dancing to *Mohe Rang Do Laal* he was turned on like he had never been before. *Uff.* Her naughty, shy eyes, those delicate moves of her waist, the rise and fall of her breasts, the beads of sweat on her painted lips, made him want to take her right on that stage. When she ended, there were collective gasps around the stage and the men looked at Deb with envy, the women with anger and the knowledge that the boy had got more than he deserved.

When the time for the *phera*s came, everyone was sleeping except Deb, Avantika, Tanmay and Deb's parents. Maa hugged Avantika for what seemed like an eternity when the chanting and the rituals were over. 'I'm glad you chose my son,' she said to her.

'I'm glad you chose me, Maa,' Avantika responded.

Later in the morning when they were getting ready to finally sleep, Tanmay confessed it was he who had told their parents about the wedding. He had still hoped their parents would come around and bless Avantika for the new life she was about to begin.

'You're naive, Tanmay. But thank you. In a weird way, had they not spoilt it, it wouldn't have been the day I would remember with so much fondness,' said Avantika.

Deb, spurred on by tiredness and the adrenaline rush of being married to her, said, 'Now if you can please excuse us, I need to consummate this marriage.'

Even after years, Deb wished he had a camera to capture Tanmay's expression.

They had tired, passionate, married sex.

Avantika clicked a picture of Deb and her and messaged it to every family friend and business associate of her father's. She posted it on Facebook walls, on LinkedIn profiles, on alumni networks, sent them to the WhatsApp groups her parents were a part of. It was a picture of Deb and Avantika in bed, bedsheet covering most of them but their naked shoulders, a thick streak of sindoor on Avantika's forehead. Tanmay as a part of his repentance reported daily to Deb and Avantika about what the picture had done to their parents.

They kept calling Avantika, and Deb kept answering her phone for her. They threatened him with legal action and Deb kept laughing at them. They gave up when they realized they couldn't do anything except get Deb beaten up from time to time.

'Brings back good memories, doesn't it?' said Shrey as he looked straight at them.

It was then that Avantika's parents picked out Deb's face from the crowd.

'They don't look happy seeing you. Look at their nostrils flare,' said Shrey.

They strode right up to Deb.

'What are you doing here?' they asked.

'I'm the *fufaji*, I'm the guy who will go to this baby's wedding and complain about the paneer. That's an important role to play in a person's life,' said Deb. 'Even more so because both of you are going to be dead anyway in a few years and after that Avantika and I will make sure he knows that his grandparents were giant pieces of shit.'

Shrey wondered if Deb shooting off his mouth was a good idea. Avantika's father looked like he could take on both Deb and Shrey if he put his mind to it.

Avantika's father broke out in a grin and put his hand on Deb's shoulder.

'Beta. Such cruel words on such a happy day. I will meet my grandson today and I don't want to soil my tongue by responding to you. But always remember, beta, we know where you live, we know where you go for work. I can come there any time. Or I can send someone. A lot of people work for me. Some are very scary ones. Just know that every day you live is the day I didn't send someone after you.'

'That wasn't pleasant,' said Shrey.

A little later, Avantika emerged with a smile from behind the doors.

'You parents went inside. You met them?' asked Deb.

'I don't want to talk about it. Shrey? Stay here and tell me when they leave. I want to come back as soon as they are gone,' said Avantika.

Avantika's parents didn't leave that night. Avantika stayed up waiting for Shrey to call them, replaying videos he sent them on a loop. In some of those videos, Deb saw Avantika's parents babbling to the child. Her fingers would hover over the delete button. But she decided otherwise.

'I feel like a bad person for not being as happy as you are with this baby,' said Deb.

'I don't expect you to. We run away from our relatives, our own blood, all our lives, wish the worst for them, and yet we feel attached to anyone who carries our genetic material. It's horrible and can't be helped,' said Avantika.

'Is that why you can't help but be hurt by them?'

'I will get there someday,' she said. 'I can't believe I'm an aunt now.'

'I can't believe that Vernita now has a baby. That foul-mouthed, sex siren, the girl we thought would never grow up, never have a relationship, has a boy to raise now. She's a mother,' said Deb.

'But look at her?' said Avantika and played a video. 'She looks like one.'

With the baby in her arms, it looked like Vernita had worn out her knees praying for a baby. She looked every bit an obsessed mother.

Deb couldn't help but wonder. How happy would Avantika be if she had a child? How beautiful would she look? It had been almost a year that they had been trying without luck. When did they go from thinking of having children as a wasteful, thankless pursuit to wanting them so aggressively that it made them so violently sad? None of Deb's failures of the past—and he had many—hurt as much as this one. Seeing

Vernita's baby made a part of Deb's body ache to hold a child of his own.

15

Vernita's baby grew cuter in the first couple of months making it easier for Deb to love him. But every centimetre that was added to his tiny self meant that Deb and Avantika were getting closer to the one-year mark of them trying to get pregnant. They would have to see a doctor soon if Avantika didn't get pregnant any time soon. As much as Deb liked the baby, he also reminded him of how long they had been trying. Seeing the three of them together, being cute, it burned something inside Deb. He longed for it, too. For himself, and for Avantika. They would be amazing, he knew that. They would be much better, more fun parents than Tanmay and Vernita would ever be. He never stopped thinking about it.

'Did you ever think it would come to this? That we would need to see a doctor to get pregnant?'

The question was on the tip of both their tongues but neither let it slip. They weren't ready for it yet.

They were both aware of the scary eventuality, and to tide over it, they loved each other fiercely and protected each other's happiness. They would not leave the other person alone for a single second, they wouldn't let a WhatsApp message, or an Instagram comment from the other person go unanswered for a single moment. They coddled each other and filled each other's lives with so much love that worry and misery couldn't find an opening. As much as the future scared them, the time that went by wasn't as hard. It was like they were in a new relationship and they had to do every little, sweet thing over again. They treated each other like little birds with broken wings.

On some nights, they wondered if not getting pregnant had gotten them closer.

'We are more intimate now, we talk a lot, we share a lot of things, and we have allowed ourselves to be vulnerable. I would say we are more in love now,' Avantika would say sometimes.

Deb concurred because on some nights he would feel so fiercely protective and possessive about Avantika that he would get jealous of Vernita's baby and their unborn child for taking away Avantika's attention. She was already thinking too much about it and it ate away at Deb. What would happen to their love five years later? Would they still be Deb and Avantika? Or would they be reduced to parents of Nayra?

Apart from the love they smothered each other with to ease the anxiety of not getting pregnant, Deb's work also helped keep him busy. The sapera track had worked well for the broadcasters and was a high point in what was a strange time for Deb and Avantika.

'I'm happy for you but you need to stop buying me stuff,' Avantika told Deb who would not come home empty-handed every evening ever since the money for the episode they had written started rolling in.

'You're uncomfortable I have cracked your code. Getting stuff for me from your salary, that's your drug isn't it? Guess what? It's mine too,' squealed Deb.

What was supposed to be a storyline for a couple of weeks had spilled over to three months and the ratings went through the roof. The sapera was loved and hated by the audience. He had slowly ingratiated himself into the family, married the younger sister of the bahu—his nemesis—and it was revealed that he could talk to snakes despite snakes being deaf. Briefly the show was even the highest-rated show on the channel. The channel made money. So did the columnists for web portals who wrote scathing pieces on the downfall of viewing standards in India. Though Deb and Shrey shared and laughed at the memes of their show, the programming head didn't take it lightly. The show was the cynosure of the TV programmer's eyes.

'Let the bastards make something good then,' the programming head would say in every meeting about the columnists. 'All of them are failed writers. Why else would they write about our show? It's low-hanging fruit! Nonsense! Our interns are better writers than any of them. They will tell us how to write a twenty-two-minute long episode every day when they can't write a three-minute article without putting everyone to sleep.'

Though, before Deb knew it, things changed.

The ratings dipped dramatically when they got the husband to help his wife get out of the sapera track.

'No one wanted to see the woman being helped. I knew it was a trap,' the programming head had said when the rating nosedived.

Deb and Shrey were meeting the entire team again. Unlike the other times, it was gloomy, there was no pizza on the conference desk, no cans of Diet Coke, no salads and no biryani. Nothing had worked after the snake track and they wanted to brainstorm new storylines as if a billion ideas hadn't already been executed in daily soaps.

'We need to think guys, we need to push ourselves. Preferably stay away from the hackneyed sapera track. I always had a bad feeling about it,' said the programming head, sipping her fourth green tea of the meeting. Her mug said *Breaking Bad*, and her iPhone cover had the Lannister emblem on it, and the way Deb and Shrey saw it, the word hypocrite emblazoned on her face.

'I have an idea,' said a smug junior whom Deb and Shrey had seen rising through the ranks with a mix of daredevilry, of questioning the writers and burying his head deep inside the programming head's asshole.

Shrey threw him a murderous glance.

'What if . . . what if . . . and I am just thinking aloud. It's all very rough in my head right now.'

Deb knew the smug asshole must have thought of it, prepared in front of a mirror for days, and aimed to stick it to them.

'What if the husband gets into an accident and—'

The programming head rolled her eyes. 'No, no, we don't want to do that. Too morose. Done to death. Think outside the box. Pretend there's no box. There's only the open blue sky.'

'Just hear me out. So he slips into a coma.'

'Too depressing,' Deb said, not wanting to encourage a junior lest he made giving them—the real writers of the show—suggestions into a habit.

The junior continued unabated. 'But then, eleven months later, the bahu becomes pregnant!'

The bastard waited for everyone to suddenly stop breathing. The programming head leaned forward.

He continued after the pause, 'Now the question is, who got her pregnant? The devar? Didn't we see them have a lot of humorous scenes? Or is it the old *mangetar*, fiancé? Is he back from the dead? Or is there a new mystery lover? Someone in the shadows?'

The programming head looked at the junior in wonder and awe.

'But don't tell me you're going to make it sleazy,' she interrupted.

'Of course, not. So where was I? Yes, the saas demands an explanation!' said the junior, his rehearsed narration hitting all the right spots.

'Build up! Build up! Build up! Charge on the saas, charge on the *maasi*, charge on the fufaji! She has none. She has none! And so she prays. Has the bahu let the *khaandaan* down? Charge! Build up! Trolley treatment! She prays to Santoshi Maa for an explanation and finds one!'

'What is it?' asked Shrey, hoping he would fail.

The junior half-closed his eyes in reverence, as if he himself was the woman praying. He said, 'It's God who had got her pregnant. Her *pati* is her *parmeshwar*, and she cites the Mahabharata! Her husband becoming God and a God comes down and impregnates her, just like Kunti. Her pati never left her side!' gushed the junior.

'Fucking brilliant. I knew we could come up with something great. This will work, I'm telling you, take my word, this will work,' said the programming head.

'That is not the worst idea,' said Shrey. 'Deb?'

'Debashish?' asked the programming head.

'No offence, but that's the worst idea I have ever heard. We can't do this.'

Shrey kicked Deb under the table. 'We will think about it. There's potential in it,' said Shrey.

'It's absolutely nonsense. Which woman would believe this, huh? Gods coming down and impregnating women? You must be out of your mind,' scoffed Deb.

'Didn't we just sell them that a woman can be a snake?' said the junior.

'Yes, because that's a fucking fantasy and everyone knows it's one. Many women watching the show will have had kids and surely they didn't come from praying. It's complete bullshit. This is insensitive shit for which television gets lampooned.'

'We are doing the pregnancy. The channel will take the onus if the ratings don't come,' said the programming head, frowning. She leaned towards Deb and said, 'Ratings, Debashish, ratings. Had the sapera track worked for another month I wouldn't have called this meeting but the sword of Damocles is hanging over our heads. You had your creative satisfaction when you came up with the sapera track, now do this track for us. And you know more than anyone else, no one's in the TV business to be Nolan. We all just want to get by and make these shows work. We need to work together on this,' she said sternly.

Shrey kicked Deb again in vain.

'It's nonsense. You can't trivialize pregnancies like this,' Deb said.

The junior butted in. 'We trivialize things all the time. That's what we do for a living. Strange that you haven't noticed!'

'We are doing the track,' said the programming head and got up from her chair. 'If you can't write it, Shrey will. Okay?'

'He will come around,' said Shrey politely.

The team filtered out. The junior skittered after the programming head, wagging his imaginary tail, yapping at her feet.

'What the fuck was that? Are you trying to get us replaced?'

'No one's going to replace us. We are the cheapest and we gave them the ratings, Shrey.'

'We are also replaceable, bro. Anyone can write the garbage we sell them. And what the hell is the difference between *ichhadhari nagin*s and Immaculate Conception anyway! The latter is way more accepted. All major religions swear by it, don't they? Fine, as she said, don't write it, I will!'

'Knock yourself out. You can write it and keep the money too. I don't give a damn. Do whatever the fuck you want. I'm done with TV anyway. I will write a fucking book instead.'

'Yeah, we all know how that worked out,' said Shrey.

Back in the office, Shrey started writing a one-pager on how the story could progress and that's when the realization struck. He went FUCK! And felt stupid for not realizing why Deb had been hesitant.

Shrey walked up to Deb who had buried himself in a bean bag and was typing away furiously. Shrey pulled his headphones off and said, 'So what are we going to do? I know, I know, I am stupid and I didn't realize it before but now I have. So tell me, how are we steering clear of the pregnancy track? And why the fuck are you making fake Twitter accounts?'

'To tell our lead couple they are fat and old,' said Deb. 'Once enough people tweet her, DM her, leave comments on her profile and tell our lead actress Sanjeeda Verma that she looks old and fat now, that she should do mother roles, there's no way she's going to agree to playing a pregnant woman. The script goes to her, she rejects it, threatens to walk out of the show and the script is rejected.'

'You think it will work?' asked Shrey.

'She has blocked twenty-two accounts up till now, been in fights with ten. You don't think it's playing on her mind?'

Shrey whipped out his phone. 'How many more accounts do we need?'

They overdid it because by that evening, Sanjeeda Verma went on a long conference call with the programming head and wanted a refresh on costumes.

'I WANT TO WEAR DRESSES ON THE SHOW, NOT SAREES. CHANGE THE TRACK SOMEHOW AND MAKE ME SEXIER. I CAN'T JUST BE AN OLD BAHU!' she had screamed on the phone.

After the actress cut the call, the programming head called Shrey and Deb, and ranted, 'Come to the office tomorrow. Let's figure out something else. Let's get the ratings up, and then we will kill off this character, okay? How dare she talk like that to us! Bloody TV actors! Bloody, my chair can act better than her! These actors think a little too much of themselves the minute they get a few thousand followers on Twitter! Once they sit at home for a few months, they will know. *Akal theekane aa jaegi*! Just wait till I spread stories of what a horror she was to work with!'

Click.

Later in the evening, they were back at the their brewery—this time without Vernita who had taken a continuous rain check until further notice—and were drunk enough to be vulnerable.

'I miss Vernita,' said Shrey. 'And I will miss you when you have an annoying little baby running around.'

'If there's an annoying little baby running around,' said Deb.

Shrey sighed and said, 'How's Avantika taking it?'

'You know how she is. She will not say anything. But it's just one whammy over another. She met her parents that day who would have unloaded shit on her and then there's this two-month old baby in Vernita's hands. She really loves that child but I know what she's thinking. What if that baby was just her own?'

'Allow me to say a platitude that it will all be fine,' said Shrey.

'To make it worse, her parents are still living with Tanmay. She told me yesterday it makes her want to throw up that they are holding her nephew,' said Deb.

'They are the worst,' said Shrey and drank a little more.

When Deb got back home and cuddled up with Avantika, the bell rang. A courier guy was outside with a big package.

'Now what did you get?'

Deb shook his head.

They ripped it apart and it was a life-size cut-out of Shrey. It wasn't the first time Shrey had done something stupid after two drinks too many. The little card with it read—*When you get busy with your lives with a baby that's going to come soon enough (I know!) and forget about me.*

'Let's hope he's right, Deb!' said Avantika.

16

Tanmay and Vernita's baby had gone three months without a name. Much to Avantika's chagrin, Avantika and Tanmay's parents still hadn't gone back to Muscat. Every day Avantika would call Tanmay and give him a piece of her mind for not asking their parents to leave. She would scream and bawl into the phone for hours on end. She would threaten Tanmay that this would be the end of their relationship but the thought of her nephew growing up without her would gnaw at her and the cycle would repeat.

'I'm not coming to see my own nephew like a goddamn thief. And how on earth can you let them raise that boy? Can't you see what they did to me?' she would say.

'It's their grandson. I can't just ask them to leave.'

'Who they will want to raise as a woman-hating monster. Not everyone ends up like you. Those people should be out of the house. Do it before I start hating you, Tanmay.'

On some days Vernita would pretend that the baby was sick and would see Deb and Avantika instead of the doctor.

Avantika's parents wanted to name their grandson Tanveer—a pandit of theirs had suggested the name—a mash-up between Vernita and Tanmay.

'Over my dead body,' said Avantika on the loudspeaker. 'Either you let them keep the name or you talk to me.'

'Can you please walk away from Deb and talk to me? This is between us,' said Tanmay.

'He has to listen in on how my brother disrespects me. He respects me unlike my own brother who's clinging on to his parents like he's still a breastfeeding boy.'

'That's unfair,' said Tanmay.

'Unfair? Tanmay, you should see what you're like in front of them. Grovelling little Mumma's boy. After all what they . . . anyway, you know where they would be if Vernita had a girl? They would be back in Muscat, that's where. THOSE ARE THE KIND OF ASSHOLES WHO ARE STAYING UNDER YOUR ROOF. Have some fucking decency and throw them out.'

'Chill, Avantika.'

Wrong choice of words to mollify someone battling with their worst baggage.

'Sometimes I think you're probably just selfish. You want all the money they have, don't you? Is that the reason why you find it so hard to cut off from them? Is it about the money? Because that I would understand and forgive. How else am I supposed to accept my brother still loves those people who would have preferred me dead?'

'Avantika, you're making a mountain—'

'Of course, I am making a mountain and why shouldn't I!' she said and stormed off.

'Avantika?'

'She's gone.'

'Can you give the phone to her?' said Tanmay.

'I won't, actually. In all fairness, you don't deserve to talk to her. And Tanmay I know you can beat me up and shit, but you got to man up in front of your parents. It's pathetic and repulsive. Also, don't beat me,' said Deb and cut the call.

Avantika had bolted the bathroom door. There was nothing Deb could have said that would make this all right.

Deb's phone rang.

'She won't talk to you.'

'It's me. Vernita.'

'She still won't talk. She's in the bathroom, crying. Tell your husband to grow some balls and throw out his parents. It's the least he could do for Avantika.'

'Don't worry, I will make him. That's what I called to tell you. Fuck his parents, they are the worst. You think I'm going to let them decide my child's name? Not a chance in hell. Tell Avantika she has that right and no one else. It's my promise to her.'

'Thank you. I owe you one.'

'You should. I'm doing it for your wife not Tanmay's sister. Tell her that I will drive his parents away in a few days. I'm planning a nervous breakdown today and another one will follow tomorrow. I will take the child and go to my parents.'

'Will you do that?'

'You think I wouldn't? I can't stand them. She expects me to stand on the cook's head and supervise her. Not just the woman, but his father too. If it's up to them I would never go back to work.'

'Is that the baby crying?'

'Yeah, got to go. You should be glad to know that I'm not making their lives easy. The maid and I left the baby on their bed without the diaper just when he was about to poo. Did it thrice. You should have seen their faces.'

'I'm proud of you.'

Click.

Later that evening, Avantika took a long walk beneath the apartment complex. Deb had asked her if he could join her. He was brutally turned down. Deb watched her as she walked round and round the apartment complex, her pace too swift for a stroll, too slow for exercise. When she came back, Deb noticed her clenched jaw, her tense demeanour. Avantika asked Deb for what she called a favour. They both knew it was more of a demand.

'Our daughter is going to take my surname,' she said.

'As in?' Deb asked.

'I don't think what I said was too hard to understand. She will be Nayra Sharma.'

'She can take your name if that's what you want. I don't see that being a problem. She can be Nayra Sharma Roy,' said Deb.

'Not even Roy Sharma? Is that what you're saying?' she asked, her gaze piercing.

'You want it to be Roy Sharma?'

'I want it to be just Sharma. Nayra Sharma. She will take her mother's surname and that's all,' said Avantika.

'That's not an exciting surname to have, reeks of Brahminical oppression.'

'And yours doesn't? Please tell me if you're okay with it or not.'

Deb realized it wasn't a suggestion, it was a deal-breaker.

'Avantika, we need to sit down and decide on this. You have to understand, what will Maa–Baba think?'

'It's not as if I have asked you to change your name. It's our daughter's name,' she said.

'I have let you keep your name as is, haven't I? I have never even mentioned changing your name.'

'Thank you for letting me *keep* my name. That's just so kind of you! I'm deeply grateful for you letting me wear the clothes that I wear, go to my job, for letting me eat at the same time as you do. After all you're the man and that's what men do—allow and let.'

'That's not what I meant, Avantika. You know that.'

'What did you mean then? That you're not like other men? That you have never stopped me from doing the things that I have wanted to do? You think you should receive a pat on the back for that? For what? For being a decent human being? Then where's my certificate? For allowing you to do what you have always wanted to do, huh?'

'You're overreacting. This wasn't even the conversation we were having.'

'Is it not? How's this different? I have got to seek your permission to name my daughter, the child I will carry inside me for nine months? Doesn't that seem a bit unfair to you?'

'See, I don't have any problem with Sharma but—'

'Maa–Baba will.'

'It would be hard for them to explain it to people.'

'Why do you think I give a damn about these people whom I have never met in my life?' she scoffed.

'Why are we even discussing this? It's not as if we are—'

'Because I don't want my daughter to grow up in a world where her name constantly makes her believe that being a boy means wielding more power, having more respect in this world. I can't let that happen.'

'You don't even know if we will have a daughter,' Deb argued.

'If it's a boy, even more so. All this nonsense is because of men like you. If my boy grows up carrying his mother's name it will change how he looks at women.'

'Wait? Men like me?'

'Yes, like you. Are you any different? You may want to believe you're different but you're not. You do the least of what's required from you, whatever you're comfortable with. You would rather bring up your child with your name for no reason at all apart from the fact that you're wondering, *log kya kahenge*, what will people say.'

'But why the hell should she get your name? Let's not give her a surname at all?' Deb barked.

She started laughing pitifully.

'Avantika, don't do that.'

'You're asking me not to laugh at your pettiness? You would rather she not have a surname than have mine? How big and fragile is your ego, Debashish? And then you say you're not like other men. All of you like the status quo, like pigs you roll in it. You want to be supportive but when it comes to decisions like these, decisions that will change the way of things, you jump ship.'

'I'm not jumping anything. I was saying it for arguments' sake. Why should she get your surname?'

'To break the status quo? To set an example? To lead? To affect a small change?'

'You're Che Guevara now?'

'Why not? And I would rather be Leila Seth, Nayantara Sehgal than Che,' she said.

'Your anger is misplaced.'

'Pray tell me how, Dr Freud?' mocked Avantika.

'I am going to ignore that tone,' he said. 'You're angry with your parents. I understand that. But you're taking it out on me and that's not done. I don't see you telling Tanmay to do the same. Make your nephew take Vernita's name.'

'See that's your problem, Debashish. You're asking me to talk to Tanmay when I don't think the decision is his at all. It's Vernita's decision and she chose to take Tanmay's name.'

'Whatever.'

'Oh, what's this? You ran out of arguments? No smart alec replies any more?'

'You can't just wake up one day and decide to go against sixty years of conditioning of my parents. I don't want to argue on this.'

'Neither do I,' said Avantika. 'And I don't think I want to have this child any more.'

She got up and left the room. Two doors slammed in quick succession and Deb realized she had left the apartment altogether.

When she didn't return for a couple of hours, a sense of gloom settled around the apartment. Deb replayed the conversation in his head and knew there would be no truce. It wasn't like those fights that dissolved after a hug without any resolution. There was no brushing under the carpet with this one. She would see this to the very end.

Avantika got no sleep till late that night. She was struggling to keep her eyes closed, had even resorted to counting sheep but to no avail. Deb's hand crept over her stomach and she brushed him away.

'Deb, sleep,' she said.

'I have come to a decision regarding that surname thing of yours.'

'I'm not holding my breath,' said Avantika.

'We could have done our bit for the nation and our society in general by not giving our child any surname. That way she wouldn't be immediately identified as a descendent of our oppressive Brahmin ancestors. She would have grown up without the privileges that would in turn have helped her be more empathetic to her friends in the future. We could have transcended caste—'

'I don't want to continue this conversation.'

'I'm going to overlook your obsession with our daughter maintaining caste, your lack of oversight, your unwillingness to help in the alleviation of our Dalit friends and agree with your decision of taking your surname forward. But if we have another child, he or she takes my surname. Deal?'

'Deal.'

She turned and kissed Deb. She smiled and said, 'Have you seen the movie *Prem Aggan*? Where the girl first seduces the guy, the guy gives in but then pulls back at the last moment and the girl says she was taking a test? To see if he sleeps with her?'

'I'm not following your B-grade movie references, Avantika,' said Deb.

'I would have wanted her to be a Sharma if I weren't trying to get rid of my family but I'm glad to know you would have stood by me. That's all I wanted to know,' she said and snuggled up to Deb.

'You spent an evening fighting for a silly test?'

'It wasn't silly for me,' she said, kept her head on Deb's chest and promptly fell asleep.

Vernita's parents got the door after they had already rung the bell twice. They apologized and said, '*Bachchhe wala ghar hai naa!* This is a household with a kid. Come, come, Vernita's waiting for you.'

Avantika and Deb touched their feet. Avantika went striding into Vernita's room ignoring her parents' overbearing love and Tanmay's presence.

'It's as if I don't exist,' said Tanmay.

'After what you did, did you expect anything different?'

Deb and Tanmay sat in the living room and waited for Vernita to finish feeding. Deb watched Vernita's mother doting and fussing over Tanmay, treating him no less than a king, and wondered if he would have been treated similarly had his marriage to Avantika been with her parents' sanction.

'He feeds a lot, doesn't he?' asked Deb after a while.

'*Chee chee*, don't say that, *nazar lagegi*,' said Vernita's mother and immediately went inside to waive away Deb's evil eye.

'How has it been? Hectic?' he asked Tanmay.

'Mom has been helping so it's easier. We have been looking for help but Vernita and her mom like no one. They reduced one to tears yesterday when she didn't use the sanitizer before holding the baby.'

'That's a valid reason,' Deb said.

'She had just washed her hands.'

'Maybe not so much then.'

They were called inside.

Vernita was inside, lying groggily on the bed, the baby was sleeping, his cheek firmly against Avantika's shoulder. Avantika was lightly tapping his back, murmuring a lullaby with all the words and the inflexions in the right places.

She had already changed her clothes.

She didn't look up from the baby. She was transfixed. Envy crept in Deb and he walked up close. He saw the baby wasn't sleeping. He was looking up at Avantika, all goggly-eyed, as if in love, and moved his lips like a little fish. His heart melted into a little puddle and instead of snatching Avantika away from the baby's grip, he wanted to do the opposite.

'Why don't the two of you get some sleep tonight?' asked Deb out of the blue.

'We will handle the baby,' added Avantika.

'Avantika, he's not an easy baby to manage,' said Vernita breaking out of her daze.

'We will manage,' said Deb.

Tanmay seemed shifty. Avantika told him, 'If we need you, we will call for you, don't worry.'

Tanmay and Vernita looked at each other, the part of them that was sleep-deprived won over, and they looked at Avantika and nodded.

'Do call us out if you need us, okay? The bottles, his milk, everything is on the table. He cries because of colic in the middle of the night. If he doesn't quieten then—'

'Don't worry, Vernita,' said Avantika and kissed the baby's forehead.

When Deb closed the door behind Tanmay and Vernita, they felt like they had kidnapped the baby. As if on cue, the baby got up and stared at his parents for the night. A few nervous seconds passed before he broke out into a silly, toothless smile.

'Now what?' asked Deb.

'Hold him,' said Avantika.

'I hope I don't break him. Tanmay won't like that too much,' said Deb before scooping the baby up in his arms. He wriggled a little bit but then settled in his arms. 'He's warm.' Deb giggled and looked at him. That's when the baby started to coo a little. 'Why is he doing that?'

Avantika handed over the bottle of milk he was having a little while back.

'I just put it in his mouth like that?' said Deb and without waiting for an answer did just that.

The baby latched on immediately and sucked furiously on the nipple. Deb and Avantika looked at each other, bright smiles on their faces, confused why a little baby drinking milk made them so happy.

'Look at him, so cute, he looks like you,' said Avantika.

'That's not possible,' said Deb.

'Not like that but like, in terms of how cute he is. Look at how he's looking at us!' said Avantika. 'Guglu! We are your parents now, forget your mumma–papa, we are everything now!'

'I feel pathetic at feeling what I'm feeling looking at this baby. Why am I not disgusted? Why do I want to hold him?'

The baby went back to sleep, still sucking on the bottle. When he finished drinking, Avantika asked Deb to keep him in the crib.

'Absolutely not, let him sleep where he is,' said Deb, cradling him closer.

'That's not fair,' said Avantika.

For the next hour, Deb sat upright, the baby comfortably sleeping in his arms. When he woke up, bawling, Avantika shot up and snatched him from Deb and tried to coo him back to sleep. Tanmay and Vernita came to the door but saw Avantika rocking him, cooing to him, and realized they couldn't do much more. Deb insisted they catch up on their sleep.

For the next hour, Avantika sang to the baby tirelessly. Deb looked on as the baby cried and cried and yet it made no difference to her. She kept smiling at him, kissing him, trying to lessen the baby's discomfort. When the baby slept, she slowly kept him between Deb and herself, a light hand over him, and looked at Deb and said, 'I love him.'

'Why do I love him? I shouldn't be feeling what I am. He's just a friends' baby. Am I an uncle now?' said Deb.

Avantika ran her hand over his face, 'As long as you're a cute uncle.'

'Rather be a hot dad,' said Deb.

'And you will be, Deb, you will be,' said Avantika.

They both looked at each other, and only then it struck them—it had been a year that they had been trying for a baby. They would have to see a doctor sooner rather than later.

17

Debashish took a cab to the flower *mandi* at five in the morning to buy the freshest flowers for the mandir. On his way back, he stopped at the Azadpur sabzi mandi. He buried his nails inside the fruits and vegetables, checked for dyes, and only when he was convinced that they hadn't been soaked in chemicals, he bought them. Just like his mother had taught him. He couldn't have gotten it wrong. Every time he shopped for groceries he would be reminded of how embarrassing his mother used to be. He was now her. Free *dhaniya* and *mirchi* was his birthright.

While he was at the mandi, Avantika's responsibility was to make the house squeaky clean. By the time he was back home, the boxes of protein supplements had been hidden, the medicine strips missing a tablet or two were thrown away as if Avantika and Deb had never been sick. The house was upturned, deep-cleaned and put back together before Deb's parents came home.

They both put face packs, made their skins glow and look healthy, and Deb sprayed Engage Yin & Yang Perfumes over both of them to complement each other's scent. They did everything right but all their efforts came to naught. Deb's mother, Maa, reached their house in the late afternoon and promptly declared that they lived in filth and suffered from malnutrition. She pulled back her bangles, and promptly got down to work while Deb's father, Baba, interrogated them about their financial health.

Both parents shook their heads in disappointment. They told Deb and Avantika that it wasn't late and that they could still make amends. They nodded, pretended to take notes.

Baba and Avantika discussed how they could save more while Deb's Maa was happy to get time with her son. 'Your father didn't even learn to boil an egg in all these years,' complained Maa to Deb when she saw Deb whip up *luchi*s with precision. 'He too should have gotten a Punjabi *bou*, wife. He would have come right on the line then. *Kichhui kaajer naa tor baba*, your father's useless.'

Maa's grouses were shoddily, unconvincingly delivered. In truth, Maa didn't even dislike anything about Baba, not even slightly. Their love wasn't a force of habit, but one of unending adoration for each other.

'*Ei! Ki korli daekh to*, see what he's done!' exclaimed Maa when Deb burnt his hand on the last luchi. She took Deb's blistered hand into hers.

'*Ki holo*, what happened?' asked Avantika from the living room in accented Bengali.

'She's overreacting as usual,' shouted Deb.

Maa held his hand under water.

'*Dekhbi to ki korchhish*. What have you done? Where's your mind at?' she said angrily. She wiped the wound and asked Deb to let it breath. All this while, her face was in a tight grimace as if it was she who was hurt. 'You can't cook a meal without burning yourself, how do you think you will raise a child? You're your father's son only. Careless. What are you looking at?'

Deb stared at his mother.

'*Ki? Aami jaanbo naa?* What? You think I don't know? *Aami shob jaani*, I know everything,' said his mother, smiling. The next few seconds that passed were awkward. It beat the time his fifth-grade crush had seen him naked and cowering behind a curtain after he had soiled his pants. It beat the time he was surrounded by school bullies and their girlfriends and he got whipped by the ends of their wet handkerchiefs.

'You want to start a family. I know. It's the right decision. You should have a child before you're too old. There's a lot of running around after kids. Now go put Boroline on this.'

Deb looked at his blister, embarrassed that his mother knew—for sure—that he was repeatedly having sex with his wife.

18

Every morning for the past sixty odd years, Debashish's father, Anirban Roy, had woken up at five in the morning, and regardless of the city, walked to the newspaper seller and bought the first copy of three newspapers. He would be in his half-shirt and trousers, hair parted to the side, moustache combed, spectacles wiped clean, before his wife woke up. His two grown daughters and son had reasons to believe he did so to impress his beautiful wife. No one confronted him with this assumption because they knew they were right.

That morning, he tripped over the chair in his room while looking for the bathroom door. His wife stirred in her sleep. It had been three months that they had been living with their son and daughter-in-law and he was yet to adjust to the new house and its tics. His wife and he had been trying to go back to Kolkata for two months now. The original plan had been to be there for a month. Avantika had made them cancel twice.

'We should stay. Avantika really wants us to stay,' Debashish's mother would say every time Avantika suggested prolonging their stay.

Baba knew Avantika was not the nightmarish daughter-in-law Maa had always been afraid of. She had envisioned a different daughter-in-law. The controlling sort who would snatch their son from them. Someone who would call them Maa and Baba but wouldn't love them as much. That way it would have been easier for them to stay away from their Deb. But Avantika, she *loved* them. She loved them, and she demanded love out of them; she would get upset if they didn't call her. Worse still, she made Deb spend more time with his parents, talk to them, scolded him if he didn't receive their calls. All this made it tough for him and his wife to go back to Kolkata and stay apart from their son. Theirs was a different predicament from all their friends with daughters-in-law who were Avantika's exact opposite. Avantika would keep reminding them that their home wasn't in Kolkata, it was with their daughter . . . and son.

Avantika called him Baba, same as Deb. Unlike his daughter's husbands, the word seemed to slip naturally off her tongue. It wasn't an obligation. 'You're her baba,' Debashish's mother would tell him, and it always brought a smile to his face. The last three months at his son's house seemed like they'd passed in a wink. Sometimes he would look at Deb and wonder how swiftly time had passed. In a blink of an eye, he had turned from a wrinkly baby in his arms to this man he was proud of.

'*Issh. Shue poro*, sleep, it's early,' said Debashish's mother.

A mild panic struck him that he had woken her up. It settled only when his wife turned to the other side without opening her eyes. In the bathroom, he cut himself thrice, as he often did these days. With every wrinkle he earned with the passing of time it had become tougher to shave. The commercials don't show what blades do to puckered skin. He wondered if he should switch to the three-blade razors his son insisted he use. He dabbed on his son's aftershave. It stung and erased the little sleep left in his eyes. He waited for the blood to clot and wiped it away when it did. He then sprayed what his son introduced him to, Engage Perfume Spray, once, and then twice, and recounted all the times his wife told him he smelt fresh, young. When his wife woke up, he was ready for her—clean and knowledgeable.

'You're up,' asked his wife like she always did.

'*Baitha kemon?* How's the pain?' he asked her, pointing at her knees. Though he knew that the arthritic pain was now also in her wrists and her back. It was slowly consuming her.

'Much better,' she said.

This conversation hadn't changed for years. Only now things were worsening at a pace neither of them was ready for.

Debashish's father peeped at her from behind the newspaper as she put the water for tea to boil. Even with the dishevelled saree, the bedsheet pattern printed on her face, eyes bloodshot with sleep, she looked beautiful. His children were right all along—he didn't deserve her. She was too beautiful for him. He had spent half his life trying to be worth her. He worked harder than anyone in his office, went to the Middle East and stayed alone for five years to give his wife everything she never asked for, and only came back when she sent him letters with her handwriting smudged with her tears.

Now he saw his son doing the same; it was the fate of Roy men, it seemed.

Like him, his wife too had a ritual of her own. On her bedside, lay a small silver box her mother had given her. Every morning before she opened her eyes, she applied a thick streak of sindoor, arrogantly displaying her *suhaag*. She didn't want to wake up in a world where she wasn't married to her husband even though she had started to bald where she applied the sindoor. Over the years, the streak only got thicker, younger. Deb's father revelled in the sight of that. Of how she held his hand wherever they went, insisted on it. Sometimes she would scold him in public to ward off the evil eye from them, to not seem too happy in front of others.

Her daughter-in-law, Avantika, had picked up the habit too.

'Marie biscuit?' asked his wife and sat alongside him.

He nodded.

'You have to talk to Tini today,' his wife reminded him.

'It's their decision. I don't want to meddle. What would he think? What will Avantika think?'

'We are not doing this for ourselves, are we? We want them to be happy. They will think that we are looking out for them. Who will tell them if not us?' asked his wife.

'Why don't you tell them then?'

'Isshh. What will Avantika think? Na, na, you will have to do it. She respects you, she will listen to you.'

'What nonsense. She doesn't respect you or what?' he said, not wanting to be bullied by her as he always was.

'But not like you. We don't sit and talk for hours about the news like the two of you. Don't pretend like you don't know she likes you more than she likes me,' she said, her displeasure and envy at Avantika's love tipping more towards her husband brimming up to the surface. '*Aami kichhu jaani naa*. I don't know anything. You talk to them today. Three months we have been here, *bhogoban*, God knows how long they have been trying for a child! They should see a doctor. Don't shake your head like this. Promise me you will talk to them today.'

'I will do it over the phone.'

'No, you will do it before we leave.'

19

'The flights are cheap next week. If we cancel tomorrow's flights and book new ones it will only take Rs 2000 more. Talk to them, naa,' said Avantika, in the middle of the night and thrust the MakeMyTrip app in Deb's face.

'They won't change now. They have packed, Avantika,' said Deb.

'I will unpack for them. How long will that take?' said Avantika.

'Baba has work to do in Kolkata. If they could stay they would have.'

'What work does he have there that can't be done from here? Or Baba can go, do his work and come back? The house will feel so empty without them, Deb.'

That much was true. Every day for the past three months had been filled with activity. They would go out every alternate evening and do touristy things in a city all of them had spent most of their lives in. Baba would tell them stories of how the city was built and razed, which rulers ruled over and which desecrated Delhi and they would all listen intently late into the night. They would visit monuments they had been to on school trips and look at them in an entirely different light. With Baba around, they rediscovered the city they grew up in. Often, Deb and Avantika would Google if what Baba told them checked out and more often than not it did. Only sometimes the portrayal of Muslim rulers tended to be despotic and unjust. But what Avantika really looked forward to were the weekends. It was when Debashish's mother would make Deb try out new recipes and after a month it had become akin to a Masterchef contest—a clash between motherly pride in home-cooked food and the ego of a man who didn't want to get beaten, not even at cooking.

What Avantika didn't say aloud though was that the parents' departure would remind them of their failure to conceive, the emptiness that awaited them. While his parents were with them, they were the children, they were a complete family. Without them around, their family would again seem incomplete. They would be the adults again.

'We will be okay,' said Deb and put his arm around her.

Avantika counted sheep, lit a diffusor, had warm milk and yet couldn't sleep the entire night. They had passed the year mark. It ate at Avantika that sooner or later they would have to go to a fertility doctor. Her relationship had gone through some hard knocks in the past ten years. It wouldn't survive the one that stared her in the face now. All these years she had hoped she would never have to face this terrible secret of hers.

She washed the car and completed the web check-in hours in advance. No amount of work she did made it easier for her to accept that they were finally going. In the morning, they loaded all the suitcases in the car. Maa, like she was wont to do, turned back once, looked at the house, shed measured tears, paused and then got into the car. 'Stay back for a few days . . .' the words danced on Avantika's lips but she couldn't say it. On the drive to the airport, no one said a thing.

Three months had seemed a lot to Avantika three months ago. This was the first time her in-laws had stayed with them for such a long time. Avantika had been concerned. She had been worried sick about familiarity breeding contempt.

'What if they don't like me? They have never stayed that long with us!' she had said.

'You're literally stressing over nothing,' Deb had assured her.

'I hope they don't end up hating me!'

Now that they were leaving for Kolkata, she wished for the flights to be cancelled, the airport to be shut down. She would miss Baba more.

Debashish's father insisted he come with Avantika to find parking for the car. Deb and his mother got down at the airport departures gate.

'There,' said Debashish's father pointing to where a space had opened. Avantika parked the car. She was always good at it, but she let Baba guide her through it. She felt her heart sink when she took out her father-in-law's cabin baggage from the boot.

'You have change, Baba? I only have 2000-rupee notes,' she said.

'They don't have change at the counter? What kind of a parking is this?' said Baba. 'This is why this country will never progress. Such little things we don't get right. Horrible, absolutely horrible.'

He gave her a fifty-rupee note.

'Thank you, Baba,' said Avantika.

Baba. Never had she thought she would use this word frequently and without pain. The word was poison to her earlier. A betrayal. Mumma, Maa, Mummy, didn't invoke the kind of malice Baba or Papa used to.

'You don't have to be in a hurry,' Debashish's father had said when he first got to know of Avantika's relationship with her parents. 'You can call me Uncle.'

She called him Uncle for the first two years. While he didn't seem to mind, her mother-in-law—who prided herself in being the antithesis of what mothers-in-law are like—squirmed every time she did that.

'Avantika, I'm going to take some sandwiches for the flight,' said Baba and stopped at a vendor. 'Deb and you will have something?'

'No, Baba,' said Avantika.

She tried to pay but Baba would have none of it. While they waited, she saw Baba pick at his nails. She had often wondered if Debashish's parents missed her and if they were as invested as she was in this relationship. They had two daughters of their own blood and didn't need another one. She had only one *baba*.

'There's something that your Maa wanted to talk to both of you about. She insisted that I do it face to face before we leave.'

'Should we go upstairs? You can tell Deb too.'

'I will tell you first. Tini can be immature about certain things. But you understand. I will talk to him too later if it's needed.'

'You're scaring me, Baba.'

Baba laughed. 'It's nothing to fear. It's just our concern. Your Maa's and mine. We could be wrong too. Please tell us if we are. Please don't mind us meddling. Your Maa was insistent or I wouldn't have said anything.'

'What's it, Baba?'

'Your Maa and I . . . we know that you have been trying . . . for a child. Your Maa knows that it's been five, six months. I know it's longer. A year perhaps?'

'We . . . we . . .'

'It's nothing to worry about, Avantika. Remember Mr Biswas's son? You met them at the reception? They went to a doctor when they wanted a child. It was fine for them. Your Maa wanted me to tell you that you have our support in what both of you decide.'

'Baba.'

'Your mother is really worried about the two of you. This kind of thing puts a lot of strain on a marriage. We know. The cracks might not be obvious at first but they are there.'

'We are fine, Baba,' said Avantika.

Baba went on like he hadn't heard what Avantika had said. 'Your Maa, she didn't want Deb. Of course, we didn't know whether it would be a girl or a boy. Your mother had had enough. She didn't want to raise another child.'

'How did you react?'

'We fought, we fought every day.'

'It doesn't look like Maa and you have ever fought,' said Avantika.

Baba laughed and continued, 'During that time you couldn't even utter the word divorce or we would have used it. By the time I thought it would be best for Deb not to be born, it was too late. The doctor refused to perform an abortion. Your mother hated Deb when he was born. His dark skin was wrinkled, he was underweight, and he cried. Oh, how he cried. Your mother was cruel to him. Post-partum depression, I understand it's called that now. She would love the two sisters in front of him out of spite. It was a horrible, horrible time.'

Avantika felt her heart slowly splinter for Deb.

Baba continued, 'I took a long holiday. I could tell no one that it's because my wife had refused to raise our son. I told them that the baby was sick and needed me. For three months she refused to hold him.'

Baba started to laugh.

'What? What happened then? You can't just laugh in the middle of the story.'

'I don't know what changed then. Your Maa tells me that it's because she could no longer see me run around with the baby leaving everything. I know that was a lie because she had other versions as well. Like we were losing money because of it, or that people were asking questions. But I know what the reason was,' he said. 'By the time he was three months and his features became prominent, he was a splitting image of his mother. He was so lovely, like a little girl. Despite what I did for him, he would still run after her. He was so clingy, he still is. Haven't you seen him hide in the kitchen with his Maa? Like her third daughter.'

'Does he know that's what you think?'

'He has a lot of pictures in frocks so I'm sure he has an idea about it,' said Baba, chuckling.

Avantika was still laughing when Baba's voice turned sagely.

'It can be a long road ahead,' said Baba, and patted her shoulder. 'But if anyone can brave it, it's you.'

They walked in silence to the Departure gate.

'Where were you?' asked Deb.

'We got stuck, couldn't move an inch, mad line at the counter,' said Avantika.

The house felt empty and ate at them when they got back. Neither she nor Deb found it in themselves to clean the house or make the bed Maa–Baba had slept in. They lay down for a nap in the guest room where Maa-Baba had stayed. Deb put his arm around Avantika.

'Maa told me Baba talked to you,' said Deb. 'Did he tell you about Biswas Uncle's son? Should we—'

'I shall see one first,' said Avantika abruptly.

'Hmm.'

'Deb? Baba said such a thing can put a lot of strain on a relationship. That there are cracks we don't notice. Are we fine?'

'Of course we are fine. What would happen to us? Nothing,' said Deb and pulled her closer.

20

Tanmay hadn't slept in days. He felt tired, fat and lethargic. The euphoria of holding his child at the end of the day was what kept him going. He would have crashed and burned otherwise.

During Vernita's pregnancy, he had promised to take care of the baby, do everything that was expected of him and more. After all it was he who had wanted the child so badly.

He kept up with all his responsibilities in the first few days. He went without sleep for the first three days, guzzling Red Bull by the crate. However, that seemed tough with every passing day. Being a father, he realized, was looking on with arms folded at your baby clinging to his mother and hoping there was more for you to do. There were times in the day the baby would not quieten down unless his skin was against Vernita's, his lips clasped around Vernita's nipple. No matter how hard he tried, he couldn't give Vernita the rest he had promised. Every day he woke up, even his bones soaked in drowsiness, and wanted to complain. He would then see Vernita cradling the baby, feeding him, powering through with even less sleep than him.

He felt weak.

'You're doing great, just great. If I need help, I will ask. We can't help it if our baby's straight from hell, can we?' Vernita had said the day before.

The baby was named Ivan by Avantika. She wanted to rub her parents' noses in it. A name derived from the daughter they had thrown out. It wasn't until a couple of days after that she realized where she had heard the name before. Ivan the Terrible, the tyrant from Russia. Ivan was living up to the name by being the trouble child everyone wished against.

Today when Tanmay woke up to twelve missed calls from Avantika asking him to meet her, he felt guilty leaving Vernita alone with the baby. Sunday meant Vernita could sleep longer without having to worry about Ivan the terrible.

'Why don't you go instead?' asked Tanmay.

'If she wanted me she would have called me. She needs you. You know what it's about, don't you?'

Tanmay nodded.

'It's tough for them, you know that. Deb won't call me unless I do, he won't talk about it. And Shrey is an asshole. He will only make it worse. But she has you, and you should be there for her. Not everyone is as lucky as we were. Go now and don't disappoint your sister again.'

'I will be back as soon as possible. Ask your mom to give him NanPro and get some sleep, okay?'

'Don't worry about me,' she said.

Tanmay showered and dressed within minutes. To make up for the time he wouldn't be there he changed Ivan's diaper before it was time, fed him though he was full. Vernita chuckled softly on the side all the while.

'Tanmay? Do you sometimes feel guilty about what you have and Avantika doesn't?' asked Vernita as she watched him bury his nose into Ivan and tickle him. It had been eating at Vernita to watch Avantika shower love on her nephew when they'd been trying for a child for a year now.

'Have you seen Avantika with Ivan? One would mistake her to be the mother and not me. He just melts into sleep in her arms,' she said. 'Every time I see her I can't think of anything else but . . . Only if she got pregnant . . . I keep feeling bad about our happiness, of what we have here. You, me, this baby. Our family. Do you think about it also?'

'All the time,' he said. 'About how happy she gets when anyone tells her that he looks like her, mistakes her for his mother.' Tanmay had often wondered how divergent their lives were despite the fact that they had been born of the same mother. Like a twin in the womb cannibalizes the other's nutrition, Tanmay felt he'd done the same to Avantika's luck. While he'd bagged happiness and acceptance, Avantika had seen only pain and rejection. It wasn't lost on him how his parents had wrecked Avantika's chances of ever leading a completely normal life. He knew one just can't shed their past like that. His guilt was heavy. Avantika would always disagree on that. *Why couldn't he leave his parents if it were so?* was her question. The truth was, he had long run out of places to hide. When he was younger, he would tell Avantika that he was conditioned to not seeing anything wrong in their parents' behaviour. That women were always treated like the way she was in the family. He would argue that even their parents were products of toxic conditioning. He was thirty-two now. He had spent half his life learning and unlearning and knew now none of the explanations held any more. Only a flickering realization that he too was responsible for what had happened to his sister remained.

'She always gets the raw deal, doesn't she? Mummy, Papa . . . that boyfriend of hers from school, and then Deb—'

'Admit it or not, Deb is the best thing that happened to her. He has done what you couldn't,' interrupted Vernita.

'She deserves someone better,' said Tanmay, who had the day he had caught Deb kissing his sister seared in his brain.

When Deb had met his sister, Tanmay hadn't felt threatened. He was an average boy; someone no one spared a second look or a thought. Avantika had looked over and ignored many brilliant and good-looking boys in the two years she had been reeling from the relationship that had broken her. It was a night-out; Vernita and Tanmay thought it would be nice for Avantika to just go out, make a couple of new friends. Next thing he knew, Avantika was kissing Deb. Of all the people, *him!* It was inexplicable.

'It's just one thing after another, Vernita. It's not fair. Can you imagine how nice it would have been had you guys had kids one after another?'

Vernita chuckled sadly. 'Can you imagine the competition though? Not every pair of siblings is equally brilliant and kind like you and your sister,' said Vernita.

Tanmay left the house and wondered what could be so urgent. Ever since she had started dating Deb—the boy she knew he hated—she had never needed him. What had changed now?

He had just sat in his car when Avantika texted him the address he needed to meet her at. It was a hospital that specialized in fertility treatments.

21

Tanmay was late by an hour and yet Avantika hadn't called once to check where he was. That was worrying. Avantika was punctual down to the second and he was too until his baby came along.

'Are you there yet? Does she have an appointment? Whatever happens, just listen and be supportive, okay? She needs you,' Vernita had instructed.

'Just reached. I will call you later. I will update you as soon as I know,' said Tanmay and cut the call.

He was asked not to run in the corridors by a bunch of ward boys wheeling stretchers back to where they came from. Tanmay found Avantika in the far corner of the cafeteria, playing distractedly with the leftover crumbs of her sandwich. She sat there unmindful of the nervous and loud conversations of anxious family members stress-eating microwaved meals. It terrified Tanmay to see Avantika look out of sorts. Even in the depths of her depression, she could fool people into believing everything was fine. Had the doctor told her something? What could he say to make it better?

'Are you here for a doctor's appointment?' Tanmay asked her.

Avantika looked up to see him. Tanmay saw that she had been crying.

'Do you want me to take one for you? Is your doctor in?' he asked again.

'Sit,' said Avantika.

'What is it, Avantika?' he asked. He then softened his tone and said, 'Everything will be fine. I know it will be fine. Let's see a doctor if you haven't seen one yet?'

'I don't have a doctor. I couldn't do it, Bhaiya. I couldn't. I'm scared,' Avantika said.

'Arre? What's there to be scared in this? Vernita and I have Googled. A lot of women go through what you are going through. You will be shocked at how normal it is,' said Tanmay.

'It's not about that. There's something else. There's something I need to tell you but you have to promise me that you won't do anything without asking me. And you won't tell Deb. It has to come from me.'

'I won't do anything?'

'Just promise me,' said Avantika sternly.

'I don't get what you're saying. Okay, I promise. Tell me. What's this about?'

'You remember back in school I had a boyfriend.'

'Paritosh Mehta, of course, I remember that bastard,' said Tanmay.

How could he forget that? Paritosh Mehta was a money-throwing, glue-sniffing, alcoholic bastard his sister had chosen to date despite all the warning signs. The boy who broke Avantika enough that she had to settle for Deb.

'Just before my boards, we . . . we did some things. We . . . were young.'

Tanmay had heard the rumours. He had dismissed them at that time. It was unthinkable. At the time, Tanmay despite being the Head Boy, and hearing from everyone that he was the playboy of the school, hadn't even kissed anyone. It was the early 2000s, what did you expect? How could his sister be . . .

'Deb's the last person to have a problem with that. And it's been more than ten years. What does this have to do with not seeing a doctor?' asked Tanmay, feeling uncomfortable.

'I got pregnant, Tanmay. That's what happened.'

'What?'

'Tanmay.'

'You?'

The words muddled up in his head. For a moment he got confused. Was she talking about now? Or the past? Did she get pregnant all those years back? Tanmay felt his heartbeat quicken. His breath grew short. Vernita's words rung loudly in his ears. *Listen to her. Be supportive.* She got pregnant? She was . . . she was . . . she was just a girl! *This is not true. There's some mistake. What's she saying?*

'Why didn't you tell us?' asked Tanmay, his voice barely a whisper, his words trained responses from his conditioning. *This is not true. How can it be true? She got pregnant and then . . . ?*

Avantika's teary gaze pierced through Tanmay. It only took him a second to conjure a scenario where his parents would hack her to pieces and bury her. Then tell all the relatives she ran away with a boy and that she was dead to them. Or keep her locked up for nine months, make her deliver and then kill the child. You couldn't tell with their parents. *What did she do? Where did she go? How can this be true?* He couldn't wrap his head around it.

'Did you tell anyone?'

Avantika shook her head and stared at the leftovers again.

'What did you do?'

Avantika looked up from the crumbs and met his eyes. Blood rushed to his head and he felt light-headed. He struggled to not think of his sister, all of seventeen and in her ink-stained school uniform, finding out about this, weighing the options that lay ahead. He was there, in the same house, blind and unmindful while his sister was . . . she was right there and yet . . .

'I found a doctor and got it aborted. Paritosh didn't know about it. I handled it.'

'You could have told me,' he said.

'Would you have done anything different? And who knew? You could have run right to our parents and told them everything. I couldn't have risked that,' she said, her voice icy cold. She continued after a pause, 'Anyway, the nurse here asked me to fill a medical history form. They wanted me to tell them if . . . if I had had an abortion or a child before. I ran out. Deb has been messaging me about what happened and I have been lying to him . . . to all of you.'

'You should tell him. The later you tell him the worse it will get,' said Tanmay without a beat.

He didn't believe in the platitudes that came out of his mouth. Sitting there, watching his sister struggle to act like what happened was forgotten and buried, he felt only raw anger towards Paritosh Mehta, and at himself.

'That boy is stupid, he doesn't deserve you anyway. If he reacts with anything more than concern for you, you should leave him,' said Tanmay, finding it hard to concentrate on the conversation.

His mind kept flitting to the young Avantika, the thought of her in a shady nursing home.

'I'm never going to leave him, Bhaiya. Get used to him.'

'If that's the kind of confidence you have in him, tell him. He's not going to leave you just because . . . you . . .'

He couldn't bring himself to say the words. *Abortion. She got an abortion done. My seventeen-year-old sister. And I kept telling myself . . . it's just a break-up? She should get over it.*

'You don't get it, Bhaiya.'

'What don't I get?' he asked, trying his best not to be irritated.

'The nursing home that I got it done from . . .' Her voice trailed away. Words came out as a soft whisper. 'It was a one-room apartment. One nurse, one doctor. What if something had gone wrong that day?' Her eyes met his and he felt a shiver down his spine. She said, 'I have been Googling and it says there could be complications and I can't stop thinking what if . . . what if I can't get pregnant again? What if that was it? What if I spoilt it all?'

'Don't say that,' said Tanmay, a sense of dread struck deep inside him.

Neither Vernita nor he had told anyone about the verbal fighting matches their relationship had devolved into before Vernita had decided to get pregnant. Of the times Tanmay would walk out and spend the night at a hotel. Things had got so bad they had considered separation after one particularly heated argument. They'd called their marriage a mistake, their relationship a lie. Over the years, Tanmay had made peace with Vernita bumping into her overly friendly ex-boyfriends of which she had many and more, but this, this he would have never made peace with. This would have sunk their relationship.

'You need to not overthink. Just go and get the tests done,' said Tanmay.

'And what if they tell me what I'm fearing they would?'

'There's no way you can know. One step at a time. If they tell you what you're so afraid of, we will see what to do then,' said Tanmay. 'Look, Avantika, he didn't even want a child. Let's get done with the tests first. We will see what we must do when it comes to that. You have kept this a secret for so long, no point bringing it up now if it means nothing. Probably, nothing will be wrong.'

'Wrong . . .' whispered Avantika.

'What?'

'If I'm not able to conceive, it will be wrong. The opposite of right, won't it be?'

'I didn't mean it like that, Avantika.'

'I know,' she said. Tanmay watched her steel herself. She said, 'I need to go now. I will take an appointment tomorrow and see this through. I will do this.'

'Do you—'

'I will do it myself,' she said.

Without a word, she put her things in a purse, hugged Tanmay and left.

22

Over the past few days, Avantika had made a list of all the best fertility doctors in the city and had been meeting up with them to see which one they would finally go to. Deb had been waiting but she was taking her time to home in on one. It was surprising for Deb to see Avantika so indecisive but then again this was probably the most important decision she would ever make.

As if the uncertainty and the nervousness of what the doctors would test and say wasn't enough, Deb struggled with the mind-bending last few scenes of the maha-episode. The hour-long episode was supposed to turn around the fortunes of the serial and to get some loyal fans to start watching the show again. Nothing had worked in the past couple of months and it wasn't for the lack of trying. They had done everything. The bahu had died twice, the husband had had plastic surgery, and in a glorious moment, there was a ghost too. Things became irrevocable when they softened the saas towards the bahu. The ratings tanked more dramatically than ever! It was as if the show wasn't the same any more.

'It's unbelievable. Which saas is like this!' the programming head had thundered in the weekly meeting. 'I can't believe I let you guys cheat my viewers like that!'

It was the turning point of the show.

'Let's make the saas murder the bahu,' the programming head had said, her eyes bloodshot, hair frizzy with anxiety. 'That will be our maha-episode. The comeback of the *real* saas!'

Since then the entire team had been scrambling to make the saas a plausible murderer—of how she could kill the bahu in cold blood and still remain relatable.

Shrey had taken two attempts at the scenes and the programming head had rejected both. This turn of events was familiar. They were told that they lacked punch. In a cowardly industry, that survived purely on TRP, that's what executives did—kept rejecting stories and screenplays till the writers gave up.

'The team feels that you're not putting in your 100 per cent. You can do much better,' a junior told them repeatedly.

Deb would have stormed out of the show but he needed the money. The more he read about IVF, the more he was convinced it could wipe off the little they had saved after their debacles in real estate. And if Avantika chose an expensive doctor, then . . .

Twice in the past week he had returned from the reception of a fertility clinic. There were other men at this one, the last name in fertility treatment for men—of different ages, balding patterns and body shapes. Nothing was common between most of them except their failure to impregnate their wives and the shame that was writ large on their faces. They had all *failed*. All of them had been dealt a bad card, been ripped of their identity. What good is a man if he can't procreate? Isn't that what every species aim to do? Multiply? Deb saw a familiar look on all their faces. They all sat there, heads hanging low, pretending they were all there with someone, to support them, when in fact there was no one else.

'I'm actually with my cousin who's gone inside. Me? No way. I am perfectly fine,' Deb practiced this sentence repeatedly.

No one asked him anything.

Both times he came back thinking he wasn't one of them. He couldn't be; he hadn't done anything wrong. He hadn't even started drinking till he was twenty-one and out of college. Something must be wrong with Avantika. Wasn't she the one who had been drinking since she was seventeen? Wasn't she the one who allowed herself to be led by her asshole boyfriend to experiment with and get addicted to coke and MDMA? Wasn't that why she wanted to see a doctor first? She insisted on it.

'Don't you think it's a little presumptuous of you to sit here while she does the rounds of fertility clinics?' asked Shrey out of the blue one day.

It took a few seconds for Deb to realize, without surprise, that Shrey had infringed upon his privacy again.

'Can we concentrate on what we have to do?'

'What makes you so much of a man that you refuse to believe that maybe it's you who is . . . medically deficient?'

'I don't want to talk about this. It's not for you to ask, and it's our decision to make.'

'You can't run away from it either. You should get yourself tested too. She can't be going through this humiliating charade of visiting clinics and choosing a doctor alone,' said Shrey.

'I didn't do anything wrong,' he said.

'Deb, that's not how these things work. You don't have to be scared. There are options.'

'Scared? Fuck you.'

'All I'm saying is that there's no harm in knowing. And it's nothing to be ashamed of.'

'Again, fuck you,' said Deb.

'I was just trying to help,' grumbled Shrey.

'Were you?' scoffed Deb. 'Put your own life together before you try to help. What makes you think you can fucking waltz into my private life and tell me what to do? We are handling it.'

'I'm your oldest friend, Deb. I'm looking out for you.'

'Are you though?'

'Why else would I be saying all this?'

'Why? Because I know you, Shrey. All you want is some excitement, some gossip, some entertainment at the cost of others. You laugh and make fun of everyone.'

'Is that what you think I do?'

'Isn't that exactly what you do? Just because you're fucking stuck at where you were when you were twenty-one doesn't mean the world has stopped too. As I said, we are fucking handling it.'

'What's wrong with you? I was just trying to—'

'Shut the fuck up, Shrey. You will tell me what to do, *chutiye*? If you think you can laugh at people, you should turn and look at what people are saying about you.'

'What the fuck are they saying, Deb?' asked Shrey. 'Pray tell me, because whatever they are saying, clearly you're being a participant in the damned conversation.'

'Don't make me say it.'

'No, now I'm interested. What do you say, Deb when they say shit about me? Let's hear that. Tell me, I can take it. I want to know what my best friend says about me to others.'

They hadn't realized but their fists had balled up.

It had been two years since they had had their last fist fight. They both bore scars from that night. Sometimes Shrey would feel a sharp pain in his ribs. It was the day they'd wound up their little publishing house, their labour of love. Their promising and surprising run had ended abruptly and without a whimper. It was just like everyone from other publishing houses, editors and distributors had said, 'Don't leave your management jobs. You two wouldn't last. You know nothing about this business. Leave it to us.'

They both loved books, though. Deb more than Shrey, and they would have regretted it had they not given it their all. What if they couldn't be bestselling writers themselves? They would always find a successful author. Their success was brief. A few writers teased success. Nothing sustained. They were trying to sell books to a country that didn't read. Writers who they thought would change the landscape of Indian publishing couldn't sell more than a hundred books.

Soon, the bad debts their distributors had run up snapped at their backs. Their calls went unanswered. Legal notices were ignored. Visits were rudely cut off.

'*Is business mein aisa hota hai* (this is what happens in this business),' they were told.

Unlike Deb, Shrey knew long before time that they were dead in the water. Deb tried pulling the dead whale back into the sea, borrowed money from Avantika and spent it all in the uplifting of the business. Nothing came out of it.

It was Friday when they tailed the last pick-up truck with their books to the pulping factory where the unsold books were to be shorn off their covers and destroyed. Shrey couldn't recall having seen Deb that desolate before. It was like a part of him had died. So on their way back, Shrey had suggested they drink. A few drinks down, Deb's demeanour changed and he unloaded on Shrey real quick. For him, Shrey had never taken the business seriously and had dragged Deb down with him. Shrey wasn't one to take it all lying down and came up with his own issues with Deb. Accusations flew thick and fast—and despite Shrey's best effort to not lose his temper, he did—and they battled it out, bang in the middle of the road. From there, they were both bundled to the hospital, bloodied, bruised, and barely conscious. Police waited outside to see if they had to file an FIR.

Shrey knew Deb wasn't any more driven to make it work than him—they were equally lackadaisical and unlucky. The only difference was Deb had someone to lose face in front of—Avantika, who had in part funded their venture. That embarrassed him the most. Deb—again—couldn't be the *man* in the relationship.

'I'm done here,' said Shrey, who didn't want to stretch it out, and got up.

'You don't have to leave, I will,' said Deb.

He slammed his laptop shut, stuffed it inside his bag and made his way out.

'I was looking out for you, asshole!' shouted Shrey from behind him.

Deb turned. 'Were you? Were you looking out for me, *bhenchod*? Why didn't you give another shot at the episode then? Why didn't you try harder to keep the job so I could afford the child I'm planning? Because no, that would be work and heaven forbid you invest anything of yours in a friendship except wisecracks. So the next time you say anything about Avantika or me or meddle in our affairs, even if I hear a word, I will fuck you up.'

Shrey sat in the office till late that night. They had no business keeping the office they ran their publishing house out of now. They were freelance writers—they didn't need the office. Deb had suggested in the past to let go of it. Shrey knew he wasn't serious then. It was a keepsake of the time they had shaped their passion into a business and neither of them wanted to let it go. Shrey made himself a strong coffee, opened his laptop, and suspended his disbelief and promised to write the most ridiculously magnificent maha-episode in the history of maha-episodes.

That night, Deb and Avantika too slept in different rooms. Avantika slept on the couch, working on the backlog that had piled up. Deb slept—or pretended to sleep—inside. They hadn't had sex in a week, or was it two? They had just stopped doing it. It's strange he called it sex in his head. Because now there was no lovemaking, there were just attempts to get pregnant. And they quit on it because what was the point of it any more? If it had to happen, it would have. Either it was him, or her; someone was, as Shrey called it, medically deficient. Of all the things he would give up in a heartbeat for Avantika, which included his life, like literally his life because he had imagined scenarios like that in his head, he wouldn't be able to give *this*. He wouldn't accept being the one unable to sire a child.

He would rather be the one who was all right.

Deb's mother called late in the night. 'Hello?' said Deb, groggily.

'Where's Avantika?' she asked out of the blue.

'Outside, why?' he said.

'Are the two of you okay?' asked Maa, her voice stern as if it was his fault.

'She's working, Maa, that's why.'

'Are you sure?'

'Yes, yes, did you call to ask me just that?'

'Fine, go to sleep. I will call tomorrow. Ask Avantika to rest a little more. She can't be working all day.'

Click.

Deb got up and went outside. Avantika had dozed off on her laptop. He sat next to her and kissed her on the forehead. What had happened to them? Avantika opened her eyes slightly. She said, 'I had . . .'

'Slept off here, I know,' he said and wrapped his arm around her. Avantika shifted and settled in the hollow of his arm, and clasped him. They stayed like that for a good part of an hour. Deb finally said, 'Avantika? Were we not enough for each other that we wanted a child? Why did we do this to ourselves? Had we not . . . this wouldn't have happened. Why are we in different rooms? This sullen face of yours? Why did we want this baby? Were we not interesting enough?'

Avantika thought for a while and said with a slight smile, 'We are. That's why we should have a child. Our story needs to carry on, doesn't it?'

'But our story doesn't need to stop just because a child's coming to our life, does it?' said Deb.

'Absolutely not. That would defeat the purpose,' said Avantika.

'Did you find the doctor?' asked Deb.

Avantika paused for a little and said, 'Not yet.'

'There's no hurry. Take your time,' said Deb.

Deb extracted his hand from Avantika and got up.

'Where are you going?' asked Avantika.

'We will fuck each other today, like we used to. With a condom. Without thinking we have a child to create. I might make love to you because you're so goddamn beautiful but mostly, I'm going to fuck you. We will be like we used to.'

'Monkeys.'

'Rabbits, animals basically. So I'm going to search for a condom and by the time I come back you should be naked and on your knees,' said Deb.

'What makes you think I will be the one on my knees, Debashish Roy? You better come crawling here. You have to lick something,' said Avantika with a smile on her face.

23

Every time Deb replayed the conversation with Shrey in his head, he felt more in the wrong. Instead of wanting to apologize, it made him angrier. It was as if Shrey was there in the bedroom with

Avantika and him every time they tried to conceive—laughing, pointing at his inability, his flawed masculinity.

Deb's fingers trembled as he filled out the form at the fertility clinic. The questions on the form were invasive and offensive. Doctors can do that—get away with anything. He wondered if Avantika had answered such questions too, and if she had, had she lied about anything? How many sexual partners? When was the first time you had sex? Do you have more than one sexual partner right now? Then again, it was Avantika. She wore the truth like a badge of honour. There were no secrets with her.

When he submitted the form, Deb was told that the urologist wasn't in that day but he was asked to give a semen sample and blood samples. Was there bad news to be given? A husband who would never be a father? The nurse—a woman with kind, accepting eyes—gave him the option of choosing which one he wanted to give first. He chose blood. He didn't wince when they pushed the syringe in, watched as his blood dripped into the tube. He felt . . . like if he could do this unflinchingly, he would be sufficient.

When he sat in the room to give his semen for collection, staring at the little transparent box with a black lid, he felt like crying.

This entire process was so—inelegant. Why couldn't they just stick a needle in and get it over with? He looked around ashamedly. The nurse had asked him to take his time.

The walls were painted a cheery blue. There was a television in the corner. An old CD player and a bunch of CDs stacked by the side. He could tell no one used it any more. They gave him the password to the Wi-Fi before he entered the room.

He hadn't watched porn in the longest time. He punched in addresses of his once-favourite website. Back in the day, he would relentlessly browse and carefully pick the clips. It would take up to an hour for him to find that perfect clip. The main act of masturbation would last only a couple of minutes. The search seemed futile when it all ended. Instead of an hour and two minutes, now he had fifteen minutes tops. There were other men outside, and no one so much as spared Deb a glance. None of them had brought their wives with them. Deb, like all others outside, stood at the ultimate precipice of manhood, masculinity. Can you father a child? Can you pass on your genetic material to an offspring? Or are you the last of your kind?

Deb browsed through the videos. They didn't work as well as he imagined they would. Was it the men outside waiting for their turn?

Twenty-five minutes, two knocks on the door, and two very close ejaculations later he gave up.

'Do you want to try after a while? This happens. Don't worry. If it's too much you can come tomorrow and do it,' said the nurse looking at Deb's empty container.

'I will try after a while,' said Deb and sat in the corner, at the end of the line. What kind of a man couldn't masturbate? Teenagers were landing up in hospitals from masturbating themselves to exhaustion. When he was their age, he could masturbate while watching TV and doing a chemistry numerical.

He watched the men go inside, finish the job and come out without any trouble and only felt worse. He closed his eyes and tried to remember the first time he had touched Avantika. A rush of blood to the head. He remembered their first kiss clear as day. That and the slaps that followed. One hour later, it was his turn again. He had just entered the room when Avantika messaged him. His heart jumped. It seemed to him Avantika always knew telepathically whenever he was doing something he shouldn't be doing.

Avantika Work
Where are you?

He lied.

Deb Home
Somewhere you're not. Though I wish you were here. Where are you?

Avantika Work
Meeting. Bored. My feet are killing me.

Deb Home
Too bad I'm not there to play footsie.

Avantika Work
Errm.

Deb Home
?

Deb Home
?

Avantika Work
Now I'm thinking about it.

Deb Home
With all your bosses around. My foot against yours. Rubbing. Inching up. Softly clawing up my way.

Avantika Work
Stop.

Deb Home
Why. What's that? A rip in your stocking? I'm not sorry for that. I'm going to rip it further.

Avantika Work
I can't text you back right now. People will know.

Deb Home
*Will they? That only makes this exciting. We have an audience now.
We better perform well. Did I tell you how my heart jumps thinking that
you're getting wet?*

Avantika Work
WHY AM I TURNED ON RIGHT NOW?

Deb Home
Because this is risky. Thrill. Adrenaline.

Avantika Work
Go on. What else will you do?

Deb Home
*Inch up. Reach the end of your stockings. My feet grabbing at them . . .
pulling them down.*

Avantika Work
Deb . . .

Deb Home
Rubbing against your inner thigh. Slowly.

Avantika Home
It's warm.

Deb unbuckled his jeans. He texted with one hand. His spellings
were awry. Texts flew back and forth. It went dirtier by the
minute. Most of the words they sent after a while were just
moaning sounds. It took him three minutes and he was frothing
at the mouth when they finished.

Avantika Work
?

Avantika Work
?

Avantika Work
?

Avantika Work
?

Deb Home
Was cleaning up.

Avantika Work
Done already?

Deb Home
Yes. That was hot. Not my fault.

Avantika Work
Loser.

Avantika Work
There?

Deb handed over the container to the nurse. As he walked out, he read Avantika's penultimate text again.

Loser.

He walked away from the fertility clinic for fifteen minutes and then took a cab.

24

Shrey named it scene_version_11_final_final. He put them all
in a zip folder and attached them in an email. He wanted to
stop at three but then thought of it as an unlucky number. Five
was too clinical, seven was just aiming for too lucky a number,
ten seemed like one was trying too hard to round it off. Eleven
was auspicious so he stopped when he was done writing eleven
versions of the same scene. Shrey and Deb were used to writing
ten scenes a day for the show, but these eleven versions of the
same damned scene took Shrey three days to write.

'If you ask *Game of Thrones* writers to write an episode a
day, six episodes a week, I dare them to write better than we do.
Sooner or later, the show will turn it into *Teen Saas, Do Damad,
Kya Hoga Simar Ka*,' Shrey would often complain when they first
started writing for television.

He remembered those days fondly. Especially the first show
they wrote and pitched. They had pitched the love story of Deb
and Avantika—Deb had insisted on it—and the producer had
loved it. 'It will change the face of Indian television,' she had said.
'It will bring the younger crowd in,' she had said. 'They will love
it,' she had said.

Within a couple of weeks, with the broadcaster's input and
the producer's insights, their story was bastardized. Avantika and
Deb were no longer college students in the story but they were
newly-weds.

'We also want the older people to watch the show!' the
producer had cried out.

A few days later, Deb was changed to a Punjabi from a
Bengali.

'We want colour in the show! Some loudness and humour
you know!' the producer had exclaimed.

A week later, Deb was no longer the average-looking,
ordinary boy from a humble background but a son of an
industrialist. He was Deb Singhania.

'No one wants to see poverty! And we want to put up a huge set. Show some production value! If we put in songs at a later date who will dance around in a two-bedroom house? Think, Deb, think! Who wants to see a poor, ugly guy!' the producer had insisted.

A month later, Deb was changed to Rohit. Rohit Singhania. Avantika Sharma was changed to Avantika Oberoi.

'Aspiration, Rohit, aspiration! Oh wait, your name is Deb. Aspiration, Deb, we need to show it in their names! No one wants a name like Deb!' the producer had pointed out.

A few days later, the relationship was tweaked.

'Deb! Make them hate each other first! That's how love stories are! Hate, hate, hate! THE BOY AND THE GIRL ABSOLUTELY HATE EACH OTHER! And then accidental kiss. That's how TRPs come. Deb, that's how it will work!' the producer suggested.

As time went by, more additions were made.

'The girl has an evil sister! She loves Rohit too! Better still, we will see if we can cast twins! The drama, imagine the drama! The episodes will write themselves.'

'The boy has an evil bua. That's where our drama will come from! It will be fun! We will make her ugly so that's why she has a problem with Avantika.'

Shrey had watched Deb go through all of it with gritted teeth. He drew the line when it came to Avantika.

'Who falls in love with such a brazen girl! No, no! We will make her coy. *Chulbuli* but coy. Much more relatable! No one will like this girl,' the producer had suggested.

'I fucking did.'

Shrey heard Deb mutter these words at first slowly, and then it came from the depths of his bowels. It felt like a demon had come to life. Deb ripped into the producer, called her names, and stormed out of the office.

Three months of work had gone down the drain. For a while none of the producers wanted to work with the two recalcitrant, conceited, arrogant novelists who wanted to change television and move away from the old ways.

'I don't regret it,' Deb had told Shrey at the time. 'What I would have regretted is what they would have done to our story.'

For someone who was usually a soft-spoken coward, Shrey was often amused to see how easily Deb could slip into the toxic masculine role of saving the love of his life. It was not much fun to see this transformation.

Shrey's finger hovered around the SEND button for a while. He wondered if he was expected to write an apology with it as well. He wanted to, he knew that Deb deserved it. The words swam in his head. All he had to do was to frame his feelings into words and paras. When he wrote them down though they seemed silly:

I'm sorry, Deb. For all the times I have needlessly poked my nose into your matters. It's only out of my love for you that I do that. Believe me I have no other intentions. You're my best friend and you will always be. There's no one more important. Please find attached the last few scenes.

He stared at it for a while, deleted it and he wrote another version.

Haan bhenchod, sorry hai. Bhaav mat kha itna (don't throw so much attitude). Please find attached the scenes.

He deleted that too and sent Deb the mail without any text in the body.

25

Dr Nikhil Sharma changed out of his scrubs, washed his hands like he had been taught seventeen years ago at UCMS, Delhi, and walked out of the operations wing. He nodded at the younger doctors who hoped to assist him someday and walked into his cabin. Outside, eleven anxious women waited for him. Some had been waiting for hours. Out of the eleven, he would have to disappoint some of them today. He would have to tell them that they would never get pregnant, that they would never be a little child's biological mother. He had experienced that by adding one extra word 'biological' he could keep women from buckling into their seats and crying. They could *still* be mothers, just not of children made from their own flesh, blood and tissue—in short, their biology. In a country with an inadequate, crumbling healthcare set-up, efficiency trumped empathy.

But things weren't like this two years ago. He had a modest stream of patients walking in, people who were mostly recommended by others but nothing like what it had become now. The Internet had made him—amongst a select few doctors—a bit of a rockstar of their profession. Two years ago, an upstart journalist had called him when he was working on a story on the rising use of IVF and was interviewing fertility doctors and women who had benefited from it for his story. His name had been suggested by a woman whom he had helped conceive and she had raved about him to the journalist, like the women who have successful IVFs often do; they start seeing the doctors as saviours. The coupling effect of the woman's words and the picture they used—he was twenty-eight at the time the picture was taken—got a lot of attention. For the next week, he was the *hot* bachelor fertility doctor who could get women *pregnant*. For the first time, he was told that his premature ageing was him sporting a salt-and-pepper look, that the bursting nerves on his forearm and the jagged, sharp jawline, were not signs of him not eating well but of his fitness. He remembered being annoyed at the time. His phone rang off the hook with calls from pesky teenagers calling him and giggling over the phone, and from women who wanted to get married to him. He took a couple of weeks off work for the hoopla to settle down which it did when a cat was found patting down two dogs.

What remained were the search results. If one typed out *Fertility doctors Delhi best* in a Google search bar, his name and his face popped up.

'Send the first one in,' he said on the intercom.

Sumitra Bhasin was the first woman to see him that day. She was accompanied by her husband who seemed cockier than he remembered from the last time. He had his reasons. His tests had come out all right. The *problem* was with his wife.

'What can we do, doctor?' asked the husband. 'We will do anything, absolutely anything. I want her to get pregnant and make it happen. I have read some articles online. It's not that—'

'Let me stop you right there on account that I'm the doctor and she's my patient and nothing you've read online matters. And if it does, you shouldn't be here,' said Dr Sharma sternly. He then lied barefacedly to put the husband back in his place. 'And your results are barely above the line.'

He broke it down for Sumitra Bhasin in as few words as she could fathom. She would never be a biological mother. No medical options were open for her. She would have to let go of the idea. They could try, spend lakhs and lakhs of rupees on it, but it would all be for naught. They could get a second opinion and some doctor may choose to fleece them but he was more than sure it would only end in disappointment. What they could do instead was adopt. If they wanted to raise a child they could do that. He watched as the wife shrunk into her seat, defeated and disappointed. The husband grew angrier with every word that Dr Sharma said. He looked at his wife in disgust. By the time they left he could see their relationship crumbling.

'Send in the next one,' he said.

'Avantika Sharma, thirty-one,' said the nurse, handing over the file to the doctor.

Dr Sharma knew the case by heart. If it were up to him, he wouldn't see her. Unlike the others the doctor attended to, this girl only had herself and the boy to blame. Why would they do this to themselves?

'Hi Avantika,'

'Hi,' said the woman as she walked in and took a seat in front of him.

Dr Nikhil Sharma took a deep breath and reminded himself that nothing would come out of him reprimanding the woman now. The damage was done, and it was none of his business what the woman and her husband did in the past; it was his job to heal them now.

'Your reports came in. I don't want to beat around the bush, the news is not good. The carelessness of you and your husband . . . the abortion that was performed on you has endangered the chances of you ever getting pregnant. In all probability you can't get pregnant naturally. There are options but that road is not easy,' he said, keeping his anger in check. He kept thinking that this woman and her husband didn't deserve a child. Half of him wanted to turn her away, send her to some other infertility doctor. For the most part, he hoped they never have a child. He asked angrily, 'And why isn't your husband here with you? It's his fault—'

'It wasn't my husband. My husband is a good man.'

At the same time, unbeknownst to Dr Sharma, a doctor, in a fancy clinic in Mahavir Enclave, was going through the blood and semen work of a gentleman named Debashish Roy and things weren't looking good there either.

26

It was too late for a coffee but Ritam thought what the heck. One more wouldn't hurt. The sun had set hours ago. They had waited for Ragini to go to bed to talk.

'I'm a bit flattered to know that you picked me to talk about whatever you want to talk about,' said Ritam, sipping his coffee, when Ragini finally turned in.

'Believe it or not, you're the only one whom I can talk to about this. Says something about the kind of people I have surrounded myself with, no? How's Ragini doing? She looked . . . happy?' asked Deb.

'She's doing quite well. You noticed that, didn't you? She was just made the head of her department last week. They had a little celebration at school yesterday. There's some leftover cake. I was going to throw it out but do you want some?'

'Glad to know I can always come here to have some cake you're about to throw out.'

Ritam laughed. 'I didn't mean it like that.'

'I know you didn't,' said Deb.

'So? What's it, Deb? What's it that you want to talk to me about? You sounded serious on the phone,' asked Ritam.

Deb pushed a file in front of Ritam. Just the kind of file he hated—one with a hospital's name emblazoned on it.

'Read it,' he said.

Ritam picked it up. He couldn't make sense of what was written in Deb's report but the fact that it was from a fertility clinic made things clear for him.

'How bad is it?' asked Ritam.

'They will tell me today.'

Ritam closed the file and slipped it back to Deb.

'Isn't it a little premature to worry, Deb?'

'I think it's a little too late. Had I worried earlier maybe this day wouldn't have come. Maybe there would have been preventive measures I could have taken.'

'I'm not sure if that's how these things work. And let the reports come out and then maybe you can freak out.'

'You think I'm freaking out right now? This is the calm me. I'm thinking clearly right now and that's why I came to you because you know . . .' said Deb. Then he looked at the cake Ritam had brought in as they talked and said, 'Do you think anything is open right now? Let's order something. I don't want to have the leftover cake.'

'I will make you something,' said Ragini.

They both turned to look at her.

'Bachchha, you should sleep. You have to get up early tomorrow morning,' said Ritam and walked up to her.

Ragini shook her head. Stubbornness was one of the reasons Ragini was where she was right now. She quickly made two paranthas from the leftover dough from the morning and wouldn't accept any help from both Ritam and Deb.

'What's it you wanted to talk about?' said Ragini and picked up the file from the table. She looked at the file and then at Deb who squirmed uncomfortably in his seat. 'So tell me?'

Ragini sat alongside Ritam. Ritam held Ragini's hand. In the brief second that followed, Ritam watched Deb's eyes follow Ragini's scarred hand. It was only when people stared that Ritam noticed. Earlier he used to feel angry about the crinkled noses. He picked up fights because of them. It took him years to realize that most were just curious to know what had happened to his wife.

Deb hesitantly began. 'Actually . . . we, Avantika and I, have sort of hit a roadblock. You know we have been trying. And things aren't working out the way we thought they would. We are seeing doctors, of course. And I'm sure things will be all right but you know . . . just in case they aren't, I wanted to know how you guys dealt with it.'

With every word, Ritam's discomfort ballooned. With every word, he saw his wife's grip on his hand loosen. Ritam would have preferred this conversation with Deb alone knowing what this would trigger.

'So you want to know from him what's it like to not have a child of your own, is it? You came to the right person—'

'Ragini, *kya yaar*. Leave that now. I thought we decided we won't talk about it.'

Ragini scoffed angrily. 'But Deb needs to know, doesn't he? You should help him out,' said Ragini.

'Ragini.'

'No, why don't you tell him?'

'Ragini, please yaa,' said Ritam, not wanting to fight again. This had been their longest stretch of peace—three days.

'He should know. He's our friend. You should totally tell him how it wrecks you inside, that despite everything you have done for me, you can't have a child of your own with me. Tell him! Why don't you tell him that?' argued Ragini.

'Ragini, you should sleep now,' said Ritam.

'Why? Why should I sleep? Absolutely not! I'm not going to sleep at all!'

'Enough, Ragini,' said Ritam.

'He needs to be ready for it, doesn't he, Ritam? Of looking at other men his age have children of their own? He needs to learn how to lie to his wife that it doesn't matter to him.'

'It's not like that, Ragini. I don't care about it,' said Ritam.

'It's exactly like that, Ritam, and I know it. YOU CARE ABOUT IT A LOT!' she exclaimed and stared at Ritam.

Ritam watched her eyes burn with anger and guilt. She *wanted* this badly. Ragini wanted to bear his child.

But Ritam couldn't let her. How could he? He had seen her lie on the bed for two years flitting in and out of devastating pain in that horrible bomb blast that burnt through her leaving 90 per cent of her body but totally scarring the last 10. She spent night after night screaming as her body developed resistance to painkillers. Then two years of skin grafting surgery to replace what had melted off her broken body. Her body was functional now. He had learned to find it beautiful again, to love it, to feel attracted towards it. He didn't want a lot from his love story but just to love someone free from pain. He couldn't have subjected that body to a pregnancy.

'The doctors said I could do it but your friend seems to think I can't. What does it say about that he thinks so of me? That I'm weak? That I don't love him enough?' said Ragini.

'Ragini! There are donor skin cells deep . . . I don't . . . I don't want to talk about it. We talked about this. If we want a child, we can adopt. That's what you wanted growing up, didn't you?' asked Ritam.

'But that's not what you wanted, is it? One thing I could do for you, one thing, and you don't let me do it. Why wouldn't you let me do it?'

Ragini's word drowned into a whisper. She looked at Deb.

'Deb, if Avantika can't give you a child, here's what you will be like, like Ritam. Pretending there's no discontent inside of him eating him up. He thinks I can't see the resentment in him but it's there! No matter how much you lie to yourself, you will end up blaming her all her life!' she said and stormed off.

Ritam turned to a horror-stricken Deb who was by now imagining the demise of his relationship because of his inability to give Avantika a child. Ragini had assumed that the problem lay with Avantika and not *him*.

'She gets like that sometimes,' said Ritam. 'She will be fine in the morning.'

'Will she?' asked Deb, breaking out of his reverie.

'Yes, yes. It's a once a week thing. She still thinks I did a huge favour to her by marrying her despite her . . . injuries. And by getting pregnant she could return the favour. It really doesn't matter to me as much as she thinks it does,' said Ritam.

'You told her this?'

'Multiples times, Deb. But now it just makes me angry, offended even, to think why she doesn't realize that she—injuries or not—did me a favour by marrying me. By falling in love with me! That's enough for me. She needs to get that.'

Ritam saw Deb nod distractedly.

'You caught us on the wrong day,' said Ritam. 'But some advice to you . . . God forbid if either of you has a problem, pray that it's you. You don't want the person you love . . . Avantika . . . to blame herself for the rest of your lives. It's painful.'

27

Paritosh Mehta felt the soft velvet between his two fingers. He had been deliberating on the decision for a week now and the interior designer had wanted an answer yesterday. He knew his friends would prefer a brown leather couch instead of the fabric he had picked. But it was time he took a few mature decisions of his own. The setting up of the new four-storied office bang in the middle of Greater Kailash had been his responsibility and he didn't want to let his father down. After years, it seemed like his father had forgiven him. He could finally be somebody. He knew people around him kept harping on and on about how he was born with a silver spoon in his mouth but only if they were in his shoes would they see how many boys like him had squandered away the family fortune. He had come close once but that was a long time back. He was a changed man now and he would show the world that. He wasn't *them*. If he played it right he could make it to the *Forbes* list of millionaire heirs under thirty-five. He had just the right suit for it too. He had picked it up last week from Spain when he was there for a concert.

Paritosh reached out to the phone to call the interior designer when his phone rang.

'Hello?'

He heard a girl sob softly on the other side. At first he thought it was a prank by his childish friends.

'Hello? Who's this? Are you sure you have the right number?'

Paritosh hadn't dated since he'd come back to India. It didn't seem right to fall in love after what he had put his family through.

'I do. It's the right number and it's the call I should have made years ago,' said the girl, steeling her voice.

'Look, I'm in the middle of some work. I don't have time to play this guessing game,' said Paritosh.

'I asked you not to do it,' said the girl. 'How many times did I ask you not to do it, Paritosh?'

The voice now rang a bell. It brought with it a rush of memories, mostly pleasant. The voice was unmistakably hers—older, stronger, but still hers. He could recognize that soft sob anywhere. He was subjected to that long after he had broken up with her. Oh, how irritated he used to feel. Like nails on a chalkboard.

'Are you—?'

'Avantika,' said the girl.

'Avantika? Hey? Hi? What? It's such a long time,' said Paritosh.

'It has been a long time, Paritosh, and I thought I had cauterized the septic wound that you were long back. I thought I had got rid of you for good.'

'Hey? You don't have to talk like that. Let bygones be bygones,' said Paritosh.

He wondered if it was one of those calls. A lot of girls from his school were now married and they had kids, even multiple kids. A few of them would call him, drop him messages and texts that were more than just texts. They were booty calls. He didn't blame them for fancying him. He had grown hotter, sharper, as opposed to the girls from his school who had chosen to get obese in this time period.

'Bygones be bygones? Haan, Paritosh? You destroyed my life, Paritosh, you did.'

'Look, we were in a relationship and you got your heart broken. Shit happens. Get over it already. It's been more than ten years for fucks' sake! Aren't you married to some writer guy? Why are you calling me now?'

'If you use that tone with me, Paritosh, I swear I will come there and slap you so hard you wouldn't know what hit you!' growled Avantika.

Paritosh was now sure it wasn't a booty call a decade too late.

'And who the fuck gave you the right to talk to me like this?'

'Because you *raped* me, Paritosh. Because you raped me! There, I said it. That's what you fucking did. There's no way around it. You cajoled me, you forced me, you made me drink . . . all for what? That I would sleep with you? Shame on me that I loved you, asshole, shame on me!'

'Hey? Hey? Let's not jump the gun here. I didn't rape you. We had sex, there's a difference,' clarified Paritosh, just in case she was recording the call.

After his long-drawn litigation in the US where he was charged with possession and assault he now knew the ins and outs of legal cases. Extricating himself from the US prison had wiped out half the Mehta fortunes. But what is fortune if it can't save the *ghar ka chirag* (the beloved heir)!

'Don't tell me what it was, Paritosh. You violated me, over and over and over again. Till the very thing made me numb. It was just something you did. You groomed me into it. You taught me, you goddamn made me do it for months.'

'Stop.'

'Fuck off. You don't tell me what to do. You need to listen to what you did to me. You broke me! I was a little girl and yet every damn afternoon after school, you made me lie down on the bed. There, just lying down, just lying down on the bed, you hiking up my skirt . . . I remember . . . I still remember watching the fan rotate, telling myself that it's what people do for love. That destroyed me. You destroyed a part of me.'

'It wasn't rape. I was seventeen too! And what is the meaning of all this? After all these years? Look I have a good life going now. If you do anything . . . anyway even if you do, it's not going to reach anywhere. It was a long time back and I'm innocent! Did you read too many #metoo posts or what?'

'You got me pregnant, Paritosh,' said Avantika, her voice down to an angry whisper.

The words hit Paritosh like a train. 'No.'

'I got it aborted. All of seventeen and I got it aborted. It makes me wonder sometimes. How brave must I have been to do that alone? But also how stupid that even after all that I was with you.'

His patience had run out.

'Avantika, I would love to get all nostalgic with you and talk about the times gone by, maybe get a cup of coffee together but I really don't have the time. And as far as our relationship goes, yes, of course you were stupid! Didn't I break up with you twice and you came crawling back to me, begging? So anything that might have happened to you is *your* own fault. Period. You got an abortion done, big deal, a lot of people do. People beg on the street to get it done. Feel lucky, bitch. Can I cut the call now?'

'There's one more thing you need to know.'

'Will you stop already?'

'I received my fertility test results today.'

'I'm cutting the call, Avantika.'

'They told me that my fallopian tubes are blocked. It happens in a lot of women, often without reason. But in mine, they said, it could be because of a botched abortion. So Paritosh I can't get pregnant again because you raped me. That's what I wanted you to know.'

'I'm cutting this call right now,' said Paritosh.

'I'm going to tell my husband and my brother today. They are good men, both of them. Deb loves me, he really does. He's a calm man but my brother isn't. This news will break them. I will ask them to lay off you and maybe they will. Maybe they will not do anything this year, or the next, or the one after that. But they will come, and when they do, I hope there's no one to save you.'

Click.

Paritosh's fingers trembled as he cut the call.

He quickly dialled the number of the head of security of his company, and then cancelled all the meetings for the day.

28

The last time Deb nervously looked over his shoulder every second minute was the year 2002 and he was watching porn in a cyber cafe. When the waiter came with his order of a cup of coffee and a sandwich he turned the laptop screen out of the way.

Since the past two days, Deb had searched far and wide to talk to someone about it. He had first searched for and entered a lesbian chat room. Soon he realized that it was a bad idea. Most people in that chat room were men. Then he set up a fake Facebook profile, Tinder and Grindr profiles with Avantika's picture and it all came to naught. They too were filled with men masquerading as women. His last resort was Twitter. He set up an account, used Avantika's picture, named it Vernita, found women who were fighting for LGBTQ+ rights and retweeted a bunch of them. He wrote 300+ tweets pretending to be a gay woman who felt aggressively aggrieved by the state of affairs as it were. He then bought a thousand followers for 200 rupees to make his account look believable. When all this was done, he sent out Direct Messages to a lot of women he had thought and researched about being gay. Within the first hour itself, a bunch of them had replied. He picked the women who were older. It wasn't until the fifth woman that he was able to steer it in the direction he wanted.

Vernita (Deb*)*
You haven't even told your brother that you're gay?

Jhanvi
No. But I will have to soon. I'm turning 34 next year and I'm not getting any younger. You?

Vernita (Deb)
No. I will have to come out to myself before I do that to anyone. I haven't dated anyone yet. Not even had a fling.

Jhanvi
It's sad not to have experienced love at the age that you are in. I fell in love at 21! It didn't work out obviously and she's married with kids . . . but you know that's how it is.

Vernita (Deb)
Kids, huh.

Jhanvi
What?

Vernita (Deb)
Do you ever think about them?

Jhanvi
My mom doesn't let me not think about them.

Vernita (Deb)
Forgive me if I come across as naive but how do you think that will work out?

Jhanvi
As in?

Vernita (Deb)
Like let's say you fall in love and by some miracle get married in India, who gets to pass the genetic material on? How do you decide that?

Jhanvi
Love? Get married? And have the opportunity to have kids? You think after all those miracles that you just named I would care about what DNA my child carries? I will feel lucky to be a parent, to be with the person I'm with.

Vernita (Deb)
? So you wouldn't mind it at all if the child has nothing of you?

Jhanvi
I'm sure the thought wouldn't cross my mind. Just to know that I would be a parent . . . damn. Wouldn't that be something!

Vernita (Deb)
That's one way to look at it. Do you think that's true for gay men too?

Jhanvi
Why don't you get to the point?

Vernita (Deb)
As in?

Jhanvi
You think I can't see that your profile is one day old? That your followers are bots from Brazil and Bangladesh?

Vernita (Deb)
So?

Jhanvi
You're a boy.

Vernita (Deb)
I'm offended that you would say that.

Jhanvi
What do you really want to ask?

Vernita (Deb)
Nothing. Why would I want to ask something?

Jhanvi
How old are you? 21?

Vernita (Deb)
30 actually.

Jhanvi
Wow. And still so juvenile. I'm going to go out on a limb and say that either your girlfriend is pregnant with someone else's child or you impregnated someone's wife and she's keeping the child.

Jhanvi
?

Jhanvi
Gone already? It was fun though talking to you. Hehe.

Jhanvi
You're still reading my messages.

Vernita (Deb)
It's neither.

Jhanvi
Don't tell me you're a failed writer who's looking for plot twists at our community's expense.

Vernita (Deb)
The first part is true. But I'm not looking for plot twists.

Jhanvi
What is it, then? The groundwork behind this profile says it's something serious.

Vernita (Deb)

I got my fertility reports. You must have heard about men with low sperm counts. My sperm count isn't low.

Jhanvi

Then?

Vernita (Deb)

I met a senior doctor. The last name in men's fertility.

Jhanvi

So?

Vernita (Deb)

My sperm count is zero. Not less, but zero. So there's a zero in a billion, trillion chance that I will get my wife pregnant. So since the past two days I have been Googling how my wife can still get pregnant and IVF seems to be an option. But it will be someone else's sperm in my wife's body, someone else's face on my baby's face. You get the drift. I won't be able to ever play the game . . . does she/he look like me?

Jhanvi

What are you concerned about?

Vernita (Deb)

I just told you.

Jhanvi

Two entirely different things.

A) *Your child not looking like you. But then there's a 50 % chance he or she will look like your wife which will be great, no?*

B) *You have a problem with someone else's sperm impregnating your wife. It's not real sex, you know? The guy won't know your wife and your wife him. It's just cells.*

So tell me is it your masculinity that's under threat? You won't feel like a man any more?

Vernita
You won't get it.

Jhanvi
Maybe I won't.

Deb closed the chat and swiftly deactivated the profile. He felt a sense of fear pervading through him. He worried if the girl would find out who he was and tell the world about his inability to get his wife pregnant. He had used Avantika's photo. Had she taken a screenshot? He had told her that he was a failed writer? Would she be able to join the dots?

Deb left the cafe. To him, it seemed he had lost a few inches of his height, grown smaller. He felt ashamed. He put himself in the shoes of men in the yesteryears, before IVF, before adoption. Men who couldn't get their wives pregnant. He thought of the childless couples, the imagined hushed conversations about them, and their lack of options. What would they have done if they had a choice? He wondered. What would it be like to love a baby with the face of another man? A man so virile he had some to share with his wife.

He missed his Metro station.

23

The third drink was stiffer than Deb wanted it to be. Deb sat there staring at the empty glass, wondering if he would have come to get drunk if it weren't hammered into him by popular culture that it was what you do when you're at your lowest. It's how you get addicted, find yourself in a downward spiral until someone intervenes, and loves and nurses you back to health. No one blames you or expects you to take responsibility for anything, you're forgiven. And right now, he wanted to be forgiven by Avantika for his infertility. Time was passing by. She was still choosing doctors and he was letting her do that. He should tell her that the problem lay with him and not her. But all the past days, he had failed to say it. He had tried to share it with Shrey but he even failed at that.

Deb stumbled out of his chair and made his way to the parking. There were no autos around. The nearest cab was fifteen minutes away. He decided to walk it down. He hoped to be a little sober by the time he got home. The disappointed face of Avantika greeted him at the door.

'Deb, there's something we need to talk about,' she said even before he could enter.

'Sure,' said Deb.

Had she found out about the test results? Was she leaving him? No, Deb, no. Stop thinking drunk.

A draft of alcohol breath must have hit Avantika because he watched her step away from him, 'Maybe tomorrow.'

'I'm sorry,' said Deb, not knowing what he was apologizing for.

'You don't have to apologize for anything,' she said and added in the same breath. 'I will sleep outside. You look like you need rest and I have some work to do.'

Deb nodded. Avantika hugged him lightly and turned away from him.

'Avantika?' called out Deb.

'I will get you lime water and keep a bottle of water inside. Keep drinking it.'

'Will we be fine, Avantika?' asked Deb.

His heart leapt to his mouth in the few infinitesimal seconds that passed. A sense of dread came over him as he watched Avantika's eyes—just her eyes—blink twice, in disappointment, in anger, in discontent.

'We will, I'm sure we will,' she said.

When she walked away, Deb replayed the sentence in his head repeatedly and every time she sounded less sure.

Three alarms rang in the night, reminding him to drink water. It's what she always did. Twice he woke up and found Avantika sitting on the side table.

'Are you okay?' she asked every time.

Deb would mumble that he was fine and go back to sleep. He dreamt scarring dreams. He saw a future where Shrey—the virile best friend—was getting married to a pregnant Avantika.

'Why would anyone be with a man like you?' Tanmay told him in one of the dreams. 'It's better this way, isn't it? My sister could have had a child with someone else but the child would have spent its entire life looking for who his or her father really was and that works well for no one. I always liked Shrey better anyway.'

Together they had a curly-haired kid who was phenomenal at calculus. He told both of them that he was happy for them, and then went back home and slit his wrists and even that he couldn't do properly.

There were other versions, with other men, and all of the nightmares ended with a pregnant Avantika and a cuckolded Deb.

He woke up with a splitting headache. There was a tall glass of warm water and a Crocin by his bedside. Guilt coursed through his body. He needed to apologize. He needed to come clean about the reports.

He walked out of the room.

Avantika was at the gym. *Perfect*, he thought, and whipped up a south Indian breakfast of rasam, idli and chutney. Just what she liked. An hour passed by and then two. She was not back. He wondered what kept her. It was then he noticed that her laptop was gone; the office ID was no longer hanging from the hook. She hadn't gone to the gym as he'd imagined. She had gone to office early.

Deb Home
Office?

Avantika Work
Yes.

Deb Home
Meetings?

Avantika Work
Yes.

Deb Home
Or are you angry?

Avantika Work
You have done nothing for me to be angry about.

Deb Home
I have come home drunk three times in a row. Won't do it again.

Avantika Work
The baby . . . it's pressure. I understand. It's breaking us.

Deb Home
So you're not angry?

Avantika Work
No. Why would I be? I get it.

Deb Home
Swear on me?

Avantika Work
Swear on us.

Deb Home
I made rasam.

Avantika Work
And idli?

Deb Home
And chutney.

Avantika Work
Sorry.

Deb Home
See you later.

Deb's fingers hovered over the keypad. He typed the words *there's something* and deleted them. Yet again, he couldn't make himself tell her.

30

Shrey knew immediately something was wrong. There was no reason why three cars would be standing in that little, crowded lane that led to their office. He asked the cigarette boy what the fuss was about.

'A bunch of men. They have come to your office only. Reached only ten minutes ago. *Unki bhi udhaari hai?* (do you owe even them money?)' said the boy.

'*Chup saale* (shut up),' said Shrey and ran towards the office. He knew Deb was already in office. The bolt of the main gate was open. He sprinted up the spiral staircase. He was at the door when he heard a man shout.

'YOU WILL ASK YOUR WIFE TO SHUT UP ABOUT IT OR YOU DON'T KNOW WHAT I WILL DO!' he heard the man bellow.

He heard Deb's voice, cold as steel, unafraid, 'I don't tell her what to do. If she told you that you raped her, then you did. And if she doesn't shut up about it, then I guess the only way I will know what you will do to me is when you do it.'

Shrey knew Deb wasn't a fighter unless it really came down to it. He could hold a grudge, he could be vindictive, but in a slow poisoning sort of a way.

The man grinned and said, 'You don't realize what you're up against, do you? She hasn't forgotten me. I'm sure she takes my name when you guys fuck. IT'S PARITOSH MEHTA, you two-paisa writer! These four friends of mine can mess up this pretty face of yours within seconds. I wonder who she will fuck then.'

'She would like the scar, I believe.'

'Saale, you have a big tongue on you, don't you?'

'And your ex-girlfriend and my wife loves how I put that to use with her. She had never experienced that before,' said Deb.

Shrey now saw the four men, each of them bigger than Deb by a few inches. Paritosh—the man's name struck Shrey immediately, Avantika's ex-boyfriend—wasn't messing around.

Deb continued calmly, 'Anway, if and when Avantika decides to file a rape case against you, she will make sure she checks with your mother. Who knows maybe you're your father's son. Maybe he raped your mother too? Your mother would need liberating then, wouldn't she?' said Deb.

At this, he saw Paritosh charge. He picked up the chair and lifted it to throw at Deb but stopped midway, the chair high in the air. Then he kept it down. 'I won't do it, asshole,' said Paritosh. 'I promised my mother I won't hit anyone. Don't make me do it.'

'Then why don't you fuck off, Paritosh? Because unlike you, I don't live on my father's alms, do I, now?'

Paritosh looked at his men and then at Deb; he was losing the argument.

'Whatever, fucker, whatever,' said Paritosh.

Shrey smiled, glad he didn't intervene. Deb needed this win. Shrey had tracked his movement to the fertility clinic, noticed the hangover and had put two and two together.

'That's a good comeback,' said Deb.

'Comeback? You need a comeback, you fucker? You need a comeback?'

'Good try again.'

'You asshole! I hope every time you fuck her you think of me!'

'Fat chance of that, Paritosh. She enjoys me way too much. The way she wraps her mouth around . . . wah . . . just amazing. So no, no one's going to be thinking of you, chutiye. Did she tell you of the first time she saw my dick? She was surprised they could be that huge and I wasn't even hard. I wonder why that was,' said Deb.

Paritosh paused for a while and then laughed maniacally. There was a certain graveness to his laugh, his pause was a few moments too long.

'That might be true, Deb,' said Paritosh. 'But you know what?'

'I can't wait to know. Is it another one of your super witty comebacks because you're killing it today?'

'I'm not sure it's witty. I'm not the writer you are so I will let you decide, Deb. From where I'm seeing things, I will be the only one who's ever had a child inside of her. And I will be the last person to ever do that.'

'What the fuck are you saying, Paritosh?' asked Deb.

'Oh, wait, wait, wait, wait. This is great! This is amazing! She hasn't told you yet? Nice! Then let me break it to you, pretty face. I fucked her, she got with child, and she aborted it. The doctors told her that she can never be a mother again because of a shitty-ass operation. You didn't know that! Wow! Love it!' said Paritosh, smiling.

Shrey saw Deb's face lose colour.

'Nonsense.'

'Why don't you ask her, bro? Ask her if there was a little Paritosh inside her. My dick left a little something inside her. Aw, that's so cute though . . . a little Paritosh inside her waving at your little dick every time you're—'

Paritosh didn't finish the sentence. The chair he had put down came flying at his face. Paritosh didn't duck in time. It hit him square on his face and sprouted blood. The other four men were on Deb in a flash, kicking him, punching him. Shrey was about to spring into action but stopped. Deb was fighting back the best he could. He had brought two men down with uncharacteristically brutal and precise jabs at their eyes. He could have gouged out their eyes. They lay writhing on the floor. Just a few seconds more, thought Shrey. Just a few more times he would let Deb hit Paritosh, he would need to remember this when he was reminded of what he was just told.

And so he waited.

Deb was pummelled. He bled through his shirt and so did Paritosh. Paritosh and the boys won, but not by much. Deb was on the ground, breathing heavily. Paritosh and the others were barely on their feet. They helped each other up.

Shrey entered once they were gone. Deb lay slumped in the corner, ragged breaths heaving through his body. When Shrey helped him up, he saw the tears. He put his arms around him and Deb broke down like a little child. In that moment, if he could, Shrey would have killed the man who'd done this to his best friend.

31

That afternoon, Shrey called Avantika and told her that he had been in a spot of trouble. 'My motorcycle brushed against a car and now I'm in the hospital,' said Shrey. He toyed with the idea of giving Avantika a heads-up on Deb getting beaten up. He didn't. Of all the people he knew, Deb and Avantika were the strongest couple, but this was unprecedented territory. He often played a game in his head—what could possibly break Deb and Avantika apart? From serious ones like infidelity to unfortunate ones like a person falling out of love to funny ones like Deb accidentally cutting off Avantika's arm and vice versa, nothing seemed to work in his hypothetical models. It was hard for him to imagine these two—they had even started to resemble each other, which was strange because Deb looked like shit, and Avantika was always the goddess—apart. But he had never thought of the situation these two were in right then.

'If you're talking to me it looks like you're fine, aren't you?'

'Yes, that's the thing. I insisted they get me to Fortis and you have no idea how expensive this hospital is. Can you come here and settle my bill so I can leave? My credit card got lost in the accident.'

'Shrey, I'm in the middle of something. Can you call Deb please?'

'Are you seriously letting your friend be in the hospital because you're in the middle of something? Deb's in an important meeting so you got to step up,' he said.

'You sound fine, Shrey. Nothing that can't wait till the evening.'

'Fun fact, Avantika, I have to check out at noon or they will charge me for another day,' he said.

'Fine.'

Avantika wouldn't have packed up her things and left for the hospital had she been able to work in office. For the past few days, she had been staring listlessly at the computer, counting hours till it was time to go home and finally face her demons and tell Deb the truth. He deserved to know it, he was a good man. She hadn't yet told Deb about her meeting with Dr Nikhil, the death knell of her news, and of the abortion. She had tried but every evening she would look at the man she loved so dearly, the one she couldn't imagine a single day without, and would balk. *What if he leaves me? What if he walks out? He's cute, which girl wouldn't snap him up in a day? How will I go on?* She knew that despite her telling Deb, he had gone and visited fertility clinics on his own, to see if he were the cause of their childlessness. It couldn't be pleasant for him. She had to put a stop to that.

Tanmay made it worse every day by reminding her that time was running out.

'I know it's a very personal thing but I can't hide it from Vernita for long. She's going to feel cheated if it comes out later that I knew something concerning her friend and I didn't tell her. You know she's possessive about Deb.'

'I'm trying, Tanmay.'

Avantika parked the car and headed to the reception. The sight of hospitals made Avantika sick.

'Which floor are you on?' she asked Shrey.

'Fifth floor. Private room. 509.'

'You took a private room too? Anyway, I'm coming up,' said Avantika and hung up.

The lifts were slow and depressing and cramped with stretchers going in and out. She took the stairs instead. By the time she got to room 509, she was short of breath and her head spun a little. She was reminded that she hadn't eaten at all in the past three days.

'Shrey?' she said as she entered the room.

And that's when she saw him.

It wasn't as much as his body as his eyes which looked battered. It was one of those moments that pass between couples that confound people who aren't together.

Deb didn't have to tell Avantika he knew about Paritosh.

Deb smiled at her weakly—a fake smile, he didn't mean it, she could see it—and it broke her heart. In the next few seconds, their entire relationship flashed in front of Avantika. Every fight—big or small—they had powered through. But this, this would break them, she knew. It was only later she saw the injuries to his body.

'I'm okay. I need to be alone for a bit,' said Deb.

'I will be outside,' said Avantika and turned to leave the room. Before she turned, she saw him looking away, and outside the window, the hurt spilling from his eyes.

Shrey waited for Avantika on a steel bench.

'I didn't know if I could tell you,' said Shrey.

Shrey gave her a cup of coffee and put his arm around Avantika. Avantika sobbed softly in his arms.

'It was Paritosh,' said Shrey. 'He told him everything. Deb was . . . shattered. You saw him. But look at the brighter side. He threw a chair at Paritosh. Brought down two grown-ass men all on his own. It was glorious to watch. I didn't think he could punch a poodle and there he was, knocking them out.'

'Deb?'

'It was like Rowdy Rathore IRL. I think I have a crush on him. He cried in my arms later to restore the balance. But you know, unpredictable.'

'I broke him. I broke us,' she said.

'Deb has already surprised us once today,' said Shrey.

She felt helpless. Her soft sobs soon turned into wails which bounced off the walls and terrified the relatives who were praying in their own corners. She felt like she was unfairly monopolizing grief in the hospital corridors. She closed her eyes and willed time to turn back. He was all she had. She didn't have a passion growing up, or a hobby as they called it. When people in her office ran marathons in their free time, or travelled, or read books like Deb did, Avantika daydreamed of Deb. Even when he would be sitting right in front of her, she would dream of him. She would look at pictures a week old and feel nostalgic and rue the time gone by. A year-old photo could make her cry. A five-year-old picture would make her angry—where did the time go? Her life with him, most of it, seemed like a chimera. Often she would try to make herself believe that she wasn't as happy as she was lest she jinxed the happiness. Many times she would feel guilty of enjoying the quiet desperation of Deb's love. She would be confused if she loved loving him more or loved being loved by him. She took an evil pleasure out of knowing that Deb would give up everything for her. She revelled in the power of their love and his dedication. She felt like a goddess; Deb was a *bhakt* who could do no wrong. What would she be without his love? Nothing, a husk, that's what. *It's all okay, he's going to call me and tell me it's all okay. This won't be the end of us. It can't be. What will happen if this is it? What will I do?*

'He will understand,' said Shrey once she quietened down.

'Would you have understood?'

'I don't want kids of my own so I would have probably counted it as a blessing,' said Shrey.

'That's not an answer,' said Avantika.

'The question's not for me either, is it?' said Shrey.

Right then, the heavy door opened, a blast of cold hospital air gushed out. Deb limped out and said, 'My Internet just ran out. Can either of you give me hotspot?' asked Deb.

'Of course,' said Avantika and tapped on her phone.

'Got it,' he said and walked back inside.

Avantika sent Shrey home after a while. An hour passed and then two before Avantika's phone beeped.

Deb Home
You should go home. I will see you tomorrow. I have recharged my phone.

Avantika Work
I need to see you, Deb. We have to talk.

Deb Home
We will talk tomorrow.

Avantika Work
Please, Deb.

Deb Home
Please, Avantika. Tomorrow. You need rest.

Avantika Work
I need you.

Deb Home
Please give me some time.

Avantika got up when she saw a nurse approach. For the split second that it took for the door to open and close, she saw him. He lay there looking at his phone, lost, tired and shattered.

It wasn't until one in the morning that Avantika's phone beeped again.

Deb Home
Are you up?

Avantika Work
Yes. How are you feeling?

Deb Home
Much better.

Avantika Work
I am sorry?

Deb Home
Don't do that. What are you apologizing for?

Avantika Work
Don't make me say it, Deb. I already feel bad.

Deb Home
But I want you to say it.

Avantika Work
That I can't . . . because . . .

Deb Home
But you can still have a child. Blocked fallopian tubes, so what? There's IVF, I searched. There are options. So what are you saying sorry for?

Avantika Work
It's wrong. And I hid it from you. I lied. It's unfair to you.

Deb Home
What's unfair?

Avantika Work
Deb.

Deb Home
What's unfair?

Deb Home
?

Deb Home
?

Deb Home
?

Avantika Work
That I was pregnant with Paritosh's child and I can't do the same for you. That I slipped and I made a mistake. There, I said it.

Avantika Work
?

Avantika Work
?

Avantika Work
There?

Avantika Work
?

Avantika Work
Are you there?

Deb Home
I'm here.

Avantika Work
Say something.

Deb Home
What you mean by that is you're sorry that you were raped and you had to get a baby aborted when you were all of 17. Is that what you're sorry for?

Avantika Work

Deb Home

You must be insane to think that you need to apologize for that. If anything I should apologize for making you think that it was unacceptable for you to tell me this happened. Why didn't you tell me?

Avantika Work

Deb Home

More than ten years we have been together and yet you couldn't feel safe to tell me this. I'm not sure you should be the one apologizing.

Avantika Work

Deb.

Deb Home

I want that man to die.

Avantika Work

:(

I heard you came close to killing him.

Deb Home

I surprised myself too.

Avantika Work

Why did you send me outside?

Deb Home

I was confused. Disgusted.

Avantika Work

Sorry.

Deb Home

Not at you, at myself. You went through hell at 17 and all I could think lying in this bed was how badly it hurt my ego. That how little I felt when Paritosh told me what he did. I kept thinking of how angry I was. Of how much bigger a man he must have felt telling me that.

Avantika Work

Deb, don't.

Deb Home

I was questioning my love. I couldn't feel sorry for you even a little bit. I kept feeling angry. ☹ That's just wrong, no?

Avantika Work

You weren't in love with a 17-year-old Avantika.

Deb Home

Why couldn't I feel sorry? Why was my anger more important? I wish I can turn back time and change that. Maybe that will make me feel something.

Avantika Work

Hmmm.

Deb Home

Hmmm.

Avantika Work

Can I come see you? I'm dying a little inside.

Deb Home

So am I. I kept switching on my Wi-Fi to check if your hotspot was still on to see if you're outside.

Avantika Work
I knew you were. I kept checking if it would connect.

Deb Home
Come here.

Avantika slowly walked inside as if she would jinx it with one wrong step. She climbed up the bed and over him.

'I'm a little injured,' said Deb.

'I don't care,' said Avantika, crying and smiling and laughing, and she kissed him. 'I'm so sorry, Deb, I'm so sorry.'

'You will get punched if you apologize. And you should know that I can do that. Shrey should have taken a video—'

'Shut up.'

Avantika didn't let Deb's hand go for the rest of the night. She couldn't get a wink of sleep. She watched him flit in and out of sleep. Every time he would open his eyes, she would feel her heart jump. Then he would smile at her and she would feel at ease. It was like him telling her that he had undergone is past him and that they would never discuss it ever again. She kept her hand on his chest, felt his chest rise and fall, and kissed him softly as he slept. It felt like she was falling in love again.

She ate what was left in Deb's hospital meal. She didn't want to go to the cafeteria and leave Deb's side. Every time she would get drowsy she would have lucid dreams about Deb getting up from the bed, walking out of the hospital and never coming back again. What would she do if he ever did that? What would anything mean without him?

It was early morning and the doctor had just seen Deb when Deb said, his words muffled with sleep and pain, 'Avantika?'

'You need to rest, Deb. Just sleep.'

'You need to know something.'

'I love you,' said Avantika.

'I love you too,' he said. 'There's something else . . . the reports, my reports from . . . fertility clinic, I got them a few days back and . . .'

32

Vernita felt her heart pound in her chest. The roads, the signboards, the lights, they were all out of focus. She kept looking at her phone. Ivan was sleeping and yet she felt on the edge. *What if he wakes up?* She felt a little guilty to be wanting to be back home when her best friend was going through what was the toughest phase of his life. In her defence, she had been texting Deb regularly through the last week. But Shrey told her that she should go meet him. Shrey said he didn't want to meddle after what happened the last time. Vernita was nervous, too. Deb had not needed anyone as an emotional crutch ever since he started dating Avantika ten years ago. What would she say to him? What did he need to hear?

When she reached Deb's house, she found him in a rather chirpy mood, confusing her further still. She spent the next hour trying to discern if it were put-on. He kept talking to her as if it happened to every second person.

Vernita said, 'Look on the positive side, Deb. I think of it sometimes. What if we never had any kids? Imagine the freedom? And not now but when we are forty and fifty and sixty!'

'Hmmm. I just keep thinking of all the time we used protection. Such a waste of time and money. I don't think there's anything sadder than that. It feels like a joke,' said Deb.

'What did the doctors say?'

'You know . . . the same, all the tests say the same. I'm incapable of what comes naturally to almost everyone around me. No matter where I look, everyone is fucking getting pregnant.'

Despite the calmness, the cracks in Deb's voice had now surfaced. She asked, 'How does Avantika stand all this?'

'Stand what?'

'This whining? This beating down of yourself that you do? Deb, I'm not going to listen to all this self-deprecating bullshit from you. You know what Tanmay told me? He told me straight to my face that he would have left me if he were faced with the choice you were faced with. That makes you a bigger man than him. That's something I never thought I would say.'

'It is easier to be the bigger man, isn't it? The real choice would have been if I had a working penis and I could actually father a child—'

'You have a working penis, I guess,' said Vernita.

'I mean if that . . . that thing had a few tadpoles. It's easy to accept that lie of hers because it's really me who's powerless. I have nothing to give her—'

'Fuck off, Deb. One more time you say something like that and I'm leaving.'

'But it's true, isn't it? Being the way I am it would have been odd for me to—'

'You could have been the most virile man on the planet and yet you wouldn't have left Avantika and you know that,' she said.

'How can you be so sure?'

'Because you're selfish with your love. You can't bear to part with the thing that gives you the most happiness. You're not stupid like other men.'

'That I'm not,' he said and smiled.

'Why are you smiling now?' asked Vernita.

'There's another upside. After this whole business of low sperm count, to not make me feel less of a man, Avantika moans a lot more now. You should hear it. It's like she's making out with Hercules. I can't say I don't love it. She's a good actor.'

'You're impossible!' said Vernita. 'Now tell me exactly what the doctor said? And not just the parts that will make me feel sorry for you? What are your chances?'

'Minimal. They told me what they are going to do in detail and it wasn't pretty when they did.'

'Tell me. Don't miss any detail.'

'They will slice open my balls. They will check if the problem is the transportation of sperm. If it is, then they harvest them.'

'That doesn't sound pretty.'

'It's not. They will then get eggs from Avantika and make a baby embryo in a lab. Once that's done they will implant it in Avantika's womb and that's how the pregnancy will start.'

'That sounds simple enough.'

'Only if they find something when they take a knife to my balls,' said Deb.

'Don't make it sound dramatic. So when is the procedure?'

'We haven't scheduled it yet,' said Deb.

'Why?'

'We haven't decided on our worst-case scenario decision. What if they cut me up and there's nothing? Fossilized sperms. Dead children.'

'Then what?'

'We could go the *Vicky Donor* way or we could adopt.'

'What do you want to do?' asked Vernita.

'I don't want to be a bigger man this time. I want to adopt. I don't know if I will be able to love the baby if it reminds me of anyone other than Avantika. Anyway this entire process is lopsided, she will carry the child, she will birth it, she will feed it, the baby will be always be more hers than mine. I don't know if I will have it in me to love it as much as I would have if it were mine. Does that make a bad person?'

'You can't help it. But adoption would make it 100 per cent not yours. If Avantika bears the child, there's at least something of the two of you in the baby. There's a chance it will look like her, no?'

'Yes, but if we adopt Avantika and I will have the struggle of trying to love the baby. We will do that *together*. The baby? It will be equally ours. We will both be in the same boat,' said Deb.

'Did you tell her this?'

'Are you crazy? Not in a million years. I don't want to take this away from her. If she wants to get pregnant she can get pregnant. I will take that chance. Why should I rob her of the happiness? If the baby . . . I will find it in myself to love her.'

'You lied to her about not wanting to adopt?'

'That's what you do for love, don't you?'

Twenty kilometres away, in an investment bank office, Avantika and Tanmay were having the showdown of their lives. Neither of them could keep their voices down.

'I don't want to talk here,' said Avantika.

'You can't run away from this,' said Tanmay.

Avantika smiled at the colleagues who passed her by. She fooled no one, it was easy to see that they were having a fight.

'What's this nonsense about adoption? If you can get a child normally, you will do that. Do you hear that? I will not hear one more word of adoption, okay?' grumbled Tanmay.

'I have made up my mind. That's not your decision to make, Bhaiya,' said Avantika.

'So now nothing I say matters, haan? And why should you adopt? If there was some problem with you, wouldn't he have tried to see if he could choose surrogacy or whatever they do?'

'He might not have,' said Avantika.

'Don't put him on a pedestal he doesn't deserve to be on.'

'You're saying this after knowing what I hid from him?' asked Avantika. 'He didn't say a thing to me, Bhaiya! Not a thing!'

'That would be mighty convenient don't you think? I would have taken him seriously if . . . he had it in him.'

'Had it in him? Really? Is *that* how you will say it? Is that what you're saying? Had you used the same words for me?' asked Avantika.

'I can't believe that you're taking his side on this.'

'His side?' asked Avantika. 'He's my husband.'

'And I'm your brother. I'm your family.'

'And what do you think he is? Bhaiya, if that's how you're going to talk about him I'm going to have to stop talking to you. You're pushing your luck now,' she said.

'For him?' scoffed Tanmay. 'Just to knock some sense into you, I have to tell you that Deb's best friend Vernita is against this stupid adoption idea.'

'What do I have to do with what Vernita thinks we should do?'

'You need to calm down and think about it. I can talk to him. He will understand. Why should you be robbed of having a biological child just because he is . . .' argued Tanmay.

'There's no point talking to him. He doesn't want to adopt either.'

'Then where's the problem, Avantika? Why do you want to adopt when you can do the IVF and he doesn't mind?'

'I can't claim the baby just as my own. It's unfair on him,' explained Avantika.

'Why would you do that?'

'That's what you do for love, don't you?'

33

Baby shops and babies and pregnant women didn't move Avantika as they once did.

She wasn't reduced to happy tears looking at little baby socks. She didn't crave to tell her own stories of tiredness, of frustration with a newborn. The future joy of having a child with Deb had ebbed away. Every morning she would look at Deb, his smiling face staring like the goddamn sun at her, with tea in the cups they had picked on a holiday to Bhutan, on a tray that they had flicked off a hotel in Raipur. Her heart would sink at the thought that their baby wouldn't have anything of him. Why would she want a child that would have nothing of the man she dearly loved?

She had imagined it so many times in the past year, of what her mornings would be like. She would be sleeping in the other room because Deb would insist on her getting sleep before her office. And he would come trotting in with their daughter clinging to him. Both of them would break out in bright smiles seeing her. They would climb up on the bed like two twins—and smother her with kisses. She would be torn trying to decide who she should kiss more. They would fight for her attention, and every morning, it would break her heart to leave them and go to office.

Of all the things she was sure of, she knew Deb's baby would be capable of unconditional love like him. What's the point of having a baby otherwise if not to feel loved like you're the only person in the world?

Deb was unmoved and undaunted by the possibility. He didn't mind that the child would have nothing of him. He found the heart to even joke about it.

'Weren't your friends disappointed that you had started looking like me?' Deb had said the day before.

'It's not funny, Deb,' Avantika had said.

'The baby might not look like me, might not inherit anything from me but you must be crazy to think he or she would mimic anyone more than me. You will be in office making money and I will be with Nayra making her a little me. She will always be on my team. You will be the cruel mother who asks her to study and perform well and what not and I will be the cool father who knows how to have fun. Our roles are set and you're the loser,' Deb had said.

'You're not fun without me,' Avantika had said sadly.

They had homed in on their worst-case scenario decision. Deb had browbeaten Avantika to find a donor in case his surgery had no results. Deb's books might not have found an audience but his words always worked on Avantika and once he started showing her repeatedly what she would miss if she didn't go through with a natural birth, Avantika was no match for him.

Dr Nikhil Sharma had been of considerable help. Unlike other doctors, he had taken a deep interest in their case and would text Deb every day to ask him about the progress, his language more friend-like than doctor. He had encouraged Deb and Avantika to pursue IVF over adoption.

'Because you need to earn money,' Deb had chuckled the first time he had said it.

'Once you wish to have the second child, adopt,' said Dr Sharma. 'These things are hardwired into us. Once you learn to love your own child, made of Avantika's flesh and bone and tissue, you will be able to love anyone. But start with IVF. Being pregnant and giving birth is an experience for both the man and the woman. You don't want to miss out on that,' he had said to Deb.

'For a single, childless man, you sure know a lot about it,' said Deb and sniggered at his own joke.

'How do you deal with him?' Dr Sharma asked Avantika and she laughed.

Despite Avantika agreeing to the decision they had made, she would dilly-dally and keep changing her mind.

'We can choose not to have children,' said Avantika.

'Why would we do that?'

'My super boss, she doesn't have kids, and look where she is. Maybe it's not okay to take a break in a career like mine. It's easy to irreversibly slip down, no?'

'That's lame, Avantika. You will be working till the very last day of your pregnancy, and you will go back to the office the day it's possible.'

'What if I don't feel like it? What if I want to stay with the baby? What if I lose my ambition, my drive?' asked Avantika.

'That offends me, Avantika. You have called me "baby", you once told me you love me more than it's possible to love anyone, and yet you didn't lose your ambition or drive, or wanted to permanently stay home.'

'How do you know I have not wanted to permanently stay at home with you?' she asked, holding his hand.

Deb smiled softly and said, 'You don't have to worry about me, not even a little bit. Anything that comes out of you is mine because you're mine. How can I not love it? I even love your shoes. Umm . . . that came out wrong.'

'That's worryingly sweet. Why are you this annoying? Can't you just be angry with me? Be frustrated? Fight. Make a big deal out of it. Why can't you make this into the worst phase of our relationship? Why are you taking this so well?'

'We are starting something new and I don't want it to have bad memories trailing with it. God knows you have had enough of them already. If you average out all the things you have been deprived of and all the things I had, me not being able to father my child doesn't leave a big dent,' said Deb.

Avantika felt her ambition waning looking at Deb saying the perfect words like he always did. It was true he was annoying. Sometimes he got on her nerves by setting standards of love so high it was impossible to match. It was only last year that Avantika noticed something Deb had been doing for years now. Every time he would go out to shop for himself, or Avantika would go on a work trip, or he would go on a trip Shrey would drag him to, Deb would always come back home or wait at home with a *gift*. Now these weren't gifts that were easily discernible. Sometimes he would clear her cupboard and set it up. At other times, it would be a leftover piece of pizza. Or a trinket both of them knew she wouldn't wear. Sometimes it would be a lone scented candle. She hadn't realized this for a long time—that these were gifts for her, to make her happy after a long absence. He was like a puppy who brings slippers to its pet-mom or pet-dad after he or she is gone for a while. It's not because the pet-mom will be happy, it's because there's no other way the puppy can show how happy it is to see her again. She had cried and laughed in the washroom when it finally struck her. And from then on, she always looked for her *gift* and then felt guilty for being not able of reciprocate the same way.

He was the nice boy who hadn't finished last in love. All she wanted was to drag Deb inside the blanket and spend the rest of her life snuggling.

She regretted ever wanting a child. The idea had festered and festered in her for a long time and now she knew she would never be complete without a child. Even though she had suggested to Deb that they could go without one, she knew there was nothing else she wanted more in life.

34

TESE.

Testicular Epididymal Sperm Extraction.

That's what the doctors were calling the procedure. Dr Sharma had booked them an appointment with a doctor in Mumbai whom he highly respected. Deb and Avantika had to fly down to Mumbai to meet the doctor and discuss their case.

'We will make incisions on the testes and get to the sperm-producing tissue. There will be an embryologist in the room who will check it for sperms. Whatever we find, will be frozen for IVF,' the doctor said. Then he looked at Avantika and said, 'Dr Sharma must have updated you on what we do next. If we find what we are looking for, we will start your IVF. We will harvest your eggs, fertilize them and we will take it from there.'

'How often do you find sperm in the tissue?' asked Deb.

'There's no such percentile. It's important for both of you to be positive at a time like this. If things don't go the way you want them to then there are other options. If you want a sperm donation we can facilitate that, if adoption is the route you want to go in, we can get you in touch with the right people,' the doctor explained.

Later, on their flight back to Delhi, Avantika couldn't help but think how rehearsed the doctor's answers were. She wondered how many times he would have said the entire same thing, then gone back home and drank tea with his wife, played with his children like nothing had changed. She thought about the couples who were his patients—how indelibly he would had changed their lives with his words.

During the week that passed, Avantika couldn't sleep, eat or work. Deb seemed to take it well, or at least he pretended to. A few times Avantika asked Deb if he wanted to talk about it and he would brush it aside. 'It's like the roll of a die. We will see what comes out of it. No point stressing over it,' he would say.

On the red-eye flight to Mumbai for the procedure, Deb promptly fell asleep with his head on Avantika's shoulder. Avantika switched on the reading light and read all the literature she had downloaded on the TESE procedure.

Deb woke up minutes before the flight landed.

'Did you sleep well?' he asked.

'I did.'

'Why doesn't your mouth smell like dead rats then?' asked Deb and promptly slept again in the cab, and shouted with joy when it stopped outside their hotel, St Regis. Avantika had stayed in this hotel before and would bring the little shampoo bottles back for Deb. Deb had always been jealous of Avantika when she would come back with stationary with her name in golden lettering on it.

'It gets boring after a while,' she would say and he wouldn't believe her.

He kept flitting from the room to the bathroom and back to the room after they'd checked-in. Watching him, Avantika couldn't believe he was scheduled for a life-changing operation the next day.

Avantika wanted Deb to get some sleep but Deb didn't want to miss the complimentary breakfast, or the chance to go to the pool. He dragged her to the complimentary fifteen-minute foot massage too.

After Deb exhausted all the things one could do for free at the hotel, clicked enough pictures in different clothes at different times to show he had been there more than once, Avantika asked, 'Do you want to go somewhere nice?'

'You have chosen nicely till now. I feel like a lamb before slaughter, a happy lamb. I allow you.'

Avantika booked an Ola cab for the day; not just any cab at that but a luxury one. The driver came in a white suit driving a Jaguar and was more handsome and confident than Deb.

'Thank God for capitalism and your investment banker salary,' Deb whispered when they got inside the car. 'We don't really need to go anywhere. We can stay in the car. Look at this leather.'

'He's listening,' muttered Avantika angrily.

'Chee. I was talking only about this leather and not what we would want to do on it. Did you feel it? Amazing, isn't it?' said Deb and Avantika realized he meant it.

Avantika took him to Jamjar Diner, a place she always went to when she was in Mumbai.

'I always thought you would like this place. It's very writerly, isn't it? I have imagined you sitting in that corner, typing away, and me in this corner looking at you, trying to come up with conversation starters,' said Avantika.

'It makes sense it's an imaginary scenario because no one comes to me when I'm writing. And you can hardly write when you know that the coffee you're drinking is for 400 rupees,' said Deb. 'Nice place though. I reckon Amish and Chetan and Ravinder come to write here.'

Deb ordered like they had not just eaten a meal fit for beasts. His fingers were sticky from pork ribs and chicken pulled burger and meat-juice dripped from his mouth like he was a little child. 'Should we talk about tomorrow?' asked Avantika when they were walking on the Versova beach, trying to digest what they had eaten.

'Didn't we have numerous talks about it? If things go right, it will be a blessing; if they don't, we will take it as it comes. I have thought about it. Why would it be any trouble loving something that's a part of you? It's going to be easy, I know,' said Deb.

Deb wouldn't talk further and it didn't help Avantika's anxiety. No matter what he said, Avantika wanted the child to have both their genetic markers. She wanted Nayra to be like Deb and no one else.

When they seemed to have digested their food, they headed to the nearest mall, bought bar-worthy clothes and went to a nearby bar where neither of them drank. Deb could see nothing of the dress; she was all skin, all legs and no fabric. Deb, on the other hand, was all fabric, layers of it. With a blazer on, he felt overdressed in the right kind of way. Avantika's constant glances, her little touches, stolen pecks made him feel handsome, sexy.

Unlike Deb, Avantika never needed alcohol to dance. Within minutes, she had turned the dance floor into the stage of *Dance India Dance*, establishing long eye contact with anyone who would try to upstage her. Even after all these years of a hectic corporate job, Avantika's steps and rhythm were razor sharp. There were still remnants of the old Avantika who could party all days of the week, knew every club manager, every bouncer and a flirtatious smile from her would be all it took to get inside any club in the city no matter how exclusive.

Avantika knew that dancing made Deb uncomfortable. He would always look at his feet, from deep inside his drink, and pretend as though he came alone to the bar. That only made Avantika throw her arms around him and point to him every time a word like *dilbar*, *jaaneman* or *dildaar* came in the song. He would shyly curl into himself and look like a little hedgehog.

'You need to stop doing that,' she said when they left the bar.

'That's never going to happen.'

The tiredness set in only when they were back in their room. They had six hours before they had to report to the hospital for the procedure.

With every passing minute, Avantika's nervousness went up a few notches.

When Deb went to the bathroom to shave his nether regions like he had been asked to do, Avantika cried a little.

'Are you okay in there?' asked Avantika from the other side when it had been some time.

Deb didn't answer. She peeked in and found Deb sitting hunched up on the corner of the bathtub. The razor was still in his hand and the shaving cream was untouched. Avantika went and sat next to him.

'It's okay, there's no need to be brave,' she said and held his hand while he cried.

'You needed a good cry,' she said when he was done, and took the razor from his hands. 'Let me help you out.'

'No, thank you. You will turn me on and that will only make it harder. To shave I mean,' said Deb and winked.

'I'm glad you're back to your old pervert self. But to answer you I would rather shave something hard than something floppy. Now show it to me,' said Avantika.

The lathering was okay. Deb even enjoyed it. 'We should do this more often. But you need to get better, put your heart into it, like really get in there,' he said to her. Avantika shook her head, smiling. But the second Deb saw the razor in Avantika's hand approach his privates, he started to freak out.

'I don't trust you.'

'What! It will be fine, believe me.'

'I have seen you sharpen pencils, you're horrible,' said Deb.

'But you have also felt up my legs. They don't shave themselves, I do,' argued Avantika.

'Legs are safe, not this. I will do it myself,' he said.

'Okay, fine, I have a better idea.'

Avantika left the bathroom and came back with a little tube of Veet, a hair removal cream. 'This is safe. It might sting a little but it's super clean. Smells good too!'

That's what they did. Avantika took to his cock and balls like an artist and aimed for perfection. By the time she finished, the place was so smooth you could skate on it.

They made jokes about it till it was time for them to leave. Avantika double-checked the files before they left. They held hands all the way to the hospital. The nurse whom Avantika had made good friends with the previous time they were at the hospital wished them luck and ushered them into the room. The sympathetic look in her eyes was unmissable. It did nothing to their confidence.

There was another couple waiting there. Half an hour passed by and neither they nor Deb and Avantika introduced themselves. They looked more nervous than Deb and Avantika. It was finally Deb who spoke, 'It's going to be fine.'

The other man, who identified himself as Ankit Gupta, nodded. The wives looked at each other. In the tiny second they held their gaze, both of them told each other their story.

Ankit and Reema Gupta, who lived in a large joint family, hadn't told anyone they were going through this procedure.

'Our friends know but our parents don't,' said Avantika.

They didn't discuss the steps ahead but Avantika knew that Ankit and Reema Gupta wouldn't go through with adoption. The thick sindoor on her forehead, the clutch of bangles, the saree, told her that they were from a conservative bania business family where adoption wasn't an option. Donation would be frowned upon too. But they would do it and lie to their entire family.

'Best of luck,' Avantika wished them, briefly thinking about the lie the Guptas would have to live through their lives if today wasn't successful for them.

Deb was called before Ankit Gupta and put under general anaesthesia. He remained cheerful through it all.

'We will get through this,' said Avantika to Deb as he started to drift off. 'You're the most beautiful man I have ever seen.'

Deb drifted off with a smile on his face. She kissed his face lightly and found herself tearing up when they took him inside.

A little later, Ankit Gupta was called too. Avantika and Reema sat in the waiting room holding hands, a strange kinship between them, waiting for their husbands to emerge from the operation theatre. Both their hearts pounded, and their eyes kept flitting towards the clock. *The surgery is not life-threatening,* Avantika kept reminding herself.

'They will be okay, they will be okay,' she kept telling Reema Gupta.

Avantika was called first. Deb had been shifted to a private room.

'I will see you later,' said Avantika to a nervous Reema.

When she walked into the ward, she was just happy to see Deb. He was waking up. For that moment, she forgot there was an operation on the result of which their lives hinged. She was just glad to see him, and hold his hand again.

'The drugs are powerful. I might have flirted with the doctor there when he reached out. In my defence, everyone sort of looked like you,' said Deb.

Avantika smiled, and then they fell silent. For the next half hour, they just sat there, waiting. The effect of the drugs wore off and the first signs of worry cropped up on his face. Every passing second made their anxiety worse.

'If they found something they would have told us by now. I have read it. Men are often told during the surgery if it's successful,' said Deb.

'Let's wait,' said Avantika, wringing her hands together, muttering prayers. She didn't need Deb's negativity right now.

Deb, too, closed his eyes in prayer but couldn't concentrate.

A little later they saw Reema Gupta outside. She was crying, her hands were clasped tightly around the doctor's and she was thanking him. Ankit's surgery was successful and he would go on to the next step. When Reema Gupta turned, she saw Deb and Avantika looking right at her. Not knowing how to react, she scuttled away trying to hide her happiness but the spring in her step was hard to miss.

'You know what that means, right?' said Deb.

Avantika squeezed Deb's hand. She looked at him and hoped she could do something to make it all go away.

'Let's wait for the doctor to come?' said Avantika.

'Accept it,' said Deb and leaned back, the truth was staring right at him, and he tried his hardest not to cry. *It doesn't matter, the child will still be mine, it will be mine, it will be Avantika's and mine.* 'It's okay, Avantika. We know what to do from here. We have talked about this. We need to look ahead.'

'I'm not talking about it till I hear it from the doctor.'

'That's just irrational,' said Deb.

It took him all his might to not cry; he wanted to. He wanted to unhook the cannulas and run away from the hospital, just keep running. *Why me? Why the fuck did I have go through this fucking fucking fucking thing!*

A little later when the door to the room opened, they were offended to see the doctor's smiling face. Had he forgotten what news he had to give to them? Deb took a deep breath. He had kept his tears in, and that's the way it would be from now, he thought. There would a long road ahead. A baby, not his, would grow inside Avantika's womb and till the time it was born with Avantika's face, he would have to keep all his tears in.

'How are we doing?' he asked, rather gleefully.

By now Avantika's restlessness had peaked. She wanted to smash the glucose stand on the doctor's head.

Both of them just smiled drily waiting for the bad news to be confirmed.

'So good news, we found quite a few sperms in the tissue. They are being frozen as we speak. We will get them transported to Delhi and Dr Sharma will take it forward,' said the doctor and turned to Avantika. 'So you know what you need to do now, don't you? You need to get ready for a pregnancy.'

Deb and Avantika made the doctor repeat what he had just said. The doctor told them, once, twice and then again, that they were cleared for IVF and if everything went well there was no reason why Avantika wouldn't be pregnant soon.

Back in the hotel that night, Deb and Avantika cried together and ate two cheesy burgers with fries and coke and watched their wedding video. Neither of them said anything because they didn't know what to say.

35

They were only half way through their journey though. After they found sperm in the TESE procedure, Deb and Avantika's days had become a painful science project. Jokes and little dates were what kept them going. They hadn't been prepared for how exhausting IVF was, no one tells you that; they kept reminding each other what they had already gone through to come to this point to power on.

The first thing they had to learn was to administer injections to Avantika to increase the egg count. And since Avantika turned out to be rather bad at it, poking and prodding and bleeding before she got the nerve right every time she tried, it was Deb who had to carry out the job.

The stress of missing an injection was immense. After pricking her countless times, he didn't want to skip one by mistake lest they had to do the entire procedure again. He would put alarms on his phone two hours prior to remind himself of when it was time to inject her. He would be at her office an hour before it was time, pacing around nervously, cradling softly the vials of medicine. Then they would go inside the women's bathroom, hang the

CLEANING IN PROGRESS signboard outside and then carry it out.

Everyone in her office figured after a few days what was happening. None of them possessed less than a post-graduate degree or a sub-100 IQ and yet they threw looks they would have imagined on aunties in their locality.

'Don't mind them,' Avantika would keep telling Deb every day.

'I'm fine, it's horrible that you have to see them every day,' Deb would say.

It kept getting more and more painful for Avantika; as if everything inside her body was being churned. The closer they got to the date they had to collect the eggs, the more tense they became.

'You need to be together in this. It's a stressful time for any couple,' Dr Sharma kept telling them. He would regularly schedule their sessions with a counsellor even when they told him they didn't need it. Every few days a friend of his would drop by their home; they would reluctantly talk to him but would feel better by the end of it all.

Deb knew Avantika had a high threshold for pain but this was on an entirely different level; the tension only made it worse. The time leading up to the day she was due to get her eggs collected was stressful. Avantika had to apply for sick leaves for the regular tests and blood work. They had to make sure everything was working fine. They had heard from others who went to the same hospital that it could be painful. The doctor had given Avantika the choice to go under local or general anaesthesia.

'You don't have to be Wonder Woman. Take general and then sleep,' said Deb.

Avantika didn't agree. She was being superstitious. She thought nothing good would come out of it if she didn't go through the pain.

'That makes no sense at all,' said Deb.

'Nothing that we are doing makes sense. Fifty years ago if you told a couple they could only have kids if they cut open the balls of the man and then extracted eggs from the woman and then fertilized them on a slide, it wouldn't have sounded real to them,' argued Avantika. 'Let me do this, Deb.'

'You have been through enough pain, don't you think?' Deb said even as Dr Sharma stood on their heads asking them for what they had picked.

'Local,' she said.

'Let her do this,' said Dr Sharma.

'You're not married to her,' said Deb.

'Wow, sass, is that what you kids call it these days?' said Dr Sharma with a smile. 'Can we hurry up now? Believe it or not, I have other patients.'

She was wheeled in for the surgery. Deb waited outside. Dr Sharma had assured them beforehand that the surgery was commonplace and all they should hope for was that they get a lot of eggs or they would have to repeat it again.

Dr Sharma had explained, 'The more we get, the more we will try to fertilize. Some don't take, others might fertilize but some embryos might die. The higher the number of eggs we get, the better are your chances. The less I see both of your faces the better for me.'

'You will miss us when we are not around,' Deb had quipped at the time.

While the anaesthetist was getting her ready, Avantika felt like she was about to take a test and she had to perform well in it; it was as if her life depended on it. Once they started harvesting the eggs, a sharp pain—nothing like she had ever felt before—shot up her body. She told Deb later it felt like someone was slowly sucking the life out of her. There was constant pain that kept ramping up all through the procedure. Twice she thought she would pass out from the pain but she held on. To tide over the pain that had taken over her body, she kept imagining Deb's stories that he had told her of what it would be like when they were finally parents and Deb's face if Dr Sharma were to tell them that she did well and they had a good chance of getting pregnant.

Later in the evening, that's exactly what Dr Sharma said. They had harvested over 100 eggs and that was a high percentile.

'Just keep your fingers crossed now. We will now fertilize the eggs, create the embryos and keep you updated on the results,' said Dr Sharma.

Dr Sharma had decided to create fifteen of them. They would monitor them over the next few days and see how many survived. They would then have to take a call on how many of the surviving embryos would they get implanted. Dr Sharma kept telling them to look happy; they were close. But neither Deb nor Avantika could wholly believe their struggle was coming to an end. It had started to seem like a mirage, a game with more misses than hits.

Back on their way home, a happy anxiousness took over them, the realization slowly sinking in. They kept tossing names of babies about. There was a possibility—although it never quite happens—that all fifteen survived. In their heads—especially Deb's—the embryos weren't a bunch of cells but little babies waiting to spring forth into the world.

'Imagine if we have fifteen babies running around, crawling all over us? Wouldn't that be something?' asked Avantika. 'We would probably want to run away leaving all but maybe two or three behind but still. Just the sight of them. Like animals, no?'

Deb didn't think of leaving even one of them behind; he would take all of them with him.

By the time they were home, they had fifteen names of babies written down. Deb stuck it on the fridge. He said, 'What? We created them, didn't we?'

Avantika was fit to go back to the office the next day but she stayed at home and together they fantasized about what the coming days would be like.

They would call the hospital every twelve hours to enquire about the fertilization of her eggs. After the first few times they were told off and warned against calling so many times.

'There are rules against this kind of thing. And no Deb, you can't bribe me into giving you sooner updates, okay?' said an irritated Dr Sharma.

It was after a week that they were called to the doctor's office. They threw questions at the person who called who knew Deb and Avantika enough to cut the call mid-sentence. In the cab to the hospital, neither of them asked the question that ricocheted in their minds. *How many of their fifteen kids survived?*

The smiling face of Dr Sharma greeted them. *Why is he smiling? Why's the bastard smiling? Did all survive? Fifteen kids? Between the two of us and one set of grandparents? And mostly one salary? How much have my parents saved?* Deb's hand immediately reached out to Avantika's and held it. He fed the insane possibility of them being parents to fifteen children. It would be like the old times. Of course, they wouldn't plant all of them in Avantika in one go. Maybe they would start with three. And then three more, and then three more. What other option did they really have? They wouldn't let their children be in a freezer forever, would they? Moreover, he had checked how much it would cost them for those little embryos to be preserved for an extra year. It was a bomb. They would be asked if they wanted to *destroy* them and they would have to select that option if not bring them into this world. *How different was it from killing a baby?* There were times he would think of the baby Avantika had to abort. It didn't matter any more if it were Paritosh's. He believed he could have still loved it with all his heart. Sometimes, in the past few days, he had dreamt up futures with that child. He would have been a teenager now. An angry, rebellious teenager who wouldn't have accepted Deb as his father, who would stalk his biological father, want to establish a connection with him, but Deb would have smothered him with love and reunited with him as his father at his deathbed.

'We have good news. We have two embryos. We started with more than fifteen but they couldn't survive,' Dr Sharma announced excitedly.

Thirteen embryos died. They were embryos and yet Deb and Avantika felt a dull sorrow hammer away at their hearts. They could have been their children. After all they had gone through, it seemed like they were meant to have fifteen children.

The doctor continued, 'What do you want to do? We talked about this. If we plant both of them, there's a higher chance. We sometimes transfer three of them as well. The couples do end up with triplets—'

'Both,' they both said without missing a beat.

It seemed crazy that they wouldn't want the best chance of being pregnant. They were meant to be parents to two kids and not one. It wasn't even a question. *Why would the other survive otherwise?*

'Then we should do the transfer as soon as possible,' the doctor said.

They left the hospital prickly with excitement. A strange energy coursed through bodies to think of what was coming next. They held their hands all the way back to their house, still trying to wrap their heads around the impending possibility.

'It's happening,' said Avantika when they turned in for the night.

'Let's not jinx it by talking about it. It will happen when it does.'

The transfer was scheduled three days later. Watching how careful Avantika was during those three days, it would seem to one that she was already pregnant.

On the day of the procedure, Avantika took Deb to Guruji's ashram and they spent an hour there, staring at Guruji's picture. Deb made no jokes; it wasn't worth the risk. If he were a real guru, this was the time to prove it.

Avantika shook with fear when they finally reached the hospital and she changed into scrubs. *What if they don't take? What if after all this, it comes to naught?* Just before she was wheeled in, Deb handed her his cell phone with a little video on it which he wanted her to see.

'This is how every pregnancy starts, baby,' he said to her while they were taking her away.

He had not followed it with a warning, telling her to watch it in private. When she clicked on it—with the nurses and Dr Sharma watching on—she saw Deb on the screen keep the phone at a distance, shift back, and turn on the music.

'What's he up to?' asked Dr Sharma. 'We don't have time for this.'

It was right then that Deb launched into a hilarious strip-tease act, tripping over twice and trying to twerk but only managing to do some kind of old-person yoga. The nurses who had been watching, chuckled.

'This is how it should have felt, right? Getting pregnant,' said Deb, laughing in the video. 'Sexy, right! You want this? You want this? I know you do! Yes, take it baby mama, take it, take my baby-making machine and dock it with yours. Give me a baby, baby!'

'Oh my God, you're married to a buffoon,' said Dr Sharma.

'I think he's pretty good,' said Avantika and smiled at the nurses who looked away shyly. 'Look how big he got? Look! Look!'

'Shall we start now?' said Dr Sharma wryly.

The procedure itself was rather painless and quick. She smiled through it, thinking of Deb and how stupidly he was in love with her.

When it got over, Dr Sharma told her that everything seemed to go off fine and asked her to rest for a week. 'Sometimes the embryos don't take. You have to know it wouldn't be your fault. It's just how bodies work. We will have to try again if they don't,' he said. 'Another round of IVF for you but don't think about that right now. Let's hope it doesn't come to that. If you get your period you will know. Let us know as soon as possible. For now, just go home and feel proud to have done this and done this well. And please delete that video from your phone. I can't rest till the time I know it exists in the world.'

'When can we take a pregnancy test?' asked Avantika.

'After a week. Don't try it before that. It's unnecessary stress. Couples keep doing it multiple times a day. There's no use of that,' Dr Sharma said. 'Knowing the two of you, you will take at least one, I know, but it's my job to tell you to try your hardest not to.'

On their way back, they wanted to stop at every chemist to buy home pregnancy tests. They wanted to know if Nayra and her unnamed brother or sister had taken root in Avantika's womb.

36

The week crawled by ever so slowly. Avantika and Deb were holed up at their place. The TV was on all the time but no one was watching it. They mindlessly went through four seasons of *Mad Men*. They would wake up in the morning and wait for the night to fall so they could clock another day. Twice in the past seven days, they had given up. They had left the house and walked to the closest chemist and bought a home pregnancy test. Both times they had dumped it in the dustbin outside their house.

But today, they had no choice. They had to leave the house. It was Ivan's first birthday.

'Ivan wouldn't even know that it's his birthday. What's the point?' said Deb, still rolling in the bed. He hadn't taken a shower yet.

'He will grow up and know,' said Avantika.

'We will just tell him that the memory card got corrupted. How hard is that?' he argued.

'My parents aren't coming because he wanted me to be there. That's the first time he has picked me over them. I am not going to turn that down no matter what you say,' said Avantika.

'You're such a puppy around him,' said Deb.

'At least I'm not scared of him, am I?' said Avantika. 'Go take a shower.'

Much to the anger and disappointment of Vernita's parents, the birthday—as Vernita had insisted—was a modest affair at their house. There would be no one, no useless relatives, no colleagues, just ten friends and that's it. In a first, Tanmay had kept his parents from coming to their grandson's birthday and that had brought an endless smile to Avantika's face.

Tanmay and Vernita had done up the house with a sailor theme—cliched but beautiful. The cake was three-tiered, blue and tasted incredible. Ivan wasn't allowed to have any of it.

'If both of you need rest then you can go home,' Vernita told Avantika when the gifts passed hands and Ivan had gone to sleep.

'I think we are going to stick around,' said Deb.

They all sat around for a couple of hours and, like people in their early thirties are wont to do, they discussed their college days, how recent it seemed, how time had flown past, how neighbourhood kids now called them Uncle–Aunty instead of Bhaiya–Bhabhi, and they all told each other that on their faces ten years hadn't gone by, maybe just five. *We all look 25 at best, not a day more.* Ragini and Avantika spent a lot of time in the balcony talking to each other while Ritam giggled nervously through the night.

'She's bullying me into it,' said Ritam to Deb. 'How can I say yes to it when I know it will be insufferable pain for her?'

'I jabbed Avantika about a hundred times with injections that I could have gotten wrong every time. She never winced, never complained about the pain. You can never be sure how they deal with pain. Let her make the decision?' answered Deb.

All of them talked and talked till their old bodies gave up, way earlier than before. There were times Deb and Avantika forgot they were going through what was one of the most testing times they had ever faced. When it was time to go, everyone promised each other that they should do this more often, knowing that they wouldn't, not because they didn't want to but because that's what adulthood meant—missing out on the smaller, easily available joys.

Deb and Avantika, dead tired and longing to get home as soon as possible, were getting inside the cab when a Volvo rolled up in the parking lot next to theirs. Deb looked at the car—which looked like the kind people with a lot of money to spare would buy—and then at Avantika to share a wisecrack when he noticed the colour drain out of her face.

'They are here,' she said.

The driver asked, '*Kaha jaana hai, Bhaiya*, where do you guys want to be dropped?'

'Get down,' Avantika said angrily and nudged at Deb.

Deb saw the door fling open and Avantika's parents step out of the car. Within that split second, anger coursed through him and a nerve in his temple throbbed.

Avantika held Deb's arm. She muttered angrily under her breath. 'He called them. He lied to me . . . he'd called them . . .'

It was then that they noticed Avantika. Avantika's mother said to her father at a volume loud enough so that Deb and Avantika could hear, 'Don't spoil your mood today. It's a good day for us. Ivan is waiting.'

'He's asleep actually and that's the best thing that has happened to him in the past year. To not see your face on his birthday,' said Deb after he saw Avantika not come up with a biting repartee.

Deb derived pleasure out of the anger on her father's face who swallowed and then smiled and said, 'We will see him tomorrow. But you? Will your parents ever get the joy of seeing a grandson? Listen, beta, what you should do is adopt one of those kids from the slums. They will look like you anyway.'

Her mother added, 'What are you saying? Don't you know how much he earns? Let those kids live in the slum.'

Her father looked at Avantika and laughed. 'So this is what you chose after running away from the boy we wanted for you? A half-man who can't even give you a child?'

Her mother chuckled. She opened her bag and took a bunch of crisp 2000 rupee notes and handed them over to Deb with a wicked smile. 'Take this. Eat something. Maybe it will help.'

Before Deb could react or throw the money at them, Avantika's parents had turned and walked away.

They noticed now that the cab had left. Deb checked on the application; the driver had cancelled, and the next cab was twenty minutes away. When he looked up, Avantika was already walking out of the parking lot and he followed instinctively, walking two steps behind her, and then with her, his heart still pounding with fury. They forgot that their house was not within walking distance and it would take them three hours on foot, and yet that's what they did. They walked briskly towards their own house, both replaying the conversation in their heads, their faces flushed with anger.

'I'm sorry,' Avantika said.

'Why are you sorry?'

'Because they are my parents, my family,' she said.

'I'm your family. And I should have hit them. I was thinking of hitting them and I don't know why I didn't hit them. You should have asked me to hit them,' said Deb. He was still burning with shame.

It was then that it started to rain. Little slivers at first and then water thick as ropes started to assault them. They walked a little at first and by the time they took shelter under a bus stand they were fully drenched. Avantika tried to book a cab but it seemed like everyone had decided to do the same at the same time.

'It's showing fifteen minutes away,' she said. 'Booked it.'

They sat at the empty bus stop watching the rain fall. The pitter-patter calmed Deb down a little. It was then that he noticed a chemist shop on the other side of the road. Avantika caught him staring at it and sighed deeply.

'It's a week now,' said Deb, looking at the watch. It was past midnight. Without waiting for Avantika to say anything, he trotted towards the shop and reached it seconds before the pharmacist was about to pull down the shutter.

He bought three brands of home pregnancy strips for Avantika. The taxi was still ten minutes away. Avantika took the strips without a word and looked around. A public toilet was a few paces away.

Deb waited as Avantika disappeared inside with the strips. His heart thumped out of his chest. He paced around, took deep breaths and tried calming himself down.

'WHAT IS HAPPENING?' he shouted over the din of the rain.

'Wait,' said Avantika.

A couple of minutes later, Deb said, 'NOW?'

'Wait,' said Avantika, her voice softer now.

'NOW?'

Avantika emerged from the washroom, the three pregnancy sticks in her hand. She looked at Deb and Deb knew.

They were *pregnant*.

37

Deb got shouted at every time he asked Avantika to do as little as pass on the remote. She wouldn't move an inch from the bed. It was an overreaction that Deb allowed her. He hadn't been completely innocent as well. When he saw her shifting the centre table as they needed to clear pathways so she wouldn't bump into anything, Deb had shot his mouth off.

The first few days after the pregnancy tests came out positive were nerve-racking for both of them. It was like they had taken a long breath, it was their last one, and they were too scared to get it go. It was important for Avantika to rest but she could hardly get herself to close her eyes as if doing that would cause her to lose the pregnancy. They weren't even cent per cent sure she was pregnant. They neglected a small detail that many pregnancies that show up on home pregnancy strips are chemical pregnancies, where there's no child cooking in the womb, just a hormonal imbalance.

They cancelled out every day on a calendar, on the daily planner on their phones and in their heads. Dr Sharma, who they had called the day after the test, had asked them to hold on. It wasn't easy, to say the least.

A week later, they took an appointment for a full pregnancy test. The blood work was done swiftly and they were due for a scan. The entire city seemed to have gotten pregnant at the same time since they were asked to wait for a while.

Deb held Avantika's hand—he had learned that from the movies—when the doctor spread the gel on Avantika's stomach.

'The blood work suggests you're pregnant,' she said and then as she peered into the monitor, she got serious. 'But this doesn't show anything. Why does it not show anything?'

Avantika's heart jumped to her mouth.

'What?'

The doctor turned to the nurse, 'How many?'

The nurse checked the file and said, 'Two weeks. She insisted on a scan.'

The doctor didn't say it out loud but she rolled her eyes and it was clear what she was thinking.

'Avantika. A two-week scan hardly shows anything. Come back two weeks later so that we can get a clearer picture, okay? We can't tell right now if the embryos took,' she said.

'Of course they took, what are you talking about? All we have come for is a picture of the two of them that we can stick on our refrigerator!' said Deb.

'Another two weeks?' shot out Avantika.

'Fine, come next week and we will see what we can find,' the doctor said and asked them to take it easy. 'It's important that you don't stress the foetus. It's early days.'

Deb wanted to correct her that it's not the foetus but Nayra and her unnamed brother.

Dr Sharma had said the same thing to them but they wanted a second opinion. More like they wanted someone to tell them that they were pregnant for sure, that there was a child inside her, not just a spike of hormones. It was like a fishbone stuck in their throat, neither here nor there.

On their way back, they picked up a kilo of biryani and had the facile argument of whether they could finish it or not. Every day had a lot of hours they had to fill up with talk about things that didn't matter any more. Aided by the stress they were in, they polished off the biryani in an hour, and wondered if Avantika's appetite was somehow pregnancy-related.

'Now ask them to do the scan!' joked Avantika and burped loudly.

'We won't talk about it for the next week, okay?'

Avantika reluctantly went back to office the next day. She had exhausted her sick leave and was slipping in her work. Deb made her promise she wouldn't stress herself with it.

'Keep reminding them that you work there. I won't want Nayra and her brother to grow up in penury,' said Deb and packed her a lunch of his home-made biryani.

The next week, they went to the doctor again—not Dr Sharma who had explicitly told them that they were banned at his hospital till the two weeks were over—and she looked at them sullenly, as if they had spoilt her mood. To help things along, Avantika hiked up her dress, rubbed the gel all over herself and smiled.

'Nothing,' the doctor said. 'Come back next week.'

That week was easier. They repeated the schedule—the anxiety, the stress eating, the trying not to talk about it—from the previous week and returned to the doctor. This time they went to Dr Sharma who was smiling his trademark half-silly, half-stern smile, and waiting for them.

'Today's the day, right?' Avantika asked.

'Yes, and don't think I don't know you have been prancing around to other clinics getting scans done. It's like the both of you are cheating on me,' said Dr Sharma.

'We weren't getting what we wanted from you,' said Deb.

Looking at Dr Sharma's equanimity, they were strangely assured that everything would go okay. In the past three weeks, they had grown certain there were two little humans taking root in Avantika's belly. If Dr Sharma told them anything different, they wouldn't believe it. They wouldn't even believe the possibility of only one of the embryos surviving.

'There's definitely a pregnancy. I can see that for sure. Of the two embryos that were planted, it's too early to say if both of them have taken. Come back in two weeks?' he said. 'Oh yes, did I say you are quite pregnant?'

Avantika smiled and said after a pause, 'There are two of them in there. I just know.'

'But why two weeks again! We already waited three weeks! THIS IS UNFAIR!' protested Deb and got nothing back.

Dr Sharma brusquely asked Deb to shut up, and stop going to other doctors.

'I hope you haven't told Shrey about it,' said Avantika on their way back home.

Shrey though had suspected it from day one. He had caught on to Deb's prolonged absences from the office. Not telling Tanmay was easier. They weren't talking to Tanmay and Vernita since the day they bumped into her parents in the parking lot. Tanmay had expected a shouting from Avantika after that night but Avantika—who had found herself pregnant—had gone radio silent on him, making him wonder if this time she had cut off ties with him for good.

Tanmay had tried explaining that they hadn't called their parents.

'I believe him but did he throw them out later? He didn't,' Avantika said. It was also better for her to not reconcile right now. It made it easier to hide the news.

It was most difficult for them to hide the news from Deb's parents. To explain the huge hole in their finances, to explain all the times Avantika had taken and was taking sick leaves from her office. Both parents would ask piercing questions, sometimes masked, other times direct, to find out what was going on with them.

This time, they waited for an extra week to go for the scan. They knew the pregnancy had happened. What they didn't want to hear was there was only one child. They wanted them both. Otherwise rare, they would now spot twins everywhere. Identical, non-identical, identical but one taller, one fatter, identical but one lighter. Dr Sharma had called them repeatedly during the week and had worriedly asked them where they were. For once, they were the ones bullying him, getting a minor kick out of not picking his calls.

'I hope you're not cheating on me again,' he would text them.

Every night, they talked endlessly about how this was going to change their lives.

'It's going to be tough, no? Vernita is struggling, Tanmay is struggling and they are masters of time management,' asked Avantika.

'Just give me two house helps and my mother and I will handle everything,' said Deb.

'It's not as easy as you're making it out to be,' she said.

'It can't be that tough either. Back in the day people were getting pregnant at twenty. They had five children by the time they were thirty. We are just having two,' said Deb.

On their way to the scan two weeks later, Deb said, 'What are we calling the other? Nayra's brother is a little unfair no.'

'Are you sure it is a boy?'

'I wanted to have a boy. Not so much any more. But maybe one wouldn't be bad?'

They debated on the names through their drive to the hospital. The one they least fought on the least was—Augustya. Deb was kicked about it because he was the protagonist of a book he had never finished but loved, and Avantika thought it was pretentious and tough on the tongue.

When Dr Sharma strode inside the scan room smiling, he found Avantika lathered up with gel and Deb running the ultrasound on her. The smile was wiped off his face as he shouted loudly making Deb drop the probe from his hands.

'You were late so . . .' explained Avantika.

'ARE BOTH OF YOU ABSOLUTELY CRAZY!' shouted the doctor, picking up the probe. 'JUST DO WHAT YOU'RE ASKED TO DO. I HAVE HAD ENOUGH OF YOU TWO!'

'You love us,' said Deb.

'SHUT THE FUCK UP!' Dr Sharma shouted back.

Deb was made to sit where husbands were supposed to sit. Avantika and Deb chuckled. They had a good feeling about this.

'So six weeks now?' she asked.

They nodded.

Dr Sharma squinted at the screen.

Avantika wrested the probe from him, and moved it swiftly over her stomach.

'Will you stop doing that?' Dr Sharma scolded her.

'Yes, you were right,' she said.

'About what?' asked Deb.

'Let me do this, Avantika,' said Dr Sharma, snatching the probe from her.

'There are twins. I can see the two gestation sacs. There,' Avantika said and pointed to the screen. 'WE ARE HAVING TWO KIDS! WE ARE HAVING TWO KIDS! TWO CHILDREN! NAYRA AND AUGUSTYA!'

Dr Sharma slapped his forehead and grumbled, 'What did I get myself into?'

'Is she right, Nikhil?' asked Deb.

Dr Sharma nodded. 'You ready to hear their heartbeats?'

He brought the volume up and the first thing Deb wondered about was if they were normal. There were loud whooshing sounds that were too quick for heartbeats.

'It's around 104. That's normal for babies,' Dr Sharma said. 'Congratulations to the two of you. I can't say I'm not worried for the babies you will bring to this world. Now get out, and come for another scan next week. Twin pregnancies are often more complex than single pregnancies. Don't worry. We have the best doctors working under this roof and they will tide you through this. Only if you promise to stop with your nonsense.'

The words bounced off their ears. Like they had not been spoken to at all.

Twins.

That's all they thought about.

'When do we tell people?' said Deb, on their way back home.

'Never. We deliver the babies, we raise them in a quaint place, possibly Bhutan, they grow into adults, we grow old and when they come for our combined funeral is when people get to know that we had kids. I want nothing to cast a shadow on this. This is for us,' said Avantika.

38

'The first three months are most critical.'

Deb and Avantika heard it from every doctor, every pregnant woman, and every nurse they talked to. What they didn't tell them was what happened when things went south. It was the word no one wanted to say out loud. *Miscarriage.* The nurses made them feel like it was normal and happened all time, but since no one shared news of a pregnancy before that time no one apart from the couple knew about it. Deb wondered how many people around him, in Avantika's office, in their gym, had miscarriages and just went about life as if nothing had happened. But no matter how hard Deb tried, his mind would wander there. He knew how it would break them. Nayra and Augustya were still only embryos, foetuses, but within a few days it seemed to them they were never not around.

And they made their presence felt in quite some way. It sure seemed like the nausea, the heartburn, the morning sickness all gets doubled when there are two babies instead of one inside the womb. Every few days, Deb would wish the pregnancy on himself rather than Avantika because the entire business of carrying this pregnancy seemed unfair and unbalanced. While she vomited, stayed up entire nights, peed a thousand times, he could only look at her helplessly do the trips to the bathroom.

'There's nothing you can do. Go to sleep,' she would say every night.

'And that's worse,' Deb would answer and hold her hand and keep asking her if he could do anything for her. She kept going to work through her nausea and her heartburn while Deb was unemployed, sitting at home, texting her every few minutes asking if she were okay.

He could do *nothing* for her.

Avantika literally felt her body being torn apart, destroyed by the lives growing inside of her, but she didn't mind it the least bit; instead she revelled in the attention Deb showered on her and sometimes told Deb she wished the pregnancy to last for two years instead of the paltry nine months.

For the first time, she didn't feel guilty at not expressing as much love as Deb often did. She would feel her heart explode every time she would feel his hands on her legs, kneading them, massaging them, and she would pretend to be still asleep. He would kiss her toes softly and she would melt into a puddle.

She had never mentioned it because what kind of ungrateful bitch would she be if she told him that she worried about ending up as an unfit mom—after the years she had spent whipping herself into shape. But Deb knew, and he kept reminding her every morning about how beautiful she looked. He had started to eat more so he could gain the weight with her.

Sometimes she would play a little game with Deb and test his patience. She would crib all day long, be unreasonable, cranky and would hope Deb would finally crack and shout back at her, storm off, say something unkind, and then she would wrap her hands around him, tell him it's a prank and then shower him with love. He never broke. He never once broke!

It got progressively tougher to hide it from people around her. Twins meant she started to show quite early. At eight weeks, she started to look like she was three months pregnant, and at ten she looked five. She stopped going to the gym and added a couple of more kilos.

Since all her clothes fit her snugly, she outgrew them within days of getting to know she was pregnant. Every evening they would have to go out and find clothes for her that would mask the pregnancy. Luckily, she didn't put on any weight on her face, making their job a little easier.

A few random people did ask them if they were pregnant and they would very obviously lie. Deb would crack some offensive fat joke and that would put it to rest.

It was harder hiding it from Tanmay, Vernita and the others in their circle. They knew about the TESE and the IVF, and the nervous week that followed the transfer.

Deb found a cruel way around it when Vernita pestered wanting to know why they weren't meeting them, or even Ivan. Deb's defence was that he had no choice.

'Tanmay already apologized for what happened! You guys can't be that unreasonable and ask him to cut off all contact with his parents just like that,' Vernita said.

'Avantika doesn't want to see him till the time he does that. He has to choose. It's either them or her. And till that time, she doesn't want to see him. Or you, because, well you're married to him.'

'Are you guys out of your mind? I'm not letting Ivan grow up without Avantika around. You guys better sort your shit out,' she pushed. 'I'm coming home tonight.'

'NO!' said Deb panicking.

'There's no reason why I shouldn't.'

'There's enough reason,' said Deb. 'I don't want to tell you what but there is a reason.' Deb didn't know what he was thinking but he said, 'The IVF failed. The babies didn't take root. Avantika doesn't want another round of IVF. She's . . . she's wrecked. We don't want you to come home.'

'Deb—'

Deb cut the call. He lied better on texts so that's what he did. Vernita bought it hook, line and sinker. Avantika wasn't too happy about it. For someone who had built a career on rationale and logic, she was strangely superstitious. 'It will cast a bad shadow on the babies,' she said and closed her eyes in prayer. That night, she dragged him to the temple nearby. On the way back home, he even saw her close her eyes the two times they passed in front of a gurdwara. She stayed up the night watching old Guruji videos and praying to him.

In the middle of the night, Avantika heard him whisper into her ears, 'I'm sorry for saying that.'

'It's fine. I was stupid to have made a big deal out of it,' she whispered back.

But it got Vernita off their backs. The next day, a bunch of flowers arrived at their house with an apology letter from Vernita. Whether it was a mood swing or a superstition, Deb didn't know, Avantika threw out the flowers and the card as soon as they came. As if their mere presence was poisoning her.

By the time they crept to the tenth week, things got worse. The weekly scan was the only thing they looked forward to. The twins were doing fine. Every time they went into the hospital the biology of it just blew their minds. They would bombard the doctors and the nurses with so many questions that the latter began to hide when they saw them approach. Both of them would hold the prints of the scan and marvel how from the biryani and the Coke and the ham sandwiches she craved and ate a lot of, two hearts, two spinal cords, little arms and legs were taking shape inside her body. The intelligent design of something they had taken for granted was unfathomable to them.

At the tenth week scan, Dr Sharma assured them, 'Just two more weeks and it will become easier. It's going to be just the best time.'

'I don't know if I should believe you. Just seems like a lie pregnant women are told so that they stop complaining about what they feel,' said Avantika, still tired from the night before when she counted and peed a total of fifteen times. When Deb said that there were two people peeing inside of her, he got smacked on the head.

'You will be able to go to the gym, do some light workouts. Swim, maybe? You can also travel. Take a little babymoon trip. A lot of couples do that. This will be the last trip you take together in a while. And since you are having twins, holidays are going to be a task.'

'I can't wear any clothes any more. I will look like a potato in a few days,' groused Avantika.

Dr Sharma looked sympathetically at Deb.

'She's doing great, isn't she?' said Deb.

'She is. She's doing incredibly well,' said Dr Sharma responding to Deb's cue

'She works twelve hours a day on top of it. Not late for work even for a single day,' said Deb.

'Not a lot of women can do that,' said the doctor.

'She drives too,' said Deb.

'Wow. Just wow.'

Avantika interrupted them. 'If you think this is making it any easier for me, it isn't. You are irritating me. And doctor, if you're wrong about the nausea then you are going to get it from me,' she said.

The twelfth week scan was the most exciting for them. They saw the spine, the little hearts, the tiny arms and the legs and heard the heartbeats which thrummed like mighty drums now.

'They are strong, both of them,' Dr Sharma said.

'Is the boy as strong as the girl?' asked Avantika.

Dr Sharma turned and met the expectant eyes of Deb and Avantika with anger. Over the last twelve weeks, they had tried different tricks to wheedle out of the doctors the sexes of the twins and had been unsuccessful.

'We know it's illegal but we genuinely want girls,' Avantika had explained.

Dr Sharma kept reminding them that it was illegal, and had asked them specifically to stop irritating him. Deb had listened to him. He wasn't insane. Avantika however, pestered on. She had her reasons. Of late, she had vivid nightmares of having two sons. She would wake up, streams of sweat dribbling down her forehead.

'There's no way I'm raising two sons. What's in it for me, then? I want two girls running eights around me in their little dresses and calling each other behen and didi and sharing everything with me. I don't want boys, period.'

Some nights she would fall off the dark edge and try to buy ultrasound equipment off the internet. She wanted to find out herself.

'What if they tell you that it's two boys?' asked Deb, exasperated, finding it a little ridiculous.

'I will learn to love them from right now. I don't want to be on the hospital bed, torn and exhausted and be told that it's only boys. I need to be ready for that eventuality,' said Avantika.

There was no end to that conversation.

They took their next, decisive, scan to Dr Sharma who smiled at Avantika cockily and said, 'So? How's the nausea?'

'It's gone,' said Avantika shyly.

'I told you so,' said Dr Sharma. 'Everything seems okay. Your blood work, the scan, the weight, the pregnancy is progressing well. You're showing a lot, aren't you? Thinking of telling people now?'

They nodded.

'Have fun,' he said. 'You will miss this time. Your mobility will be restricted once you get to your sixth, seventh month. Though we recommend activity till the day before the delivery date, women find it tough. Another thing: your mother-in-law and your aunts will keep telling you to eat for three. Don't do that. Just take care of your nutrition, okay? Don't overeat. I will see you in a couple of weeks?'

They were beaming when they left the hospital. They still didn't want to tell anyone. It wasn't about jinxing it any more. The last three months, they had spent as much time as it was possible together and it had become an intensely private affair.

Deb, for one, didn't want to share this with others. His strongest claim apart from the fact that it was his genetic material was that only he knew the twins apart from his wife who carried them. He didn't want to lose that sense. He didn't want people to guess what the sexes were, he didn't want people calling out the name of the twins, he didn't want people thinking of things to buy them, he didn't want anyone of think of them as their nephew or their niece—he wanted them all for himself.

If it was possible he would create a universe for the four of them and never emerge from that.

39

Shrey couldn't remember the last time he had got this drunk. His head spun like a hurricane and he spent a good hour after coming home vomiting his guts out. However, unlike others he was determined not to promise himself that he wouldn't drink again. Whether he would be this happy when he drank was another question.

Shrey had anticipated things this far and that's why he had started drinking before he'd got to their house. Due to the nature of what was going to happen, he was not sure about the presence of alcohol at the event.

He was the first one there, the first one to know, the first one to see Avantika's distended stomach in all its pregnant glory. The lies became clear all too soon. Avantika hadn't failed IVF, and she hadn't buried herself in an investment deal that wasn't going through. She was pregnant. She had been pregnant all this while. Three months. *I knew it! I knew it!*

'I didn't think you were capable of that sinister lie. A miscarriage? Really? Also, that doesn't look normal for three months,' said Shrey, pointing to her stomach.

'There are two of them,' said Deb, shyly. Shrey felt like Deb would curl into a ball. It was cute. The way Deb mouthed those words. *Deb would be a* father. *This was insane. That* boy *who had no sense was going to be a father! What was this world coming to? Will we have to deal with a fit Deb and a fat Avantika?*

'I have no idea how you guys are doing this,' Shrey said once Vernita reached and screamed her head off when she was told about Avantika being pregnant with twins. Tanmay had broken down. Avantika had taken Tanmay to the room and through the ajar door, Shrey had seen them have a poignant sibling moment.

'HE'S SUCH A FUCKING LIAR! YOU DIDN'T EVEN FLINCH WHILE LYING OVER AND OVER AGAIN,' shouted Vernita once Avantika and Tanmay left the room.

'I'm not sure that's what we should be talking about. Deb, do you realize what you have done? Two kids. Not one, but two! Vernita's struggling with one.'

'I'm not sure this is the right time to be talking about it,' said Vernita.

'I'm sure it is. This is exactly the time we should be talking about this. We need to look for solutions now. You know what I mean? To tide this. The kids deserve good parents and we both know Deb's only half a man,' said Shrey.

'Excuse me?' asked Vernita.

'Too soon? What? I can crack the joke now! His sperms were working, only the conduit was a little fucked up. See, the point is, the kids need people who can take care of them and to that I might have a solution,' said Shrey.

Deb, who had been too caught up in the happiness, finally spoke, 'And what might that be?'

'Don't tell me none of you see it?' said Shrey.

Vernita rolled her eyes and said, 'Can you say it and get over with your joke?'

'It's not a joke. This is my serious face. You seriously don't see it? I'm the solution.'

'What are you talking about?' asked Deb.

'I can see Deb's already struggling with Avantika's nausea and the mood swings. The bags underneath his eyes? Hideous! You don't want our cute boy to look 100 in a few months. What I suggest is simple. I move in with them. It's an elegant solution. No one knows these two better than I do. I work with Deb, which means he no longer has to come to office and we can raise the two kids when Avantika's not here,' he looked at both of them and spoke again, 'I can see by the look on your faces that you're not on board with this and that you think it's a crazy idea.'

'There's no way you're raising anyone,' said Vernita.

'You blew up a lot of money on IVF, didn't you? I will pay rent. In cash. You need it,' said Shrey to Deb. 'My bags are packed and I can come in tomorrow. You know I make the best chicken in the world. You need the protein.'

That much was true. He did make the best chicken in the world. He learned it mostly to piss of his fanatically vegetarian family. He would make it every weekend and send it to his house to screw with his mother. He had seen her in the past wash herself vigorously and not eat anything even if she accidentally touched eggs.

'That's not a bad idea. The logistics at least are in place,' said Deb.

'See? He knows I'm right!' said Shrey and lit up.

'It just seems that you should do this alone, Deb, and not drag him into it,' said Vernita.

When Avantika and Tanmay emerged from the room, holding hands, having cried a little and now smiling, Vernita complained to them about what seemed to her a diabolical plan. However, Avantika seemed strangely relaxed. She didn't say anything at that time and everyone thought the plan was junked.

It was only later when everyone except Avantika and Vernita were a little drunk that she spoke. 'That's not bad. It will take some pressure off Deb,' said Avantika.

'Are you out of your mind? Tanmay, can you knock some sense into her?' said Vernita.

'She must have her reasons,' said Tanmay.

'That I'm awesome, that's the reason, that I'm up to it, that's the reason!' said Shrey.

'That's debatable,' said Deb.

'There's nothing he can possible gain out of this. He has seen you struggle at this, Vernita. Shrey never volunteers for something that's thankless and if he wants to do this it means he's up to it. I'm not stupid enough to turn down his offer. It could be the best decision or the worst decision we have ever taken in our lives. Maybe we will have to just try it out,' said Avantika and then looked at Shrey. 'If you screw up, the littlest of mistakes, I will rip your throat out and eat it. You have no idea how hungry and cranky I am these days.'

Shrey raised his glass and drank to that. Once, twice, thrice, and then forgot how many he drank. He knew it was going to be the last time in months he could drink that much. Not that it would matter if he drank and didn't come home for a day or two. But it was how he wanted to commit to it. Avantika put it rightly; he wanted to do this. If life had taught him anything, it was that you must make your family. He didn't know if he would fall in love enough to actually marry, have a bunch of kids of his own, but he knew Deb's kids were the closest he would get to having his own children. He felt responsible for the children already. They would be little Debs and he loved Deb, and he could already feel him and the kids being great friends. He would accept no other future. These children—at least one of them—was his now. That was the way it was going to be.

He called Avantika and Deb after three tall glasses of lime water he had at home later that night.

'We could have been sleeping,' said Avantika.

'Had you been, you wouldn't have been online on WhatsApp and Instagram ten minutes ago.'

'Why are you calling, Shrey?' asked Deb.

'I'm coming tomorrow morning. If the hangover stays, maybe afternoon. My bags are packed,' said Shrey.

'See you tomorrow,' said Avantika. 'I hope you don't screw up.'

'I won't.'

Shrey disconnected the call soon after. Then he daydreamed of the time when their son, Augustya, liked him better than he liked his own parents. He woke up fresh and was at Deb's house before they even woke up. Deb was mildly annoyed and asked him to clear out the guest bedroom and make space for himself. It wasn't as much a guest bedroom as a servant's quarter. There was the other guest bedroom where Deb's parents lived when they came to visit but it was a bit much for Shrey. And he knew Deb's parents would land up sooner or later then he would be asked to shift to this one. He didn't want to get used to the bigger room.

The next day he didn't get up early and make breakfast, he didn't want to set expectations he wasn't going to follow up on.

Instead he fixed his two routers that he had got along which meant every corner of the room had high-speed Internet. He also cleaned the AC filter which meant no one would have to wonder why an AC he had purchased recently was performing so badly.

When they woke up, the usage of bathroom, the cold water of the fridge, the comfortable temperature of the thermostat automatically adapted to three people. The three of them ate breakfast in silence, looking into their phones, and then watched the fourth season of *Vampire Diaries* together.

It seemed like they were back in college, that nothing had changed, and it was a hostel mess and they'd always lived together. That evening it was Shrey and Avantika who went out for a walk and Deb slept soundly.

By the time night fell, Shrey made them feel like he was never not there.

40

All through the past week, the men in her office had assured her that her position would be safe in office and that she would be back before anyone knew it; that missing a year in one's career was a minor blip. The women though toed a different line. They didn't say anything out loud. But they looked at her with pity. They shook their head and she could almost hear them say, 'She could have gone only so far.'

It was an echo and Avantika couldn't bring herself to push it out of her head. She felt selfish about not being thankful enough for the lives she carried in her womb. There were still a few months to go before she would be called a mother and yet she already felt like a bad one. She felt undeserving for it crushed her heart to lock up her things and leave her desk. She wouldn't be back the next day, or the day after that. She had thought she would be happy about the sacrifice she was making, a sort of a bittersweet thing. But in the cab back home, she could only taste the bitterness and the resentment in her mouth. She wondered if Deb would see past her artifice of happiness and sense her disappointment.

Unwittingly, she had started to form her arguments.

'You wouldn't know, Deb, you wouldn't know. This is for me to carry. The babies are in my body and this body and this mind and what this mind can achieve will suffer.'

She knew her anger was misplaced. She knew if she would have asked Deb if he would bear the child for nine months or twelve or preferably longer, Deb would enjoy being pregnant. Just lying around, bored and sick and having people to fuss over him. He would have enjoyed it immensely.

She got dropped off outside Vernita's office. She felt bad for having to get her out of her office.

'I'm so sorry,' said Avantika as Vernita ushered her into her cabin.

'Don't worry about it. I'm easing into work anyway and with you dressed like that, it would be more like a work meeting,' said Vernita.

'It's either losing the weight or getting an entire new wardrobe,' said Vernita. 'Do you know how much it costs to educate a baby? My college has increased its fees by six times since I left. Figure that! Plus I love my old clothes!' Then she looked at Vernita's face, 'So? So? How are you feeling? Hey? Do people with twins get twice as sick?'

'I don't want to leave my job. This . . . these twelve months will undo whatever I have achieved. The banking industry doesn't take kindly to pregnant women and mothers.'

Vernita frowned. 'Did you come all the way to throw shade at my job? Have you tried selling mouthwash in Benaras?'

'You know what I mean, Vernita. I'm sure it's difficult.'

'No, it's not, Avantika. You just have to shout the loudest, take the most room space and flail your arms around, and smile the hardest and lie shamelessly when shouted at. Turns out I do that well. It's none of the hoodwinking, life-destroying, economy-crumbling mumbo-jumbo you do at your office.'

'I can't say if you're being sarcastic right now.'

'I'm not. I know what you're feeling and there's no way it's not going to be tough for you out there. It's going to be horrible when you get back to work. You see all my colleagues out there?'

Avantika turned around and watched the young men and women scuttle around with laptops in their hands, tapping furiously at their phones.

Vernita continued, 'At least half of them would have betted on me not coming back. A fairly large percentage still thinks I won't be able to take the pressure and will go running back home to take my child into my arms. And let me confess, it's not something I haven't thought about.'

'Why don't you do it, then?'

Vernita sighed. 'The baby's annoying most of the time. He cries and cries and cries. But there are moments that he smiles and makes it all worth it. Throws everything we learned in economics and return on investment out of the window. But then again there are moments like that, here in the office, which make me feel the same. It would be unfair on me, on Tanmay and the baby, if I just relegate myself to being a mother. It's unacceptable to me.'

'And you don't feel selfish when he cries alone and you're here laughing with your colleagues? Out on a business lunch which maybe could have been avoided?' asked Avantika.

'Avantika. You don't have to feel guilty. It's all right. That's what I keep telling myself every day. I feel lucky to be a woman, to have made an entire human and birthed it. Tanmay or Deb will never have that. They will never have the dependency, the selfless love of a baby. Why do you want to rack yourself with guilt and spoil it all? So if you don't want to feel selfish about leaving work or going back to it when it's time, think of it as time-off!' she said and held Avantika's hand. 'Moreover, I'm sure you will kick ass when you go back to work.'

Just then, Vernita's phone rang.

'Hey? I got to go and shout at some people and get shouted at.'

'Of course. See you later.'

On the cab back home, Avantika felt a lot better. She was allowed to feel the potential loss of the job and feel sad about it without the guilt.

She wanted to take off her heels, order a huge lunch— preferably biryani—and get into her own bed as soon as she got home. She flicked through Zomato and changed her mind a dozen times.

41

After the nineteenth-week scan, Shrey and Deb peered at the 3-D sonographic image they had been given. They had paid extra for a more in-depth scan. At a coffee shop nearby, they kept comparing the ultrasound image with others uploaded on the baby sites. But there was no way of telling the sex of the babies.

'It all looks the same,' said Shrey.

'Maybe we should give up, they are not doctors for nothing,' said Deb.

'We need to know,' said Avantika and looked at Shrey who nodded back at her like a righteous *senapati*.

'This is childish to be honest,' said Deb but Shrey had already gotten up and left.

During lunch, Shrey had taken the image of the ultrasound to a few doctors he knew. He was surprised by how upright they were! They chased him away and threatened to call the police on him.

'Assholes, every one of them. If only they knew how hard we would celebrate if it's a girl,' Shrey groused.

Despite their failed attempts to find out the sexes of the children, they were quite certain in their belief that there were one girl and one boy. Nayra and Augustya, they were sure of it. All this running around was only supposed to confirm this belief. For Avantika, she wanted to know if her imagined future with Nayra were real; and for Shrey it was with Augustya.

'You know what we should do? We should take a vacation. To Dubai, or say, Bali? Close by, nothing too far. We can know the sexes then, no?' suggested Shrey. 'As the doctor said, it will be our babymoon.'

Avantika interrupted him, 'First, it can't be *our* babymoon if you're included in it. And second, we can't go without asking Deb's parents and you know they are already a little angry at us.'

'They are not angry. You're overthinking this,' argued Deb.

'Of course they are, Deb. And what was the need for you to tell them that we don't need them yet?' complained Avantika.

Deb's parents had not taken this lightly. As Avantika was telling Maa of the pregnancy, Deb's father was booking his and his wife's tickets to Delhi. By the time the call ended, they had tickets to Delhi on their phone. Slowly and steadily, Deb told them they weren't needed as of now. His parents—who had always been wary of intruding into their son's life—had stepped back and decided to wait for Deb and Avantika to call them on their own.

'BECAUSE YOU TOLD ME TO TELL THEM WE DON'T NEED THEM!'

'I told you. I didn't tell you to tell them. And I told you that it would be a waste of time since I'm fine right now and I can do all the things on my own. If Maa comes she will insist that I rest and I will blow up like a hot air balloon. That's what I said! You made me sound like a villain, that I didn't want them to come,' she said.

'There you go again,' said Shrey.

'Maa doesn't think of you as a villain. If anything she likes you more than she likes me.'

'WHY DOESN'T SHE CALL ME AS OFTEN AS SHE USED TO!' said Avantika.

'Because she then feels like coming. Ask Shrey how many times she calls him to ask about you! Ask?' said Deb.

'I don't want to sound creepy,' said Shrey, 'but it's become very awkward at dates when your mom calls me incessantly and it keeps flashing "Deb's mom calling". It's weird for the person sitting with me.'

'See? She likes you more than she likes me!'

'What will I do with liking? I want her to love me more than she loves you.'

'Of course she loves you,' said Deb. 'When did she ask last how was I doing? It's just you and the babies, just you and the babies. It feels like this is all she had been waiting for. For you to get pregnant and her real nature to burst out of her—the suffocatingly loving grandmother who spoils the daughter-in-law and the kids silly. Like I was just a means to that end. Nonsense,' said Deb, who had been feeling rather ignored by his mother.

'But anyway, the point is we can't tell them we are leaving the country just to do sex-determination. They will flip out and never talk to me,' said Avantika. 'Anyway, she thinks I should have left the job a month earlier.'

'You're overthinking this,' said Deb. 'I can call them tomorrow if you want me to.'

'No, don't. She will think we are just calling her because we think she's angry. Just don't do anything,' said Avantika.

'Frankly, with me around, you don't need anyone else, do you?' asked Shrey.

'You're a liability, Shrey,' said Avantika.

'Choose your words wisely or I will leave,' Shrey countered.

'You say that every day and yet every day you are on the couch watching television,' said Deb.

'Well I would leave but I don't trust Augustya with you guys. You're gender-discrimination pricks and I want my nephew to get all what he deserves. And c'mon, you guys would have been bored without me. You can't deny that.'

They couldn't, and they wouldn't have it any other way. Yet every evening they went through the same charade. Avantika would complain she was too zapped to do anything, Deb would try the best of his words to comfort her and Shrey would give them options to go out and do new things. Sometimes it was the bowling alley before it shut down for good, at other times it was a restaurant tucked in the farthest corner of Delhi; it was something new every day, something they wouldn't have done on their own. An hour of cajoling from Shrey would convince them and they would come back home satisfied. The next evening, the same thing would repeat again. He had even made them start learning Spanish with him. Of course, Shrey regretted that since Deb and Avantika would try out Spanish phrases on each other through the night and would be better in the next class. But now that he had been living with them, they couldn't imagine doing it without him. It was like Shrey had decanted the parts that made him annoying and thrown that away. Now the only parts that were left were the eccentric but nice-boy parts. Avantika saw why Deb had stuck around with him for so long. It seemed like what everyone said about Deb was true. He fed off good people, that was his thing. He trusted his life and handed it over to people who he could count on and in return loved them with all his heart. That's not a bad way to live a life.

Every morning, Avantika would wake up to Deb and his best friend fussing over her, fighting with each other about what she wanted, and she felt . . . *special*. In the classes for pregnant women that she used to frequent to pass the time, she would find women talking about how the process is easier with their mothers around and she would feel a hole open up inside her. But she would leave the hospital and find these two boys—and they were boys, not men, and she liked it that way—waiting for her. It was as if she had another brother in Shrey.

On other days, she would take the piss out of other women by bringing both these boys along to classes where it was mandatory to bring a husband. Deb, Shrey and Avantika would pretend they were in a polyamorous relationship and they had no idea whose children she carried. After a few times, Dr Sharma put a stop to it, telling them that it was hurting his business.

'And stop enjoying this pregnancy so much, Avantika. The other women don't appreciate it. Can you at least act that it's hard on you?' said Dr Sharma. 'And you, Shrey, is it? As if it wasn't enough for me to deal with Deb, now you have also walked into my life. Who are you, again?'

'He's Deb's best friend,' said Avantika. 'And an okay friend of mine.'

'An okay friend? I can live with that,' said Shrey and smiled at her.

But it wasn't so much the running around, the show of affection, the nights Shrey stayed up for Avantika that mattered as much as what she had stumbled upon on Shrey's laptop. She had snooped to find out more about what had happened to their old publishing venture—Deb hadn't shared much with her and had deleted every trace of the company that ever existed when they folded up, and never discussed with her why it didn't work—and instead had stumbled on Google searches he had made. In the past couple of months, he had saved a couple of lakhs and bought government bonds and investments that didn't mature until twenty years later. It was odd because Shrey was one of the first bad influences in Deb's life—the one who had convinced Deb that all money should be spent. The name of the nominee in all those investments was Augustya Roy Sharma. Of course, Avantika knew none of these would be valid but the thought was what mattered for her. When she talked to Deb about it, he brushed it away as if it was something quite expected from Shrey.

She didn't mention it to Shrey.

42

'This is all nonsense,' said an exasperated Deb, his hand travelling all over Avantika's stomach.

'Let me try,' protested Shrey.

'Like hell you will! There's no way you're feeling the babies kick before me,' said Deb and turned to Avantika. 'Are you sure you didn't imagine it? You know, influenced by all the movies Shrey made you see?'

Avantika shot him a murderous look.

'You need to be patient. Just keep your hand there and wait. Maybe the babies are getting scared by your touch,' said Avantika.

'What nonsense! Why would they be scared of me? Do the babies know I let doctors take a knife to me for them to be born? Bloody ungrateful foetuses,' said Deb.

'Language,' said Avantika.

'Let me try, I will be patient,' said Shrey.

'Not before him. He's got to feel it,' said Avantika.

'You guys are making it a bigger deal than it is, let me check instead,' said Shrey. 'And don't worry I will only feel Augustya's kick. I don't care about the girl really.'

'NOW!' shouted Avantika.

Deb shot his hand out and kept it where Avantika's hand was.

'THERE IS NOTHING!' he complained.

'Why can't you feel it?' said Avantika.

To Deb, the words seemed like an allegation. Like he wasn't trying hard enough as a father. Scared? That only conjured up images of two little children cowering away from him—a belligerent, violent father.

'Seems like you're getting two mama's children,' said Shrey and only made it worse.

For the rest of the day, Avantika called out to Deb numerous times to feel the kicks. Deb was always too slow, or too fast and missed them. As night fell, Avantika stopped calling Deb.

'Maybe it's too soft to be felt outside the womb,' said Avantika, on their late night stroll.

'OR MAYBE DEB IS A LOSER!' Shrey shouted, a few steps ahead of them.

They never strayed too far from the house after an incident which all three of them had vowed they wouldn't talk about or even refer to again. They'd named that situation *Code Kilimanjaro*. Back during the days when Deb and Avantika had scaled Kilimanjaro mountain, there were a lot of times they had to go poop behind the rocks with nothing but a tissue roll in hand, hoping no one else would choose that exact spot. The first day was tough, shameful even, but later it became a part of the routine. Sometimes they would run out of toilet paper and they would end up using leaves. It had become their second nature. It did take the sexiness out of the trip. But when they came down from the mountain and used a real toilet after so long, it felt charmless to shit without the birds squeaking and that little mist hiding them from other hikers.

Something akin to that had happened on the street Shrey, Deb and Avantika used to walk on during their midnight strolls. This road would be largely deserted. Twice before that day, Avantika had buckled in the middle of the street wanting to go to the bathroom. They had been lucky to find autos. But that fateful day, there were no autos. Time was running out. Avantika had started to sweat like a pig.

'I NEED TO GO! I NEED TO GO! I'M DYING HERE!' she shouted.

She really needed to go.

'I'M BOOKING AN OLA!' shouted Shrey.

'THERE'S NO TIME!' said Avantika.

'WE WILL MAKE IT!' shouted Deb.

'I WON'T!'

'YOU HAVE TO! YOU CAN'T GIVE UP NOW!' screamed Deb.

'I CAN'T DO THIS!'

'YOU ARE STRONG! BELIEVE IN YOURSELF! YOU CAN!'

'ETA FIVE MINUTES! JUST WAIT FOR FIVE MINUTES AND WE WILL BE CLEAR! YOU CAN DO IT! FEMINISM!' shouted Shrey.

'I CAN'T! FORGIVE ME!' said Avantika.

Deb and Shrey looked the other way. Avantika hobbled over the footpath, crossed the road and found a spot. An awkwardness descended on Shrey and Deb.

Shrey said to break the silence. 'When I was younger, I didn't think pretty girls went to the bathroom. Like why would they do the same nasty thing we do? Sit like us? And then wash? Chee.'

None of them spoke that day on the way back to their house.

Since then, they always took a roll of toilet paper roll with them and never strayed too far.

'Should we go back? I feel winded,' said Avantika walking alongside Deb.

'Sure,' he said.

It wasn't lost on Avantika why Deb was quiet during most of the walk. In her defence, it was annoying her to not be able to share this moment with him. The kicks were strong and frequent, and he was taking his hand away too quickly, and bringing it in too fast. They slept without talking to each other about it.

Like every night, she woke up dozens of times to go to the washroom. And every time she would come back, she felt Deb's hand brushing against her stomach. She knew soon enough what Deb was doing and felt bad about the way she did about it. After the surgery, this would be his first interaction with the babies, unlike her who had been carrying them for weeks now.

She caught him doing it and asked, 'Did you feel it?'

'I did. Quite a few times,' Deb said, his voice a low, tense whisper.

'Then why is your hand still on me?' asked Avantika.

'Because it feels too real, too intense. It finally feels real. They are not images on the screen any more. They are not just a bloated stomach. They are . . . are children. They are making decisions, Avantika, like okay, now I'm going to kick my mother, now I'm going to make her go pee. Nayra and Augustya are somersaulting inside of you. Who knows why they are doing that? They must be feeling something, no? Happy, sad? Hungry? Restless? Sleepy? Do you feel that? They have things they can feel now. They are real. They can feel us feeling them, I'm sure of it, and I want to be there telling them that I'm here. Maybe they will kick me and say, no, enough of touching, Baba, now go away, and I will say no, I will be here, I will tell them that.'

Deb calling himself a *baba* of someone gave Avantika goose pimples, that little boy she loved would be a father. And she . . . she would be a mumma, two little kids calling her *Mumma*. *Uff*.

'And how will you tell them that?' asked Avantika, amused.

'By tapping Morse code on your stomach. They are your children. I'm sure they are intelligent.'

Avantika shifted close to Deb and made his hand rest on her stomach for the rest of the night. Nayra and Augustya kept making their presence felt. And by the time it was morning, Deb's hand felt like a punching bag for his two babies.

'Of course I can do that,' said Deb trying to convince Avantika that he could differentiate between the babies. 'The quicker punches are from our daughter, I'm sure of it. The more contact is Augustya.'

'As long as both are fighters I'm fine with anything,' said Avantika, finally conceding.

43

It was Deb who cried first. Shrey wanted to put his arm around him, say something to alleviate the situation. He was too scared he would end up crying himself if he tried doing that. And who were they to cry when it was Avantika in there?

Avantika was in the hospital room and a bunch of doctors, led by Dr Sharma, was attending to her. Avantika had held up better than Deb and Shrey on their way there despite the bloodied towel between her legs and worst-case scenarios ricocheting in her head.

'It could be nothing,' the nurse in the ambulance had said. 'Most times it's nothing.'

Avantika had held on to it. She kept repeating it. *It could be nothing, it could be nothing.*

The bleeding was profuse when it started. It was an unnatural amount of blood. Avantika had screamed when she had woken up from her afternoon nap and found blood streaking down her thighs. Shrey and Deb had rushed from the living room and had panicked when they saw her. They drew a blank. They stood there, frozen, trying to not think but still thinking what they shouldn't.

They are dead.

'Augustya,' whispered Shrey in horror.

Avantika had dialled the number of the hospital. 'HURRY,' she had screamed.

Deb broke out of his daze. He collected towels and rushed to her. Shrey left the room to hide the tears that were damming against his eyes.

'Nothing will happen,' said Deb as he helped Avantika change. 'Has the bleeding stopped? Has it stopped? How do you feel? How do you feel?'

Avantika nodded, her eyes now welling up. The bedsheet was still drenched. Deb tore it off the mattress and threw it in the corner of the room so that they didn't look at it and give the thought more power. The mattress was soaked in blood too.

'Come outside,' he said and helped Avantika. 'Is it hurting? Nothing will happen. Trust me, nothing will happen. It's fine.

We have read about this. Sometimes . . . it's just . . . bleeding, nothing more.'

Outside, the three of them sat holding their breaths. Every few seconds they would look at the clock. Deb called the hospital thrice to ask where the ambulance had reached. Their eyes would flit to Avantika's stomach? Were they still there? Avantika kept her hand lightly on it to feel kicks, anything. *She would have said if there was anything*, Deb thought. He kept staring at the phone. *Will the ambulance call when they are here? Where the fuck are they? Was there traffic? Why the hell aren't they here yet?* It was when he called them for the fourth time that he heard the siren right outside their building.

Two nurses helped Avantika into the back of the van.

'You can walk, good, that's very good,' said the ward boy.

Shrey sat in the front and Deb climbed in the back.

'What could it be?' Avantika kept asking the nurse.

The bleeding started again. It wasn't as profuse but it was there. It was blood from their children—Nayra and Augustya. How badly Avantika wanted it to be hers not theirs! What did they do to deserve this?

Shrey Googled from the front seat and kept switching tabs every time he read something bad.

'They are fine,' said Deb to Avantika. 'They're fighters, remember? Maybe they kicked too hard and you couldn't take it?'

Avantika smiled unwillingly.

'We have plans, Avantika. We have plans for them and for us. They have to make our lives miserable. So they are still there, doing exactly that, making plans of their own. How they will bang their heads into places they shouldn't, make their diapers leak, intentionally have bad handwriting, throw ink at the teacher, date boys and girls they shouldn't, not listen to our career advice, lock us out of their lives? You know, we talked about this. They are still there, I'm sure of it,' said Deb.

The nurse and ward boy exchanged apologetic smiles. When they reached the hospital, Avantika wanted to jump off, run inside, grab the doctors and demand an explanation. The nurses helped her on to the wheelchair and paged ahead for the doctors.

'You have to wait outside,' Dr Sharma told Deb and Shrey as they wheeled her into the emergency room.

'It's going to be okay,' said Avantika to Deb as she left his hand. 'It's still going to be four of us.'

'Five of us,' said Shrey.

Avantika smiled and for a moment everything felt like it was okay.

'He's going to be fine,' said Shrey to himself. 'He's going to be fine.'

'So is she. Both the girls,' corrected Deb.

'They are going to be fine. Who knows what goes on inside the body, right? It's going to be okay. I know it's going to be okay,' said Shrey. 'See, I pulled some Google results why it could have happened.'

'I don't want to read anything right now,' said Deb and pushed the phone away from him.

They waited outside. It wouldn't have been twenty minutes, but it felt like they had been there for days.

Deb tried to think good thoughts. He forced himself to imagine a future where Nayra and Augustya were two problem children, driving Deb and Avantika to madness, or worse still, Nayra and Augustya were both boys, horrible boys who made Avantika and Deb regret that they had had children in the first place. And yet, he could only think of a future where they were back in the infertility clinic, ten years down the line, trying again for a child. He imagined them as middle-aged people who had been broken by the premature deaths of the twins they were supposed to have. He got up and paced around, to drive those thoughts out, but they clung to him.

'They are going to be okay . . . they are going to be okay . . .' said Deb and then started chanting what a Buddhist friend of his had once taught him. *'Nam myoho renge kyo.'* Deb didn't believe in it but the simplicity of it had attracted him. *Chant and ask for what you want and you will get it.* It was now a reflex, he couldn't help but chant the words whenever he wanted something. Often it didn't work but it gave him hope. And so he chanted. He put in everything within him behind it.

Shrey started mouthing it as well.

'Nam myoho renge kyo, nam myoho renge kyo,' they both muttered under their breaths.

Deb felt his head grow light, and just when he thought he would pass out, he saw her. Dressed in a faded hospital gown, she was in the wheelchair, talking to Dr Sharma. She was smiling. Deb stopped chanting. He ran up to them.

Dr Sharma said to Deb, 'We wanted her to be in a stretcher but she said you will freak out. Come, let's walk to the ward and I will update you on what happened.'

Shrey joined them.

Dr Sharma started speaking and his words were like the annoying buzz of a housefly. Deb got only snatches of what the doctor said. He told them something about something being wrong with the placenta and that they would be keeping her under observation and the worse-case scenario after they ran some tests was that she would require a lot of bed rest.

Later that evening, the scan and test results came out. They were testing for a condition known as placenta praevia and it was negative. There was nothing to worry about, Dr Sharma told them later. It was a one-off incident and changed nothing. He told them he would like Avantika to be in the hospital for a couple of more days to keep an eye on her. Shrey went home and got a change of clothes and toothbrushes for both of them. When he came back, Deb wondered if Shrey had taken the time-out to do some light, relief-fuelled crying.

The two days in the hospital went without incident. They spent their time playing Uno and Scrabble. They had a lot of questions about the incident and the nurses and the doctor kept assuring them that twin pregnancies were always trickier and more complex but there was nothing to worry about.

'The time around the twenty-fifth week is the most sensitive for twin pregnancies,' said the doctor.

'Is the boy okay?' asked Shrey.

'I'm not falling for that,' quipped the doctor.

'And the girl?' asked Avantika.

'Stop trying,' said the doctor and laughed.

Their restlessness was only put to rest when they made friends with other women with twins—in the maternity ward and on online forums—who had had bleeding incidents. Some had been diagnosed with placenta praevia and they had done just fine despite that.

Shrey, who had been making profiles on all the forums of baby websites—first to ask and later to answer questions—had grown to be quite popular. His research on twin pregnancies was reaping him benefits. He started getting friend and follow requests from new mothers.

'I think I'm in love with a few of them. Though I think it's a little odd trying to hit on a new mother. I'm hoping some of them are single,' said Shrey.

'I hope you don't find anyone. Augustya will be quite pissed to have your attention diverted,' said Avantika.

'That's not going to happen. I'm going to close my account down right away,' said Shrey.

None of them said anything about what they were thinking when they saw her bleed, or in those tense moments in the ambulance, or that time the doctors were running scans on her. They didn't talk about how indelibly their lives would have changed had something gone wrong. The realization lay heavy on all their hearts. Fear had made its home in them and the permanence of that fear was terrifying.

While Avantika signed her discharge forms, she said, 'We will never be the same without them, will we?'

Deb shook his head and said, 'Now I know why my parents always look so scared. I can see it now. The deep-set lines of dread. We will need to stock up on anti-wrinkle creams. Being a parent is about being worried all the time. I get that now.'

'Maa called again, asked whether we were still in the resort. I lied again. They asked me what Shrey was doing there. I don't think they suspect anything,' said Avantika.

'Did Tanmay call?' he asked.

'Lied to them as well. There's no need to make a big deal out of this.'

Avantika came back home to see the old bedsheet and mattress gone, thrown away and replaced by Shrey. It was like the bleeding incident never happened.

44

Standing in front of the hideous seven-seater Innova, Deb saw Tanmay's face and felt sorry for him while he kept overcompensating to his sister to make up for his relationship with his parents.

'You didn't have to sell it for me! You loved that car,' Avantika protested.

'All of us wouldn't have fitted in a Fortuner,' said Tanmay who everyone knew was practically married to that car. It was the first car he had bought, fully loaded, way more expensive than it should have been, and he was still paying off its loan. He said, 'This has enough space for us. Three car seats for the children and four of us.'

'Five of us,' Shrey corrected.

'Five, yes,' said Tanmay.

'I call shotgun for all of eternity,' said Shrey.

'Fuck off,' said Vernita. 'For the record, I love this car so much more than the last one. That guzzled petrol like crazy. This one is much better.'

'You didn't need to do it,' repeated Avantika.

'Oh please, shut up. Now start the car. We have been waiting!' said Vernita.

'Why should I do it?' asked Avantika.

'Just do it. They will not rest till the time you do,' said Deb, a little envious of what Tanmay could buy for Avantika and he couldn't.

'Fine,' said Avantika. 'Hop on.'

Shrey ran and took the passenger seat. The rest of the three crammed in the back seat. Ivan slept in Vernita's lap. Avantika pushed the key and turned on the ignition. The car came to life. It was way more silent than Deb had expected it to be.

Avantika drove around in circles taking in the feel of the car. She said, 'It's not as bad as I thought it to be. Pretty good, I would say.'

'He bought the top model,' said Vernita.

'Show off,' said Shrey. 'Love it. So nice. The kids are going to love it when they are little and then hate it when they grow up. They are going to ask us to park it away from their school entrance.'

'We will buy a better car by then,' said Deb.

They drove the car to a famous biryani restaurant because that's all Avantika wanted to eat and they all ate like everyone was pregnant with twins.

'Drive it home,' said Tanmay when they reached Tanmay's house. 'We don't need it right now. Give it to me once you deliver.'

'We don't need it, Bhaiya,' said Avantika.

'You do. Just keep it. Not listening to any arguments. Vernita will drive her own car and this will rot at home. You need it more than I do,' said Tanmay.

'We will keep it,' said Shrey. 'Thank you very much.'

And that was that. On their way back home in their newly gifted car, Shrey got off at the supermarket to get a few things for the house and asked them to carry on home. 'See you in a couple,' said Shrey.

Avantika connected her phone to the Bluetooth of the car and put on her playlist.

'He got the speakers changed too,' said Deb.

'Do you remember this song?' asked Avantika.

It was the song from the Abhishek Bacchan–Aishawrya Rai starrer *Guru*, 'Ai Hairathe'. It used to be their song when they started dating. They would listen to it on loop for hours on end. Unlike the other songs which they listened to repeatedly they never tired of this song. They would hear the song at least once on every date despite it not being that kind of song; they had made love to it countless times.

'We were such animals then, no?' said Avantika.

'You couldn't keep your hands off me,' said Deb.

'Yeah, right. It was all me. You never wanted to do it, yes?' chuckled Avantika.

More than once they had been caught by Delhi police constables, making out in deserted places, behind filmed windows. They had seen those deserted places being slowly populated in the last ten years. Lights. Buildings. Malls. Where would a horny couple go in Delhi?

'Delhi isn't deserted any more,' said Deb.

'Maybe we don't look hard enough,' answered Avantika.

That much was true. Times had changed, and they had come quite far from making out in cars. When you don't have a place to make out, you crave for one, and when you do, you crave the thrill of kissing at random places and the possibility of being caught.

'You had to take a left,' said Avantika.

'I know. I'm looking to see whether a part of Delhi is still deserted,' said Deb and winked at Avantika.

Avantika's heart leapt a little. It was surprising to her that after all these years, Deb and his restless touch could still jumpstart her like that. She felt nervous, excited. The past year had been hard for them. First came the mechanistic sex to reproduce, then the anger at their failure to conceive and the disappointment that they couldn't procreate like others, and then the pregnancy. Ever since they got pregnant—despite the doctors telling them it was okay to be sexually active—they had kept their hands off each other. So now when Deb turned into the parking lot of the half-constructed and deserted shopping mall, she felt tingly all over.

Deb parked the car and pulled the handbrake. He turned to her and said, 'That we are doing it in your brother's new car only makes it better. Years later I am going to tell him. I can imagine what his face—'

'Shut up,' she said and pulled his face close.

And just like that they started kissing with the practiced efficiency of a married couple, and the unbridled passion of two drunk teenagers making out for the first time. They surprised themselves with how hard they bit, how deeply they sucked at each other's lips and throats. They didn't remember the last time their kissing had lasted this long. They were out of breath and incredibly turned on when they separated.

Avantika reached out for the lever of Deb's seat and pulled it till the seat was pushed back all the way.

'Love the car,' she said.

'Only the best,' said Deb.

She then reached out for Deb's belt buckle and undid it lightning fast.

'Still got your touch,' said Deb.

'Shut up,' said Avantika and kissed him.

Her hand reached down and she grabbed him. He had grown in his pants.

'You're bigger than I remember,' whispered Avantika in Deb's ears.

'Took the cock enlargement pills they advertise on porn sites,' joked Deb, biting her ear.

'Let me give you something so you don't have to look at porn again,' she said and took out her phone. Swiftly, she hit the record button and gave it to Deb. 'Record,' she said.

'This is nasty,' said Deb. 'I love it.'

She unzipped Deb's pants and pulled them down in swift motion. She held him and slapped it over her face.

'Whoa, you're watching more porn than I am,' said Deb.

She looked at him and let her tongue slide up from the bottom of his shaft. Deb moaned, and a tiny part of him wondered if it were the feeling of Avantika's tongue against him, or the way she looked at him, the raw lust in her eyes, that gave him more pleasure.

And then, without warning, she took him inside her mouth. He watched himself disappear, slowly and then all at once. The warmth and the wetness enveloped him sending pulses of ecstasy through his body. His back arched, eyes rolled, as if being exorcised. She rolled her tongue against him, and slid it inside and out. Deb felt like he would come any minute and had to jolt himself out of the throes of pleasure to prolong this.

At first he thought it was her, but then the banging noise intensified and he knew what it was. Deb and Avantika both looked up and there was a man banging at the window of their car. In a flash, they both sat up. The constable peered in as Deb helplessly pulled up his jeans and his seat.

'KHOL MADARCHOD,' shouted the constable.

Deb, now dressed, rolled down the window.

'Come outside,' said the constable who had parked his car next to theirs.

Before Deb could get off, Avantika did and walked to the other side. The constable, who had been angry at the outrage of modesty by this horny couple, was now ashamed and confused. His eyes were on Avantika's rather pregnant stomach.

'We are sorry, sir,' said Avantika.

'Madam . . . madam . . . *aise thodi naa hota hai* (this is not done),' said the constable, now shy, finding it hard to keep up the pretence of his righteous self, of being angry at this obscenity and his duty towards pregnant women.

'His parents are the worst, sir. They don't give us time only. So we had to do this,' said Avantika. 'I have twins by the way. Nayra and Augustya.' She looked at her stomach and said. 'Bachha log? Say Hi to police uncle? Say Hi?'

'Madam, but . . .'

'We are sorry, Bhaiya. We will leave right now. It's our fault.'

'Haanji . . . *aisa mat kijiye aage se* (yes, please don't do it again),' said the constable.

Avantika got back in the car.

'Drive,' she told Deb.

Deb put the car in gear and backed out of the parking lot. They watched the confounded constable scratching his head in the rear view mirror of the car.

'Too bad,' she said.

'I have the video. I will finish off later,' said Deb.

'And me?' asked Avantika.

'I know another mall nearby,' said Deb and slipped his spare hand inside her dress.

45

Deb's parents hadn't picked up the phone in days now.

He had been calling them incessantly all the way from the house to the airport. The last time they talked, Deb's mother had told them off badly for not letting them help Avantika all this while, going to all the scans alone, trying to be adults, and now this, this was the last straw.

She had gone as far as to tell them she was not going to talk to them till the time Avantika delivered. The phone was then disconnected, and it was switched off. Since that time, they had stopped picking up Deb's or Avantika's calls. Even Deb's father—who usually was the voice of reason—was not talking to them.

'Do they still require you to take printouts of the visa? Or can you show them on the phone?' asked Deb as the cab stopped at the airport. He was trying to fill the silence with conversation. They hadn't told anyone of the trip—not even Shrey—till the very last minute. They wanted it to be just the two of them.

Moreover, they knew everyone would disapprove and poke holes in their plans. This would be the last time they could do this together. And plus, there was this other thing.

'Showing them on the phone is all right. That's what people said online. Don't worry, Deb.'

'I'm not worrying, I'm not a child.'

Deb picked up the single suitcase both had stuffed their clothes into and walked towards Departures. It would be their first holiday where they decided to travel light and managed to do it.

'We should have gone ahead with my plan. We should have lied, gone underground for a while. You didn't have to tell them the truth,' said Deb. 'I had handled it. I had lied before about the IVF, didn't I?'

'I didn't want to lie. I wanted this to be perfect.'

Of course, she did! After all that they had been through, to reach the point that they could be pregnant, she'd wanted everything post that to be *perfect*. And apart from that one mishap, that trip to the hospital, things had gone well.

True, the past four months had been a lesson in military precision and discipline. She ate on time, carefully measuring and double-checking what she put in her mouth, slept on time, powered through her nausea, read the material people recommended, made notes and bullied doctors to answer all her questions. She trained Shrey and Deb well too. Together they could have written a book or two on the subject by now. Despite this overwhelming, all-consuming pregnancy the number of things they had done in the past few weeks had far surpassed what they'd done in years. There had been way too much work to do the *stupid* things. Like watching three stand-up specials in one-day. Doing a Marvel movie marathon twice. Going to a laughter club and enjoying it.

'They are not okay with this decision and they are titling my decision towards theirs. No one wants us to go. Like, literally no one,' said Deb, echoing the sentiment of his parents, Tanmay, Shrey and everyone who knew what they were doing.

Everyone was strictly against Avantika sitting in an airplane and going to an alien country just to know the gender of the twins. Even Shrey, who had suggested this in the first place a couple of months ago.

'It's a holiday! It's a babymoon! Didn't every pregnancy website suggest this? To take that one last holiday before the babies come? That's what we are doing, nothing else,' lied Avantika for the thousandth time as if saying it would make it true.

'If it's a babymoon, we could have gone to Kerala, no? Kashmir, maybe? Why Dubai?' said Deb.

'Look, if you want to talk about this and spoil it, count me out,' said Avantika.

'Why can't you just accept why you're going there? You can at least say that to me, right? That we are just going there to know the gender of the babies,' said Deb, exasperated.

'Because it's not *just* that! We will get some time together, just the two of us. After this we will always be way too many people in the house. Us, the kids, your parents, my brother and his family . . . And yes, I want to know whether I'm having boys or girls, or as we have always thought—Nayra and Augustya. I really want to know what's inside of me.'

'I understand that but Maa–Baba, they worry,' he said.

'The scans came out all right, didn't they? The doctor has cleared us. Everything is going to be okay.'

'Reading a few books doesn't make you an expert,' said Deb.

'Why don't you say that to the doctor instead?' said Avantika.

Deb rolled his eyes.

'Okay. I get you don't want to go because of Maa–Baba. I won't go if that's what you think we should do. It's not one of those trick questions. I swear on my children I wouldn't feel bad if you decide against it. I leave it up to you. What would you do?' asked Avantika. 'It's not as if I want to go with everyone being upset with me.'

Deb sighed. 'That's true,' he said.

Had she been excited about this trip—had they had sanction—she would have shopped and they wouldn't be travelling with one paltry suitcase. They would have cargoed Avantika's clothes beforehand.

They sat in a restaurant outside the airport. Deb finally spoke, 'Let's not leave like this. Let's call them and put forth our argument.'

And that's what they did. Deb sent his parents a long sentimental message and they answered his call the next time he tried. Deb put everyone on a conference call and Avantika told them why it was important for them to go on this trip. No one was convinced and everyone wanted to jump in and shoot down the idea but Avantika dropped in a sentence that brought an end to the conversation, 'It's important for us for you to be happy for us. We won't go if this makes you unhappy. That's all that matters to Deb and me,' said Avantika.

Deb wondered if it was a sales pitch manipulation or she meant it. Nevertheless, it worked and all of them feebly agreed one by one.

'It's settled then,' said Deb.

They checked in their only suitcase and walked to the security check. That phone call had cost them all the duty free shopping time and their boarding was announced soon after. Every time they announced the zones whose passengers were asked to board, Deb's heart jumped a little. The reluctance had melted away. It had been a long time since they had gone on a trip.

'For someone who didn't want to go in the first place, you're strangely chirpy,' said Avantika.

'Because unlike you, I don't get to leave the country for business trips and such,' argued Deb.

'Oh please, the last time I went on one was a year ago and let me tell you it was not fun at all. They packed us in a hotel like sardines and we slogged harder than usual,' said Avantika.

'I don't believe a single word of that.'

They were the first ones to board in their zone. Deb didn't stop giggling through the boarding, the bad airplane food, the immigration at the Dubai airport and their check-in at the hotel.

'Room service! The only magic I believe in,' squealed Deb and then ordered half the midnight menu.

'You know you have to pay for room service.'

'Wasn't this a vacation? Why are we worrying about the bill then?' he asked.

While Avantika slept soundly on the hotel bed that was five times as thick and soft as the one in their house, Deb stayed up late, ate two club sandwiches, French fries, mutton *roganjosh* in no order or combination, and watched things on television that he would have never otherwise watched. Then he spent a good part of the morning in the bathroom expelling most of what he had eaten the night before.

He got a good sounding off on their way to see the Burj Khalifa soon after. It turned out to be a bad idea. The height made Avantika puke all over the glass wall. Since she was so obviously and heavily pregnant, no one turned up their noses. Instead they all asked if she was fine and if they needed anything.

For the rest of the day, they flitted from one restaurant in Dubai Malls to another. Avantika didn't feel well during the entire time, vomiting thrice.

'At least the washrooms are incredible. If someone has to vomit, they would choose do it here rather than anywhere else in the world,' said Avantika.

'I'm not dying to find out the truth in that,' said Deb.

When she felt better, she shopped like a wild animal that was let loose after years of captivity. It was mostly clothes she wouldn't have fit in even before the pregnancy. She said, 'They will hang like corpses in my cupboard. A scary reminder that if I don't lose the pregnancy weight soon enough I will never fit into those clothes.'

'For an incentive, it's an expensive one,' said Deb.

They turned in earlier than usual that night. The next day's itinerary had a bunch of places—some carried over from the previous day. Despite the minor hiccups of Avantika's feet killing her, an odd bout of vomiting, the day whizzed past. It was a blur of one tourist attraction after another and Dubai never falls short of that. They construct one every year and they execute it to perfection. If it fails to fire a tourist's imagination, they break it and make something new. Dubai's a city where ugliness is intolerable.

Avantika had kept the best of the lot for the last. They had dinner on the top deck of a yacht owned by a prince of Bahrain.

'Where did you find out about this?' asked Deb.

'Groupon, 65 per cent off,' said Avantika. 'And frankly, I didn't know it would be this beautiful. A part of me was thinking this was an elaborate way to kidnap someone. I thought it would be a boat but this . . . this is super *nice*.'

The advert hadn't done justice to the product. The multi-decked yacht was surreal in its opulence. It almost bordered on offensive, that's how luxurious it was. As if a country had been destroyed, stripped apart of its natural resources, including men and women, to pay for this. Even walking on the felt carpet felt like one was soiling it.

There were only five more couples on the beautifully lit-up yacht and they were all newly married and dressed up in what seemed like their finest clothes. Clearly, they knew what they were getting into.

'I feel underdressed for this,' said Deb complaining.

'How would I know it would be better than it looked in the pictures?' asked Avantika. She thrust the pictures in Deb's face. 'Look,' she said. 'Just look, do you think someone would sell such a deal at this low a price! It looked unreal.'

Deb didn't blame Avantika; if the pictures were unreal, too good to be true, the yacht itself looked straight out of the matrix, too perfect. Deb wondered if they had paid the entire fee or they had bought it off Groupon as well.

'Why the fuck did they have to sell it on Groupon?' asked Avantika.

The hostess—who Deb thought was breathtakingly beautiful—was surprised to see Avantika come there, heavily pregnant as she was. She had at first refused to give them the table close to the railing. Avantika—who had been refused quite a lot of things because of her pregnancy—would hear none of it and chose a seat closest to the railing.

'You can call the prince if there's a problem,' said Avantika. 'Also if I need to vomit I would rather do it on the other side of the railing than spoil your floor. It can really raise a stink, I'm telling you.'

The hostess didn't say a word after that.

'We deserve this,' said Avantika confidently to Deb and then added. 'But we also need to make the most of it.'

That meant they had to let the food go cold and click pictures they could send in their WhatsApp group. It was too beautiful to just sit back and enjoy.

'The pictures will let us enjoy it repeatedly, even when our memory fails,' said Avantika.

When they were done, Avantika sent the food back to be reheated. 'I have paid for it,' she said even as Deb wanted to jump off the yacht in embarrassment.

But soon enough, they found three other couples doing the same—having their money's worth. There were shameless looks exchanged between all of them. By the time they finished their meal, the other couples were drunk enough to come to their table and congratulate them for the impending babies. Nayra and Augustya were introduced to them and none of them could pronounce the names.

'You guys are goals.'

They heard this in four different languages, and in different stages of inebriation. Slowly, what should have been a long, romantic dinner with hand-holding and stolen kisses, turned into the couples teaching each other expletives in different languages. Deb learned to say bhenchod in Polish, German, Spanish and Portuguese. Though none of them felt as effective on the tongue as it did in Hindi. When the music came on, the dancing wasn't slow and lovely, it was drunken and for a while everyone danced to Bappi Lahiri songs. They all sang songs they knew, and it turned out even after decades, Backstreet Boys was a unifier. When it was time, they exchanged numbers, knowing they would never call each other. It was a good time and the numbers, and their faces on Facebook suggestions would remind them of this night which was possible only because Avantika had stumbled on a 65 per cent discount coupon on Groupon.

Deb and Avantika went back to the hotel and started to drift off within seconds of putting their heads on the pillows.

'Nervous about tomorrow?' asked Deb, his voice down to a whisper, already halfway to REM sleep.

Avantika had already drifted off by then.

46

Their anxiety and excitement was palpable. Everyone felt it; the guard who opened the door, the receptionist who talked to them, the nurse who asked them to wait, the pregnant women who streamed in and out of the maternity ward, the ward boy who told them that the doctor was ready for them. Wherever they went, eyes turned towards them. All morning they had been playing little games. If Deb managed to throw that crumpled paper into the basket, it would be one girl and one boy, if he failed, it would be two boys. When they weren't getting the answers they wanted, they stretched it—best out of three, best of out seven. The hospital staff kept looking at them and giggling.

Dr Sreedhar came out wiping his hand twenty minutes later. Avantika had researched the best hospitals before they'd come here and bought an insurance plan that could support a few hospital visits. All they needed was one. A quick in and out, as Avantika had put it.

'So? All the way from India, eh?' Dr Sreedhar asked, a bright smile on his tired face. He was in his mid-fifties, and had a kind of face that suited a doctor—rimless spectacles, bright eyes and balding. 'Couldn't wait, could you?'

'Do you get people like us a lot?' asked Avantika, her hands all clammy from the nervousness.

'Unfortunately, yes, I do. A lot of people from north India, Haryana and Punjab, they come to know if they will have a son. Imagine having the money to come here and yet,' said the doctor, the laughter he had greeted them with had slowly died.

He continued in a grave voice, 'What do you say to those people also? When I was young and foolish, I used to sometimes lie to them. Especially to women in an advanced stage of pregnancy. I didn't want the blood on my hands.'

'What happened then?' asked Deb.

'A senior made me stop. He told me it was a lost battle trying to keep the sex from these people. That the girl children I saved would be living substandard, inhuman lives in their families. The girls would pay the price for their doctor's lie, he told me. Worse still, they might kill the children after they were born. So I stopped.'

'That sounds horrible,' said Avantika.

'Why I am telling you this is because I want you to tell me that you're not going to make this into a bad day.'

'Avantika wants girls. Two girls to be honest. What I want is a boy and a girl. We have names down too. Nayra and Augustya. We had a little debate on the latter but now it's settled,' said Deb, the words dribbling out of him nervously.

'But what if you have sons? What will be the names then? Not decided?' asked the doctor, gleefully, the happiness back on his face.

'We have back-up names for a boy but none we are too happy about. We have a lot of time to come up with another name, don't we?' asked Avantika and smiled at the doctor.

'Great, then! Let's do what you're here for! Two sons, two daughters, or a son and a daughter. I feel good about this,' said the doctor. 'Can I see your reports once again?'

Avantika slid her reports in front of the doctor. The doctor studied them for a bit and said, 'Everything seems fine. You went through a bit of a struggle, didn't you? I'm glad both of you persevered.' He rubbed his hands in obvious delight. 'Are you guys ready?'

Deb and Avantika looked at each other, clasped their hands tighter around each other, and nodded.

'We can't wait to know,' said Avantika.

Dr Sreedhar called the nurse and asked her to take Avantika away for the preliminary testing.

'You will have to leave his hand for that,' said Dr Sreedhar.

Before she disappeared behind the curtain, Avantika winked at Deb, and mouthed, *best of luck.*

Deb closed his eyes and said a small prayer for them. He tapped his fingers on the table, nervously thinking what their family pictures would look like—two brats making faces, climbing over them, pulling each other's hair. It would be *perfect.* Two babies.

Dr Sreedhar scrubbed his hands clean, looked at Deb and said, 'We will start now. Stay put right there and I will keep telling you whatever's happening. Shall we see how Nayra and Augustya are doing?'

'Yes, doctor,' said Deb and beamed.

Dr Sreedhar disappeared behind the curtain. Deb heard the nurse, Avantika and Dr Sreedhar mumble and giggle from behind the curtain. He felt a little left out. 'Please let one be a boy . . .' he muttered to himself. He wondered how many arguments he would have to let go if there were three girls prancing about in the house. He muttered a silent prayer for Augustya. He needed that boy. He closed his eyes. *Let there be him, let there be a boy. I need him, I need him so much*. The boy would be his insurance policy against the girl gang in the group. Thinking of how teams would be split in the house, Deb smiled a little.

'Are you ready, MR DEBASHISH?' shouted Dr Sreedhar. 'Are you ready, Avantika?'

There was silence from the other side for a few moments. Deb's heart thumped. Was it two girls? Was the doctor murmuring that to Avantika? What would they name the other girl? Augustyi? Would that work? He waited for the familiar gurgling sounds of amniotic fluid, of the two whooshing heartbeats. After a few seconds, he heard them. A big smile spread across Deb's face. The sound of the heart beating, the blood flow, the signs of life. He heard Avantika laugh.

'Ah, there she is! I can see your Nayra! Congratulations, people! You have a daughter!' said Dr Sreedhar. 'And now you don't have to worry about the second boy's name. Come, let's find Augustya and let's see if he's a boy!'

Avantika was laughing. Deb imagined her lying back now, relaxed, unfazed with whatever the doctor was going to find. She'd got her daughter! Deb felt his eyes tear up. He was happy for her. He could imagine her eyes lighting up like Diwali diyas. Nayra was *real*. Deb found his hands clamming up now. Was Augustya *real* too? It was his turn to get his boy.

A minute passed by, and then another.

Deb heard Dr Sreedhar instruct Avantika. 'Can you turn a little to your left.'

There was silence again. No gurgling sounds, no whooshing, no signs of life. Another minute passed by. Dr Sreedhar asked Avantika to turn on her side again. The nurse rushed out. Deb felt his breath get stuck in his throat. He got up and strode towards the curtain but was stopped.

'GET OUT!' the nurse shouted this time and the curtain was closed.

'IS EVERYTHING OKAY?' shouted Deb from the other side.

'Is everything all right, doctor?' asked Avantika.

Just then, an old woman strode in wearing a white lab coat and a stethoscope hanging limply around her neck. She looked a few years senior to Dr Sreedhar. She promptly disappeared behind the curtain.

Deb got up and followed after.

'You can't be here,' said the woman doctor, voice stern, and closed the curtain.

For a brief second, he had seen Avantika. What was that he saw? She looked terrified. A certain gloom gripped Deb.

'IS EVERYTHING ALL RIGHT?' shouted Deb. 'WHERE IS AUGUSTYA! PLEASE TELL ME WHERE HE IS! TELL ME!'

There was silence.

'Please! Please!'

His knees buckled and he stumbled to his chair all hunched up.

His eyes flooded with tears. His knees shook, and with it the chair wobbled, filling up the silence. There was no heartbeat, there was no sound of the blood flow. No sign of life!

The curtain jerked open. Faces, confused, scared, terrified faces stared back at him. Deb and Avantika looked at each other. It had dawned on both even before the doctors spoke. What had happened had struck them straight in their faces. As they both were locked in a gaze, they knew . . . they knew . . . they had talked about this . . . they would never be the same. Things had changed forever, as if their DNA itself was being rewritten, their destinies rescripted. In that moment, their account, the state of their lives was being cruelly, unjustifiably edited, the number of laughs, smiles, times of extreme joy, were being cut down, and to tally the two sides, the tears, the sadness were being added. They felt it, they felt this change, and they felt helpless.

'Something was *wrong*,' that's what the doctor said. The words swam in and out of their ears. They heard only snatches of the doctor's sentences. *Fear. More tests. Can't be sure. More tests. Where's Augustya?* The words died in Deb's chest. Only his lips moved. A button was pressed and three ward boys came running in, Avantika was shifted to a bed and she was wheeled out for more tests. The light in Avantika's eyes was long gone. Snuffed out, extinguished. The old lady doctor rushed out with her.

Dr Sreedhar patted Deb's arm before he walked out, 'It will be fine.'

Deb finally found his voice and said, 'Where's my son? Where's Augustya?'

It wasn't a question borne out of hope. It was a question of despair. It was more of an answer. He could have said *let me see him, I know what happened but let me see him*.

The door closed the curtain on Deb's face. He sat there in silence. His soft sobs filled up the empty room. The curtain was now drawn open. He looked up at the ultrasound monitor. A strange, empty darkness stared back at him. Deb and Avantika would never be the same.

47

They came back to the hotel the same evening. Dr Sreedhar said there wasn't any need for her to stay back in the hospital. The tests were done and they were conclusive. Nothing could be done. *Everything else,* they were told, was all right, and there was *nothing* to worry about. They should carry on like normal. No precautions needed to be taken. Just the regular scans that they had been doing anyway. It seemed unreal that they were asked to lead their lives again like everything had not changed.

'I need to sleep,' said Avantika when they reached the hotel.

'You should eat something first. The doctors said that—'

'I'm fine,' she said before tucking herself in.

Deb watched her pull the blanket over her head, and crunch into a ball inside it. She was still. A few minutes passed by and then some more did. There was stillness. And that's when Deb heard the sobs that she was keeping from him. Deb ordered for food, club sandwiches, and asked room service to keep the food outside the room and not ring the bell.

He then walked out of the room leaving Avantika to cry in peace. Deb would have held her hand, like he always had. But what could he have said to her? *Nothing.* Back in the hospital, she had listened to the doctors intently, and taken down notes. Her face had betrayed no emotion. The doctors had been surprised. They had expected tears, screams, a sedative shot up the mother's arm. When they were leaving, the nurse asked him twice if she was going to be okay. They didn't want an untoward incident pointing back at their hospital or just their consciences.

He walked down to the lobby of the hotel.

'Can I help you with something?' asked the receptionist.

'Can you?' asked Deb and left the hotel.

The city was dead but lit up like a Christmas tree; it looked like Dubai was always celebrating something. What? For whom? Why was the city still functioning? Why hadn't it come to a fucking standstill? Why was the world still spinning around its damned axis? How was everything still okay? How were people sleeping when one of their children . . . how was that possible?

He walked listlessly in circles around the hotel. He wanted to think, think about anything, anything to distract himself from the reality that stared him in the face. He drew a blank. A couple looked at him strangely after he passed their car a few times. He changed his route. What explanation could he have given them? Where would he begin?

He fiddled with his phone wondering whom he could call to talk about this. Should he call Shrey? Would that make sense? He knew the decision lay with Avantika and not him. How do you even begin to tell something like this? Had they believed it themselves? Or would they only after they had . . . the baby in their arms? Though Dr Sreedhar and the other woman doctor assured them that the 'miscarriage' wasn't due to her air travel no one would believe them. The last thing Avantika needed were the questions and accusations, said or unsaid, hurled at her.

Augustya was dead.

She would have to carry Augustya for four more months. It would be her burden to carry for the next four months. It was her burden to birth that child, to go through the pain of bringing a life to the world only to also bring death into it.

'The delivery will happen normally with the other child,' said Dr Sreedhar about the dead child. 'The pain might be a little less because the child won't be a fully grown one.'

'His name is Augustya,' said Deb even though they hadn't asked the gender of the child who expired.

Deb had watched Avantika's eyes flicker when he told her that the pain would be a little less. Would the pain be less? It would be her on the doctor's table four months later, waiting for the happiest and the worst moment of her entire life. When they would first let her hold a living child, their Nayra, kicking and crying, she would have to forget in that moment about the other baby, Augustya, who would never breathe out in the world. The child that didn't get to live. Deb wondered which child would see the light of day first—Nayra or the one she'd lost.

But was it just her loss? Was it not his? Deb wondered if he would want Avantika's pain for himself instead. He closed his eyes and imagined himself to be in Avantika's shoes. It didn't

take a second for the tears to come flooding down his cheeks.
He snapped out of it; he knew he couldn't bear it. Deb found
himself outside the hospital. He had walked for an hour to
get here. He hadn't meant to go there, or maybe he did, he
wasn't sure about anything any more. He entered and asked the
receptionist if Dr Sreedhar was still there.

'No, he's not. Is this an emergency?' she asked.

Deb shook his head. His legs were giving way so he trudged
to the sofas where other women and their husbands sat. He
leaned back and closed his eyes. The husbands kept their hands
on the wives' stomachs. Was it to protect the child? Should he
have done it too? Didn't they tell Augustya that they loved him
too? That he was equally wanted in their lives? How were they
supposed to go on now? He wondered if Avantika had eaten
something. He closed his eyes and willed himself to not think
anything, anything at all.

He was tapped on his shoulder.

'Excuse me?'

He opened his eyes. The nurse from the morning was
standing over him. She handed over a chit.

'This is the doctor's personal number. He's awake now, I
checked. If there's something you need to ask him you can call
him.'

'Thanks,' said Deb.

The nurse smiled at him—because what else would you do
in such a situation—and turned away from him.

Deb stared at the number for a while. He dialled the number
twice and disconnected. An unjustified anger towards the doctor,
towards the nurse, towards the airline, the aircraft, the taxi driver
to the hospital, rose inside of him, and he wanted to hit someone.
He wanted to murder someone, have his revenge on the world,
do something rather than just sit and stare at the number. He
got up and strode out of the hospital. He needed to be with his
wife. It took him longer this time. His heart beat faster, his fingers

trembled, he worried how Avantika must feel, and how foolish he was to assume she would be okay without him. He started to run.

He ran up the stairs of the hotel. The door was ajar. For some reason he assumed the worst. And then thought how stupid it was to think that. She would never do that, not in a million, million years. Nayra was still there, still with them, like she had always been. The *one*. The one that they wanted from the very beginning. Was it their fault? Did children in the womb sense what their parents wanted?

Deb found her sitting up in the bed, staring at nothing. For a moment, he thought she was watching TV but it was off. The sandwich lay half-eaten, little crumbs of French fries strewn on the bed. Deb gingerly climbed up on the bed and sat next to her. Avantika reached out for his hand and held it. Deb pulled her close. What could he say to her to make all this go away? Would all the words in the dictionary, in every language dead or in use, in every order they could put them in, make it go away?

'You didn't eat the entire sandwich?' he asked.

'. . . I left some for you,' she said.

The day was reminiscent of the second time they had met, that night outside the club. They had kissed then and the world seemed a lot better in that instant. Deb knew he couldn't kiss her now. The sadness was deep, in her bones, in his bones, inside her body, and this wound couldn't be cauterized by all the love in the world.

'Did you go to the hospital?' she asked.

'How did you know?'

'I saw you circle the hotel. I saw that couple watch you,' she said. 'Did you meet the doctor?'

'I got his number. Couldn't bring myself to call him. I didn't know what would come of it . . . and yet . . .'

Avantika slipped her hand into Deb's jacket and fished out the cell phone. She stared at the number in the last dialled list for a long time.

'Should we text him? We have to know, we have to know, don't we? How can we not know?' she asked after a while.

'It's your decision to make, Avantika. I'm okay with what you're okay with.'

'Is it?' she asked. 'I got the daughter I wanted. Should I have wanted a son too? Is that why . . . I should have asked for a son. Maybe . . .'

She turned to look at Deb. Did she know he had wanted one to be a boy? Someone who would be in his team? They texted the doctor. The reply came almost instantly. As if the doctor had been waiting for them to text him.

It was a boy.

It was Augustya.

48

Three weeks passed by, and they were still in Dubai.

Avantika had thought it would get easier with time. It only got worse. The reality sunk in slowly, as if there was an abyss it was sinking into, no end to the grief they felt. It seemed like it was just yesterday that the doctors shook their heads and told them. The silence still haunted Avantika. The moment of panic on the doctor's face, his frantic movement of the device on her stomach, the unmoving lump of tissue and bones on the monitor, the apologetic and scared shake of the nurse's head. She saw it repeatedly, and with every time, more details came into the picture. Sometimes, they would look at the pictures of the old ultrasounds when Augustya was still alive, when they were parents of two children and not one and they would want to reach out and ask him to hold on, not die on them. The more they looked at the ultrasounds—the same one which were indecipherable to them earlier—the more they could tell Augustya apart. The baby in the back, the weaker baby, there he was, clearly visible. Of course it was him.

A few days after they knew they had visited the embassy to extend their visa. The visa officials told them they would have to furnish a hefty fine for overstaying, and they might be blacklisted from coming to the UAE again. They didn't care. Avantika knew they wouldn't come back again. It was the city that had killed Augustya and left him dead in her womb.

Deb had been a rock these past few weeks, doing all the right things, saying all that was needed to be said, keeping silent when it was necessary. But she thought the cracks in him were too stark to be missed. She knew how Deb lived as much in his imagination as he lived in real life. Sometimes she wondered how much time Deb would spend in his imagination. Avantika could nurse that grief, really indulge in it, it was in her womb to hold but Deb had nothing. He couldn't be angry or sad because he knew she would get sadder, and no one knew better than her that he placed her before anyone else. It was the same that had happened with Paritosh and the baby she had had to kill, but he had no claim on that grief. It wasn't him who'd got pregnant and carried the baby.

After the news was broken to them, the doctors told them it was advisable to postpone their travel plans for now and wait for a few days. They were asked to postpone their departure by a week but the days ticked by and they couldn't get themselves to leave the city. Deb cancelled the tickets and saved what little they could out of them. They moved out of the hotel and shifted to a small motel in Bur Dubai. Neither of them were sure how long they would stay in Dubai. Deb's parents called and fussed and worried about the cancellation. Deb lied to them.

'We like it here. We will stay a few days and then come back. Everything is fine, Maa. Why wouldn't it be?' he had told them.

Deb's parents had taken to calling them twice, thrice a day to check on them. Deb consistently lied to them that they were fine, always putting on his bit-too-cheerful voice. His parents were slowly losing patience. More than once, Shrey had threatened to come to Dubai. On one occasion, he sent them a picture of him outside the visa office and warned them he would come over if they didn't come back soon. More lies were told, and Deb did most of the lying.

Every night they would take a long walk to tire themselves out. They would take the same route. One hour to the hospital, fifteen minutes more to get back. Sometimes they would go in, sit on the chairs of the reception, and play out the entire thing in their heads. On other nights, they would station themselves outside the twin pregnancy division of the hospital and watch women with distended stomachs complain about how difficult their pregnancy was. They would distractedly walk towards the labour section and stare at the twins delivered that day. Only rarely had those parents decided the names beforehand. Was that their mistake? They had put in so much already that they jinxed it? Every day they would pass the scan room and there would be a little voice in Avantika that told her maybe Augustya had come back to life, that they should check. After all, he was still inside of her, swimming in her blood, maybe he had drawn a little life for himself. How could it be that his sister was still living, and he wasn't, that she was still growing, turning somersaults, sucking her thumb, and he wasn't?

Deb would always try to stop Avantika from going to the hospital. He would tell her that it couldn't be good for her to be doing this. They were all unconvincing lies he said every day. He would ask her to move on, concentrate on what was coming ahead. They were all lies.

He wanted this as much as she did. Avantika knew that. It was how he was grieving, there was no way out of it so why not make it their home. They found themselves in a strange situation. The death of Augustya in her womb was an open wound. They couldn't move on. How could they?

In a few months, all the hurt and the loss would come back again and this time it wouldn't be a black and white grainy, unmoving image on a little screen. They would have the tiny, limp body of Augustya in their hands—what could have been their son. They would either have to cremate or bury or leave him in the Ganga. Any which way they would have to go through that. They would have to go through his death again.

As much as Avantika mourned the boy, she felt it was Deb who found it hard to chip away at the pain. After their long walks to the hospital and back, Avantika would be tired, her feet would hurt and she would promptly go to sleep. Unlike her, Nayra didn't demand anything from him. She didn't kick in Deb's womb to remind him that at least she was there. Deb would stay up sometimes till late afternoon. He would smile at her whenever she would get up. If she would ask, he would always reassure her and tell her that he was doing okay. He hardly ate and on more than one occasion she found the food she would order for him lying upturned in the dustbin. She would often catch him staring at her belly.

'You're worrying too much. I'm okay. I just . . . I just want to go back to India as soon as possible. So whenever you think you're ready, we should go,' he would say every time Avantika confronted him.

Not once had he asked if they should tell his parents or Tanmay about what had happened. He could sense that she wasn't ready for it yet.

'I know you're sad,' she told him one day.

'We can't afford to be sad. It's a new beginning for us and we can't let this overwhelm us. We just hit a roadblock, didn't we?'

'Dead Augustya is a roadblock?' she asked.

'What do you want me to say?'

'You keep smiling at me. You think it will be better, but it won't be. Nothing will be the same again. Stop saying all the right things, stop trying to make it okay. I know you're hurting as much as I am. Stop making us okay, nothing is going to be okay.'

'Should I order you something? You should eat and not stress over these things. Didn't you hear what the doctor said?'

She had and she had heard it well. Dr Sreedhar had recommended them to a counsellor. Deb had refused to go. The counsellor had repeatedly stressed on the need for the husbands to open up about how they felt.

'The loss can change him as a person if he keeps his feelings bottled inside,' the counsellor had told Avantika. 'It's not an easy loss, to be parents of a dead child before you can be a parent. It can be confusing.'

And for Deb, it was confusing. He had lost Augustya, and he wouldn't lose Nayra because he couldn't help Avantika emerge from the hurt and the loss. To him, it was important he fought this with everything he'd got. What was his use if he couldn't even do this?

When it was finally time to leave the city, a sense of hollowness filled them. It was the city where they last imagined Augustya to be their living child. Was it why they couldn't leave the city earlier? They reminisced the last time they had talked to Augustya. They had been flitting from one tourist destination to the other. 'LOOK! DUBAI CANAL!' 'LOOK BURJ KHALIFA!' 'LOOK! DUBAI GLOW GARDEN!' Even then they had always taken Nayra's name first and then Augustya's.

On the way to the airport, Deb had yelled twice at the taxi driver.

'CAN'T YOU DRIVE SLOW OR WHAT! YOU CAN'T SEE THERE IS A PREGNANT WOMAN!'

The taxi driver had frowned and apologized.

'So what's it? Boy or girl?' the driver asked.

'Both,' said Deb. He looked at Avantika and said, 'We will land, drop all our bags at the house, and go straight to the doctor, okay? We will do a scan there. Everything is going to be all right. Nayra is going to be okay.'

The doctors in Dubai had repeatedly said that air travel couldn't be a reason behind what had happened, but Deb wanted this flight back to end safely. They checked in their luggage and held on to their boarding passes possessively. He checked the air route to Delhi for turbulence. It showed all clear. Deb walked faster than he usually did. He did not stop at any of the duty free shops and went straight to their boarding gate. He sat near the gate, tense, his knees shaking violently.

'Do you want to get something to eat?' asked Avantika.

'There will be food on the flight. They will start the boarding any time now,' he said.

'There are two hours. We can't just keep sitting here, can we?' she asked.

'We can't roam around in the airport. There's too much commotion for you to be walking around. If you want something, tell me, I will get it.'

Avantika looked at Deb.

'Why are you looking at me like that? Do you want something?' he asked.

'Nothing.'

They fell silent and looked at the boarding gate. They took out the books they had got from Delhi and hadn't even started reading. Time ticked by slowly. Deb's mother called, and Avantika told her they were fine and that the boarding was going to start in a bit. Deb was the first one on the boarding line and insisted that Avantika sit tucked in far towards the window.

Avantika stuffed her ears with earphones. By the time the boarding ended, an hour later, she had dozed off. She didn't get to know when the flight took off. When she woke up, she found Deb with his eyes closed, tears streaking down his cheeks, his hand firmly on Avantika's stomach. Nayra kicked lightly inside of her. She kept her hand on his. He opened his eyes and looked at her.

'The worst part of all this?' he said. 'Despite what you're going through? I blame you for it.'

'Do you?' said Avantika, knowing that was how he would feel. Dr Sreedhar and the counsellor had prepared her for this. The powerlessness of the men when they lose a child often turns to blame.

'I do and then it just becomes worse,' he said. 'I'm sorry.'

'You don't have to be. It's okay to allow yourself to feel,' she said. 'Your loss is as big as mine. Augustya was as much yours as he was mine.'

She saw his eyes flit towards her stomach and then back at her.

'Can we . . . we pretend he's not dead yet? He's a part of me still, isn't he? He's a part of us,' said Avantika. 'We will mourn him when the time comes, okay? Till then he's as much there as Nayra is.'

Deb nodded.

'Did you feel that?' she asked.

'I did.'

'Your girl is lazy, she's sleeping. That one was Augustya, he was the one who kicked,' she said and watched Deb smile behind the tears.

They slept like that. She had no idea how much time had passed when she heard her name being called out. She thought it was a dream at first. When she woke up, she saw Deb's eyes boring through her.

'Avantika!' he cried out.

Behind his silent screams, the pilot exhorted everyone to fasten their seat belts for they were about to encounter turbulence.

'BUT I CHECKED! THE AIR POCKETS WERE CLEAR!' shouted Deb at the flight attendant who was checking if everyone was buckled in.

She didn't respond. Deb and Avantika held their breath while the plane shook and trembled for what seemed like an eternity. For the rest of the flight, they sat with the seat belts on and were the first ones out of the door.

They went straight to the doctor. While Avantika waited in the scan room, Deb informed Dr Sharma of what they had found in Dubai. Dr Sharma listened with a bowed head and offered his expertly worded condolences; he had seen this before, he said. Deb handed over the scans and Dr Sharma pored over every page. The helplessness was writ large on his face.

'It was a boy,' said Deb.

The doctor pretended to read on. What could you say to a to-be parent at a time like this? Deb smiled his practiced smile at him to put him at ease.

'I'm sorry,' Dr Sharma said, before he went to the room to carry out the ultrasound. When he emerged, he said, 'She's okay.' And then added after a pause, 'I wish Augustya was too. He would have been lucky to meet the two of you.' He looked at Avantika and said, 'Please know you had nothing to do with this, *nothing*. I'm your doctor. I asked you to travel. If there was anything wrong I would have told you. If this had to happen it would have happened sitting in your living room. There's a healthy child inside of you and she needs all the love you have got. Look at me, the two of you. I'm also your friend, okay? I care about you too. Be strong and you will get through this. Okay? Look at me and nod?'

It was only later when they got back home with the scan results showing everything normal—Nayra, healthy and alive, Augustya, dead and still—that they realized that they had left everything they had bought from Dubai in the cabin baggage in the aircraft.

They didn't bother to fetch the bag. The airlines staff kept calling them. They didn't take the calls and eventually blocked the numbers. They didn't want anything they bought in Dubai back.

They got back home from the hospital to a big banner that screamed WELCOME HOME NAYRA AND AUGUSTYA! They were received by Shrey, Tanmay and Vernita who screamed their heads off when they saw Avantika and Deb. They were admonished and loved equally by them.

'You have been gone forever,' said Shrey.

'We liked the place,' said Deb.

'I was talking to Augustya, not you,' said Shrey.

Tanmay made them promise they wouldn't go on another trip till the pregnancy came to fruition. Vernita was the only happy one, who wanted to see pictures of the trip, and was happier when Deb told them they didn't take a lot. 'That means it was quite some trip,' said Vernita and nudged them naughtily.

Later that night, Shrey asked Deb and Avantika for the reports and the scans from Dubai. 'I need to stick them in Augustya's file. I don't want him growing up and telling me I don't have enough pictures of his,' he said.

Deb lied that they'd left them all in Dubai; he made a mental note to get rid of the reports. These things had a way of coming out later. Shrey wasn't pleased about it.

'Let this be the last time you're cavalier with Augustya. I'm reminding you again that I'm raising that child. Nayra is yours, do whatever you want with her but he's mine,' said Shrey in all seriousness before going to bed.

43

The guilt weighed down heavily on Avantika. With every passing day that she swelled, the lies Deb and Avantika told Tanmay, Vernita, Shrey and Deb's parents kept getting more elaborate. Four weeks had passed since Deb and Avantika had taken that nervous, turbulence-ridden flight from Dubai to Delhi, four weeks since Deb and Avantika had been lying to everyone on their faces about Augustya. It was exactly three months to the date of the delivery when Deb's mother called them to say that they were going to move in with them.

'Twin pregnancies can get difficult. Your mother needs to be there. *Etto o bodo hoyo ni tomra* (you are not that grown up),' Baba said over the phone from Kolkata.

Deb and Avantika tried dissuading them, that they were doing fine, but the parents wouldn't hear a word of it.

'There's Shrey here, he helps out. You don't have to worry at all, Maa,' Avantika said but it fell on the deaf ears of Deb's mother.

Deb's mother scoffed, 'Shrey? What are you talking about, *mamoni*. I don't want my grandchildren to grow up and tell me I didn't take care of their mother when she needed me. I'm coming and that's final.'

Deb and Avantika destroyed all the reports from Dubai and Delhi doctors that showed the *damage*. They didn't discuss even once if they should come out with the truth. The lies had piled on and it sounded like a betrayal now. They had gone too far and there was no return from there. It was the hardest to lie to Shrey. He had nothing to do with the two of them; his commitment to Augustya was unwavering and complete.

If only he knew . . .

He was deeply uncomfortable with Deb's parents coming to stay with them and threw a huge tantrum when Deb bowed down to their wishes. He warned them that he and he only would be the first one after Deb and Avantika to hold Augustya, he would be the one to give him the formula milk for the first time, and he would have a picture with the baby before anyone else. He threatened to stop being friends with them if any of his demands were compromised.

A day before Deb's parents landed, Avantika broke down in Deb's arms. The presence of Shrey, Tanmay and Vernita, and their heartbreaking secret had made it difficult for them to cry in peace. They smiled so much, faked happiness so often, that sometimes they themselves believed that Augustya was still in there, alive and kicking, fighting with his big sister.

'We have to tell them. They are going to be outside the labour room expecting two children. We can't do this to them.

They will know Augustya didn't die at childbirth. It's not a secret we can keep,' said Avantika.

From the way Deb looked at her, she knew that he had been waiting for Avantika to come to this realization.

'We can't tell anyone we found out about this in Dubai. We will tell them we found out much, much later. Maybe last week or the week before today. I have talked to Dr Sharma. He will play along,' said Deb.

'So we keep lying? For how long?' she asked.

'All our lives. You know no one will forgive us if we tell them it happened right after the flight everyone asked us not to take. Everyone will blame—'

'Me.'

'And I won't have that,' said Deb. 'Because it's not your fault, it's not our fault. It could have happened to anyone.'

'So we tell them tomorrow about Augustya?' asked Avantika.

Deb wiped Avantika's tears which refused to stop.

'I will tell them.'

'And Shrey?' asked Avantika.

Deb had no answer for that.

50

Deb and Avantika were an hour early at the airport. They had their story straight. They couldn't tell them they just found out because they would have to act out a lot so they decided that it had been a month since they found out and they were too devastated to share the news with them.

'The flight is late by half an hour. We should have checked before we left,' Deb told Avantika as they waited at the coffee shop outside the airport.

'Do you want this?' asked Avantika, pushing the half-finished tea in front of Deb.

Deb sipped on the now lukewarm tea.

'How do you think they will react?' she asked.

'You know how Maa is,' he said. 'She will try her hardest not to cry but will end up crying for days. Baba will read and read and read about it till the grief is all science and words and he will be older and weaker from it.'

'I'm sorry,' said Avantika.

'Please—'

Deb was interrupted by his phone ringing loudly.

'Why is Tanmay calling?' asked Deb. He picked up the call. 'Hello? Yes. What? Why? Yes, yes. We are just outside at the coffee shop.'

Deb disconnected the call.

'They are here. Both of them,' said Deb.

Avantika's face lost colour.

'Will they come home?' asked Avantika.

'He's your brother. Of course, he will,' said Deb.

Before Avantika could say anything to that, Tanmay and Vernita came striding in, big smiles on both their faces, an excited Ivan hanging from a contraption from Tanmay's chest. Ivan lunged at Avantika when he saw her and tried climbing out. Avantika took him from Tanmay and kissed him all over. Deb watched Avantika try to muster up the affection she had once felt for the boy. She babbled in a cute voice and kissed and hugged the baby but it all seemed ridiculous to Deb. Deb felt nothing for Ivan. The boy wasn't Deb's blood so it wasn't expected of him to entertain him for long. There was a relief on Avantika's face when the boy started to cry and Vernita started to feed him. With every passing day Ivan had started resembling Tanmay. It wasn't lost both on Deb and Avantika that their son could have looked like the boy in Tanmay's arms.

'We got you something,' said Vernita. 'But let your parents come, only then we will show you.'

Deb and Avantika didn't insist on it. Between the crying of the boy, the diaper changing, the passing of him from one to another, time passed by quickly.

'Wait here,' said Tanmay to both the girls when it was time.

Tanmay couldn't stop talking about the things Ivan was learning, how intelligent he had become, and what playschools they were choosing for him while Deb and he walked to the gates. Deb blocked most of it out. He was guilty enough anyway for not feeling any love for Vernita's baby. If anything, he felt a mild hatred for their happiness.

'Avantika seemed a bit off? Is something wrong?' he asked.

Deb paused for a bit and said, 'You know, pregnancy brain. She's feeling too hot. So a little down.'

'I know,' said Tanmay. 'Talk to her about post-partum pregnancy. It's pretty common for women to not feel quite motherly or loving towards the child after the delivery. Especially since she has taken such a long break from work.'

'I will.'

'Don't mind it, Deb. It's just that she didn't seem to love Ivan as much as she did earlier, that's why I asked. I could be wrong but I'm saying. It's important that you talk to her about this.'

Minutes later, Deb's parents walked out of the gates, grinning and looking for Avantika. Tanmay was onto their trolley in a flash, playing the good brother-in-law to Deb. Deb's parents had always looked at Tanmay a little goggly-eyed.

'The flight was good? Vernita checked online and found out that it was late. Hope you ate something?' he asked.

They both nodded.

'Where is Avantika?' Deb's mother asked.

'Just around the corner,' answered Deb.

'You shouldn't have got her. She should have rested at home,' she said.

When they got to the coffee shop, Deb's mother didn't allow Avantika to bend to touch her feet.

'No bending, *shona*. You will hurt the babies. Don't tell me you have been doing that all this while,' she said sternly. 'Have you?'

'No, Maa.'

They all huddled in Tanmay's car, with Ivan in Deb's mother's lap. Tanmay and Vernita were jumpy during the entire ride home, excited about what gift they had bought for Deb and Avantika. Deb and Avantika were nervous, texting each other, talking about how and when to break the truth to them. When they reached home, Tanmay rudely cut off Deb's father's plea and insisted he carry all the suitcases to the apartment.

'Don't open the door till I get there,' said Tanmay to Deb and Avantika. 'I want to capture it on camera.'

Shrey had been kicked out of the house to plan this. He wasn't happy waiting outside the locked door of the house he had been living in for the last so many months. Tanmay and Vernita had always had a key but they had put an extra lock to keep Shrey out of the apartment.

'Where's he?' said Vernita, impatient.

'You shouldn't have got us anything, really,' said Avantika.

'Oh, shut up,' said Vernita.

'I'm sure it will be something nice,' said Deb's mother, smiling.

'Now open,' said Tanmay once he dragged the last suitcase to the floor. He switched on the camera on his phone.

Deb jimmied the key in and turned. Tanmay and Vernita waited with bated breath for all of them to react to what they had bought for them. It had taken them two months to get this. They had downloaded the designs off the internet, looked for the people who could executed them, and then paid them extra and made subtle changes. It was *perfect*. Gorgeous.

In the living room were two beautiful teak, not cheap wood or MDF, cribs waiting for them. They were ornate and huge, cribs for giants, not regular babies, that lay bang in the centre of the room.

'That one's for Nayra, and that one's for Augustya,' said Tanmay excitedly.

'They look the same to me,' said Shrey, annoyed, and trying hard not to be impressed with the craftsmanship of the royal cribs. He had to give it to Tanmay and Vernita—it was quite something.

'They have their names engraved on them. The mattresses heat up in the winter. There's a baby monitor attached to the railing and a little camera that can beam images directly to your phone,' explained Tanmay, his chest puffed up with pride.

Tanmay moved to capture Deb and Avantika's astonished smiles and found only tears.

'Is something wrong?' asked Deb's father.

51

Debashish's mother didn't sob softly as Deb had expected.

She burst out in a barrage of tears when Avantika told her. At first, she didn't believe it. She thought she'd misheard what Avantika had said or misunderstood her words. The words slowly sunk in. The reality of it hit her—her grandson was dead. Her body trembled, and she would have slumped on the ground had Deb's father not held her. She muttered to herself in Bengali, repeating the same thing, 'It can't be true . . . it can't be true . . .'

She held Avantika, looked at her stomach in disbelief, kept her hand on it, and cried and cried and prayed, and got down on her knees and talked to Avantika's stomach, pleaded for this to be a lie. She said words but all everyone could hear were her inhuman wails. Avantika made her get up, held her face. 'Maa, Maa . . .'

'You're fine, you're fine, everything is fine,' Deb's mother kept saying to Avantika. 'You will be fine. We will go to a doctor and everything will be fine. Listen to me, it will be fine. Tell her everything will be fine.'

She exhorted everyone to see the doctor again, a better one. She walked up to Avantika, held her hand and begged her to see a doctor she would choose. She kept insisting that there must be a mistake, that there's no way this was true. She refused to believe it. She alternated between crying, shouting and mumbling incoherently to herself. The shock Tanmay, Vernita and even Shrey felt—who had begun to cry softly—dwarfed in front of the mad grief of Deb's mother.

Only when Baba pulled her away from Avantika, whispered softly in her ears, did she calm down. She couldn't tear her eyes off Avantika's stomach. She mumbled the names she had chosen for her grandson, and there were many. She mourned his loss loudly and wildly. Within minutes, her face was streaked with tears, her hair was in disarray, she looked like a broken, homeless woman. It seemed like the grief had coursed through her entire body and destroyed her. She would always be the woman whose grandchild died. It was right there, on her face, anyone could read it. Avantika watched her mother-in-law crumble in the helplessness, anger and grief. Deb clasped his hand around Avantika's hand.

'Shona,' murmured Deb's father in his wife's ears.

She broke out of her reverie and looked up at Avantika. A wave of guilt washed over her. She wiped her tears and straightened the grief out of her face, realizing she wasn't at the centre of the tragedy. She turned to Avantika, who at once seemed to her shrunken and sick. She went up to Avantika, asked Deb to leave her hand, clasped her hands around hers, made her sit down, kissed her on her forehead, hugged her and apologized. More tears sprung to her face. Her eyes turned to Deb and it was after years that Deb saw them burn with anger towards him. She was madder than the time she had seen the crown of a beer bottle in the house, angrier than the time he had failed to clear his entrance examination, and more livid than she was when he quit it all to pursue writing. Deb's mother had found someone to blame—it wasn't the flight they took, it wasn't her womb, it wasn't plain bad luck; it was Deb, her son, whose carelessness had resulted in this.

She wouldn't leave Avantika's hands for an hour.

She spent the rest of the evening clearing out Deb's stuff from Deb's and Avantika's bedroom.

'I'm going to stay with her till the delivery. I have seen how responsible you are. From now on, I will take care of her,' she said, her eyes still piercing through Deb as if he had failed to keep his wife and child safe.

Then she looked at Deb's father and said, 'Didn't I tell you we should have been here from the first day. Your confidence in your son is misplaced. He's not like his sisters.'

She looked at Deb and asked, 'Did you tell them?'

Deb shook his head. All this while, Ivan screamed in Vernita's arms. Neither Vernita nor Tanmay could find it in themselves to quieten him down. Did babies sense tragedy? Could they hear the slowing of a beating heart?

Deb's mother took Ivan, cooed to him a Bengali lullaby, a song from a grandmother to her grandson, till Ivan was asleep. It struck Deb, she wouldn't be able to do so to her own. She put Ivan in the crib meant for Nayra and let him sleep there. Everyone's eyes turned to the empty crib of Augustya which seemed to have grown and taken all the space in the world.

Deb's mother looked at Tanmay, sharply, and shouted, 'YOU'RE A FATHER YOURSELF. YOU SHOULD HAVE KNOWN THAT BUYING NEW THINGS FOR UNBORN BABIES IS INAUSPICIOUS. DIDN'T YOUR PARENTS TEACH YOU ANYTHING?'

Deb's mother's voice seemed to shake the foundations of the house. Tanmay listened, head hung low. Ivan cooed in his sleep, sat up, eyes still closed. Deb's mother tapped his shoulder and apologized to him. Ivan went promptly back to sleep. No one said a word.

Deb's mother opened her suitcase and unpacked a large canister. Deb recognized it immediately. It was a payesh made from jaggery, Deb's favourite. Deb knew it wasn't for him. She stood over Avantika and made sure she finished it.

'You need the energy. Eat, eat all of it,' she said and Avantika ate dutifully.

Since the time Avantika broke the news, they had all been standing where they were and they only moved when Ivan woke up an hour later. 'He needs to eat,' said a scared Avantika.

'Go home,' said Deb's mother.

Tanmay called a cab for Vernita to go home.

'Keep the other crib on the terrace,' Deb's mother demanded of Tanmay when Vernita left.

Deb and Tanmay and Shrey carried the crib upstairs to the common roof of the apartment building and kept it there.

'You should return it,' said Deb, and handed over the bill.

'I can't do that. This will always be his,' said Tanmay.

'I will take it home,' said Shrey.

'Home?' asked Deb.

'Your mother's here. You don't need me any more. I will be gone in the morning,' said Shrey, his voice breaking.

'You don't have to go.'

'I do. If I stay here I will only remind you . . .'

He embraced Deb and told him he felt sorry for him. He told him he would always be there if Deb needed to talk. From the tears that streaked down Shrey's face it seemed like it was he who needed to talk. The three of them stood there, staring at the crib, at Augustya's name emblazoned on the side of it. Ten minutes passed and then some more, and they kept sitting there, staring at the crib, thinking of their futures with Augustya, their boys' club, now missing a member. When they went back down, Deb's mother had unpacked all the food she had made and heated it up. Unlike other times when she would serve and fuss over who ate how much, it just lay there in glass bowls. Shrey packed everything he had brought with him within ten minutes in one lonely suitcase. The room stripped of Shrey's character seemed bare, lifeless. It felt like he had never lived with them. His suitcase lay near the door while they ate and Deb kept looking at it. None of them ate a lot. Avantika was made to by Deb's mother.

Deb knew he wanted to talk to Avantika but Deb's mother wouldn't let Avantika out of her sight for a single second. Maa wouldn't let him close to Avantika, as if he was cursed. For not a single moment she had met Deb's gaze.

'You have gone through a lot,' she said to Avantika. 'Eat and go to sleep. Give me your phone. You shouldn't look at screens before sleeping.'

She tucked Avantika in like a little girl. She closed the door behind her and announced, 'She's sleeping. Don't call her before morning and I don't want anyone to talk about Augustya from this moment on. She's still carrying my Nayra and I want her to be healthy.'

Tanmay and Shrey got up from the dining table, washed their hands, touched Deb's parents' feet and walked out of the house.

Deb's parents had come with twenty used pairs of infant clothes, a number of pairs of baby diapers and mats and mittens. Before sleeping, they lay one of each in the crib on the terrace and covered it with a plastic sheet. When they came down, Deb's father made tea for his wife and made her drink it sip by sip. She hadn't eaten anything since morning. He softened a rusk and made her eat it.

It was three in the morning and Deb found himself at the terrace, staring at the discarded clothes, at the beautiful crib. Little did he know, Shrey hadn't gone back home. He was there, sitting on the water tank, his suitcase on the side. When Shrey saw him, he came and stood near Deb. He offered Deb a cigarette.

'The hurt doesn't stop, does it?'

Deb and Shrey turned around.

'Does Maa know you're here?'

She slipped her arm into his and snuggled next to Deb.

'It's beautiful, isn't it?' said Avantika, pointing to the crib.

'Augustya would have loved this,' said Shrey.

And then without a word, she walked towards the crib. She took off the plastic sheet and kept it on the side. She took the locks off and the bars came down. She pushed the clothes to one side, patted the mattress, felt it beneath her fingers and gingerly sat on it. She looked at Deb and Shrey.

'Come,' she said.

Deb and Shrey sat next to her. All three of them leaned on the back railing of the crib. A collective sigh escaped their lips.

'It's comfortable,' said Deb.

Shrey took the little blanket from the pile of clothes and kept it over them. 'He would have liked it a lot,' he said.

'He would have liked you even better, Shrey,' said Avantika. She added in a soft voice, 'Thank you for everything.'

52

Deb wasn't supposed to be in office, he should have been home, trying to mend his relationship with his mother, to be around Avantika who was constantly reminded of Augustya because no matter how hard Deb's mother tried, there would be one time in the day that she would cry and remind everyone of what they had lost, and yet he was there.

It was Shrey's week to handle all the meetings of which there weren't any. Yet Shrey had called him earlier that morning to tell him he was needed urgently. He hoped it wasn't another one of the field days Shrey insisted they would take to *recharge* their batteries. The entire idea was ironical given how free they were most of the time.

It had been three hours since Deb had been there and Shrey hadn't reached the office and wasn't taking any calls. Deb had come only because Shrey had not taken the news well. He had moved into an even smaller house—Deb didn't think it was possible—and lived even more poorly. His spiral of self-destruction was inexplicable.

It had taken an intervention from Deb's father to leave Deb's house finally. For a week, Deb's father had looked for a flat Shrey could move into. He got all the paperwork sorted and even put in the deposit amount which he refused to take back from Shrey. Deb's father—who Deb now believed wanted to spend as little time in the house as possible because he often found himself struggling to deal with Augustya's loss—spent another week with Shrey looking for the right furniture. Together, they set up the tiny one-bedroom flat Shrey had rented. He scoured through dozens of washing machines and refrigerators and televisions before he recommended the right ones for Shrey. He interviewed maids and cooks before he hired them. By the end of the exercise, both Shrey and Deb's father emerged a little less damaged. Despite this, Deb would find Shrey mindlessly scribbling Augustya's name on the margins of the books he had. Deb sometimes wondered if the depth of the loss felt by everyone around them lightened their own load.

'Lock the office and come down. We are waiting. Quick, there's no time,' said Shrey and cut the call.

Deb locked the office, went down the stairs, trying to think of a pretext to get out of whatever Shrey was about to suggest. He saw Tanmay's car at a distance and Shrey begging Tanmay to let him drive it.

'What's happening here?' asked Deb.

'Get in. We need to be somewhere. We are already late. I told Shrey we didn't need you but he insisted. He told me you would be good help. If not for anything else, at least in holding the camera,' said Tanmay.

Then he told Shrey, 'From what I had heard he hadn't done well in front of Shawar. From what Vernita tells me, he would have been beaten to pulp had Avantika not intervened,' said Tanmay.

'In my defence, I was up against a hooligan,' said Deb, trying to pretend as if that day didn't still give him the heebie-jeebies.

It was from a time in college. Avantika and he had just started dating much to the chagrin of Vernita and Tanmay. Vernita was pulling no stops to make life hell for Deb because apparently Deb betrayed her by dating the girl she had expressly asked him not to. She had stooped low when she told Avantika's ex-boyfriend, part-time ruffian from Delhi-Ghaziabad, Shawar—boyfriend according to the boy himself—where he could find Deb and Avantika on a date. Shawar, smarting from the loss of a girlfriend, had come in two big cars and a policeman to beat Deb up. Had Avantika not saved Deb, he would have had at least a few broken ribs and his face messed up.

'Where are we going?'

Tanmay and Shrey both looked at the rear-view mirror at Deb. It struck Deb.

'Stop the car,' said Deb.

'I told you he would say that,' said Shrey.

'He's scared,' said Tanmay. 'Don't be, Deb. We are there. We need to do this. He can't get away with this. It doesn't matter whether you come with us or not, it's going to happen. He needs to get beaten up.'

Deb leaned back in the seat.

Shrey turned to look at him, surprised. 'I thought it would take us more convincing.'

'No, let's do it. Paritosh has to be taught a lesson,' said Deb. 'So tell me? What do you guys have? Hockey sticks? Rods? A bat?'

'We don't have anything,' said Tanmay.

'No knuckledusters? No chains?' asked Deb.

'No,' said Shrey.

'You seem to be a little underprepared. We should take an unlicensed gun just to be sure,' said Deb.

'We don't want to kill him, Debashish. What's wrong with you?' said Shrey.

'I was just thinking what kind of lesson are we thinking of teaching him? What's appropriate? How many ribs? Or just a couple of fingers? What?'

'We just want to beat him up,' said Tanmay.

'It's the stupidest thing you have ever said, Tanmay.'

'You're scared, we get that,' said Shrey.

'Maybe I'm a little bit scared and I should be, that's normal. What's not normal is what you guys are doing. Does Avantika know? Does this have her sanction? And why the hell did you think I would like to do this?' asked Deb.

'Revenge,' said Tanmay.

'Revenge for what?' asked Deb.

Tanmay didn't say anything.

'My revenge is done,' said Deb. 'He doesn't matter to me or to Avantika. Why would I go there and give him the satisfaction that he still matters? My daughter is happy and kicking inside of her, that's all I want. I don't want revenge.'

'But—'

'If you really seek revenge, ask Avantika to file a sexual assault case against him. Can you do that, Tanmay? Go with her to a police station and set an example for your unborn niece and Ivan. That's how you have revenge,' asked Deb.

Tanmay drove silently.

'I didn't think so,' said Deb. 'So if you will be very kind, please drop me home and then go on to do whatever you want to do. I won't be a part of this. I have a wife to take care of who I'm sure would gladly stop talking to you if you pull this off.'

At the next red light, Tanmay took a U-turn.

Later that night, Avantika got a call from Tanmay. He asked her if she wanted to lodge a complaint against Paritosh. Avantika was surprised to hear him offer that. Tanmay's idea of respect always revolved around how the women in the family behaved. She wondered if years of chipping away at it by Avantika and Vernita had finally changed him a little. Avantika turned him down. She told him it wasn't the time.

'The world's a nasty place and I don't have it in me to put up a fight right now. When the right time comes, I will do it, and I will need you to stand right behind me,' said Avantika.

53

Avantika often woke up to Deb and his mother exchanging high-pitched volleys in Bengali of which she understood only some bits. It was a daily skirmish between the son and the mother. Ever since his mother had moved in, Avantika had noticed Deb flail around uselessly, his purpose wrested away from him while his mother went about doing everything that needed to be done. Deb's mother's anger had slowly transformed to a rankling irritation with her son and his interfering ways in how the house and Avantika's pregnancy should be managed.

'That's my calling, managing the house and sometimes working on the side, and I'm fucking great at it,' Deb often used to tell Avantika. And now with every passing day since Deb's mother's walking in and taking control of *all* of the housework, a silent resentment had built up in Deb. At first, he didn't do anything about it. He kicked back and even enjoyed it.

His mother, who had mollycoddled him when he was growing up, wasn't used to asking her son to share in household activities. For her, they had turned back time to when she would take care of three children without a groan. It was her purpose in life. She hadn't learnt to sit and twiddle her thumbs or watch television. Even after the kids had grown up and left the house, she would spend hours in the kitchen, doing everything painfully slowly, or just hover around and clean the tabletops to keep herself busy, and for a moment, forget how empty the house was without the children.

'Let me at least make breakfast,' said Deb after a couple of weeks had passed by.

'No, you do your work, I will do it. And you don't know how to make it the way Avantika likes it,' said his mother.

It was business as usual for Deb's mother. It seemed to her like the most natural thing to do—to handle housework while the kids worked. For her what was odd was to think that her son could pick the ripest tomatoes of the bunch or could replicate the mutton she had made for him all these years. It was even more unacceptable for her when she would spot him dusting or mopping the house. No matter what she would be doing she would leave everything and snatch the duster or the mop out of his hands. To her, it was sacrilege to let her children do these things in her presence.

'This is my house and I can run it without anyone's help,' he had said one day when he had found out that his mother hadn't eaten till late afternoon because she was too busy doing everything herself. 'The least you can do is take some help from us.'

His mother scoffed. 'I don't need anyone's help. And what do you mean us? You think I will take Avantika's help? I would rather die than do that. She is into her seventh month and you want me to make her work. This is why I don't ask you to do things. I will leave it to you and you will make her do things. No way!'

'He never does that, Maa,' said Avantika.

Deb's mother had more trust in Avantika's word than her son's so she let Deb start making breakfast from the next day.

Through little victories like these, Deb wrested back his place in the house. It was fraught with difficulties since both of them didn't want to cede space to the other. It was the homely version of *Game of Thrones*.

'He's his mother's son after all. There's nothing your mother can do that he can't,' said Deb's father to Avantika one day. 'Always suspected that. If he would have taken after me, he would have gone to IIT. Seems like you're not that unlucky after all.'

Avantika chuckled at it and they both watched the everyday skirmish with amusement.

Slowly and surely, Deb clawed back into a position where he had reduced his mother's work to half. She would groan and moan and emotionally blackmail Deb the entire day, but he developed a thick skin quite soon. He would do the same to her and they would reach a stalemate.

'I didn't call you to turn you into a maid. You have worked enough already. If you don't stop I will hire someone full time,' he would say.

'Things I do for my children make me a maid? Then I have been a maid all my life. Is it not so?' she would answer.

The same conversation would play out in differently worded sentences every second day, and the fever pitch of the conversation would reaching a tipping point. It wasn't just the housework that irritated Deb but also how his mother had entirely hijacked his fatherhood. She would spend hours after hours with Avantika. She would read stories to Nayra, sing boring *Rabindrasangeet* to her, and coo to her if she kicked too hard. All the things that Deb should have been doing. She didn't let Deb and Avantika alone out of the house. The evening walks to the Kilimanjaro point meant they all went out. Deb's mother would carry an umbrella and swat at any motorist who drove too close. After a while it became too embarrassing for them to go for a stroll. Deb feverishly missed those days when it was just the two of them. Now he struggled to find time with his own wife and his unborn child.

'If it goes this way, my daughter will end up calling my mother Baba,' an exasperated Deb had said to Avantika one day.

Avantika continuously slipped into the role of a mediator and often bungled it. She stopped doing it after a while and let them be. Sometimes she wondered if this was good for Deb. All the little battles with his mother took his mind off the loss they had endured.

'He will get thrown out of the house,' Deb's father had said to Avantika one day when things got really bad.

It sure looked like that was the direction it was going in. The tension between mother and son had been simmering for quite some time and it would have exploded any time, had it not been for Rashmi Sharma.

Rashmi Sharma—the inimitable TV producer—had a history of producing TV shows that lasted a minimum of 1500 episodes and she had expressed the desire to work with Shrey and Deb. She made her assistant call Shrey and tell him that she loved the sapera sequence of the show they had written earlier.

It was just the kind of break Deb and Shrey had always dreamt of. If they could crack this, and if their show worked, it could mean four years of assured income for episodes that a toddler could write.

After that exciting phone call, Deb's father had taken to watching all the TV shows Rashmi Sharma had produced before. After going through five episodes each of the twenty-three shows she had helmed, he announced emphatically, 'She's a cancer to the society and I don't want you to work for her.'

It was only after a long conversation of how it's partly the audience who decides what will sell and not an evil daily soap maker who wants to earn a quick buck, and a short course on Deb trying to tell him it was how he made money, that he bent a little.

'If that's the legacy you want to leave for Nayra,' his father said.

'If we do this show we wouldn't have to do any other show for a really long time,' Shrey added helpfully.

Of all the people, it was Deb's mother who was the happiest. If they decided to do this show, they would have to go to Mumbai for at least a week.

'You should do the show, secure Nayra's future,' Deb's mother kept saying repeatedly.

She could barely contain her glee. She kept telling Deb to take as long as it did to make this happen. It was finally decided that this was too good an opportunity to let go, today they were to write *Mayka Sumita Ka* (Sumita's Mother's House), tomorrow they might even get to write *Ishq ka Rang Kabhi Dhale na Dhale, Hum Saath Rahenge* (Whether Love Fades or Not We Will Be Together). It seemed there was no end to Deb's mother's happiness.

'Did you see her grinning?' Deb asked Avantika sourly.

'You can't blame her. You have been a pain in her ass ever since she moved in. Not without reason but you have.'

'Tell the *bartan wali* help who comes to do the dishes to come twice a day, okay? She shouldn't be washing the utensils herself. I have no idea how she keeps finding work for herself.'

'She doesn't listen to me. You tell her.'

'Fine. And make sure that Maa doesn't scold her too much. She's a good help and we won't find anyone like her again,' said Deb.

Avantika nodded. She could see that Deb didn't want to go.

'This will be good for us. We could use the extra money,' said Avantika.

'I know but that doesn't make it any easier to leave. Why couldn't it have happened six months later?'

'When we would be even busier with Nayra and not sleeping a wink?'

'But the difficult part would have been over,' said Deb.

'Don't overthink this. You will be back in a week and nothing is happening in a week. I have everyone here. They will take care of me,' said Avantika.

Despite reservations from Deb's mother Avantika went to drop him to the airport. She raised a racket. 'He's not a child, he can find the departure gate himself,' Deb's mother had complained. When Avantika wouldn't back down, she tagged along and cribbed all the way from the house to the airport.

'It's going to be so crowded in the airport,' she complained in all the three languages she knew. She even frowned when she saw them hold hands. They kept the taxi they had hired because his mother didn't trust a radio cab to arrive on time.

'Don't overeat just because there's room service,' said Avantika when it was time for him to enter the airport gates. Just being there reminded Deb of the last time they had been at the airport. Avantika noticed that and said, 'Only you're travelling now. Nothing is going to change in a week. You will just find me twenty-nine weeks pregnant and even fatter.'

'And still very hot . . .' whispered Deb so his mother couldn't hear.

'Why don't you say it a little louder?' winked Avantika.

'Can we go back home?' Deb's mother spat out angrily.

When Deb boarded the plane, his phone beeped.

Avantika Work
Nayra and I miss you.

Deb Home
I miss you too. I will be back soon.

54

One week turned to two, and the meetings didn't go anywhere.

Shrey and Deb slaved inside the producer Rashmi Sharma's windowless office which was only done up in white and silver and gold. It seemed like an exercise to brainwash more than anything else. They ran around in circles.

'It's assured money,' Deb would tell Shrey every night before going to sleep. 'Just a few days more, we do the channel meeting, get the whole thing passed and we are done.'

Every day, Avantika would send him a long video asking him to stay back, to work at this, that things were fine there. Deb had never been away from Avantika for such a period of time for the longest while. He felt pathetic to miss her as much he did. *Does she even miss me? Or is she just having fun with my mother?* Being away not only made him miss her, but also helpless and restless. *What if something happens? Who would take care of her?* As much as his parents were doing for her, he knew she needed him. Of course, Avantika didn't say that to Deb and it would bug him to no end.

'If she does, you will take the next flight and fly home, won't you?' said Shrey.

At times, he would get irritated with the distance and the sadness and vow not to talk to Avantika or Maa till the time he went back. He would then drag Shrey out to drink with him, be the irresponsible one. But after three drinks, he would end up calling Avantika and pouring his heart out to her as if they had just started dating. He would quickly Google and search poems by ancient Bengali or English poets and start reciting them for her. He would then crib that if he had to be a failed writer, he would rather be a failed poet, because at least he would have been more romantic. Avantika would giggle and laugh through all of it. She would be happy that he was being his old self again. Sometimes Maa would snatch the phone away from Avantika, scold Deb for keeping her awake and then switch it off. Like a teenager, Avantika would then take the phone from below Maa's pillow and then go to the washroom and call Deb. Sometimes they would talk through the night.

But some days were not as easy.

Deb Home
I miss you.

Avantika Work
I miss you more.

Deb Home
I can't do this. I want to be around you. What's this nonsense of having a career and what not.

Avantika Work
This is what you like to do as well. And it's just a few days.

Deb Home
What's Nayra doing?

Avantika Work
Sleeping now. Because I'm awake. She will wake up just when I'm going to sleep. She's a prankster.

Deb Home
She's going to be so awesome, no?

Avantika Work
She is.

Deb Home
C'mon.

Avantika Work
What?

Deb Home
You're thinking about it.

Avantika Work
No.

Deb Home
You're lying. I know that.

Avantika Work
I am. Had to lie again today.

Deb Home
What?

Avantika Work
There was a scan. Dr Sharma and I lied that it's better for me to not have anyone in the room. Maa of course felt odd.

Deb Home
You can't help it. Maa cries and then everyone's mood is screwed.

Avantika Work
I saw Augustya. I can see him clearly now. He's so much smaller than his sister.

Deb Home
Don't think about it.

Avantika Work
I'm trying my best.

Deb Home
☹

Avantika Work
Don't be sad! Work now! Last text. Bye. I love you.

Deb Home
I love you.

The next day the tables had turned. It wasn't Avantika who needed Deb, but Deb who needed her.

Avantika Work
Shrey told me what happened today.

Deb Home
Nothing happened today.

Avantika Work
Are you sure?

Deb Home
Of course.

Avantika Work
That's why you walked out of the meeting? And didn't go back? Deb, you can't do that to people. Or to Shrey.

Deb Home
I was missing you.

Avantika Work
I didn't see any calls.

Deb Home
I was missing you and thinking about him. I'm sorry.

Avantika Work
What did we talk about this?

Deb Home
That we will call each other when something like this happens. I'm sorry.

Avantika Work
I love you, Deb. You're forgetting what we are. We need to be with each other.

Deb Home
I'm sorry. I miss you so much. I feel so lost here without you. Why can't you be here?

Avantika Work
You know I want to be. ☹

Deb Home
I just want to feel your touch for once and then you can go back.

Avantika Work
Just once.

Deb Home
For now, even once would be a lot.

And then there were days that were absolutely great! There would be things that reminded them that in the longer run they would be happy—that there was no other choice. Despite the cruel hand nature had dealt to them, they would be fine. Deb couldn't stop texting her from the meetings.

Deb Home
Audio Note

Avantika Work
HAHAHAHAHA!

Deb Home
Did you hear that? Rashmi wants the hero to lose his memory twice in the second month!

Avantika Work
Heard that. Can you stop making fun of her and concentrate on the meeting!

Deb Home
Now she's suggesting we make Ghajini.

Avantika Work
Hehe.

Deb Home

Wait! Wait! She said no one will get to know because our hero doesn't have the body. This is amazing.

Avantika Work

DEB. CONCENTRATE! AND STOP LAUGHING AT HER FACE.

Deb Home

Me? No. I just said we should make both hero–heroine lose their memory so we could repeat their love story.

Avantika Work

And?

Deb Home

It was a joke but she loved it. Hold on, hold on.

Avantika Work

What now?

Deb Home

What I was waiting for! Supernatural element.

Avantika Work

No.

Deb Home

Old boyfriend. Is now a bhoot. The ghost inhabits the hero's body!

Avantika Work

Fuck.

Deb Home

This show is amazing!

That day of the meeting, Shrey and Deb felt like they were back in college, about to take an exam. There was almost as much at stake. Deb couldn't wait to get it over with and go back to Delhi to Avantika and his baby.

In the morning, Avantika and his parents video-called him. Avantika's belly seemed to have grown twice as much in the past week. It seemed like he had been away for months.

'You will be great,' said Avantika just before Deb left the hotel for the meeting.

'I don't care any more. I just want to come back already. It seems like I was born here,' said Deb.

'We better get this show, we have come too far now,' said Shrey. 'You know what this means. We get this cleared and we won't be kicked out of the show. Even if we do, as the creators of the show, they will have to keep paying us royalty. Imagine that! Just sitting at home and getting paid!'

'What if we get this show and I have to stay here for extended periods of time,' cribbed Deb.

'Don't wish against it. Do your best and get the show. Nayra and I aren't going anywhere. And Shrey and you can take turns to travel to Mumbai,' said Avantika.

'She has a point,' said Shrey. 'Moreover, if this happens, your first impression on Nayra will take a major spike. You won't be a failed writer then. You will be a big-league TV scriptwriter and that counts for something, right?'

'I'm sure she will be embarrassed of me,' said Deb.

'Still better than unemployed,' said Shrey.

'And I have seven weeks to change that, don't I?' said Deb.

'Unless Nayra wants to come out early. Then you have even less time,' said Avantika.

'Don't make me nervous,' said Deb. 'Chalo, got to go now.'

Deb disconnected the call. *This is important.* He closed his eyes and hoped the job would go well. Not for him, not for Shrey, not for the money, but so that when Nayra came along and asked for things, he could provide them. The huge car Tanmay had bought, for instance.

The final meeting started off rough.

The channel heads, the programming people and their minions had a lot of questions; everyone, in a bid to justify their jobs, tried poking holes into their story. They didn't have a creative bone in their bodies but they did wrestle themselves into the cushy chairs through group discussions. They couldn't create but they could debate and that's what they did. Shrey and Deb were grilled like murder suspects who, after the first few hiccups, cruised through it like Hannibal.

Their story was unassailable. A girl from a small town gets married to the youngest son of the great Singhania family that has a terrible secret. There are two elder bahus in the family both of whom married for money. The youngest scion is a chauvinist and hates the girl. The mother-in-law is an orthodox Hindu woman who believes the small-town girl should stay at home but the girl has plans, big plans! It was a combustible family with a lot of intrigue. And then, of course, there were the masterful additions Rashmi Sharma had made. Two memory losses, a supernatural element, and the girl having a twin no one else knew about. The team had fallen silent as they could already hear the pitter-patter of TRPs, the loud clanging and the jarring edit pattern that would help the show break all records. The conviction writ large on Shrey and Deb's face made it seem like the story wasn't fictional. They had lived this story. At one point, Shrey had elicited tears in his eyes—the heroine's *shaadi ka kangan* (her marital bangle) was being taken off, slowly, over a span of two episodes and was being handed over to the doppelganger; the doppelganger later threw it away in the garbage and the heroine had to sift through the trash over a period of three more episodes to find it. It was as if Shrey was that heroine. Deb had to pat him to calm him down.

It took three hours more than what the meeting was scheduled for.

Deb and Shrey felt like their voiceboxes were paralysed, but they had finally browbeaten the team into submission. They came up with a storyline and side tracks on the spot. There wasn't supposed to be two rebirths and three time leaps but they put them in. The feeling of an impending win sent them into overdrive. Deb and Shrey changed voices and narrated the impromptu storyline like theatre actors in their prime. The naysayers slowly came to their side. They bought every character, every incident of the same old story that the duo put in a nice new bottle, wrapped with a neat little bow and presented to them. Every time Deb saw a plotline fit, he would think of the money and what it could buy Nayra. The last part of the meeting was the hardest for Deb. They knew they had the show in the bag; now they were just sitting around and exchanging pleasantries. He wanted nothing of it. He couldn't wait to bolt out, catch a flight no matter how expensive and get to hold Avantika. This was the starting of something new and he couldn't wait to share it with her. Years later, when the young kids in colleges across India got stoned, his would be the show they would watch and trip over. It would be right up there with the movie *Gunda*, and the laptop-washing scene from *Saath Nibhana Saathiya*. They would be a part of history.

The meeting ended with wide smiles and tall promises.

'Seems like it's going to happen. Both of you did extremely well,' said Rashmi Sharma. 'We need to start scripting the show as soon as possible. We need to make this show something different, do things the way no one has ever done before.'

'We will do that,' said Shrey.

'Send me a six-month story bible. We won't follow that but the channel will want to have something in their hands. It's more a formality than anything else. You know how it works,' said Rashmi Sharma.

'Give us three days,' said Deb, which was a fair enough time in Indian television to come up with a six-month story.

Anything more than that was sacrilege. People came up with a year's storyline in a meeting, three days was an eon.

'Both of you flying back to Delhi?' asked Rashmi Sharma.

'I have to. My wife's alone there,' said Deb, keeping up the lie that he had told multiple times to hurry up meetings and wrap the trip up.

'She's seven months along right?'

Deb nodded. 'And she's alone. Our maid also left. She's managing everything on her own.'

Rashmi Sharma continued, 'Oh, you don't know how strong women are. I have made my actors work till the last day of pregnancy. They have given shots in the hospital too. Of course we had to change the storyline accordingly.'

'Nice,' said Shrey, trying to be genuine.

'We could have celebrated our successful meeting today. You could have met some people who will form the crew of this show,' said Rashmi Sharma. 'Come back soon, eh?'

'We will,' said Deb.

And with a flourish, she fetched a bag from beneath her seat and handed it over to Deb.

'What's this?'

'A little something for your daughter. Open it,' she said.

Deb took out the little box from the considerably large paper bag. He opened it gingerly.

'Got it made especially for her, the name's engraved,' she said and smiled.

Deb didn't know a lot about jewellery but the way it gleamed in his hands, and the way Shrey was looking at it told him it was obscenely expensive. Deb thanked her and hoped he sounded grateful. Rashmi Sharma got off at her office and asked the driver to drop them at the hotel.

'I will see you soon?' she said. Shrey and Deb nodded eagerly.

The driver drove towards the hotel.

'Check the flights. Let's get out of the city,' said Deb. 'My phone's off. Fuck, how long was that meeting!'

Shrey checked his phone and it was switched off too. Deb could see that Shrey wanted to celebrate. It was a big win for them. A show they had created, a show that they wouldn't be kicked out of. It was their first big creative win in years. He felt a little sorry that he was dragging him back to Delhi, but there would be enough time for celebration.

'Let's stop somewhere, get it charged? If we get the tickets, I will call the hotel and they can check us out? We will save some time,' he suggested.

They went to a cafe nearby, ordered sandwiches for themselves and put their phones to charge.

'We cracked it wide open, didn't we? That Rashmi, it was like you could see the money in her eyes,' said Shrey. 'But you get the credit, man, you did that. I would have floundered. But you, you were like a rock there. I might have developed a crush on you. You did fumble once though.'

'That was embarrassing,' said Deb.

'Who keeps the phone on vibrate any more?' said Shrey.

'I do.'

'But who says "Oh, I forgot it's on *vibrator*",' said Shrey and laughed out aloud.

'Is the phone charged yet?' asked Deb.

'10 per cent,' said Shrey. 'Let it charge some more. Don't make that face. Nothing is going to happen, you won't die if you don't talk to her for fifteen more minutes. Let this sink in. An entire show, man, an entire show. I can't wait to discuss the commercials with her. Though Avantika and her vibrating call would have spoilt everything!'

'Oh please, stop overreacting,' said Deb.

'But I will still tell Avantika that her stupid vibrator phone call could have messed things up for us. It will be nice to see her squirm in guilt,' said Shrey.

'Don't be so dramatic. Keep it for the show,' said Deb.

They ate their sandwiches and ordered another one each. They hadn't eaten well in days. Shrey asked for the cheque and

Deb fetched his phone from behind the cashier's counter. He switched it on.

'Shrey?' said Deb.

'What?'

Deb's fingers trembled. He struggled to open the notifications.

'Forty-five missed calls,' muttered Deb, his voice down to a whisper.

Shrey leaned over and peeked at Deb's phone. There were forty-five missed calls, countless messages and texts asking Deb to call back.

'Open them,' said Shrey to Deb who had frozen with fear. 'Deb? Open them?'

Shrey snatched the phone from Deb's hands and started going through the texts one by one. None of them had any details. They just kept asking Deb to call back immediately. *No details*. They were all sent an hour ago. Shrey's heart jumped to his mouth. Forty-five missed calls in sixty minutes. Twenty-three texts. Someone was calling every thirty seconds and sending a text every second minute. What had happened? What was so urgent? Where was Avantika?

'CALL THEM!' said Deb.

Shrey called Avantika, then Deb's mother and then finally Deb's father.

'WHY ARE THEY NOT PICKING UP!' Deb shouted. 'WHY THE FUCK AREN'T THEY PICKING UP!'

'Sir, you can't shout in here,' said the waiter.

'Fuck off,' snapped Shrey.

Shrey's hands went cold. He reached out for his own phone and switched it on. Same story, same number of calls. Shrey looked at Deb and stayed quiet. He didn't want to speculate, he didn't want to say or think a single thought. He saw Deb's feet buckle from under him and caught him just in time. He made him sit down.

'Don't think, don't think anything. It could be anything,' said Shrey.

He dialled the numbers again. Still no response. Shrey opened the travel app and furiously tapped on it.

'We have to go to Delhi,' said Deb. 'WE HAVE TO GO TO DELHI NOW! NOW, NOW!'

'I have booked the tickets. The cab's on its way.'

Three minutes later, Shrey and Deb ran out and boarded the cab. Deb incessantly kept calling his father but he didn't pick up the calls.

'It will be okay, it will be okay,' Shrey kept telling Deb who hadn't cried yet. 'Keep holding on, man. It's going to be fine. We will be in a plane soon. We will be right there.'

They hit a pocket of traffic right outside the airport.

'We can't wait, we can't wait!' screamed Deb and threw open the door of the cab.

He leapt out of the car, Shrey followed, and they ran straight for the departure gate. They skipped the line, pushed a few people out of the way and got to the front.

'Oye!' said someone from the back of the line.

'*Maa chuda chutiye,*' Shrey bellowed at them to fuck off and made way for Deb.

They were entering the airport when his father finally picked the phone up.

'*KI HOCHCHHE OEIKHANE*! Why the hell are you not picking up the phone? Is Avantika okay? WHAT'S HAPPENING THERE!' shouted Deb.

The others in the line turned to look at them. Tears dammed against Deb's eyes, the phone shook in his trembling hands.

'We are at the hospital, we have just reached. She's . . . her water broke,' said Baba.

'What?'

'Her water . . . it broke, Tini,' he said.

It took Deb a little time to register what his father had just said. *Her water broke.* That meant . . . Avantika was going to have a baby. His heart leapt with joy but . . . His father's voice was sombre, not a hint of happiness in it. Why would he be sad? Why wouldn't he be happy? And then, it dawned on him.

Deb and Avantika had downloaded a bunch of pregnancy apps on their phones when they first knew of it. They had put in the conception date in the app and it updated them daily on how far along they were in the pregnancy. Along with that, every week the app would send them details on how big their baby was growing. *Your baby is now as big as a pear! Your baby is now as big as a cabbage!* Different apps compared Nayra to different vegetables.

'Nonsense these apps are,' Maa would say every week when Deb would read out the mail from the app.

Deb remembered the last update from a couple of days ago.

Congratulations! Your baby is now 7 months old! It's as big as a cantaloupe! Her lungs are now forming! Her skin's getting thicker and her brain is gaining mass! Her fingers are getting shape! She's slowly getting ready for the world!

Deb muttered under his breath, 'Her lungs were not formed, her skin is not thick enough, her brain is weak, her fingers still bunched up, she isn't ready for the world, she isn't ready for the world.' He looked at Shrey, his voice a whisper. 'She wouldn't survive.'

The baby was not due for another 7 weeks.

'She's less than 30 weeks! How? There must be something—'

'Come to Delhi, quickly,' said Baba.

'How's Avantika?'

'They have taken her inside, Deb. I don't know what's happening,' said Deb's father.

I don't know what's happening.

These words broke Deb. How can *he* not know?

His father, though old, never said these words. He might be short and slightly hunched over, but he was a strong man in every sense of the word. He had a strong mind, an unbreakable one. It wasn't the words that he said but the way he said it. Like a defeated man. Deb's heart pounded out of his chest. Seven weeks early. Nayra wasn't even a baby yet. He remembered from the scans. How little, how incomplete. She wouldn't survive. She wasn't ready to come to the world. This wasn't her time.

'Baba?' said Deb.

'I'm here,' Baba said, the strain on his voice clear. Deb had never heard his father cry outside of tragic, old movies.

Never.

'Please don't cut the call, please don't cut the call,' said Deb, breaking down. He had never cried in front of his father too. He said, 'Tell me what's happening there. What's she doing?'

Deb couldn't take the name. What did he mean? Avantika? Nayra? What if he meant Nayra? Could she be doing anything? What if she's not doing anything . . . what would that mean?

Shrey showed the passports to the guard. He made Deb sit on a chair, and ran to check them both in. He watched Deb from afar as his wails shook the entire airport. Everyone looked at him, and made up their own stories. Shrey wondered what they thought. A dead parent? A sibling in an accident? A broken father of possibly two dead children?

'Your Maa is inside with her,' said Deb's father.

'Baba? Will the baby . . . she's . . . she's so small.'

Deb knew his father would find and say the right thing and he did.

'Let's not speculate. Let's wait for the doctors,' said Baba with the familiar stern, assuring voice.

Deb's tears wouldn't stop. He felt like he was dying bit by bit. Deb and Shrey were late for the flight. The counter had closed by the time Shrey got there. He screamed at the woman at the counter, and told her what was going on. She looked at Shrey and then at the man Shrey had pointed at. In a rare, fortuitous moment, something happened that Deb had never faced before— the girl recognized his name and put a face to it.

'I know him,' said the girl at the counter. 'He's that writer, isn't he? Who wrote about the girl he loved?'

She had read his first book.

Frantically, she called the supervisor and Shrey explained the situation breathlessly. The supervisor had heard Deb cry.

'PLEASE JUST LET US GO!' cried Deb from a distance.

The supervisor took the desk from her junior and sat in her seat. She quickly tapped and typed and the machine spat out two boarding cards.

'You have to run. You can't check in your baggage. Just take him and run,' she said.

Deb and Shrey ran all the way from check-in to security, to the gate down the aerobridge.

'Baba, don't cut the call. Baba, don't cut the call,' Deb cried into the phone.

'What the fuck are you looking at,' Shrey shouted at the co-passengers who kept staring at Deb.

They were the last ones on the flight and the plane started to taxi minutes after they had boarded it.

'Sir, you need to calm down and ask your friend to disconnect the call. We are taxiing now. He can't talk on the phone any more,' said the flight attendant.

'Deb?' said Shrey.

'Huh?'

Shrey pulled the phone off him. The phone was already disconnected. He was shouting on the phone but Baba wasn't there on the other side.

The aircraft took off.

Deb's body shook and trembled. Shrey reached out for his hand but he pulled it away. Shrey called for water but Deb wouldn't have any. Shrey felt like Deb would pass out any second. He had booked business class tickets, Deb noticed only after twenty minutes into the flight.

Shrey got up from his seat once the seat belt signs were turned off. He walked around the plane, shouting out aloud, 'Is there a doctor on board? Is there a doctor on board? A paediatrician?'

He found one before the flight attendant asked him to quieten down. He requested the doctor to come talk to Deb. Shrey explained the situation and Avantika's medical history to her.

Deb had only one question for her, 'How likely is her survival?'

'I can't say that for sure. I can't tell you without the reports.'

'Just give me a number,' he said.

'It depends on the hospital, the doctors, the condition—'

'JUST TELL ME A NUMBER!' wailed Deb.

'50 per cent,' said the doctor. 'I would say there's a 50 per cent chance she would survive the delivery. That's what the hospital rates are in India.'

Shrey thanked the doctor, apologized for Deb's outburst, and walked her back to her seat.

Deb's heart still felt like it would explode. Every few minutes he would see his phone knowing fully well it was irrational to expect network. Would the baby be born? Maybe it was a false alarm? He had read about premature babies. Babies born a week, or two weeks, before the due date. His daughter, she was a lot earlier. Everything he had read came rushing back to his mind. The last two months were critical for a baby's development. The lungs are formed, the nails take shape, the heart develops its capacity to pump blood in the amount necessary, and the eyes take shape and colour. What will his baby be like if she's born now? The questions took the form of an unbearable physical pain in the pit of his stomach. He threw up twice in the vomit bags the attendant gave to him. The third time he got up and went to the washroom. He threw up everything he had eaten or drunk. He washed his face; the pain didn't lessen even in the slightest bit. It had settled in a lump in his stomach. He stared at his reflection in the mirror. He should have been there; he should have never gone to Bombay.

The flight attendant knocked at the door. 'Are you okay, sir?'

'I'm fine,' he said, his words barely a whisper.

'Are you okay, sir?' she asked again.

'I'M FINE!' said Deb louder this time.

He came out a few minutes later, his body giving up, still dry heaving. Shrey helped him to his seat.

'Is he going to be fine? Should we call the captain?' asked the attendant.

'He's going to be okay,' said Shrey. 'Everything will be fine.'

The flight attendant gave him ORS and he couldn't keep it down. He vomited all over the floor. Shrey offered to and then cleaned the carpet. He needed to do something, occupy himself.

Time crawled by, the two hours seemed like a month. Deb couldn't sit down or stand up. His head spun.

Deb was already at the door when the flight landed, being shouted down by the flight attendants.

'PLEASE SIT DOWN, SIR!'

'I'M NOT SITTING THE FUCK DOWN, OKAY! MY CHILD IS DYING!'

The door opened, and the aerobridge locked into place. Deb prepared himself to run.

55

Two hours ago, Avantika had been wheeled into the hospital, her water had broken, and the labour pains had set in. The nurses and Dr Sharma waited for her at the entrance. Everyone's faces bore a funereal look. *She shouldn't be here, not right now, it's too early.* This was clearly written on the hospital staff's faces.

'HOW IS THIS HAPPENING! IT CAN'T BE!' she had screamed in the ambulance. Deb's mother had held her hand and she had buckled over to the floor of the ambulance.

Her voice had given out by the time she had reached the hospital. Her screams were now silent, haunting wails. Her hand was firmly around her stomach. It was as if she was stopping

Nayra from getting born, not right now. *It's not your time, Nayra, please don't, it's not your time.*

Dr Sharma had rushed to her side and held her hand, asked her to relax, and told her sternly that she should do what she was told.

'Where's Deb, I want Deb!'

'We will do everything possible,' said Dr Sharma. 'But we need you to cooperate. We will make everything okay. Listen to my voice. Everything will be okay. We are calling Deb. He will be here soon. Just be with me.'

And that's what she did. An irrational dread had crept in. These were the people who would deliver their delicate baby and she shouldn't behave unwarrantedly with them or who knew . . . she might never see Nayra.

She blocked the uncertain future out and pretended that forty weeks were up, and that she would deliver a healthy Nayra. Not a dead one, or one barely hanging on for life. They put a foetal monitor on her. Nayra was breathing, she heard Dr Sharma say. But they were losing her. What did that mean? *What do you mean? Why do you say we are losing her?* Her voice wouldn't leave her throat. The pain was to be minimal, Dr Sharma said. Both babies were smaller than they should have been. This thought came ricocheting in her mind. She closed her eyes shut and did what Dr Sharma and the assistants asked her to do.

'YOU NEED TO BREATHE!'

She pushed as asked. Most of her effort was spent in trying to visualize that everything was going to be just fine. 'The baby will be healthy . . . the baby will be healthy . . .' she kept saying this to herself. She thought of Deb, of disappointing him, of losing . . . both his children. *The baby will be healthy, Nayra will be healthy . . .*

The instructions kept coming from Dr Sharma who shouted to get through to Avantika. Avantika's body was half on auto-pilot. Fifteen minutes later, she felt it. A gasp escaped her lips. She knew. Relief? Happiness? Pain? She knew she was a mother. A mother of a dead child but a mother nonetheless. What she always wanted, to have a family, but it came wrapped with so much sorrow. It was Augustya. It was her son. She had to welcome him with a smile on her face. His soul was in that body that left her. *He's watching me, he's waiting for me, I have to smile for him, I love him.* She felt the doctor hold him in his arms. She opened her eyes and looked at the doctor. She noticed that slight twitch of pity in his eyes. A dead baby, the worst sight in the entire world.

'I want to hold him, keep him on me,' she said, her voice a whisper. 'He's my son. My firstborn, Nayra's elder brother.'

Her heart beat faster. The nurse cut the cord and quickly wrapped him up. And that's when she saw him. 'Augustya,' she whispered again. 'A part of me, a part of Deb, a part of us. I love you. My little *jaan*, my *bachcha*, my baby.' So little, barely human. The nurse kept Augustya on Avantika's chest for barely a second and then took him away. Avantika closed her eyes, the image seared itself into her brain. In that moment, she promised herself she would never forget him. He would always be her first child. There would always be an empty chair for him.

The dead baby—Augustya, their son, Shrey's godchild, Deb's parents, grandson—was taken away.

The nurses looked at each other, felt sorry for the woman in front of them, but knew the worst was over.

'Hold on for a little bit,' said the doctor. 'Just keep doing what you're doing. Stay with us.'

Avantika tried to tear herself away from the thought of Augustya and concentrate but she couldn't. The screams and shouts of the doctor were just noises at a distance. Then the screams slowed down; she found it hard not to slip away. There were encouraging words which were spoken. Avantika was told she was doing great and the baby would come any moment. Avantika tried staying in the moment, struggled hard to single-mindedly focus on Nayra but it wasn't to be. She thought of death. She thought of not one but two dead babies. Siblings who didn't want to get born. Brother and sister who would take everything from her. She couldn't tear herself away. And then she saw him. *Deb*. He was there, as clear as day, right there by her bed. He was holding her hand, that dimpled face, that smiling face, crying and smiling. He told her things would be okay, that he loved her, that Nayra was about to be theirs. Everything would be okay. She needed to be positive. *I love you, Avantika*. She heard his voice, the love of her life was speaking to her. *Of course it will be okay*, she said. She came back and she pushed.

The baby came.

'IT'S HERE!'

The last of her strength drained away. From what Avantika had read, seen, heard from people, she had prepared herself for a loud, angry cry of a baby torn away from the womb where she previously rested. A baby disturbed from her sleep. All she heard was a whimper.

She saw the doctor before she saw Nayra; a face contorted with fear. She began to cry. Big drops of tears streaked down her cheeks, and a tearing want to hold Nayra overtook her body. She was *hers*. She had whimpered, she had breathed out in the world, she had made Avantika her mother. Nayra was a part of her; she wanted to hold her right that instant. She felt empty. It felt discomforting that in a moment both her children weren't inside her, resting, but outside, crying and dead.

She saw her as the doctor lifted her.

She was the big sister, she was the bigger baby of the two she saw today, yet she was so tiny. She saw little fingers, still a little webbed, move. The doctor kept the baby on her chest and she looked at her.

'Nayra,' she whispered. 'You're loved.'

Nayra heaved and her lips turned into a small curve to cry but her voice stuck in her throat.

'Your father will be here soon, he will make everything okay,' said Avantika and cried. She wanted to clasp her, hold her tight, love her, but she felt if she held her any tighter, she would break.

Before she could tell her who she was, and how lucky they
were to have her, tell Nayra her father's name, they took her away
from her. She watched helplessly as they put her in a plastic bag, not
somewhere a little child should be in, and took her behind a curtain.

'Why did you put her in a bag? She was moving. She's not
dead,' she said, her voice barely a whisper. When she wasn't
answered she mustered all the strength she had and screamed,
'WHERE ARE YOU TAKING HER! WHY ARE YOU
USING THAT BAG! GIVE ME MY BABY BACK! I WANT
MY BABY!'

'She needs to be protected against infections, she's too small,'
said the assistant doctor calmly. 'You need to rest.' He held her
and made her lie down. Avantika wanted to protest further but
she had nothing left her in. Her body was giving in.

Avantika strained to hear her cry but she got nothing. She
heard faint murmurs from the doctor and that was the last thing
she heard before she passed out. She dreamt of two babies, both
alive and crawling into her lap, and then she dreamt of two
babies, both covered in a grey slime and dead. She laughed and
cried and even as she dreamt she knew she was dreaming and she
tried willing herself to wake up. She fought the sedatives and lost.

'I NEED TO SEE MY BABY NOW!' screamed Avantika
two hours later even before her eyes opened.

She found her throat dry and her voice gone, she saw Deb's
parents in the room. She saw them before they saw her. Deb's father
was on his phone, nothing like she had ever seen him—tense and
out of depth, his shirt dishevelled and his stature shrunken. Deb's
mother was crying, bunched up in the corner of the sofa, muttering
to herself in incoherent Bengali, swaying from front to back like
a lunatic. Seeing her Avantika let out another silent scream. Deb's
mother rushed to her, wiped her tears.

'Is she . . . dead?'

'No!' exclaimed Deb's mother. 'Why are you saying that?
They took her away but—'

Deb's father took over lest she uttered something that wasn't supposed to be said. He said, 'She's under observation. The neonatal paediatrician will see us in a while. Till then you're supposed to rest.'

'Rest, Baba? Just tell me about her, please! What's she doing? How's she doing? Please? They . . . they kept her on my chest and she didn't cry. She didn't cry as they told me she would. I read that if that doesn't happen . . . the baby . . . the survival rates.'

'Avantika, you need to take care. You have gone through a lot today.'

'Tell me anything! Please, Baba, I'm begging you.'

'She's . . . 0.6 kg. That's her weight,' said Deb's father, his voice barely a whisper.

Avantika's shoulders drooped before she slumped completely. Her hand went instinctively to her stomach. It felt empty, hollow, like the very life force of her, her entire world had been sucked out of her, snatched before time.

Going by her pregnancy, the doctor had estimated the baby's weight to be at least 3.5 kg. She couldn't think of anything else but how small Nayra was, how tiny her fingers were. Every time she played it in her head, the time she held Nayra in her hands, she got surer her child wouldn't survive. Her brain started rummaging up memories of all the accounts she had read of mothers of twins and triplets, many of whom had premature deliveries, and she remembered how many of them hadn't made it.

Of all that she had read, her child was the tiniest.

Nayra wouldn't survive.

She looked at Deb's parents and realized they didn't know any more than she did. Deb's mother had taken to sitting on the floor and praying. She had her eyes closed and a constant stream of tears kept running down her face.

She pressed the bell button as hard and as many times as she could.

A nurse came rushing in. She asked her the same question she had asked Deb's parents, at first politely and then threatened her with her job. She held the nurse's collar and demanded to know if the baby would be all right. When the nurse stalled and refused to answer, Avantika slapped her. She tried to clamber down and fell. It took two nurses to put her back in her bed and hold her down.

'The doctor will come soon. We can't tell you anything,' said the nurse, gave her the medicines that she had to take and rushed out as hurriedly as she had come.

Deb's father held Avantika's hand and asked her to be patient. She wanted her father-in-law to keep the hollow platitudes to himself and get her Nayra.

'Where's Deb?' she asked him.

'He's on his way,' said Deb's father.

'Will she live? Baba, please tell me she will live?' she asked him.

'I have read a few articles,' said Baba.

Deb's father read out whatever he had found in the past two hours. He used the word *miracle* and *critical* one too many times. Avantika was sure Deb's father had cherry-picked incidents to make her keep her faith. She knew too much herself to believe in the rosy picture he tried to paint.

It was only now that she thought of Deb that she remembered the other child. *Augustya.* A wave of guilt washed over her. She cried and closed her eyes, 'I didn't mean to forget you, I didn't mean to forget you, baby. Sorry, Augustya. I love you, I love you, Augustya. And I will see you again. Please forgive me. I love you and I will always remember you.'

Soon, the pain returned, and she passed out.

56

When she woke up again, the physical pain came in all its force. She felt a hand on her forehead. She opened her eyes and saw Deb standing over her. She thought she was home, in her own bed, and Deb was waking her up to tell her there was chai waiting for her and that it would get cold. She could almost smell the tea and she smiled for that brief second at him. Everything was normal. She was still pregnant. The babies were still inside her. There had been no visit to the hospital. No delivery.

Then it all came back to her.

'Deb?' she said, panic in her voice. She stared at Deb, searching for signs of worry, panic and dread. She couldn't read his face. She searched his face for disappointment.

'We need to go see Nayra. She's in the NICU. Dr Sharma needs to see us,' he said.

He didn't use the term Neonatal Intensive Care Unit because she didn't need to hear that.

'You saw her? She's okay?' asked Avantika.

'The doctors told me I should come when you wake up. I haven't seen her yet,' he said.

He searched for reassuring words but he couldn't find any.

Deb's father had been outside the hospital when Shrey and Deb reached. When Shrey saw Deb's father's helpless face, he had assumed the worst.

'So she's alive, she's alive, right?' Deb, who had been deathly quiet on the cab ride to the hospital, had asked and his father nodded.

That's all Deb had wanted to hear. It was like he wasn't prepared to hear anything else. The tense nerves that had been throbbing through the flight, the taxi to the hospital—Shrey saw them all relax at once. Did he catch a faint smile? How could he . . . be sure?

'Where's she? Where's Dr Sharma?' he had asked as if this was routine.

Both parents needed to come together, he was told by the nurse. Deb had then gone and sat near Avantika's bedside. He felt sorry for her; she had been through it alone, all that pain, all alone; he should have been there. He had tried to Google what entailed such premature births but Shrey had taken the phone from him. 'Nothing will come out of it,' he had told Deb. Deb watched Avantika sleep restlessly. Her lips quivered continually, and her fingers kept twitching. He kept imagining what she might have gone through in the past few hours. He cursed Rashmi Sharma and his greed; he should have been here, holding her hand. Instead, she had to bear all this pain alone. Quite a few times, Deb wanted to ask his parents if they saw Augustya. He couldn't find the courage to; seeing his mom sit in the corner of the room, muttering prayers and swaying broke his heart. He reminded himself that they needed to concentrate on Nayra now.

'I'm so sorry I wasn't here, I'm so sorry, baby,' he said to Avantika.

Avantika tried sitting up.

'You don't have to—'

Avantika kept a hand on Deb and interrupted him. 'She's alone. We need to see her. She needs us. She needs us.'

Deb said, 'Are you sure you're okay to go?'

'I won't be till the time I see Nayra. We have to see her. She's our daughter,' she said.

'We do, we do, we are parents now,' said Deb, held her hand and clasped it tight. He managed to smile at Avantika.

The nurse brought a wheelchair in. Deb and the nurse helped her on to the wheelchair. 'Will she be okay?' asked the nurse.

'Of course,' said Deb. 'We will be back soon,' said Deb to his parents as the nurse pushed the wheelchair out of the room.

It was then that for the first time Deb's mother opened her eyes. They were bloodshot; she struggled to adjust to the light. Deb's father helped her towards Deb. Deb saw her lip turn up in a half-cry. She composed herself, held Deb's face and kissed him.

'You deserve everything in the world. You're always so nice. *Tumi dekhbe, kono dukkho hobe naa tomar,* you don't deserve any pain,' she said and embraced Deb.

'Thank you, Maa,' he said.

As he left the room, he saw his mom go back to the corner of the room and start praying. Deb said to Avantika, 'Nothing will happen.'

In the lift, Avantika asked Deb, 'Does Tanmay know?'

'Baba told me you asked him to not tell him. Do you want to call them?' he asked.

'Not yet,' said Avantika.

The fear of seeing Nayra again burned through her. Whatever awaited them behind the lift door, behind the ominous glass walls of the Neonatal Intensive Care Unit—it was for them to deal with, just her and Deb. It was their grief to be felt, no one else's.

'Here we are,' said the nurse outside the NICU. 'The third bed,' she said. 'You can't touch the baby yet but still make sure you sanitize your hands once you get in. I will give you some time alone with the baby and then you can come see the doctor. He's waiting for you. You will meet Namrata inside. She will guide you through this.'

A heavy metal door waited for them. The word NICU was written in light pink lettering. They could have had a clown holding up the sign and it wouldn't be less heartbreaking. Avantika imagined Nayra hooked to ventilators, cannulas piercing her body, machines barely keeping her alive. In her head, she had seen the worst. Every few seconds, a rogue, sinister situation entered her head, of a doctor telling them that Nayra didn't have a chance at a good quality of life and they should switch off the ventilator. She kept pushing it away and yet it clung to her.

Deb opened the door and pushed the wheelchair inside.

'Don't worry,' he said to Avantika.

You haven't seen her, she thought to herself, otherwise you would worry too.

There was a long corridor with curtains dividing the passages. Behind every curtain was a baby like theirs. Avantika counted three. The nurse in the NICU asked them to sanitize their hands.

'I will be with you the entire time. I'm Namrata,' said the nurse. 'You're Nayra's parents? She's a brave girl.' She smiled at Deb and Deb smiled back at her.

Avantika got up from her wheelchair. She washed and sanitized her shaking hands. Deb did so excitedly, as if nothing was wrong.

'It's going to be okay,' Deb said to Avantika.

Deb hurried, Avantika walked behind slowly. Behind the first curtain were two glass boxes—incubators and not ventilators as Deb would learn later—with two little babies in them. A woman looked over at them and babbled. The tiny children, obscured partly by the glass case and a blanket, looked to be fast asleep. Behind the second was just one and no one was around. There was silence other than the little beeping sound. It looked less an incubator and more like a glass coffin.

They stopped at the third; their daughter awaited them. The lights were off. A blanket kept over the incubator to block out the light. On the side, there was equipment. Multiple screens with green and shifting red numbers on them. It wasn't the way they had imagined they would see Nayra together for the first time.

They walked slowly towards her. Deb gingerly removed the blanket, preparing himself for the worst. *No matter what she looks like, she's my daughter,* he reminded himself of that.

Avantika switched on the light. They bent over and stared.

It's just like the womb, is the first thought that came to Avantika. She cried the moment she saw her.

Her Nayra. She lay face down on her bed behind the glass wall. They created her, she was theirs. That broken, too–soon-into-the-world child was theirs. She saw the light too soon, too soon, her face was still a smudge of features, her skin translucent, the veins visible. She looked at Deb, and wondered if he saw what she saw, the fragile child fighting to live, but she saw that he was smiling and tapping his fingers across the glass impatiently. It was like he wanted to reach out to her this very moment.

'Looks like a little frog, a little cuddly frog, cute, so cute, cute like a button,' said Deb, tears flooding his eyes, his words jumbled up. 'I made you. You're so cute! You're so damn cutuuuuu! Look at you! Aw! So sweet! So little . . . where's the chocolate, let me lather you up in it and eat you. Nom, nom, nom. You stayed inside your mother, now stay in my stomach.'

'I made you,' repeated Avantika and she looked at Deb. For a split second, she saw the look she was used to seeing on his face earlier in their relationship. That look of him falling in love. She looked at the two of them . . . and her broken heart melted in a puddle.

Nayra wasn't bigger than a fist. Tiny eyes, small fists, so little, so delicate. Even so there were countless probes on every part of her body. It was all you could see. Two little pipes went through her nose and her mouth and it made Avantika physically sick to watch that.

'That's not right,' she heard herself mutter.

'She is a like a spaceperson, a cosmonaut. A cute cosmonaut! So cute though,' said Deb.

Her back rose and fell—and that was balm for Avantika's heart. A sign of life. Avantika felt scared even keeping her hands on the glass. Deb on the other hand . . .

'Can we touch her? I want to touch her. I want to touch Nayra right now,' asked Deb. He ran out and got Namrata inside. 'We can touch her, right?

'Why don't you do that after you meet the doctor?' Namrata said.

'That sounds about right. Where's she going anyway? Space?' asked Deb and laughed, who in those little moments he had spent looking at that face, imagined a future with her. There were no alternatives but for Nayra to live and fulfil the destiny Deb had imagined for her. They had made pacts and promises to each other and she couldn't bow out of them just because they hit a little hiccup of her getting born earlier.

'Will she survive?' asked Avantika.

'What nonsense? Why would she not?' said Deb.

The nurse paused nervously and then said, 'I don't want to lie. She's the youngest premature baby we have had in the hospital. The rest the doctor will tell you.'

'I know what the doctor is going to tell us. She's going to be up and about in a flash,' said Deb, smiling.

The nurse didn't know how to react to that.

'That's exactly what the doctor is going to say,' said Avantika and held Deb's hand. They both smiled at each other, and stood there and watched their little daughter. They cried together. They didn't wonder if she would live or die, they *knew* she would survive. After seeing the future with her, they knew it was the only way forward.

'That's our daughter. It's unbelievable, isn't it?' said Deb.

'Please tell me she will always be.'

'She will always be.'

57

The first word Dr Sharma said was *congratulations*, and that itself made her feel like the weight of the world had been lifted off her shoulders. He got up and hugged Deb, shook hands firmly with Avantika. He wouldn't have said that had he not felt Nayra would survive. Deb smiled widely.

'Didn't I tell you everything will be fine?' said Deb.

There was a knock on the door and Shrey peeked inside. Dr Sharma called him inside.

'I will cut straight to the point, Deb, Avantika. We have never had a baby as premature as Nayra. You have seen her, you know. There are more babies in the NICU but she's smaller and weighs lighter than them. It decreases her immunity to fight against any infections. That's why we had to immediately put her in a plastic bag and into an incubator. We can't take any chances with her. The slightest infection can—'

'Nothing's going to happen to her. I just—' said Deb.

'We get your point though,' said Shrey helpfully.

'Will she be okay?' asked Avantika again.

'Why do you keep asking that?' asked Deb.

'I have always been honest with you. Can I continue being so?' asked Dr Sharma.

'It's not going to be an easy journey. Nayra's lungs are weak and the trauma her body has gone through due to this early delivery is too immense. We must be extremely careful with her. Her lungs will take a lot of time to develop and she still might require oxygen support for upto a year. She's going to have to stay in the NICU for at least two months. It will give her time to fully develop in a controlled environment. Both of you must be strong for this. It can be a harrowing process. We have counsellors on board whom you can talk to.'

'But she's going to live. Is that what you're saying?' asked Avantika, another iteration of the question she had been asking since morning.

'Of course she is,' snapped Deb.

'We can't talk like this, Avantika. You understand that. You can't put a number to this,' said Dr Sharma. 'The average rate of survival across the US and Europe, in good hospitals, is 60 per cent.'

Deb threw his hands up in the air. 'I don't know why we are talking about this, Dr Nikhil.'

'You're saying that there's a 60 per cent chance? You're saying that my daughter won't survive this hospital?' said Avantika, her voice cracking.

'That's nonsense,' scoffed Deb, feeling a mild hatred towards the other children who were fighting a percentage battle with Nayra.

'Listen to me,' said Dr Sharma, his voice booming. 'What I told you means nothing. Every child has its own recovery rate. As parents, it's your duty to do what you can, and as her doctor, I will do what I can. Do you understand that it's my job to see the children healthy? That's what I do.'

Deb said, 'But—'

Avantika stopped Deb and said, 'Let him finish, Deb.'

Deb leaned back into his chair and muttered inaudibly. He was already fishing out his phone to Google the best hospital for premature babies.

'Now there are some things I need to tell you right away,' said Dr Sharma.

'Even when Nayra leaves, you will have to be extremely careful with her for the first two years. We will give her a lot of oxygen in the coming two months and that could have some lasting effects.'

'What kind of lasting effects?' said Deb, keeping his phone aside.

'On the brain. We will carry out brain scans to see. Even if there aren't any anomalies, she will be a little slow on physical developments too. She will catch up after two years. You need to constantly get her checked . . .'

The doctor went on for the better part of an hour outlining all that was needed to be done, the money they would need, the kind of treatments they should opt for, the kind of attitude they should keep towards the process. Both had tuned out after the first few minutes. It was Shrey who was taking notes on his phone.

They wanted to get back to their daughter. All they wanted was for her to survive. They didn't care about brain bleeds, or if she had reduced motor capacity, or was even disabled, or if they lost all that they had to see her survive, all they wanted was for her to live.

As they walked back into the NICU they realized why parents spend decades caring for the unfortunate children who have no future. They would do that in a heartbeat. They just wanted Nayra, wheelchair or not, brain damage or not, bedridden or not, they just wanted her.

Looking at her, the worst-case scenarios flooded Avantika's mind.

'If what the doctor says . . . if she needs constant help . . . what if she grows old and . . . if we are not around for her and . . .' Avantika's voice trailed off.

'We will find a way to live forever,' said Deb, and he put his arm around her, and Avantika almost instantly felt safe, as if she were in bubble wrap and nothing would happen to her, or her daughter. She looked at him, and muttered a soft love you, not to tell him, but to herself, to remind herself how lucky she was to be allowed to be in love with a man like him.

58

Tanmay and Vernita reached the hospital a couple of hours later and texted Avantika.

Deb and Avantika asked them to wait in the ward with his parents. Neither Deb nor Avantika were there to see how they reacted when Deb's parents and Shrey relayed the sequence of events to them. But they could imagine all of them Googling and calling people they knew, checking for references, and searching for alternate hospitals for Nayra.

Deb and Avantika stood near the glass casing for an hour, sanitizing their hands repeatedly. Yet neither of them had the courage to touch the baby. They were scared down to their bones to hurt her. With every passing second, it started to seem that she was normal-sized, as if all babies were supposed to fit in your palm, and spend months in an incubator. What didn't seem to get acceptable were the tubes and the wires that went in and out of her. That one tube that went up her tiny nostril to pump in oxygen felt most uncomfortable for Deb. It seemed unnatural, cruel. Even though she slept she didn't look at peace. Deb wanted to rip it out, hold her in his hands. What could a daughter want more than to nestle in her father's arms and sleep?

'Touched her yet?' asked Namrata.

They turned to see Namrata watching over them, smiling. They shook their heads.

'She technically has. They placed Nayra on her after the birth. So yes, I haven't. She's so little. How do you hold her? You need to teach us,' said Deb, a tingling sensation bolting through his body.

'Here, sit. Let me help you,' said the nurse. She held Avantika's hand and made her sit. 'You need to pump milk for her every hour. In your body she was getting that nourishment, we need to keep up with that. This is an electric pump. You have to get one but for today we will use this. So what you do is . . .'

'I know how to use it. I have one at home. I practiced and saw videos for . . . I wanted to know,' said Avantika. 'I will get it tomorrow.'

'Seems like you're set, then,' said Namrata and clasped Avantika's hand. She looked at Deb watching Nayra unblinkingly. 'She's a miracle, isn't she?'

'She is,' said Deb.

'She's yours. You can't do anything to hurt her. She's waiting for her parents. You can touch her through those little circular holes on both sides. Don't pick her up though. She's a little baby and needs her rest. I will leave you to it,' said Namrata with a wide smile. She pulled the curtains and left.

Deb and Avantika stood on the sides of the incubator, their breaths stuck in their throats. They watched the circular holes for them to put their hands in. They sanitized their hands again.

Deb pushed his hands in. A fear gripped Avantika that she would knock one of the probes off and her hands stayed outside.

Deb held her hand, calmed her down. Their hands hovered over her body for some time. Deb was the first to touch Nayra.

He let out the breath he had been holding all this while. He let his finger slowly drop over her arm and then ran it from her elbow to her closed fist. Her skin was like paper, thin. It moved over her body like it would come off. For a moment, it was like the world slowed down. She was *his*. After months and months of her being just an idea, just a name, a mound of flesh inside Avantika, she was here, breathing and living.

'It's real, she's real. She's real, Nayra is real,' said Deb. 'Look! She moved! Touch her! She's ours, Avantika. Touch her! She's so soft!'

Avantika reached out to touch her.

'Careful,' said Deb.

Then Avantika touched her. There was the tiniest of tugs at the probes and all the alarms started to beep violently. The screens went red and green and sirens blared angrily. Deb and Avantika pulled their hands back in a flash. They watched in horror as Nayra squirmed about in her bed, and groaned in pain and discomfort. Namrata came rushing in with another nurse and studied the monitors.

'DO SOMETHING!' shouted Deb.

Namrata and the nurse just stood there watching the monitors. Deb and Avantika were motionless, their eyes on Nayra.

'Can you tell us what's happening? She's moving, isn't she? She's moving, right! She's definitely moving,' exclaimed Avantika.

And just like that, the beeping stopped. The other nurse left the room without saying a word, like nothing had happened.

'What the hell was that?' asked Deb.

Namrata looked at them and answered calmly, 'She's weak.'

'Let's not call her weak,' said Deb.

Namrata smiled. 'Did I say weak? I'm sorry, my bad. It's been a long shift.'

'We won't touch her till she's ready. We will wait as long as it takes. We are in no hurry,' said Avantika.

'How did you feel when you first touched her? Did you feel good? That's what she felt too, baba. That explains the spike in the stats,' said Namrata with a grin. 'Her heart must have jumped feeling your touch.'

'It was mostly me doing the touching,' said Deb and returned Namrata's grin.

'Don't get her too excited,' Namrata said and left the room.

Deb and Avantika pulled up chairs next to the incubator and watched Nayra sleep. It was much later that Deb pulled out his phone and clicked numerous pictures of Nayra alone and together with the both of them.

'I miss him,' said Deb, soft as a whisper, thinking of the twins that were in the same NICU. 'He would have been here, right here, with his sister.'

'I miss him too.'

Avantika had been scared to talk about him and every now and then she would wonder if they could bring him into the incubator and bring him to life.

'I saw him. They gave him to me for a few seconds,' she said.

'I need to see Augustya,' said Deb.

'Are you sure?' asked Avantika.

'Augustya is as much ours as Nayra is and he deserves to be held, to be told that he is loved, that he would be remembered, and he has a family that would have done anything for him if he had decided to stay. We are parents of two children and not one.'

Avantika nodded. They called their doctor and expressed their desire to see Augustya. They had made it clear to the hospital that they would want to spend as much time as they wished with Augustya's body when she delivered.

Deb led the way as they were taken to where the hospital had kept Augustya's body. The room was cold, and they were offered lab coats which they refused. They were asked to wear gloves which they took and kept on the side. They weren't doctors. They were his parents and they needed to feel him just like they felt their daughter.

They brought Augustya's body wreathed in a white sheet. He was cleaned and prepped for them.

Deb cradled his phone. They had read that it was important to do that. It would be the only memory they would have of him. When they unwrapped him, Deb couldn't bring himself to click a picture. Nayra was small, a baby in the making, but their son—he was barely even Nayra's size.

'Camera?' said Avantika. 'Click my picture with him.'

Him? There was no him. The boy was barely there. Unlike his sister who had a semblance of a face, he had none. Just a structure where a face would have come, where there would have been eyes, a nose, two ears. Deb could feel his heart break with every picture he took of the two of them.

'Your turn,' she said.

'I don't love him like she does,' thought Deb, and it made him feel guilty. He didn't want to hold him. He was even angry at him for not existing, for breaking his heart, for making him feel the way he felt. Was it true what they said? Mothers and sons have a sacred bond? Like fathers and daughters?

As she made him hold the boy, his skin against him, the repulsion—he didn't want to use the word but that's what it was—dissipated instantly. It didn't feel odd, instead it felt natural. Of course, he wanted to hold *him*. There was a him. Augustya. The boy of his team. The member of their boys' club. His insurance policy against the girls in the house. He was everything he wanted. The boy was his, and he fell more in love with him every second that passed. With every passing moment, he saw Augustya grow in his hands, to a fully grown baby, to a child and then a toddler, he saw him climb out of his grasp and be an adolescent, a teenager, and then an adult, he saw him grow old, and then he himself grew old and was in Augustya's arm, shrinking and shrinking till he was small, and then looked up at an old Augustya. Suddenly, he didn't want to let him go.

When Avantika clicked a picture he even managed a bright, sunny smile. They clicked a few more pictures and uploaded them on the cloud so as to not lose them ever. They panicked they would lose them and mailed the photos to themselves. Deb draped him in the outfit Shrey had got for him. It was a Liverpool jersey. He looked handsome in it, said Deb.

'Are you done?' asked the nurse.

Giving him back to the nurse was harder than they thought it would have been. A few minutes more. They kept saying that every time a nurse came inside. They knew it was the last time they would get to hold Augustya. The only time their family would be whole. They wanted to stretch it for as long as it was possible. When they left the room, they were crying.

The hospital would take care of him now. What wouldn't they give to have him in the incubator next to Nayra!

'I can't stop thinking what it would have been like if he were in the cot next to hers, if he grew up,' said Avantika.

'You don't have to. He would have been beautiful, I can see that. He would have been a beautiful kid but he would have been gorgeous as an adult.'

'Would he have been?' asked Avantika.

'Yes, it's obvious. Couldn't you see that? He would have looked like you. Tall, stately, a prince. Just incredible. Heads would have turned wherever he went. He wouldn't have been very good at academics though. That's for sure.'

'Why? I'm good and you're good. Why would Augustya not have been good?' asked Avantika.

'Too busy making boys or girls or both fall in love with him. Football captain, or basketball captain, maybe both. He would have done history honours, or political science. He would have his first great love story in college, and it would change him, destroy him, make him find himself.'

'Would he talk to us about it? Would we help?'

'No. We wouldn't understand him and he would think that we wouldn't get what he was going through,' said Deb. He continued, 'He would grow a stubble, be less flamboyant, talk less and read more, organize student protests, give us heartburn by getting hit by water cannons. He would want to change the world. Stupid, stupid boy. We wouldn't understand his need to put himself in danger and he wouldn't understand our cowardice.'

'He would think of us as cowards?' asked Avantika and then realized they would be. They were worried about Augustya feeling cold inside the room that kept his dead body. She imagined the fear they would have felt for him if he grew up like his sister would. 'Go on,' she said.

'Augustya would get his heart broken by us, by the people he loved. He would start something of his own, to change something. He would spend a decade failing and succeeding. Our relationship would be on rocky ground. But then in a twist, he would run out of money and come to us. We, happy to establish a relationship with him again, would help him out.'

'We would have been lovesick parents?' she asked.

'Absolutely. We would fall for his charm like everyone did, except his sister. She would call him out on his charming bullshit all the time. Nayra would have asked us not to give him money but we would have done so.'

'We would have picked him over Nayra?' asked Avantika.

'Yes but not without reason. Nayra would be the strong one, Augustya, the vulnerable one. And this time, Augustya would have soared. He would have done well. He would have found love too with a woman like you and made babies. He would call us to live with them, raise the babies and we would do that.'

'Would we? We would leave everything for our grandchildren?'

'At first reluctantly but then we'd fall in love with our grandchildren. He would fight with us on how we were raising his children but would have always been thankful for us staying with them. His kids would love us more. He would have protested our decision to move to an old age home, to have nurses and doctors to take care of us instead of him or his sister. He wouldn't listen to any of our logical arguments and stop talking to us for a while. But he would come around every month to see us. Till the time the last breath left our bodies . . .'

'That's quite a life,' said Avantika, and smiled.

'Augustya's our son after all.'

They cried for the beautiful life their beautiful son would never live. When leaving, they filled up the form that asked the hospital to bury Augustya. They had decided that weeks ago. They wanted tangible memories of Augustya. The tombstone was to say—*He was loved by all*. Deb's mother in particular didn't want it—it was too Muslim/Christian for her—but she held back her words.

Deb and Avantika went back to the NICU to show a sleeping Nayra pictures of her brother. She would miss him during Rakshabandhan, they both thought; she would miss a confidante, someone who would always have her back. They emerged from the NICU two hours later. They were surrounded immediately by Tanmay, Vernita and Deb's parents and questions were lobbed at them. Though Shrey had answered most of them earlier they wanted to hear it from them. Deb didn't stay long, and went straight to buy the things that were needed for Nayra—diapers, wipes, bottles and a freezer for Avantika's breast milk. Avantika answered their reluctant questions. Deb's mother found it hardest to check her tears. These were no longer of fear but of hopefulness, of wanting.

'Show me pictures?' asked Vernita.

'We didn't take any,' lied Avantika. They wanted Nayra just for themselves.

59

Tanmay cried when he first saw Nayra. He cried when he saw how small she was, and how easy it was for her to not be alive. With him, watching over his shoulder, clutching Tanmay's arms, Deb's mother cried. Their shock was understandable. It wasn't until one stood there and watched her, that it hit one just how delicate Nayra was. Deb and Avantika had prepared them for what they were going to see, and yet when they all saw Nayra, they couldn't help feel the pity and the fear.

'She's happy seeing you guys, see that little flicker on the monitor?' said Avantika, smiling.

Deb and Avantika didn't mind Tanmay and Deb's mother's reaction. They had expected it. Instead, they were surprised themselves how in a matter of hours, they had developed a thick skin made of their love for their child. They also knew that the shock wouldn't last for long. They watched them watch Nayra. They could have gone back—Namrata had come twice to remind them that more than two people weren't allowed inside—but they kept standing there, peering inside the glass cage.

By the time an hour passed, Tanmay and Deb's mother were in a bit of an argument over who was going to hold Nayra when it was time, and who would feed her for the first time.

'My husband is an IITian,' said Deb's mother. 'You guys are from lowly DCE.'

The conversation ended there.

'She's beautiful,' said Deb's mother to Avantika once they were outside the NICU. She held Avantika and kissed her forehead. 'She will be home soon. I could feel it. I just know it. She needs us, not this incubator.'

Avantika tried to not cry; others loving Nayra would mean so much to her, she hadn't imagined how much.

'I'm glad she looks like Avantika,' said Tanmay to Deb.

'Actually she doesn't,' said Avantika.

'Of course she does. And she's a cute guggul. I can't wait to hold her,' argued Vernita.

'You guys are just having a hard time accepting that she's like Deb because that would mean Deb is cute too,' said Avantika.

'Whatever,' said Vernita.

They stood there arguing for a good part of the hour despite all of them knowing that she was too young to have any sharp features to make an argument. They were happy, and they wanted to stretch this for as long as possible. In that moment, no one wanted to think that her being that small was also what was killing her. No one wanted to discuss the percentage of survival the doctor had given Nayra. At that time, they wanted to imagine that there was nothing wrong, that all children went through a two-month stint in the hospital and battle through 40 per cent chance of not making it. Shrey put his arm around Avantika and smiled at her. *Thank you for everything,* Avantika seemed to say with a smile.

As they stood there talking, Deb's father bought a bunch of flowers and a banner from the hospital shop that said, IT'S A GIRL.

'They won't let you keep those in the room, Baba,' said Deb.

'We will keep them in the ward,' said Avantika.

She couldn't stop smiling and weeping and laughing; it finally felt like what she had thought it would be like to start a family; people around, joyful smiles. The thought that Nayra was out there, waiting for her to love her, someone who was her own, someone who would cling to her, someone she could raise to be a beautiful person, filled her heart with so much joy it felt like it would explode. In that moment, everything people had against having children felt like just words. Nothing, absolutely nothing, beat the feeling she felt right then. This concentrated happiness. This unbridled joy. *This* was what it felt like. She knew from the start that having a child was a selfish pursuit—a want of the complete human experience. It was, but now, now that she had Nayra, the selfishness was to see Nayra be happy all her life. What wouldn't she do to capture this moment in a bottle and relive it over and over again? Seeing Tanmay and Vernita laughing, Deb's mother and Deb's father calling themselves Dada–Dadi, and Deb flitting around, wondering restlessly what Nayra must be doing, she felt like this was the beginning of the rest of her life. She hadn't noticed it but when Deb hugged her—and he seldom did in front of his parents—she realized she had been crying like a lunatic.

When she separated, Avantika saw them. They were at the door, looking as resplendent as they always did.

'What are they doing here?' Avantika asked Tanmay.

Avantika's parents were standing next to a stroller with a little bow on top. Deb had seen that ludicrously expensive Stokke stroller online; it cost more than a small car. He had asked Avantika if they would get it when it was time. Avantika had shot down the idea and reminded him of how expensive schools were.

'I can ask them to leave,' said Deb, stepping ahead in a way that was uncharacteristic of him. He usually left Avantika alone in her battles against her parents.

'I didn't know they would come here,' said Tanmay. 'Do you want me to talk to them?'

He was about to step forward. Vernita held his hand and threw him a murderous look. Tanmay stepped back. Avantika caught their gaze head-on, anger bubbling to the surface. They had smiles on their faces but these betrayed something else they felt. Was that guilt in their eyes? Would they ask for forgiveness? She searched for what they felt for her and it seemed a lot like fear. After all these years, they could still hurt her. She had given them that power. She felt tears welling up in her eyes. Deb's parents stepped away as Avantika walked towards her parents.

'I will be fine,' said Avantika to Deb.

'Hi, Beta,' said Avantika's father as he came close. 'Congratulations.'

'We got a little something for you,' said Avantika's mother and pushed the stroller in front of her. There was no mistake, it was the said model and yet it felt like dirt. The balloons Baba had bought for her seemed much more substantial than the leather-finish stroller that lay in front of her.

'We talked to the doctors. They are saying your daughter has a good chance. If you need anything, let us know. We are your parents, we will help you out,' said Avantika's father.

Deb watched Avantika listen to them steel-faced. He wondered if she would melt in a puddle of tears and hug them or she would punch them in the gut.

Avantika's mother continued, 'This is an expensive hospital. They told us what the cost would be to keep your baby here for two months. Plus there can be incidentals. Your insurance won't cover it. We can help you out.'

Avantika had thought about the money and had already made calculations about how they could spare the amount that would be needed to keep Nayra alive. It would set them back by five years, at the minimum. They wouldn't be able to buy a car, or make the down payment on a house. She also knew Tanmay would bully her into taking help from him and she would have to fight hard to refuse that. When the doctor laid out the possible costs, all she was thinking of was the Ketto.org and Milap.org campaigns where desperate parents with no generous relatives asked for money to save their children. She had decided she would direct anyone who offered them help towards those campaigns.

'You look happy,' said Avantika's mother.

'Can we see the baby?' asked Avantika's father.

'You're not allowed,' she said.

'We get it. She's in the NICU. Maybe later then?' said Avantika's mother.

'Why don't we sit?' said Avantika sweetly.

She led them to the coffee shop of the hospital and sat in front of them. 'Would you like some coffee? I can get it added to the final bill,' she said. 'Deb insisted we don't cut costs. He's doing a new show so that will mean some money.'

'When will we be allowed to see her?' asked Avantika's father. 'Is there a timeline?'

'Yes, there is,' said Avantika and smiled. 'It's never. You are never going to see her.'

'What are you saying?' said Avantika's mother.

'I am asking you to fuck off, that's what I'm doing. Can you understand that? You can't? Wait, I will say it again. Fuck you. Fuck you for what you did to me. I have waited so long to say this. Now I wonder why did I not say it earlier? Maybe because you were still family and there has to be a set of parents in a family, right? But now . . . now that I have a child, I'm one of that set of parents. So you, I don't need you. So yes, fuck you, and fuck you, again. I just held my daughter and you know what I felt? I felt like I was the luckiest damn person in the world. I can't put in words what I felt. That one minute that I held her gave me more happiness than spending eighteen years with you, way more happiness. So imagine how fucked up you were *Mom* and *Dad*! You were horrible to me, just the worst, you should know that.' She paused and felt so much lighter. She started again, 'What kind of people do you have to be to hate your own daughter, huh? I don't understand it. How can you desecrate something so pure, so raw? I don't understand. How both of you could be so evil, so sinister. I realize now that there's something rotten inside of you. How do you guys look yourselves in the mirror? Don't you hate yourself?

'And you keep fucking justifying it in your head with oh, the society and the conditioning but screw that bullshit. You are just bad people, horrible people. I know that now. And you know what? I'm free of that. I know that I'm going to be nothing like you. I know I'm nothing like you. I will love my daughter and will give her everything that I can. I will love her till my last breath. I don't know why you came here but I'm glad you did so I could tell it to your face that I hope you die alone and miserable. I will certainly not be at your side when you rot from the inside and I hope that Tanmay sees that someday too.

'I will make sure Ivan sees you for the people that you are. I will make sure he hates you as much as I do. Trust me, he will abandon you like I have abandoned you. That will happen sooner than you think. And Nayra? She will wish you dead. And you will die alone. You will grow old alone. Trust me on that. What were you saying about my husband? That writer, yes? Well, he's a good storyteller and he told me one about you. Where ten years down the line, you call us, our kids, every day for us to just talk to you once but we don't pick your calls. You get into little accidents, break your pelvis once, one of your knees and yet no one comes to see you in the hospital. The doctors look at you and wonder what's wrong? Why aren't your kids here? You will call us but we will laugh at you. We will even call the police and report you for harassment. How much fun would that be? You go back home to wallow in your loneliness and your sickness. You grow old in that big house with no visitors. We, meanwhile, we will be happy. And we will check once every few months to know if you're dead in the house. Which you will be sooner or later. Because you know, we could use your money for our vacations and stuff. One of you will die in your sleep. The other won't know what to do. When they finally take away the body, the one who survives will be half nuts. It wouldn't matter much because you too will die soon. Of course, we won't know it until months later and by then your body will be decomposed beyond recognition. That's what your end is. So please take your poisonous selves and get out of here. You have no daughter and no grandchild. My parents are waiting for me right there, and they love me, and they are the only grandparents she deserves and needs. So get the fuck out of here.'

She looked at them with a murderous smile and turned away.

'Deb?'

'Yes?'

'Take the stroller from them. I deserve it,' she said and walked to where Deb's parents were. Deb's mother quickly took her in an embrace and muttered lovingly into her ears.

'Did you not hear what she said?' said Deb and took the stroller from them. He had a bright, victorious smile on his face.

Avantika's parents met Tanmay's eyes and stepped forward to hold Ivan but Vernita stepped in front and said, 'Don't even think about it. Just leave.'

Tanmay met their gaze and said solemnly, 'You should leave. Don't spoil this for us. Not this time.'

It took them a few moments to collect themselves before they upped and left.

'*Shotti daekho to kotto nirlojjo*, so shameful,' said Deb's mother and held Avantika's hand. 'You don't have to worry about them. We are always here for you. Your baba wanted to ask you something. Ask her?'

Deb's father hesitantly said, 'Your mother and I, we wanted to . . . see our grandson.'

'So do we,' chimed in the others.

And while all the others tried not to cry, Avantika and Deb were smiling. It wasn't time for them to say goodbye to Augustya yet.

When they walked back to the room they had kept Augustya in, the person-in-charge tried to express his displeasure. He changed his mind when he saw their faces.

'We can't let more than two people inside at a time,' he said. 'Who will go in first?'

'Shrey and I will go first,' said Avantika.

60

Deb and Avantika slowly settled down into a routine in the next three weeks. It wasn't the routine they had expected to settle into; it was nothing like the routine Tanmay and Vernita had when Ivan was born—there were no diapers to be changed, they couldn't get to bathe her, and all the other things new parents get to enjoy—but they didn't mind it at all.

The nurses and the doctors kept telling them that there was nothing that they could do there or send, yet they wouldn't be anywhere else but next to her. Nayra was not living like a baby, she was being kept alive so she could grow into one. Nayra woke up only when it was time for her to take her feed or when she soiled her diaper. Even then she wouldn't cry like other babies would. She would whimper softly. The beeping of the monitors would drown out her soft cries. Crying was too much strain for her underdeveloped lungs.

They weren't allowed to change her diapers. The nurses did that. There was a risk of them knocking out one of the tubes or setting off the probes. To think of it, it was what people kept telling them they would have to do for their children. 'It would be disgusting cleaning potty,' they said. They found themselves begging the nurses to do that. They had tried it on dolls and on Ivan; they just weren't allowed to do it for their own child. All they wanted was to touch her constantly, hold her, clean her, kiss her, be what was asked of parents. Instead all they could do was watch her, and wait, wait for her to grow into the empty spaces of the incubator.

Deb's parents asked them to go home and get some sleep on a real bed but they wouldn't listen. Every hour of every day and every night, they would stay right by Nayra's side. They now knew what every number on every screen meant. Every change, every flicker of a needle, they knew what that meant for Nayra. There were times the nurses would come running in hearing the siren and Avantika would tell them why the siren had gone off. They knew whether it were the oxygen levels or the blood saturation levels, and there were time they wanted to turn the knobs and fix it themselves; at least do something but they didn't take the chance. Nayra slept soundly through the night. And yet, it was either Deb or Avantika who would stay up the entire night looking at her. Avantika and Deb looked at her for entirely different reasons; Avantika out of fear, and Deb out of love. On some days, Deb's behaviour rubbed off on her but most of her days went in worrying about Nayra. She felt guilty, guilty that her body couldn't keep Nayra for two more months. She cursed herself, for all the time she hadn't given her body the respect it deserved, all the senseless abuse, and she cursed Paritosh and the child she had to lose. Just two more months and . . . Nayra would have been home, in her new crib.

Despite the doctors and the counsellors asking them not to, Avantika scoured every page of the Internet for cases like theirs. Avantika would sometimes drag Deb down that road. Scores of children, many younger than Nayra, had passed away in their sleep. Every time they read a case on the forums, it reminded them of how delicate their situation was. Avantika followed hundreds of parents on these forums. They would update the situation of their preemies every few hours after they were shifted to NICU. Gradually, they would slow down to a trickle. A few months down the line, there would be one of two things—either an abrupt end to the posts, or a post celebrating a six month or a one year birthday.

Avantika would search for the parents who suddenly stopped posting on Facebook and Instagram, Twitter and LinkedIn and confirm her worst fears. She would do this behind Deb's back and he wouldn't take it kindly when he would find out.

'You need to stop doing this, Avantika. Nothing will happen to Nayra, baby. Don't you see her? She's fine. Look at how beautiful she is,' Deb would tell Avantika every day.

Children way healthier, with better vitals than Nayra, died in their beds and incubators every day, and they both knew it. Dr Sharma reacted adversely when they brought this up with him.

'It's not something that you can predict, can you? Be positive and look at the brighter side of things. She has come thus far, and we hope she will be out of the incubator soon,' said the doctor.

That's what they did. They tried to celebrate every day that Nayra lived. It wouldn't have been possible without the other parents who filtered in and out of the NICU.

Twice in the last three weeks, children died in the NICU. Deb and Avantika both knew the parents and had spent an inordinately long time staring at their babies, taking their names, babbling to them. They made plans of play dates in the near future, discussed the possibility of the babies dating each other and lying to them. Karuna Makhija and Harsimrat Singh were both older than Nayra and yet their little lungs and their feeble hearts had failed them. Deb and Avantika had heard the screams of their parents when the children died and kept hearing them for days after that. It served as a reminder of how every breath Nayra took was a miracle, how her life was hanging by a thread. Ten years ago, she wouldn't have lived for an hour but now . . .

The empty incubators Karuna and Harsimrat left behind struck a deep fear in their hearts. When two more babies took the places of Karuna and Harsimrat, it only made things worse. It seemed wrong. For another baby to be in the same incubator someone died in a few hours ago.

After Karuna and Harsimrat, they tried not to get close to the parents. Their own grief and fear were enough for them to handle. No matter how hard they tried, they failed. All parents—young people—were in this maze of parenthood together, confused and in pain. Grief always brought them together. Most of all they couldn't keep the pesky Mandals, who were NICU seniors, out of their lives; they had been there three weeks before Deb–Avantika moved in. They had seen the Mandals on the very first day they been in the NICU; they had talked amongst themselves of how cute they looked together, and felt bad that they were going through the same thing as them. Their baby boy was six weeks premature.

Every now and then, the Mandals would peek from the other side of the curtain and strike up a conversation. They would get them food and sweets and four different newspapers. The Mandals and they had too much in common—a dying child—for them to not be friends. Deb and Avantika made an exception and started planning play dates between Nayra and Randhir Mandal.

Unlike Deb, Karan and Smita Mandal had day jobs and would come to the hospital straight from the office. And despite that they never went home. Every night they would unwrap their bedding sharp at eleven and go off to sleep. The next morning, they would wake up at 5 a.m., look for an empty hospital room, use the shower and leave for office. They had been doing this for three weeks before Nayra was moved into the NICU, and unlike Deb and Avantika, they were allowed to hold their Randhir for an hour every day. And while they held Randhir, Deb and Avantika would take videos and pictures of the three of them.

Even so, Randhir Mandal was the weakest of the two babies in the NICU. He had had two surgeries, and yet he didn't seem to get any better. That did not discourage the Mandals; they were very optimistic. They were younger than Deb and Avantika and sometimes they wondered if that's what made them so. Babies came and went, and Randhir Mandal didn't seem to get any better. One piece of adverse news after another followed, one medicine change after another, screaming monitors in the middle of the night, it never ended; everyone else felt lucky their baby wasn't in his condition; the Mandals kept telling themselves that their Randhir was a fighter. When the only baby older than Randhir Mandal was taken out of the incubator and sent home, the Mandals felt it.

To tide over the guilt of envy in someone's happiness, they played board games instead that night. The next morning, the Mandals sought a second opinion about their baby. They were desperate, they just didn't show it. That broke Deb a little. Despite the warning signs, the babies dying around them, or in the world, he had been optimistic and even more so seeing the Mandals hold fort without a groan. Seeing their faith waiver struck deep inside Deb for the first time, but not for long. He and his parents behaved like Nayra was just another baby—truant, a pain in the butt for the new parents, but also someone who deserved the best. Deb's parents would come to the hospital every day bearing new clothes for her. None of which fit Nayra because she was too small for even the smallest clothes. There was no market for premature, dying babies. But the mere gesture and Deb's mother's words, 'She will wear it when the time comes,' made it so much better. With time, they even started getting new clothes for Randhir.

'So what will we tell them? Randhir is like a brother? Or like—'

The answer stared at them in the face. They settled that Randhir was Augustya, the brother she didn't get to meet. When Shrey was told this he didn't take it lightly. He had to spend an entire day and a half with Randhir to start liking him and see him as someone taking Augustya's place in their lives. How he judged a baby, God only knew.

'He seems like a nice boy. Fine, I will be his godfather if you insist,' he said to the Mandals and then flooded their room with gifts. Shrey had an eye for the cutest, quirkiest gifts for babies. The Mandals groaned, tried to return them to Shrey who would hear none of it. Deb was sure the Mandals loved them as much as they did.

On one weekend, Tanmay and Vernita came to the hospital with Ivan to spend an entire day there. They had dropped over every day in the initial days but their frequency had slowly dropped. They didn't see a point of peering at their niece from a glass wall for hours at an end. It was unfair on them too—to drive all the way to the hospital after work and miss crucial time with Ivan. Or to just rest. This time, they had food packed for the afternoon and the night. A couple of hours in, Avantika called the Mandals to join them.

'I thought it would be just us,' Tanmay told them.

'We wouldn't have survived it without them,' said Avantika.

That much was true. Neither Deb's parents nor Tanmay nor Vernita could possibly know what they were going through. They were with them all through their struggle but they hadn't been on the path. The Mandals had been. Randhir was conceived after six months of trying and he meant the world for the Mandals. Both had sacrificed their careers for this. They were the embodiment of what model parents should be like.

It was a Monday morning when the Mandals, Deb and Avantika woke up with a start. They were used to the beeping of the monitors of their own children; they knew it wasn't them. They rubbed their eyes and ran out to see what the commotion was all about.

Incubators were being moved, equipment snapped into place, floors scrubbed. Three babies were moved in the NICU within the hour. A little later the Sharmas, the Iyers and the Ahujas were bent over three incubators, their hearts in their mouths, tears flooding their eyes. By the time it was evening, an unavoidable kinship set in. The Mandals were the elders, Avantika and Deb the younger generation and the three new couples wide-eyed rookies. The more experienced couples took them through the paces and put them at ease. Little did all five couples know that their first parent group would be with people with babies battling for their lives.

A few days later, the desperate Mandals left for Vaishno Devi. Deb and Avantika hadn't taken them to be the religious kind. For the three nights and three days they weren't in the city, Deb and Avantika video-called them every few hours and made them see their son. They had walked up the entire way, red, sparkly bands around their heads, and they chanted '*Jai Mata Di*' till their throats were dry. They paid every pandit, every beggar, every sadhu on the way. Deb wanted to point out the futility of it but he let them be. What can you say to a parent? When they came back, they were wearing rings on their fingers and holy threads on their wrists. They got everyone holy threads; no one batted an eyelid before wearing them.

A week after they were back from Vaishno Devi, Randhir Mandal was cleared and declared medically fit; he was to be shifted to the general ward. At first the Mandals didn't believe it. So much time had passed in the NICU, they thought this was all there would be. It took time for the news to sink in. All the other parents contemplated going to Vaishno Devi as well. Desperate parents would do anything, believe anything. A lot of them visited their local temples that day.

The news of Randhir being shifted out also scared the Mandals. No longer would Randhir Mandal be safe inside the incubator—there weren't nurses or doctors on call, no machine measuring his vitals all the time. By the time Randhir was taken out of the incubator, the Mandals were shaking in fear.

When they held their baby, the fear dissipated in a matter of seconds and they held him like they had been holding him all their lives.

They clicked a few pictures near the incubator—with Avantika and Deb in the frame. That night, despite the other parents being around, Deb and Avantika felt alone in the NICU.

In the middle of the night, they both took turns to visit Randhir. Without the tubes and the probes and the incubator, Randhir looked adorable. He wasn't sleeping. He was watching his parents in awe and wonder. Sometimes he launched into a full-throated cry. Neither of the parents tried quietening the boy. He was alive, living, and in a baby bed.

For two days, the relatives of the Mandals streamed in to see Randhir. Deb and Avantika started feeling left out. After all, family was family. And now that the Mandals' son was all right, the thread that connected them had snapped. Their grief was not theirs to be shared any more. Maybe when Nayra too emerged healthy, they would . . . The doctors kept monitoring his progress over the next few days. He was making rapid recovery.

Then the Mandals were told he was okay to go home.

'We will miss you,' they said when it was time to go. 'We can't wait for Nayra to come out and visit us. It will be so much fun.'

They saw the sadness on Deb and Avantika's faces, and knew no amount of words from them would alleviate what they felt—a mix of happiness, rage and envy. They had been where Deb–Avantika were way too many times to not know. It was a difficult place.

At the gate of the hospital, Kiran Mandal fought for twenty minutes—crying all the while—that she couldn't accept the crib that Deb and Avantika had sent to her house. It was a crib matching the one Augustya had.

Avantika would have none of it. 'Am I not his *mausi*? Is that what you're saying?'

Once back in the NICU, Deb and Avantika wanted nothing more than to go back home. They both looked at Nayra and prayed for her to get better, to lie in her own crib like the queen they would raise her to be.

61

Two more weeks passed after Randhir was shifted out of the hospital. Nayra was making progress but it was slow; her weight gain had been a problem for the doctors and they had to constantly monitor her feed. But she was beginning to get better. Even Deb–Avantika, who were constantly watching her, could tell that she was beginning to look more like a newborn baby with sharper features. The day they had been waiting for, with excitement and fear, was now near. They had to pull Nayra out of the incubator and hold her for a while.

Their hands trembled the entire morning. Deb paced up and down and around the incubator, hands clammy, nervousness taking over his entire body. He was more nervous than he had been during the entire five weeks that Nayra had been in the hospital.

'Are we not rushing into this? She's our daughter, she's not going anywhere. We can do this any time' asked Deb for the fourth time that morning and received the same answer yet again.

'It's not our call. It's important for Nayra that we do this. It helps. You have read the blogs yourself,' said Avantika.

The doctor was running late. Namrata told them there was a complication with one of the babies and he was looking into it.

'Are you excited?' Namrata asked.

'We are but we also scared,' said Avantika.

Frantic calls to the Mandals and their reassuring words didn't change anything. The past few weeks, Nayra had been steadily gaining weight, her vitals were stable and the flow of oxygen she required had been reduced. They could touch her through the little holes in the incubator more frequently. She responded to their little touches well too. Sometimes she would smile in her sleep. That little dimple on her right cheek always knocked the wind out of them. Her features were sharper now and it became clear that she was more like Deb than Avantika. Every time someone said that Deb felt a strange warmth in his chest. How close had she come to not look or have anything in common with him? It felt worth it; everything that they had been through. She was his daughter, it was undeniable.

But today they would have to hold her; they would take her out of the incubator. 'Kangaroo technique' is what they called it. They would have to hold the baby for a little while. They said to feel the parents' skin against her helped with the baby's development.

'What if something happens? Avantika, you're the adult here, did you think about it? You need to think these things,' said Deb.

Avantika knew no matter what she said it wouldn't calm him down.

An hour later, the doctor waltzed in with a confidence that almost mocked the tension Deb and Avantika wallowed in. In a flash he had sanitized his hands, and without warning he was opening the incubator. He pulled off the probes from Nayra like they were unnecessary, as if the weeks that had gone by were just play-acting, the probes and the cannulas were toys. He picked up the baby with practiced efficiency and fearlessness and said, 'Are you ready? Who's going to go first?'

Deb and Avantika looked at each other.

'He will,' said Avantika.

'I will,' said Deb.

'Right, then. You need to take off your shirt and make sure the baby rests on your skin, okay? She needs to feel your warmth. That's how it works. We will do ten minutes today. Once you're done, the nurse will put her back. Any questions?'

Deb shook his head; he had already read too much. He took off his shirt and sat on the chair. The doctor slowly lowered Nayra down on his chest. She was two palms big.

'Hold her,' said the doctor and let go. 'Does that feel okay? Don't press her too hard. Let her sleep like that. Yes, you're doing well. Everything seems set. So ten minutes, okay? Tomorrow Avantika can do it. The nurse will help you out. See you later, okay?'

The doctor left just as he had come in—in a flash and with a smile on his face. The nurse followed.

'How do you feel?' said Avantika.

'Strange. Good strange. Like a warm frog is on my chest,' said Deb, who could feel Nayra breathe in and out. That quick breath of babies. He breathed quickly too to match her rhythm. He had felt this way before and he knew exactly when. It was the day of the wedding and the pandit had made Avantika put her hand on his and tied them together with a string. Their fates were interminably entwined that day. This was like that. They were now for life. There was no other option.

'She can hear you call her a frog.'

'But she is one. Look at her, look at how small and tiny and cute she is,' said Deb and looked down.

She felt warm to him. She felt *his*. It felt like this was what he was waiting for. Something inside of him filled up with love. Nayra opened her eyes for a split second, looked up, and then closed them again. She looked irritated that they had taken the bed away from her. Deb didn't care about it. She could cry and squirm and wriggle and want to free herself all she wanted, but Deb wouldn't let go. He felt complete.

Avantika watched on, jealous. She wanted to hold her. Her heart ached. So did her breasts, always full with milk, wanting a child to latch on to them. It seemed natural.

Ten minutes later, they kept Nayra back in the incubator, and Deb felt like something precious had been taken away from him. He wanted to hold her for a little more time. A few lifetimes to start with.

'Do you think you get the same kids when you're reborn? I would like to have Nayra and Augustya again,' said Deb, still thinking about how it felt to have Nayra sleeping on him.

'I can't wait for tomorrow,' said Avantika.

'You have no idea,' said Deb, smiling like someone who had unpacked the mystery called life and couldn't wait for others to find the truth. 'It was like us. Like we struggle to tell people how much we love each other? Of course they think they love their partners as much as we love each other but they don't. It was exactly like that. I can't explain it.'

The night was long and Avantika could barely sleep a wink. Her nervous energy was taking over her by the time it was her turn to hold the baby. She dreamt that she would hold the baby and the baby would find her breast and latch on to it and would grow, her lungs would fortify, her heart would pump stronger and they could all just go home. She kept seeing the same dream repeatedly, so much so, she started believing that it's exactly what would happen. She woke up in a disturbed state of mind.

When Avantika held Nayra, all of her anxiety dissipated in a second. She felt an inexplicable energy course through her.

Deb stood over her, grinning, 'So?'

It was now their secret.

'Everything you said was true. Nothing I have felt before has felt like this,' she said.

'Surprisingly, I am not jealous,' said Deb.

She smiled weakly. Her body was suddenly jelly; she felt drugged. It was like the first time she had smoked up. The world slowed down, she could feel everything, but she could also pick out that feeling and magnify it a millionfold. She picked happiness and she indulged in it. Deb tried talking to her but she just sat there with her eyes closed, tears streaming down her face, her baby on her chest, and her fingers slowly stroking that little face.

The tape on Nayra's face holding the tubes together hid most of her expressions but Avantika could bet she was smiling.

When the nurse kept Nayra back in the incubator, she asked them, 'The day's coming soon when you will be able to take her home. Are you excited?'

Both of them nodded like little children.

62

The day came out of the blue. Just like it had come for the Mandals. They woke up to another morning of looking at the monitors and hoping the numbers would be better, when they were called by Dr Sharma and the other paediatricians who were looking after Nayra. The news was given to them like it wasn't the happiest news the world had ever received.

It was Dr Sharma who came out and hugged the two of them. 'Congratulations,' he said. 'The earlier diagnosis was a little premature.'

'I like the way you're using that pun,' said Deb, crying.

'Shall we go now?' said Dr Sharma.

'You are coming with us?' asked Avantika who hadn't started crying yet.

'You think I will let that Shrey take my place? Naah,' he said and goaded them on.

The three of them walked towards the NICU.

'It's your last time here,' said Dr Sharma when they entered. He waved at Namrata to come help him get Nayra out of the incubator. It was time for her to start her journey home.

Avantika hadn't cried till now but she burst out into tears when they took off the last probe. Namrata cradled Nayra in her hands and whispered to her, 'You're ready for your mumma.'

'And for your baba,' Deb added.

Slowly, she gave her to Avantika to carry her to the general ward. Everyone watched on as they prepared the incubator for the next child. The only home that Nayra had seen till now.

In a moment of weakness, Tanmay asked the nurse if they could buy the incubator, as a memory for Nayra. Deb's mother thought it was stupid and they would never keep something that would remind them of the time Nayra spent in the hospital. Deb and Avantika were too much in a daze to reply to Tanmay. He finally backed off when the nurse told him how much it would cost the hospital to buy a new one.

'It was a stupid request anyway,' said Tanmay to Deb's mother.

'Shall we go?' asked Namrata. 'You will be okay or do you want me to carry her to the ward?'

'She will be fine. She is with us now,' said Deb.

'With her mumma and papa,' said Avantika, lightly kissing Nayra.

That's something they hadn't done till now; the risk of infection always seemed too high. *She will always be around to do that later*, Deb and Avantika kept telling each other this. But now, Nayra was a grown-up baby. They could love her the way she deserved to be loved. Just a few months old and she had been through enough. She only deserved love and happiness now.

'She will grow up spoilt now,' said Deb.

'I realize that. Had she been born like Ivan, you know, I would have locked a three-year-old Nayra at home and gone out partying. Now, she is staying in my lap till she's nineteen,' said Avantika.

'Great, congratulations, you have a brat,' said Deb, and she smiled.

Avantika led the way. She walked carefully and slowly and the rest of them cleared the way for her, shouting instructions as if Avantika was carrying a stack of glass flutes that might crash and break. They took the lift to the suite they had booked.

'There's no way she's going to the general ward,' Tanmay had insisted, and paid for it. Deb protested lightly but then thought they could use the rest. For the past two months they had been sleeping on the cold hard ground of the NICU.

'Let him buy us whatever he wants. He has felt useless as a *mama*, and you know how Punjabis are,' Avantika had said.

The suite was nothing like they had imagined a suite to be. There were no monogrammed handkerchiefs, no stocked mini-bar, or soft light, no flat screen TV.

All they had done was to paint the wall to make it not like a hospital room. But the white bed with the adjustable controls, the harsh white lights and the poor furniture gave it all away. There was a little crib with a little mattress on the side. It was a far cry from where Nayra had been sleeping all this while. It looked *human*.

'Just keep her there,' said Namrata.

'I would rather hold her,' said Avantika.

Namrata smiled and said, 'Fine, but when you do just cover the crib with the net to keep out the insects. There aren't any but it doesn't hurt to be careful.'

She showed them the bell they needed to press to call her, told them that she would return for Nayra's next feed and left.

Sitting in the suite, no one knew what to say. They all sat around Nayra and watched her sleep and squirm in Avantika's hands. Later on, they all took turns to hold her while she slept away to glory. Sometimes they would panic and hold a hand to her chest to check if she was still breathing.

No one went home that night except Vernita who had to go back to Ivan. A bunch of doctors came and went. They gave them an entire bunch of instructions all of which they listened to carefully and made notes of. They couldn't sleep the entire night out of excitement. Whenever Nayra would cry all six of them would be on her in a flash. They would take turns to feed her and pat her back to sleep. They were all hands on deck. They were glad they could do something for her.

The next morning, Deb's parents went back home to get clothes so they could stay the rest of the two days in the suite without leaving. More doctors came to see them—some were scheduled visits, other came to see the baby that survived. They made them and Nayra feel special, like they had achieved something. Some of them even came bearing gifts and dangled them in front of Nayra. Avantika got jealous when Nayra giggled and looked like sunshine seeing Namrata's toy.

The second night, Avantika slept soundly. She passed out like a log. She had underestimated how much this journey had taken out of her.

'She's okay, we are taking care of her. She's beautiful, like you,' Deb would whisper in Avantika's ears from time to time in the night.

The others looked after Nayra.

The next morning, the number of doctor visits slowed to a trickle. That was good news. Avantika and Deb managed Nayra mostly on their own; after all they had gone through for her, it just didn't seem okay to them to see her in someone else's arms. She spent most of the time in their laps and not in the bed. Deb's father kept telling them they would find themselves in trouble if Nayra got used to sleeping in their arms.

'Wouldn't that be just the best thing ever?' Deb kept telling his father. He turned towards Avantika and said, 'We should work towards that.'

It was Deb and Avantika who gave Nayra her first proper bath. It was against the wishes of the attending nurses. The nurses had asked them to just watch for the first time. But they had seen too many YouTube videos to wait around and watch. Moreover, it was on their arms that she lay most calmly. They didn't need a nurse to bathe their own daughter.

They held a crying Nayra and gave her a good rub-down. She shrieked like a hyena and nobody who passed by the corridor would have believed that this baby still had weak lungs. They changed her diapers, clothed her, fed her, the whole deal. They stole glances at each other and hid their smiles. They didn't want to jinx their own happiness.

'This is inexplicable. This is the most satisfying thing I have ever done,' said Deb after it was done.

'Isn't it?'

'The next time a writer says writing a book is like bringing a baby into the world, he's going to get punched in the face. Only bringing a baby into the world feels like bringing a baby into the world.'

Avantika laughed.

That night they slept with her between the two of them. They took turns to keep their hand over her. Nayra didn't need the pats to go to sleep; they did it to remind themselves she existed. They cooed to her the lullabies they knew, in Bengali, in English and in Punjabi. They wanted her to recognize their voices as soon as possible.

The nurses came running in whenever it was time for Nayra to get fed or changed but found themselves redundant. It was the same for Deb's mother who had literally brought up her daughters' children. She had built up dreams of bringing up her son's daughter but her son didn't give her a single responsibility. She was disappointed in her son whom she often found fighting with Avantika for things that needed to be done. The resentment of not being able to do things a grandmother is wont to do rose within her.

'Let her grow up a little, they will need me then,' she said.

They had been expecting it and yet when Dr Sharma broke the news to them, they couldn't believe it.

Avantika lunged at Dr Sharma and hugged him and didn't let him go for a long time.

'That's a bit awkward,' said Deb looking at his parents.

Everyone left Deb and Avantika alone with Nayra. Deb and Avantika held her and tried hard to make the tears stop. It was the first time it hit them.

'Now. We are a family now. The three of us, our own world, my own family,' said Avantika.

'Our own family,' repeated Deb. 'Everything you wanted and now everything I want. Maybe this is what family means. A part of you lives in someone else.'

They both looked at Nayra who smiled, the dimples on both her cheeks sharply in focus. Deb's parents left earlier the next morning to fix the house, to get Avantika's and now Nayra's room in order. They knew it wouldn't just be fixing. They weren't good at lying. Their eyes had lit up every time they talked about Nayra being welcomed in their house. They would make up for what they couldn't do.

'I'm guessing a cake, decorations, lots of food, because obviously, and a bunch of my relatives,' said Deb.

'I think we deserve it. Nayra needs to know that she's welcomed and loved, doesn't she? It's her big day.'

Neither of them was looking forward to indulging in anything like this—all they wanted was to go home and sleep by their baby—but they knew the parents deserved this. That day was for *the others*. Deb and Avantika had shut them out for most of their journey; Nayra had to seem theirs too. They too had gone through their share of pain.

Deb and Avantika filled out the billing formalities in their suite itself. A bunch of nurses and doctors came to see them when they were checking out. They all congratulated them and clicked pictures.

The doctors seemed almost sad that Nayra was leaving the hospital. She had literally grown in front of their eyes. They had seen her ears develop, her features sharpen, and her lungs get stronger. They were all bystanders to her development. Their room was chock-a-block with gifts they had received. The biggest of them all was a bunch of gifts they had received from the Mandals—a high chair, a rocking chair and a tiny dining set. They were of the same navy blue colour with Nayra engraved on them. There was a sign at the bottom. *Randhir Mandal, you can also call me Augustya.*

A coterie of the nurses and doctors saw them off to the parking lot. They checked if the baby was safely strapped in her baby seat. They hugged Avantika when she tried thanking them.

'I will drive,' said Avantika.

'I was hoping you would say that,' said Deb.

She was a much safer driver than he was. Deb slipped into the seat next to Nayra. They were waved off by the nurses who had big smiles on their faces. Tanmay drove his car ahead of them, taking the slowest road, and driving more safely than was required.

'She's going home,' said Avantika, looking back.

'Can you look ahead?' said Deb for the tenth time in the twenty-minute drive.

'Just keep an eye on her, okay?' said Avantika.

'What do you think I'm doing?' said Deb who had slipped his finger inside her palm. She wrapped her fist around it.

'Did you see that? Did you see what she did? She . . .'

'You asked me not to look back.'

They were taking the last turn around the corner nearest to their house when Deb noticed it. He first thought he was being paranoid. She had let go of his finger. He tried making her hold his finger again but she wouldn't do it. Deb leaned towards her face. He brought his ear close to her nose, to feel her breathing. It looked like she was sleeping but . . . Deb lightly tapped her face, tried waking her up.

'Avantika?'

'Fine! I'm not looking!' she exclaimed.

'Avantika,' he said and bent over Nayra.

'What?'

'Avantika . . . something is wrong.'

'Deb?'

Deb spluttered. He kept his hand over Nayra's little chest. He waited for the infinitesimal rise. He looked for signs of life.

'She's . . . '

'What, DEB!'

'She's . . . she's . . . not breathing.'

63

Avantika slammed the brakes. She turned to look back at Nayra. She was turning blue. She looked at Deb who was now frozen, a tear resting precariously at the edge, his hand still on her chest. And then with a big heave, Nayra spluttered and took two long breaths. Deb sat up with a start.

'Nayra? NAYRA?'

She was heaving, struggling to breath. She leaned in.

Tanmay stared into the rear view mirror. He noticed that Avantika had stopped. He honked and shouted out to her asking her what had happened. From where he was he saw her turn in her seat and shout something.

'WE HAVE TO GO BACK,' Deb shouted suddenly.

He unstrapped Nayra in a hurry and cradled her. 'It's going to be okay, it's going to be okay,' he said to her and tapped her back lightly.

'JUST DRIVE,' he shouted at Avantika.

Avantika broke out of her reverie and clutched the wheel. She looked at her one last time in the rear view mirror and took a deep breath. *There's no time to panic.* She put the car into reverse and drove against the traffic. In the rear-view mirror, she watched Tanmay do the same.

Her phone rang—at first it was Tanmay and then Deb's mother and she didn't receive either call. She watched as Deb tried to do CPR on the baby. He held her little mouth open and tried to help her breathe. Nayra's body was limp; she was no longer struggling to breathe. She wasn't heaving any more, her little hands were flopping around lifelessly. Deb was relentless, he kept shouting out the count and trying to make her breathe again.

'CALL THE DOCTOR,' said Deb. 'NAYRA!'

Avantika fumbled with her phone and on her third attempt called the doctor and asked him to come to the gate immediately. When the doctor tried to ask what happened, she bellowed at him.

She screamed into the phone refusing to tell the doctor that her child had stopped breathing and was probably . . . She heard Deb mutter as she drove.

'Don't die, don't die, wake up, Nayra. Wake up, please, please, please, please,' Deb kept repeating, his voice a soft whisper.

The fifteen-minute drive which they covered in seven minutes seemed like an hour. In those seven minutes, Avantika imagined all the miserable ways their lives would be as a childless couple, a couple which didn't lose one but two children. She didn't see how they could survive that. How could they live on after suffering the loss they had? In those moments, she didn't think it made sense to live on if they lost Nayra too. All she could wonder was how long before the two of them decided to end their lives after Nayra left. Nothing would make sense if Nayra didn't breathe again. How would they pass every single hour of every single day for the rest of their lives knowing that the two people who brought them the most joy were dead now? How could they live on? How would they go on after this? They would . . . they would have to join their children. That's where they were supposed to be . . . with them.

Avantika parked the car right in front of the hospital door. When Deb jumped out with a limp Nayra in his hands, their gazes met, and both knew what they were thinking. They wouldn't survive this. It would be the death of them. In that infinitesimal moment that passed between the two of them, they made that pact. If they had to see Nayra for the last time in that cold room, they would not leave the hospital alive. They would be in the same room with their daughter. They had had enough.

The nurses who had been smiling bore a deathly countenance when Avantika parked the car near the entrance of the ICU.

'I DID EVERYHING!' screamed Deb as a nurse took Nayra from him.

Avantika watched her hand fall from Deb's lap. It just flopped down. Avantika and Deb ran after the nurses. The hospital felt colder than they remembered. The friendly faces no longer smiled.

'She's not breathing,' they heard a nurse say.

'What's happening?' shrieked Avantika.

Namrata stopped Avantika and told them to wait. The steel doors opened and Nayra was taken inside the OT; there were people screaming over each other asking for medicines, equipment and doctors. Avantika jostled with Namrata to go inside. Two other nurses had to hold a screaming Avantika down.

Deb had slipped past the nurses who tried to keep Avantika down and away from the ICU, and he was inside. The door slammed shut behind him. The nurses kept Nayra on the bed and two doctors converged over her and they pressed her chest.

'SAVE HER!' he wanted to scream but the words died in his throat.

'SHE'S NOT RESPONDING,' Deb heard a doctor say. The nurses looked at the monitor.

It was a flatline. No signs of life. They kept pressing her little body, it looked cruel how they pressed her chest, and it didn't respond. She just lay there like Augustya in the cold, hard bench in that room. Deb stepped forward, each step breaking his heart a little, making him a little dead inside.

That's when the other nurses spotted the horror-stricken father.

'HE CAN'T BE IN HERE!' said the doctor.

The nurses charged at Deb, held him strongly and shoved him towards the door. Deb had no strength to fight back. They pressed the call button and two more nurses came in and pushed him outside. Outside, Avantika was on her knees crying; Namrata was sitting mute by her side. Avantika looked up and met Deb's gaze. He didn't have to say anything. Avantika looked away and stared at her feet and more tears came. Her body was shutting down. He took Namrata's place who looked at them and said, 'She will be okay,' and it seemed like a lie. She just mouthed the words; no voice came out of her.

Deb watched her walk away. They both looked up at the cold steel doors and heard frantic murmurs from the other side. The tone of the voices, the intonations, the fear and the panic in those murmurs were familiar. They had heard it before. It was in Dubai and it was Augustya and the next thing they were told was that he was dead.

'What will we do now? What will we do without her? How will we live without Nayra?' asked Avantika.

'We won't live,' said Deb and met Avantika's eyes.

Avantika clasped Deb's hand tighter, and in a moment of clarity, she nodded. 'We won't live.'

Tanmay and Vernita came running and saw Deb and Avantika crumpled in an embrace at the foot of the waiting chairs, crying. The nurses stood at a distance, watching them cry, and weeping themselves.

'What happened?' asked Tanmay to the nurses. 'WHAT THE HELL IS GOING ON!'

They held Tanmay's gaze for a while and then shook their heads. Tanmay and Vernita sat next to Deb and Avantika. They held each other's hands and stared at the cold steel doors that separated them from the limp body of their beloved Nayra. From the little glass window, they could see the doctors shake their heads. Their lives as they knew it were over.

Epilogue

Neither of them had the energy or the will to move a muscle, look at each other, say something. The silence was better. Tanmay and Vernita had insisted that they check into this hotel, take some time off, spend a day away, without thinking about Nayra.

'You can't stop living your life,' Vernita had said.

Yet nothing changed. A year had passed and not a moment went by when they were not thinking of her.

Today they took a long shower, Deb shaved off his two-month-old beard, Avantika took the pain to wash her face, shave her legs, and put on a nice dress. She was surprised when she fit into it. Maybe women like her lost all the pregnancy weight as a consolation. Both of them looked human again, the dark circles, the collar bones sticking out, the dull skin notwithstanding.

It had only been a couple of hours since they woke up and came to St Regis and yet they were already tired, their eyes sunken in their sockets, their bones crying for help. Both sat next to each other on the bed, their bodies and their hands acting like strangers, or more like of a couple who had broken up and had no hope now. They looked at each other and then looked away. They realized they didn't have anything to say. Since that time in the hospital, they weren't Deb and Avantika, they were just people who went through that painful ordeal and what followed.

Avantika spoke, her voice barely a whisper, 'Will we always be like this?'

For the past year, they had either whispered at each other or shouted, nothing in between. Anyone who saw them, thought, *This was it, their marriage would not last this pressure*. Deb's parents wanted

Deb to go to Mumbai and write the show which Shrey was helming alone so far—sometimes Shrey would fake panic and tell Deb they would lose the show if he didn't shift to Mumbai—but Deb refused. He refused even to leave the house. Avantika fared no better. Her date of rejoining work had come and gone. She had taken three extensions and Tanmay had used every trick in the book to get her back to office, in the dire hope that things would change.

It was not that they were morose all the time. There would be a few odd moments in the day when Deb and Avantika would laugh and they would laugh like they used to. They looked like they were in love again. But most times, they would be cranky and insufferable to each other and to the people around them. All in the name of Nayra.

'We chose this, didn't we?' said Deb.

'And this will be the way it is,' sighed Avantika.

Deb reached out for Avantika's hand—the first time in many, many days—and Avantika clasped it tight. They stood up—they hadn't made love in months now and slept on opposite sides of the bed. They walked to the edge of the fortieth-storey room, to the row of ceiling-to-floor windows that overlooked the entire city. This was the USP of this suite—the view. They looked ahead and stared at what lay in front of them.

'Beautiful,' said Avantika.

'Reminds me of the time we climbed Kilimanjaro. Remember that?' asked Deb.

'You didn't even look at the sunrise, the famed view,' said Avantika.

'You know I looked at the view all right—I looked at you, and there was nothing more beautiful than you,' said Deb.

'And now? Now I'm here and yet you find something else to look at, don't you? A different view?' said Avantika with a tinge of sadness.

'I can't help it, can I?' said Deb. 'It's not like you love me as deeply as you once did.'

'I was always allowed that, Deb, you weren't. You were always supposed to be obsessed with me and nothing else. You were supposed to keep us deeply in love with each other, and let nothing affect that. It was your responsibility and it's your fault,' said Avantika.

'It's all your fault actually,' said Deb. 'You started it.'

'So now it's entirely my fault, eh?'

'Of course, we wouldn't have been here had it not been for your silly quest to have a child. So if there's someone to blame in this entire scenario, it's just you and no one else,' said Deb.

'OH PLEASE!'

'We are not having this discussion again. Keep your volume low. We can't talk if you're going to use that tone again,' said Deb.

'I AM USING THAT TONE?' scoffed Avantika.

'OF COURSE YOU ARE! JUST HEAR YOURSELF!'

'LOOK AT WHAT YOU DID!' said Avantika.

'LOOK AT WHAT YOU DID!' screamed back Deb.

And drowning both their screams, were her screams. She was up, and she was bawling, big drops of tears already at the corner of her eyes. And even with her tears, her upturned lips, her pitiful eyes, she was still the most beautiful sight in the world—Nayra. Often, Deb and Avantika would first think, *Look how cute she looks when she cries*, before picking her up to soothe her. The bird's eye view of the city from the window of their hotel suite was nothing in front of their daughter.

Avantika and Deb both lunged at her in a flash. Deb was a split second quicker.

'You will of course do that! You will make her yours and I will be the bad mumma who wakes her up and goes to office and only comes back late,' said Avantika. 'I know your plans!'

'And what do you do, huh? Lure her with your breasts! First you did that with me and now her!' said Deb.

'That's nonsense.'

'See? This is what you do. You're paranoid about everything and when I say anything you say I'm paranoid.'

'Am I paranoid? For two days straight you let her sleep on your chest and the third day she wouldn't come to me. Don't I see what you do with her?' said Avantika.

'And what about you? You're not careful enough with her. That milk—'

'Oh please, shut up with that milk! That milk was not hot for heavens' sake,' said Avantika.

'I'm not taking chances with Nayra.'

'And you think I am?' said Avantika and threw her hands in the air. 'Give her to me,' she said and reached out for Nayra who leapt from his hands to hers.

'See? She knows you. She loves you more and yet you keep taking her away from me. Why can't you just get some fucking sleep and leave her to me?' said Deb. 'You are paranoid, that's it. You're the problem, not I!'

'I am? I'm the one who sleeps like three hours a day? I'm the one who insists that we sterilize everything thrice?' asked Avantika.

'And you? You wouldn't let her into the mall because the temperature is not 24° C!'

'Deb, you know her respiratory system is weak,' said Avantika.

They were both paranoid. *How can we not be!* was their response to anyone who pointed this out to them. After that near-death scare, Nayra spent another month in the hospital, the doctors trying everything to bring her back from the brink of death. She had to undergo eight surgeries—that little child—before she emerged healthy. The doctors refused to put a percentage rate on her survival, her respiratory system was that weak. She was sent back home with a file full of instructions and an oxygen tank which she would have to carry along with her till she was at least two years old. It was that moment and this, Deb and Avantika, hadn't let her out of their sights for a single moment. They hadn't trusted Deb's parents, Tanmay, Vernita, anyone, with her responsibility. Earlier the others would try to reason with them but soon they realized that there was no point. At least once in a day, they would collectively shout like barbarians at anyone who wouldn't use a sanitizer. They wouldn't listen to anyone or even each other. They wouldn't let anyone near her.

'When will all this stop?' Deb's parents, Tanmay and the others kept asking them.

Over time, Deb and Avantika, who hadn't slept well, eaten well, or lived well, spending every waking moment thinking or fussing over Nayra, had found an answer.

'Let her be a year old and then we will relax,' they would promise everyone.

And it would be a year today. Nayra would turn one. They had given this a long thought over the last couple of months.

With time, despite their paranoia, their love and their obsession with Nayra, they had realized that they would have to let go at some point. *Let others do a little bit of work.* Deb's parents, maids, anyone. They were wrecking their health and that couldn't be good for anyone. Avantika had to get back to work and Deb couldn't forever be paid for work Shrey was doing for him. But this was not going to be easy.

'Will we keep our promise?' asked Deb.

'We have to, don't we? It's time,' asked Avantika.

'It wouldn't have been so hard if Nayra wasn't as cute as she is. Who asked her to be this cute? She could have been like one of those ugly kids we see—'

'Shh. No kid is ugly,' said Avantika as she often did.

'But ours is . . . God. Look at her!' said Deb. 'Look at her goddamn eyes.' He pointed to Nayra who was waking up now from her half-sleep, her face turning into a smile, both of her dimples deep, her eyes like two little black suns, warm and deep, and hypnotic.

'We are obsessed, aren't we?' said Avantika, who had two of her phones filled with baby pictures, pictures she never posted online because, '*Nazar lag jaati hai* (to keep off the evil eye).'

'Talk about yourself,' said Deb, who had videos upon videos of Nayra, careful not to miss a single moment of hers.

Nayra was now awake. She cooed for Deb. If a one-year-old could be spoilt, she was already way beyond gone. She wanted not one but both of her parents and every morning she wouldn't be fully awake till they were in bed with her, showering her with smiles and kisses. She would then giggle and open her eyes fully and paw at their faces.

'Tomorrow?' asked Deb.

'But if she as much as looks at someone else when I'm around, we are going back to the earlier arrangement.'

'We are going to suck so much at this letting go business,' said Deb.

'I admit it, it's my fault. I brought this on myself. If it weren't for her, you would still be as much in love with me as you were before.'

'I'm still in as much love as I was,' said Deb.

'But there's someone you love more, don't you?'

'Do you?' asked Deb. 'Do you love her more?'

It was a question that they had asked themselves often.

'I love her as much as I love you,' said Deb. 'But this is a new person in our lives and she needs to fall in love with me, and she needs to fall in love with you, and maybe that's why we love her more. But there's no one, including this baby, this cutest damn baby in the world, I love more than you.'

'I love you.'

'I love you too, Avantika.'

'Daa . . . dob . . . do . .' said a jealous Nayra and interrupted their kiss.